# THE CROWN CONSPIRACY

## MICHAEL J. SULLIVAN

An Aspirations Media Publication

An Aspirations Media™ Publication
www.aspirationsmediainc.com

Copyright © 2008 by Michael J. Sullivan
Cover Art and Map by Michael J. Sullivan
Layout: Jennifer Rowell and Robin Sullivan
Design: Jennifer Rowell and Robin Sullivan

LIBRARY OF CONGRESS CONTROL NUMBER: 2008924101

ISBN: 978-0-9800034-3-7

PRINTED IN THE UNITED STATES

First Printing: September 2008

*To my wife, Robin, (my biggest fan, critic, contributor, and publicist)
whose hard work and dedication made it all possible.*

*And to my daughter, Sarah, who would not read
the story until published.*

THE
SOUND

TREN

Lanksteer

Ervanon
Ghent
Sheridan

Lake
Windermere
Melegar
WESTERLINS
Winds Abby
Galilin  Medford
Windham
Chadwick

Roe
AVR

Glouston
Rilan Valley
Colnora

Warric
Aquesta

Ratibor

Rhenydd
Kilnar

Maranon
Manzar

DELGOS

SHARON
SEA
Ter Del Fur
Tierre

Elan

DAC

w i l d e r l a n d s

T

Lingard

ERIVAN
elvenlands

Dunmore

Glamrendor

Dalhgren

Avempartha

Amber
Heights

Y N

Alburn

GOBLIN
SEA

BA
RAN

Archipeligo

Vilan Hills

G a l e a n n o n

Vandon

Wesbaden

CALIS

Gur Em

Dagastan
Bay

Dagastan

GHAZEL

SEA

CA

# TABLE OF CONTENTS

Part 1:  Stolen Letters . . . . . . . . . . . . . . . . . . . . . . . . . . . . 1

Part 2:  Meetings. . . . . . . . . . . . . . . . . . . . . . . . . . . . . . . 13

Part 3:  Conspiracies . . . . . . . . . . . . . . . . . . . . . . . . . . . . 44

Part 4:  Windermere . . . . . . . . . . . . . . . . . . . . . . . . . . . 89

Part 5:  Esrahaddon . . . . . . . . . . . . . . . . . . . . . . . . . . . 125

Part 6:  Revelations by Night. . . . . . . . . . . . . . . . . . . 154

Part 7:  Drondil Fields. . . . . . . . . . . . . . . . . . . . . . . . 185

Part 8:  Trials. . . . . . . . . . . . . . . . . . . . . . . . . . . . . . . 215

Part 9:  Rescuers . . . . . . . . . . . . . . . . . . . . . . . . . . . . 249

Part 10:  Coronation Day. . . . . . . . . . . . . . . . . . . . . . 285

# PART 1
## STOLEN LETTERS

Archibald Ballentyne held the world in his hands, conveniently contained within fifteen stolen letters. Each parchment was penned with meticulous care in a fine, elegant script. He could tell the writer believed that the words were profound and that their meaning conveyed a beautiful truth. Archibald felt the writing was drivel, yet he agreed with the author that they held a value beyond measure. He took a sip of brandy, closed his eyes, and smiled.

He sat by the fire, savoring the moment and appraising his future. As Earl of Chadwick, he already possessed ample wealth, a modest position at court, and of course, his exceptional good looks. Most ruling nobles were potbellied, gout-ridden, old bores. He, on the other hand, was in his prime: fit and tall with a full head of auburn hair, chiseled features, and piercing blue eyes. Archibald was proud of his appearance. He could obtain wealth and fame through any number of means, but to be born handsome was a gift for the deserving. He accentuated his natural virtues by wearing the finest imported fashions made with expensively dyed silks, embroidered linens, and feathers from exotic birds. His fellow nobles admired him for his elegant style. Soon his prestige would be elevated to the same enviable level.

"M'lord?"

Reluctantly, Archibald opened his eyes and scowled at his master-at-arms. "What is it, Bruce?"

"The marquis has arrived, sir."

Archibald's smile returned. He carefully refolded the letters, tied them in a stack with a blue ribbon, and returned them to his safe. He closed its heavy iron door, snapped the lock in place, and tested the seal with two sharp tugs on the unyielding bolt. He then headed downstairs to greet his guest.

When Archibald reached the foyer, he spied Victor Lanaklin waiting in the anteroom. He paused for a moment and watched the old man pacing back and forth, and it brought him a sense of satisfaction. While the marquis enjoyed a superior title, he had never impressed Archibald. Perhaps he was once lofty, intimidating, or even gallant, but all that was lost long ago, shrouded under a mat of gray hair and a hunched back.

"May I offer you something to drink, your lordship?" a mousy steward asked the marquis with a formal bow.

"No, but you can get me your earl," he commanded, "or shall I hunt for him myself?"

The steward cringed. "I am certain my master will be with you presently, sir." The servant bowed again and hastily retreated through a door on the far side of the room.

"Marquis!" Archibald called out graciously as he made his entrance. "I am so pleased you have arrived—and so quickly."

"You sound surprised." Victor's voice was sharp. Shaking a wrinkled parchment clasped in his fist, he continued, "You send a message like this and expect me to delay? Archie, I demand to know what is going on."

Archibald concealed his disdain at the use of his childhood nickname, *Archie*. This was the moniker his dead mother had given him and one of the reasons he would never forgive her. As a youth, everyone from the knights to the servants had used it, and he always felt demeaned by its familiarity. Once he became Earl, he made it law in Chadwick that anyone referring to him as such would suffer the loss of his tongue. Archibald did not have the power to enforce the edict on the marquis, and he was certain Victor used it intentionally.

"Please do try to calm down, Victor."

"Don't tell me to calm down!" The marquis' voice echoed off the stone walls. He moved closer, his face mere inches from the younger man's, and glared into his eyes. "You wrote that my daughter Alenda's future was at stake and you had evidence of this. Now I must know—is she, or is she not, in danger?"

"She is most certainly," the earl replied calmly, "but nothing imminent, to be sure. There is no kidnapping plot, nor is anyone planning to murder her, if that is what you fear."

"If you've caused me to run my carriage team to near collapse while I worried myself sick for nothing, you will regret— "

Holding up his hand, Archibald cut the threat short. "I assure you, Victor, it is not for nothing. Nevertheless, before we discuss this further, let us retire to the comfort of my study where I can show you the evidence I mentioned."

Victor glowered at him but nodded in agreement.

The two men crossed the luxurious foyer, passed through the large reception hall, and veered off through an ornate door that led to the living quarters of the castle. As they traversed various hallways and stairways, the atmosphere of their surroundings changed dramatically. In the main entry, fine tapestries and etched stonework adorned the walls, and the floors were made of finely crafted marble; yet, beyond the entry, no displays of grandeur were found, leaving barren walls of stone the predominate feature.

By architectural standards, or any other measures, Ballentyne Castle was unremarkable and ordinary in every respect. No great king or hero ever called the castle home. Nor was it the site of any legend, ghost story, or battle. Instead, it was the perfect example of mediocrity and the mundane. For twelve generations, the Ballentynes lived there. Each earl, including Archibald's father Albright, had tried to advance his position, but in the end, his failures left the House of Ballentyne anchored to the morass of nobility's middle tier. Only time would determine if Archibald would succeed, where so many others had previously failed.

After some time, Archibald led Victor to a formidable door made of cast iron. Impressive, oversized bolts secured the door at its hinges, but it displayed no visible latch or knob. Flanking either side of the door stood two large, well-armored guards bearing halberds. Upon Archibald's approach, one rapped on the door three times. A tiny viewing window opened, and a moment later, the hall echoed with the sharp sound of a bolt snapping back. As the door opened, the metal hinges screamed with a deafening noise.

Victor's hands moved to defend his ears. "By Mar! Have one of your servants tend to that!"

"Never," Archibald replied. "This is the entrance to the Gray Tower—my private study and treasure room. This is my safe haven, if you will. I want to hear this door opening from anywhere in the castle, which I can."

Stationed behind the door, Bruce greeted the pair with a deep and stately bow. Holding a lantern before him, he escorted the men up a wide spiral staircase.

Halfway up the tower, Victor's pace slowed, and his breathing appeared labored. Archibald paused courteously.

"I know it's a long way. I've climbed these stairs a thousand times. I used to hide up here when my father was Earl. This was the one place I could be alone. No one ever wanted to take the time or effort to climb these stairs to the top. While it may not reach the majestic height of the Crown Tower at Ervanon, it is the tallest tower in my castle."

"I'd think people would make the climb merely to see the view," Victor speculated.

The earl chuckled. "You would think so, but this tower has no windows. After I became Earl, I decided it was the perfect location for my private study, and I added doors to protect the things dear to me."

When they reached the top of the stairs, they encountered another door. Archibald removed a large key from his pocket and unlocked it. He gestured politely for the marquis to enter. Once they were both inside, Archibald left Bruce outside to stand guard and closed the door behind them.

The room was large and circular with an expansive ceiling. The furnishings were sparse: a large disheveled desk, two cushioned chairs near a small fireplace, and a delicate table between them. A fire burned in the hearth behind a simple brass screen, illuminating most of the study. The candles, which lined the walls, provided light to the remaining areas and filled the chamber with a pleasant, heady aroma of honey and salifan.

Archibald smiled when he noticed Victor eyeing the cluttered desk overflowing with various scrolls and maps. "Don't worry, sir. I hid all the truly incriminating plans for world domination prior to your visit," he quipped. "Please do sit down." Archibald gestured toward the pair of chairs near the hearth. "Rest yourself from your long journey while I pour us a drink."

The older man scowled and grumbled, "Enough of the tour and formalities. We are here now. Explain what this is all about."

Archibald ignored the marquis' tone. He could afford to be gracious now that he was about to claim his prize. He waited while the marquis took his seat.

"You are aware, are you not, that I have shown an interest in your daughter Alenda?" Archibald asked, walking to the desk to pour two glasses of brandy.

"Yes, she's mentioned it to me."

"Has she told you why she has refused my advances?"

"She doesn't like you."

"She hardly knows me," countered Archibald with a raised finger.

"Archie, is this why you asked me here?"

"I would appreciate your addressing me by my proper name. It is inappropriate to call me *that* since my father is dead and I hold title. In any case, concerning your question, it does have a bearing on the subject. As you know, I am the twelfth Earl of Chadwick. Granted, it's not a huge estate, and Ballentyne isn't the most influential of families, but I am not without merit. I control five villages and twelve hamlets, as well as the strategic Senon Uplands. I currently command more than sixty professional men-at-arms, and twenty knights are loyal to me—including Sir Enden and Sir Breckton, both of whom rank in the top fifty on the tournament circuit. Chadwick's wool and leather exports are the envy of the whole of Warric, and there is talk of the Summersrule Games being held here on the very lawn you crossed to enter my castle."

"Yes, Archie—I mean *Archibald*—I am well aware of Chadwick's status in the world. I don't need a commerce lesson from you."

"Are you also aware that King Ethelred's nephew has dined here on more than one occasion? Or that the Duke and Lady of Rochelle have promised to invite me to Wintertide this year?"

"Archibald, this is quite tiresome. What exactly is your point?"

Archibald frowned at the marquis' lack of awe. He carried over the glasses of brandy, handed one to Victor, and took the remaining seat. He paused a moment to sip his liquor.

"My point is this. Given my position, my stature, and my promising future—why would Alenda reject me? Certainly, it is not because of my appearance. The rest of her suitors are old, fat, or bald—in several cases all three."

"Perhaps looks and wealth are not her only concern," replied Victor. "Women don't always think about politics and power. Alenda is the kind of girl who follows her heart."

"But she also follows her father's wishes. Am I correct?"

"I don't understand your meaning."

"If you told her to marry me, she would."

"That is not a certainty. Alenda has been known to disobey me."

"As her father perhaps, but would she refuse a command from the Marquis of Glouston?" Archibald pressed. "You could *order* her to marry me."

"So, this is why you coerced me into coming here? I'm sorry, Archibald, but you have wasted your time and mine. I refuse to force her to wed a man she doesn't want. She would hate me for the rest of her life. I care more about my daughter's feelings than the political implications of her marriage. I happen to cherish Alenda. Of all my children, she is my greatest joy."

Archibald took another sip of brandy and considered Victor's remarks. He decided to approach the subject from a different direction. "What if it were for her own good? To save her from what would be certain disaster."

"You warned me of danger to get me here. Are you finally ready to explain, or would you prefer to see if this old man can still handle a blade?"

Archibald disregarded what he knew was an idle threat. "When Alenda repeatedly declined my advances, I reasoned something must be amiss. There was no logic to her rebuffs. Look at me. I am a rich and handsome man. I have connections and my star is rising. The reason for your daughter's refusal is quite simple: she is already involved with someone else. She is having an affair—a secret affair."

"I find that difficult to believe," Victor declared. "Who is this man? Why would she not tell me?"

"It is little wonder she's kept it from you. She is ashamed. You see, the man she is entertaining is a mere commoner without a single drop of royal blood in his veins."

"You're lying!"

"Perhaps you've heard of him. His name is Degan Gaunt. A troublemaker I hear, part of the Nationalist movement out of Delgos. They rendezvous at Windermere near the monastery. They meet on nights when you are away or occupied with matters of state."

"That is ridiculous. My daughter would never— "

"Don't you have a son there?" Archibald inquired. "At the abbey, I mean. He's a monk, isn't he?"

Victor nodded. "Myron. He is my third son."

"Perhaps he has been helping them. I've made inquiries and it seems your Myron is a very intelligent fellow. Perhaps he is masterminding liaisons for his beloved sister and carrying their correspondence."

"You *are* insane," Victor shot back, suppressing a bitter laugh. "I sent Myron to the abbey when he was barely four years old. He hasn't set foot outside its walls in thirty-two years. All he is good for is scribbling books. To my knowledge, Alenda has never even spoken to him. This whole story is obviously a pathetic attempt to have me pressure Alenda into marrying you, and I know why. You don't care about her. You want her dowry. The Rilan Valley borders ever so nicely against your own lands. Not to mention, marrying into my family would be quite a boost for you, socially and politically."

"Pathetic, am I?" Archibald set down his glass and produced a key on a silver neck chain from inside his shirt. He rose and crossed the room to a tapestry depicting a Calian prince on horseback abducting a fair-haired noblewoman. He drew it back revealing the hidden safe, and inserting the key, opened the small metal door.

"I have a stack of letters written in your precious daughter's hand that proves it. They tell of her undying love for her disgusting peasant."

"How did you get these letters?"

"I stole them from her. I knew she was seeing someone and wanted to know who my rival was, so I had her followed. Once I discovered she was sending letters, I arranged to have them intercepted." From the safe, Archibald brought forth a stack of parchments and dropped them in Victor's lap. "There!" he declared triumphantly. "Read what your daughter has been up to, and decide for yourself whether or not she would be better off marrying me."

Archibald lifted his brandy glass victoriously; he had won. In order to avoid political ruin, Victor Lanaklin, the great Marquis of Glouston, would order his daughter to marry him. Finally, he would have the borderland, and perhaps in time, he would control the whole of the marchland. With Chadwick in his right hand and

Glouston in his left, his power at court would rival that of the Duke of Rochelle.

Looking down at the old, gray-haired man in his fine traveling clothes, Archibald almost felt sorry for him. Once long ago, the marquis had enjoyed a reputation for cleverness and fortitude. Such distinction came with the title. The marquis was no mere noble, nor was he a simple sheriff of the land like an earl or a count. He was responsible for guarding the king's borders. This was a serious duty, which required a capable leader, an ever-vigilant man tested in battle. However, now that the frontier was no longer under threat of attack, the great guard had become complacent, and his strength had withered from lack of use.

As Victor opened the letters, Archibald contemplated his future with relish. The marquis was right. He was after the land that came with his daughter. Still, Alenda was attractive, and the thought of forcing her to his bed was more than a little appealing.

"Archibald, is this a joke?" Victor questioned.

Startled from his thoughts, Archibald set down his drink. "What do you mean?"

"These papers are all blank."

"What? Are you blind? They're— " Archibald stopped when he saw the empty pages in the marquis' hand. He grabbed a handful of letters and tore them open, only to find still more blank parchments. "This is impossible!"

"Perhaps they were written in disappearing ink?" Victor smirked.

"No…I don't understand…these aren't even the same parchments!" He rechecked the safe but found it empty. His confusion turned to panic. He tore open the door and called anxiously for Bruce. The master-at-arms rushed in, his sword at the ready. "What happened to the letters I had in this safe?" Archibald shouted at the soldier.

"I…I don't know, my lord," Bruce replied. He sheathed his weapon and stood at attention before the earl.

"What do you mean, you don't know? Have you left your post at all this evening?"

"No, sir, of course not."

"Did anyone, anyone at all, enter my study during my absence?"

"No, my lord that is impossible; you hold the only key."

"Then where in Maribor's name are those letters? I put them there myself. I was reading them when the marquis arrived. I was only gone a few minutes. How could they disappear like that?"

"I'm sorry, my lord, I— "

"Shut up. Shut up, you imbecile! I need to think."

Archibald's mind raced. He had them in his hands only moments ago. He had locked them in the safe; he was convinced of that fact. *Where had they gone?*

Victor drained his glass and stood up. "If you don't mind, *Archie*, I'll be leaving now. This has been a tremendous waste of my time."

"Victor, wait. Don't go. The letters are real. I had them!"

"But of course you did, Archie. The next time you plan to blackmail me, I suggest you provide a better bluff." He crossed the room, passed through the door, and disappeared down the stairs.

"You had better consider what I said, Victor," Archibald yelled after him. "I'll find those letters. I will! I'll bring them to Aquesta! I'll hold them up at court!"

"What do you want me to do, my lord?" Bruce asked.

"Just wait, you fool. I have to think." Archibald ran his trembling fingers through his hair as he began to pace around the room. He re-examined the letters closely. They were indeed a slightly different grade of paper than the ones he had read so many times before.

Despite his certainty of placing the letters in the safe, Archibald began pulling out the drawers and riffling through the parchments on his desk. He poured himself another drink and crossed the room. Ripping the screen from the fireplace, he probed the ashes with a poker to search for any telltale signs of parchment remains.

In frustration, Archibald threw the blank letters into the fire. He drained his drink in one long swallow and collapsed into one of the chairs.

"They were just here," Archibald said, puzzled. Slowly, a solution began to form in his mind. "Bruce, the letters must have been stolen. The thief could not have gotten far. I want you to search the entire castle. Seal every exit. Close every door, every gate, and every window. Do not let anyone out. Not the staff, not the guards— no one leaves. Search everyone!"

"Right away, my lord," Bruce responded and then paused. "What about the marquis, my lord. Shall I stop him as well?"

"Of course not, you idiot! He doesn't have the letters."

Archibald stared into the fire as he listened to Bruce's footsteps fading away as he ran down the tower stairs. Alone, he had only the sound of the crackling flames and a hundred unanswered questions. He racked his brain but could not determine exactly how the thief had done it. Still, it was the only answer.

"Your lordship?" the timid voice of the steward roused him from his thoughts. Archibald glared up at the man who poked his head through the open door, causing the steward to take an extra breath before speaking. "My lord, I hate to disturb you, but there seems to be a problem down in the courtyard that requires your attention."

"What kind of problem?" Archibald snarled.

"Well, my lord, I was not actually informed of the details, but it has something to do with the marquis, sir. I have been sent to request your presence—respectfully request it, that is."

Archibald descended the stairs, pondering if perhaps the old man had dropped dead on his doorstep, which would not be such a terrible thing. When he reached the courtyard, he found the marquis alive but in a furious temper.

"There you are, Ballentyne! What have you done with my carriage?"

"Your what?"

Bruce approached Archibald and motioned him aside. "Your lordship," he whispered in the earl's ear. "It seems the marquis' carriage and horses are missing, sir."

Archibald held up a finger in the direction of the marquis. With a raised voice, he replied, "I'll be with you in a moment, Victor." Then he turned his attention to Bruce and whispered, "Did you say *missing*? How is that possible?"

"I don't know exactly, sir, but you see, the gate warden reports that the marquis and his driver, or rather two people he thought were them, have already passed through the front gate."

Suddenly feeling quite ill, Archibald turned back to address the red-faced marquis.

# PART 2
## MEETINGS

Several hours after nightfall, Alenda Lanaklin arrived by carriage at the impoverished Lower Quarter of Medford. The Rose and Thorn Tavern lay hidden among crooked-roofed hovels on an unnamed street, which to Alenda appeared to be little more than an alley. A recent storm had left the cobblestones wet, and puddles littered the street. Passing carriages splashed filthy water on the pub's front entrance, leaving streaks of grime on the dull stone and weathered timbers.

From a nearby doorway, a sweaty, shirtless man with a bald head emerged carrying a large copper pot. He unceremoniously cast the pot's contents, the bony remains of several stewed animals, into the street. Immediately, half a dozen dogs set upon the scraps. Wretched-looking figures, dimly lit by the flickering light from the tavern's windows, shouted angrily at the canines in a language that Alenda did not recognize. Several of them threw rocks at the scrawny animals, which yelped and darted away. They rushed to what the animals had left behind and stuffed the remnants into their mouths and pockets.

"Are you *sure* this is the right place, my lady?" Emily asked, taking in the scene. "Surely Viscount Winslow couldn't have meant for us to come here."

Alenda re-examined the curled thorny branch with a single bloom painted on the warped signboard above the door. The red rose had faded to gray, and the weathered stem looked like a coiled snake. "This has to be it. I don't think there's more than one tavern called The Rose and Thorn in Medford."

"I just can't believe he'd send us to such a…a…place!"

"I don't like it any more than you do, but this is what was arranged. I don't see how we have a choice," Alenda replied, surprised by how brave she sounded.

"I know you're tired of hearing this, but I still think this is a mistake. We shouldn't be dealing with *thieves*. You can't trust them, my lady. Mark my words: these people you hired will steal from you just like they steal from everyone else."

"Nevertheless, we're here now, so we might as well get on with it." Alenda opened the door and stepped out onto the street. As she did, she noticed with concern that several of those loitering nearby were watching her intently.

"That'll be a silver tenent," the driver told her. He was a gruff, elderly man who had not shaved in days. His narrow eyes were framed with so many wrinkles that Alenda wondered how he could see to drive the carriage.

"Oh, well, you see, I was expecting to pay you at the end of our journey," Alenda explained. "We're only stopping here for a short while."

"If you want me to wait, it'll cost ya extra. And I want the money ya owe me now, in case ya decide not ta come back."

"Don't be absurd. I can assure you we will be coming back."

The man's expression was as pliable as granite. He spit over the side of the carriage at Alenda's feet.

"Oh! Well, really!" Alenda pulled a coin from her bag and handed it to the driver. "Here, take the silver, but don't wander off. I'm not exactly sure how long we'll be, but as I told you, we *will* return."

Emily exited the carriage and took a moment to adjust Alenda's hood and to ensure her ladyship's buttons were secure. She brushed the wrinkles out of Alenda's cloak and then repeated the procedure on herself.

"I wish I could tell that stupid driver who I am," Alenda whispered. "Then I'd tell him a few more things."

"Don't even think that way. Maribor forbid your father should ever learn you came here."

The two women were dressed in matching woolen cloaks, and with their hoods up, little more than their noses were visible. Alenda scowled at Emily and brushed her fidgeting hands away.

"You're being such a mother hen, Emmy. I'm sure women have come into this establishment before."

"Women, yes, but I doubt any ladies have."

As they entered the narrow wooden doorway of the tavern, the pungent odor of smoke, alcohol, and a scent that Alenda had previously smelled only in a privy assaulted them. The din of twenty conversations fought each other for supremacy while a fiddler worked a lively tune. Before a bar, a small crowd danced, hammering their heels loudly on the warped wooden floor, keeping time to the jig. Glasses clinked, fists pounded on tables, and people laughed and sang far louder than Alenda thought dignified.

"What do we do now?" Emily's voice emanated from the depths of her woolen hood.

"I suppose we look for the viscount. Stay close to me."

Alenda took Emily's hand and led the way, weaving through the tables and dodging the dancers and a dog that was gleefully licking up spilled beer. Never in her life had Alenda been in such a place. Vile-looking men surrounded her. Most were dressed in rags, and more than a few were shoeless. She spotted only four women in the place, all were barmaids dressed indecently in tattered gowns with plunging necklines. To Alenda, their manner of dress invited men to paw at them. A toothless, hairy beast grabbed one of the barmaids around her waist. Dragging her to his lap, he ran his hands along the length of her body. Alenda was shocked to see the girl giggle instead of scream.

At last, Alenda spotted him. Viscount Albert Winslow was dressed, not in his typical doublet and hose, but in a simple cloth shirt, wool pants, and a neatly tailored suede vest. His vestige was not entirely without noble adornment, sporting a lovely, if not ostentatious, plumed hat. He sat at a small table with a stocky, black-bearded man dressed in cheap work clothes.

On their approach, Albert Winslow stood and pulled out chairs for them. "Welcome, ladies," he said with a cheerful smile. "So glad you were able to meet me this evening. Please sit down. May I order you both something to drink?"

"No, thank you," Alenda replied. "I was hoping not to stay very long. My driver is not a considerate man, and I would like to conclude our business before he decides to strand us here."

"I understand and, might I say, very wise of you, your ladyship. But I am sad to say your delivery has not yet arrived."

"It hasn't?" Alenda felt Emily give her hand a squeeze of support. "Is there something wrong?"

"Unfortunately, I don't know. You see, I am not privy to the inner workings of this operation. I don't concern myself with such trifles. You should understand, however, this wasn't an easy assignment. We have taken days to prepare, and any number of things could have transpired that might create delays. Are you sure there's nothing I may order for you?"

"Thank you, no," Alenda replied.

"At least take a seat, won't you?"

Alenda glanced at Emily, whose eyes were awash with concern. They sat down, and as they did, she whispered to Emily, "I know, I know. I shouldn't deal with thieves."

"Make no mistake, your ladyship," the viscount said in reassurance. "I would not waste your time, money, or risk your station if I didn't have the utmost confidence in the outcome."

The bearded man seated at the table chuckled softly. He was dark and seedy with skin as tan as leather. His huge hands were callused and dirty. Alenda watched as he tipped his mug to his lips. When he withdrew the cup, droplets of ale ran unchecked through his whiskers and dripped onto the tabletop. Alenda decided she did not like him.

"This is Mason Grumon," Winslow explained. "Forgive me for not introducing him sooner. Mason is a blacksmith here in Medford's Lower Quarter. He's—a friend."

"Those chaps you hired are very good," Mason told them. His voice reminded Alenda of the sound her carriage wheels made when traveling over crushed stone.

"Are they?" Emily asked. "Could they steal the ancient treasures of Glenmorgan from the Crown Tower of Ervanon?"

"What's that?" Winslow asked.

"I once heard a rumor about thieves who stole treasure from the Crown Tower of Ervanon and replaced it the very next night," Emily explained.

"Why would anyone do such a thing?" Alenda asked.

The viscount chuckled softly. "I'm sure that's merely a legend. No sensible thief would behave in such a way. Most people don't understand the workings of thieves. The reality is that most of them steal to line their pockets. They break into homes or waylay travelers on the open road. Your bolder variety might kidnap nobles and hold them for ransom. Sometimes, they even cut off a finger of their victim and send it to a loved one. It helps to prove how dangerous they are and reinforces that the family should take their demands seriously. In general, they are an unsavory lot to be sure. They care only about making a profit with as little effort as possible."

Alenda felt another squeeze on her hand. This one was so tight it caused her to wince.

"Now your better class of thief, they form guilds, sort of like masonry or woodworkers guilds, although far more hush-hush, you understand. They are very organized and make a business out of thievery. They stake out territories where they maintain a monopoly on pilfering. Oftentimes, they have arrangements with the local militia or potentate that allow them to work relatively unmolested for a fee, as long as they avoid certain targets and abide by accepted rules."

"What kind of rules could be acceptable between officers of a province and known criminals?" Alenda asked skeptically.

"Oh, I think you'd be quite surprised to discover the number of compromises made to maintain a smoothly functioning kingdom. There is however, one more type of malefactor—the freelance contractor or, to put it bluntly, thief-for-hire. These rogues are hired for a particular purpose, such as obtaining an item in the possession of a fellow noble. Codes of honor, or *fear of embarrassment*," he said with a wink, "require them to seek out a professional as their only recourse."

"So, they'll steal anything for anyone?" Alenda asked. "The ones you hired for me, I mean."

"No, not anyone—only those who are willing to pay the number of tenents equal to the job."

"Then it doesn't matter if the client is a criminal or a king?" Emily chimed in.

Mason snorted, "Criminal or king, what's the difference?" For the first time during their meeting, he produced a wide grin that revealed several missing teeth.

Disgusted, Alenda turned her attention back to Winslow. He was looking in the direction of the door, straining to see above the tavern patrons. "You'll have to excuse me, ladies," he said, abruptly standing up. "I need another drink, and the wait staff seems preoccupied. Look after the ladies, won't you, Mason?"

"I'm not a bloody wet nurse you daffy old sod!" Mason shouted after the viscount as he left the table and moved off through the crowd.

"I'll...I'll not have you referring to her ladyship in such a way," Emily declared boldly to the smith. "She is no infant. She is a noble woman of title, and *you* had best remember your place."

Mason's expression darkened. "This *is* my place. I live five bloody doors down. My pa helped build this infernal pub. My brother works here as a ruddy cook. My mother used ta work here as a cook too, up until she died being hit by one of yer fancy noble carriages. This is *my* place. *You're* the one who needs to be remembering yours." Mason slammed his fist down on the table, causing the candle, and the ladies, to jump.

Alenda pulled Emily close. *What have I gotten myself into?* She was starting to think Emily was right. She should never have trusted that no-account Winslow. She really did not know anything about him except that he attended the Aquesta Autumn Gala as a guest of Lord Daref. Of all people, she should have learned by now that not all nobles are noble.

They sat in silence until Winslow returned without a drink.

"Ladies, if you'll please follow me?" the viscount beckoned.

"What is it?" Alenda asked concerned.

"Just please, come with me, this way."

Alenda and Emily left the table and followed Winslow through the haze of pipe smoke and the obstacle course of dancers, dogs, and drunks to the back door. The scene behind the tavern made everything they endured so far appear virtuous. They entered an alley that was almost beyond comprehension. Trash lay scattered everywhere and excrement, discarded from the windows above, mixed with mud in a wide-open trench. Wooden planks, serving as bridges, crisscrossed the foul river of slime, causing the ladies to hold their gowns above their ankles as they shuffled forward.

A large rat darted from a woodpile to join two more in the sewage trough.

"Why are we in an alley?" Emily whispered in a quivering voice to Alenda.

"I don't know," Alenda answered, trying desperately to control her own fear. "I think you were right, Emmy. I should never have dealt with these people. I don't care what the viscount says; people like *us* simply shouldn't do business with people like *them*. I can just imagine what my father would think."

The viscount led them through a wooden fence and around a pair of shanties to a poor excuse for a stable. The shelter was little more than a shack with four stalls, each filled with straw and a bucket of water.

"So good to see you again, your ladyship," a man out front addressed them.

Alenda could tell it was the big one of the pair, but she could not remember his name. She had only seen them briefly through an arranged meeting by the viscount, which had been on a lonely road on a night darker than this. Now, with the moon more than half-full and his hood thrown back, she could make out his face. He was tall, rugged in feature and dress, but not unkind or threatening in appearance. Wrinkles, which may have come from laughter, tugged at the edges of his eyes. Alenda thought his demeanor was remarkably cheerful, even friendly. She could not help but think he was handsome, which was not the reaction she expected to have about anyone she might meet in such a place. He was dressed in dirt-stained leather and wool, and was well armed. On his left side, he had a short sword with an unadorned hilt. On his right, was a similarly plain, longer, wider sword. Finally, slung on his back was a massive blade, nearly as tall as he was.

"My name is Hadrian, in case you have forgotten," he said and followed the introduction with a suitable bow. "And who is this lovely lady with you?"

"This is Emily, my maid."

"A maid?" Hadrian feigned surprise. "For one so fair, I would have guessed her to be a duchess."

Emily inclined her head and for the first time on this trip, Alenda saw her smile.

"I hope we didn't keep you waiting too long. The viscount tells me he and Mason were keeping you company?"

"Yes, they were."

"Did Mr. Grumon tell you the tragic tale of his mother being run down by an insensitive royal carriage?"

"Why, yes, he did. And I must say— "

Hadrian held up his hands in mock defense. "Mason's mother is alive and well. She lives on Artisan Row in a home considerably nicer than the hovel where Mason resides. She has never been a cook at The Rose and Thorn. He tells that story to every gentleman or lady he meets to put them on the defensive and make them feel guilty. You have my apologies."

"Well, thank you. He was rather rude and I found his comments more than a little disturbing, but now," Alenda paused. "Did you... I mean, do you have...were you able to get them?"

Hadrian smiled warmly, then turning he called over his shoulder in the direction of the stable.

"Royce?"

"If you knew how to tie a proper knot, I wouldn't be taking so long," said a voice from inside. A moment later, the other half of the pair emerged and joined them.

Alenda's memory of him was easier to recall because he was the more disturbing of the two. He was smaller than Hadrian was and possessed elegant features, dark hair and dark eyes. He was dressed in layers of black with a knee-length tunic and a long flowing cloak that gathered about him like a shadow. Not a single weapon was visible upon him. Despite his smaller size and apparent unarmed state, Alenda feared this man. His cold eyes, expressionless face, and curt manner had all the warmth of a predator.

From his tunic, Royce drew forth a bundle of letters bound with a blue ribbon. Handing them to her, he said, "Getting to those letters before Ballentyne presented them to your father wasn't easy. As far as races go, it was very close but ultimately successful. You might want to burn those before something like this happens again."

She stared at the package as a smile of relief crossed her face. "I...I can't believe it! I don't know how you did it, or how to thank you!"

"Payment would be nice," Royce replied.

"Oh, yes, of course," she handed the bundle to Emily, untied the purse from her waist, and handed it to the thief. He quickly scanned the contents, snapped the purse closed, and tossed it to Hadrian, who slipped it in his vest as he headed for the stables.

"You'd better be careful. It's a dangerous game you and Gaunt are playing," Royce told her.

"You read my letters?" she asked fearfully.

"No. I'm afraid you didn't pay us that much."

"Then, how did you know— "

"We overheard your father and Archibald Ballentyne talking. The marquis appeared not to believe the earl's accusations, but I am certain he did. Letters or no letters, your father will be watching you closely now. Still, the marquis is a good man. He'll do the right thing. My guess is he's so relieved Ballentyne doesn't have proof to take to court that your affair won't bother him much. However, as I said, you'd better be more careful in the future."

"How would the likes of *you* know anything about *my* father?"

"Oh, I'm sorry. Did I say your father? I meant the other marquis, the one with the appreciative daughter."

Alenda felt as though Royce had slapped her across the face.

"Making friends again, Royce?" Hadrian asked as he led two horses from the stable. "You'll have to forgive my friend. He was raised by wolves."

"Those are my father's horses!"

Hadrian nodded, "We left the carriage behind a bramble patch by the river bridge. By the way, I think I might have stretched out one of your father's doublets. I put it and the rest of his things back in the carriage."

"You were wearing my father's clothes?"

"I told you," Royce repeated, "it was close, very close."

# 2

They called it the Dark Room because of the business conducted in it, but the little back room at The Rose and Thorn was anything but gloomy. Several candles set in sconces on the walls and on the meeting table, along with a nice-sized fire burning in the hearth, gave off a warm, friendly light. A row of copper pots, reminders of the days when the Dark Room doubled as kitchen storage, hung from an exposed wooden beam. There was only enough room for one table and a handful of chairs, but it was more than enough for their purposes.

The door opened, and a small party filed in. Royce poured himself a glass of wine, took a seat near the fire, removed his boots, and wriggled his toes before the hearth. Hadrian, Viscount Albert Winslow, Mason Grumon, and a pretty young woman opted for chairs at the meeting table. Gwen, the owner of the tavern, always prepared a fine feast when they returned from a job, and tonight was no exception. This evening's selections included a pitcher of ale, a large roast, a loaf of freshly baked sweet bread, boiled potatoes, a cloth-wrapped cask of white cheese, carrots, onions, and the big pickles from the barrel normally kept behind the bar. For Royce and Hadrian, she spared no expense, which included the black bottle of Montemorcey wine she imported all the way from Vandon. Gwen always kept it on hand because it was Royce's favorite. Despite how appealing everything looked, Hadrian showed no interest in any of it. He focused his attention on the woman.

"So, how did it go last night?" Emerald asked, sitting atop Hadrian's lap and pouring him a frothy stein of the inn's homebrew. Her real name was Falina Brockton, but all the girls who worked at the tavern, or Medford House next door, went by monikers for their own safety. Emerald, a bright and cheery waif, was the senior barmaid at The Rose and Thorn and one of only two women allowed in the Dark Room when a meeting was in session.

"It was cold," he told her, encircling her waist with his arms. "As was the ride here, so I desperately need warming." He pulled her to him and began kissing her neck as a sea of brunette waves engulfed him.

"We did get paid, didn't we?" Mason asked.

The blacksmith had started to prepare a heaping plate almost the instant he sat down. Mason was the son of the former preeminent Medford metalworker. He had inherited his father's shop but had lost it through a gambling habit coupled with bad luck. Forced out of Artisan Row, he landed in the Lower Quarter, where he fashioned horseshoes and nails, making enough to pay for his forge, drinks, and the occasional meal. For Royce and Hadrian, he offered three benefits: he was cheap, he was local; and he was solitary.

"We did indeed. Alenda Lanaklin paid us the full fifteen gold tenents," Royce said.

"Quite the haul," Winslow declared, happily clapping his hands.

"And my arrows? How'd they work?" Mason asked. "Did they anchor in the tiles?"

"They anchored just fine," Royce said. "Getting them out was the problem."

"The release failed?" Mason asked concerned. "But I thought —well, I'm no fletcher. Ya should'a gone to a fletcher. Told ya that, didn't I? I'm a smith. I work with steel, not wood. That fine-toothed saw I made—that worked, didn't it? That's a smithing product, by Mar! But not the arrows, and for sure, not ones like you wanted. No, sir. I done said ya should'a gottten a fletcher and ya should'a."

"Relax, Mason," Hadrian said, emerging from Emerald's mane. "Of the two, the anchor was the most important, and it worked perfectly."

"O'course it did. The arrow tips are metal, and I know metal. I'm just disappointed the rope release didn't work. How did ya get the rope down? Ya didn't leave it there, did ya?"

"Couldn't, the guard would have spotted it on his next pass," said Royce.

"So, how'd ya do it?"

"Personally, I would like to know how you did the whole thing," Winslow said. Like Royce, he was sitting back with his feet up and mug in hand. "You never let me in on the details of these operations."

The Viscount Albert Winslow came from a long line of landless gentry. Years ago, one of his ancestors lost the family fief. Now all that remained was his title. This was enough to open doors closed to the peasantry or merchant class and was a step better than the common baronage, at least on paper. When Royce and Hadrian first met him, he was living in a barn in Colnora. The pair invested a little money on clothes and a carriage, and he aptly performed the delicate duties of liaison to the nobles. With an allowance funded by them, the viscount convincingly attended every ball, gala, and ceremony, patrolling the political pressure cooker for business leads.

"You're too visible, Albert," Hadrian explained. "Can't afford to have our favorite noble hauled to some dungeon where they cut off your eyelids or pull off your fingernails until you tell them what we're up to."

"But if they torture me, and I don't know the plan, how will I save myself?"

"I'm sure they'll believe you after the fourth nail or so," Royce said with a wicked grin.

Albert grimaced and took another long drink of his ale. "But you can tell me now, can't you? How did you get past the iron door? When I met with Ballentyne, I had the impression a dwarf with a full set of tools couldn't get it open. It didn't even have a lock to pick, or a latch to lift."

"Well, your information was very helpful," Royce said. "That's why we avoided it completely."

The viscount looked confused. He started to speak but instead remained silent and cut himself a piece of the roast beef.

Royce took a sip of his wine, and when he did, Hadrian took over the tale. "We scaled the exterior of the east tower, or rather Royce did, and he dropped me a rope. It wasn't as tall, but it was the closest to the one Archibald had the letters in. We used Mason's arrows to connect the two towers and, with our knees wrapped around the rope, inched our way across the length hand over hand."

"But there are no windows in the tower," Albert protested.

"Who said anything about using a window?" Royce interjected. "The arrows anchored in the taller tower's roof."

"Yep, as I said, that was quality craftsmanship," Mason said proudly.

"So, that gets you to the tower, but how did you get in? Through the chimney?" Albert inquired.

"No, it was too small, and last night there was a fire burning," Hadrian said, "so we used Mason's second little tool, a small saw, and cut the roof on a bevel. All in all, the night was going pretty much according to plan, until Archibald decided to visit his study. We figured he'd have to leave eventually, so we waited."

"We should have just slipped down, cut his throat, and taken the letters," Royce insisted.

"But we weren't being paid for that, were we?" Hadrian reminded him. Royce rolled his eyes in response. Ignoring him, Hadrian continued. "As I was saying, we lay there waiting and the wind on the top of that tower was bitter. The bastard must have sat in that room for two hours."

"You poor thing," Emerald purred and nuzzled him like a cat.

"The good news was he actually looked at the letters while we were watching him through the cuts, so we knew right where the safe was. Then a carriage came into the courtyard, and you'll never guess who it was."

"The marquis arrived while you were on the roof?" Albert asked with his mouth full of roast beef.

"Yep—that's when our timetable got really tricky. Archibald left the tower to meet the marquis, and we made our move."

"So," Emerald chanced, "you opened the roof like the top of a pumpkin."

"Exactly. I lowered Royce into the study. He picked the safe, dumped the dummy letters, and I hauled him back up. Just as we replaced the roof section, Archibald and Victor walked in. We waited to make sure they did not hear us. Incredibly, he presented the letters right there and then. I must say, it was hilarious watching Archibald's reaction when he discovered the blank replacements. Things got pretty loud at this point, so we decided we better take the chance and rappelled down the tower to the courtyard below."

"That's amazing. I was telling Alenda sometimes problems occur during a job, but I had no idea I was telling the truth. We should have charged her extra," Albert interjected.

"It crossed my mind," Royce replied, "but you know Hadrian. Still, we've made a nice profit on both sides of this one."

"But wait, you didn't explain how you got the rope off the side of the tower if my releases didn't work?"

Royce sighed. "Don't ask."

"Why not?" The smith looked from one to the other. "Is it a secret?"

"They want to know, Royce," Hadrian said with a wide grin.

Royce frowned. "He shot it off."

"He did what?" Albert asked, sitting up so abruptly his feet hit the floor with a clap.

"Hadrian used another arrow to cut the rope at the roofline."

"But, that's impossible," Albert declared. "No man can shoot the width of a rope at—what was it—two hundred feet maybe, in total darkness!"

"There *was* a moon," Royce corrected. "Let's not make more out of this than it already is. You forget I have to work with him. Besides, it's not like he did it in a single shot."

"How many arrows?" Emerald inquired.

"What's that, sweetie?" Hadrian asked, wiping foam from his mouth with his sleeve.

"How many arrows did it take for you to cut the rope, silly?"

"Be honest," Royce told him.

Hadrian scowled, "Four."

"Four?" Albert said. "It was much more impressive when I imagined it as one lone shot, but still—"

"Do you think the earl will ever figure it out?" Emerald asked.

"The first time it rains I figure," Mason said.

There was a triple tap on the door and the stocky smith pushed back his chair and crossed the room. "Who is it?" he challenged.

"Gwen."

Sliding the deadbolt free, he opened the door, and an exotic-looking woman with long, thick black hair and dazzling green eyes entered.

"A fine thing when a woman can't get access to her own back room."

"Sorry, gal," Mason said, closing the door behind her, "but Royce would skin me alive if I ever opened the door without asking first."

Gwen DeLancy was an enigma of the Lower Quarter. A Calian immigrant, she survived in the city as a prostitute and fortune-teller. Her dark skin, almond-shaped eyes and high cheekbones were uniquely foreign. Her talent for eye makeup and an eastern accent made her an alluring mystery that the nobles found irresistible. Yet Gwen was no simple whore. In three short years, she turned her fortunes around, buying up shop rights in the district.

Only nobles could own land, but merchants traded the rights to operate a business. Before long, she owned or possessed an interest in a sizable section of Artisan Row and most of the Lower Quarter. Medford House, commonly known as The House, was her most lucrative establishment. Despite its back alley location, gentry from far and near frequented this expensive brothel. She had a reputation for being discrete, especially with the identities of men who could not afford to be seen frequenting a brothel.

"Royce," Gwen said, "a potential customer visited The House earlier this evening. He was quite anxious to speak to one of you. I set up a meeting for tomorrow evening."

"Know him?"

"I asked the girls. None of them have ever seen him before."

"Was he serviced?"

Gwen shook her head. "No, he was just after information about thieves for hire. Funny how a man always expects prostitutes to know everything when he is looking for answers but assumes a girl will take *his* secrets to her grave."

"Who talked to him?"

"Tulip. She said he was foreign, dark-skinned, and she mentioned an accent. He might be from Calis, but I didn't bump into him so I can't tell you for sure."

"Was he alone?"

"Tulip didn't mention any companions."

"Want me to talk to him?" Albert asked.

"Na, I'll do it," Hadrian said. "If he's poking around these parts, he'll probably be looking for someone more like me than you."

"If you like, Albert, you can be here tomorrow and watch the door for strangers," Royce added. "I'll keep an eye on the street. Has there been anyone new hanging around?"

"It has been pretty busy, and there are a few people I don't recognize. There are four people right now in the main bar," Gwen mentioned, "and there was a different party of five a few hours ago."

"She's right," Emerald confirmed. "I waited on the five."

"What were they like? Travelers?"

Gwen shook her head. "Soldiers, I think. They weren't dressed like it, but I could tell."

"Mercs?" Hadrian asked.

"I don't think so. Mercenaries are usually troublesome, grabbing the girls, shouting, picking fights—you know the type. These guys were quiet, and one was a noble I think. At least some of the others referred to him as baron something—Trumbul I think it was."

"I saw some like that up on Wayward Street yesterday," Mason said. "Might'a been as many as twelve."

"Anything going on in town?" Royce asked.

They looked at one another doubtfully.

"Do you think it has anything to do with those rumors about killings out near the Nidwalden River?" Hadrian asked. "Maybe the king is calling up support from other nobles."

"Are you talking about the elves?" Mason asked. "I heard about that."

"Me too," Emerald said. "They say elves attacked a village or something. I heard they slaughtered everyone—some even while they slept."

"Who said that? That doesn't sound right," Albert commented. "I've never known an elf to look a man in the eye, much less attack one."

Royce grabbed his boots and cloak and headed for the door. "You've never known an elf, Albert," he said as he abruptly left.

"What'd I say?" Albert asked staring at everyone with an innocent expression.

Emerald shrugged.

Hadrian took out Alenda's purse and tossed it at the viscount. "I wouldn't worry about it. Royce can be moody at times. Here, divvy out the profits."

"Royce is right, though," Emerald said. She appeared pleased that she knew something they did not. "The elves that attacked the village were *wild* elves, full-bloods. The half-breeds from around here are nothing but a bunch of lazy drunks."

"A thousand years of slavery can do that to a person," Gwen pointed out. "Can I have my cut, Albert? I have to get back to work. We've got a bishop, the magistrate, and the Brotherhood of Barons visiting The House tonight."

Hadrian was still sore from the previous day's exertion when he took a seat at an empty table near the bar and observed the patrons of the Diamond Room. The name came from its odd, stretched rectangle shape, caused by how the addition fit into the space between the tavern and the brothel next door. Hadrian knew, or was familiar with, almost everyone in the room. Lamplighters, carriage drivers, tinkers, they were the usual late crowd who came in after work for a meal. They all had the same tired, worn-out, dirty look about them as they sat with their heads bowed over their plates. Each was dressed in a coarse work shirt and poor fitting britches gathered at the waist like the mouth of a sack. They chose this room because it was quieter, and they could eat in peace. One individual, however, stood out.

He sat alone at the far end of the room his back to the wall. His table remained bare except for the standard tavern candle. He had not bought a drink or a plate. He wore a wide-brimmed felt hat with one side pinned up by a lavish blue plume. His doublet, worn over a brilliant gold satin waist shirt, was made of rich black and red brocade with stuffed shoulders. At his side was a saber attached to a fine-studded, leather girdle matching his high, black riding boots. Whoever he was, he was not hiding. Hadrian also noted a bundle beneath the table on which he rested one boot at all times.

Once Royce sent Emerald over with the news that the street was clear of associates, Hadrian got up and walked the length of the room, stopping before the empty chair in front of the stranger.

"Care for some company?" he asked.

"That depends," the man replied, and Hadrian noted the slight saucy accent of a Calian native. "I am looking for a representative of an organization called Riyria. Do you speak for that group?"

"That depends on what you want," Hadrian replied with a small grin.

"In that case, please sit down."

Hadrian took the seat and waited.

"My name is Baron Dellano DeWitt, and I am looking to hire men of talent. I was told there were a few in the area that could be had for a price."

"What kind of talents are you looking to buy?"

"Procurement skills," DeWitt said simply, "I have an item I need to make disappear. If at all possible, I would prefer it to disappear completely. But it has to happen tonight."

Hadrian smiled. "Sorry, I am quite certain Riyria won't work under such tight constraints. Too dangerous. I hope you understand."

"I'm sorry about the timing. I tried to reach your organization last night, but I was told you were unavailable. I am in a position to make it worth the risk."

"Sorry, but they have very strict rules." Hadrian started to get up.

"Please, listen. I have asked around. Those who know the pulse of this city tell me there is a pair of independent professionals who take on such jobs if the price is right. How they manage to work with impunity outside of the organized guilds is a matter of speculation, but the fact remains that they do. This is a testament to their reputation, is it not? If you know these men, the members of this Riyria, I beg you, implore them to assist me."

Hadrian considered the man. Initially, he thought him to be another of the many self-absorbed nobles looking for a chuckle at some royal banquet. Now, however, the man's demeanor changed. There was a hint of desperation in his voice.

"What's so important about this item?" Hadrian asked as he eased back into his seat. "And why does it have to disappear tonight?"

"Have you heard of Count Pickering?"

"Master swordsman, winner of the Silver Shield and the Golden Laurel? He has an incredibly beautiful wife named... Belinda, I think. I've heard he has killed at least eight men in duels because of how they have looked at her, or so the legend goes."

"You're unusually well informed."

"Part of the job," Hadrian admitted.

"In a contest of swords, the count has only been beaten by Braga, the Archduke of Melengar, and that was in an exhibition tournament on the one day he didn't have his sword. He was forced to use a replacement."

"Oh, right," Hadrian said as much to himself as to DeWitt. "He's the one with the special rapier he won't duel without, at least not in a real fight."

"Yes! The count is very superstitious about it," Dewitt said nothing more for a moment and looked uncomfortable.

"Did you stare at the count's wife too long?" Hadrian inquired.

The man nodded and bowed his head. "I've been challenged to a duel tomorrow at noon."

"And you want Riyria to steal the count's sword." It was a statement not a question, but DeWitt nodded again.

"I am with the retinue of Duke DeLorkan of Dagastan. We arrived in Medford two days ago, part of a trade negotiation hosted by King Amrath. They held a feast upon our arrival and Pickering was there." The baron wiped his face nervously. "I've never been to Avryn before—for Maribor's sake, I didn't know who he was! I didn't even know she was his wife until I was slapped in the face with a glove. I'm scheduled to duel him tomorrow at noon so the sword must be stolen tonight."

Hadrian sighed. "That is not an easy job. Taking a prized sword from the bedside of— "

"Ah…but I have made it easier," DeWitt told him. "The count, like me, is staying with the king for the negotiations. His quarters are very near my duke's room. Earlier this evening, I slipped into his room and took his sword. There were so many people around I panicked and dropped it in the first open room I found. It must be removed from the castle before he notices it is missing since a search will surely find it."

"So, where is it now?"

"The royal chapel," he said. "It's not guarded and is just down the hall from an empty bedroom with a window. I can make certain the window will be open tonight. There are also ivy vines just outside the wall below the window. It should be a simple thing really."

"Then why don't *you* do it?"

"If thieves are caught with the sword, all that will happen is the loss of their hands, but if *I* am caught, my reputation will be destroyed!"

"I can see the reason for your concern," Hadrian said sardonically, but DeWitt appeared oblivious.

"Exactly! Now, seeing as how I have done most of the work, it doesn't sound so bad, does it? Before you answer, let me add this to the proposal."

With some strain, the baron pulled the bundle from beneath his foot and placed it on the table. A hearty metallic jingle sounded when the saddlebag hit the wood. "Inside you'll find one hundred gold tenents."

"I see," Hadrian responded, staring at the bags and trying to breathe at an even pace. "And you are paying up front?"

"Of course, I'm not a fool. I know how these things work. I'll pay you half now and half when I get the sword."

Hadrian took another controlled breath of air, still nodding and reminding himself to stay calm. "So, you're offering *two hundred* gold tenents?"

"Yes," DeWitt said with a look of concern. "As you can see, this is very important to me."

"Apparently, if the job is as easy as you say."

"Then you think they will do it?" he asked eagerly.

Hadrian sat back in his chair, just as DeWitt leaned forward anxiously. He looked like a man set before a judge awaiting sentencing on a murder charge.

Royce would kill him if he agreed. One of the basic rules they had established for Riyria was that they would not take jobs on short notice. They needed time to do background checks, verify stories, and case potential targets. Still, DeWitt's only crime was choosing the wrong moment to look at a beautiful woman, and Hadrian knew he held the man's life in his hands. There was no chance he could hire anyone else. As DeWitt mentioned, no independent thieves, other than them, would dare take a job in a guild city. The officers of the Crimson Hand would not allow any of their boys to do it for the same reason Hadrian felt he ought to turn it down. On the other hand, Hadrian was not really a thief and was not familiar with all their various deliberations. Royce was the one who grew up on the streets of Ratibor, picking pockets to survive. He was the professional burglar, the ex-member of the infamous Black Diamond Guild. Hadrian was a warrior, a soldier who preferred his battles to be fair and in the daylight.

Hadrian was never completely comfortable with most of the tasks they did for nobles. They wanted to embarrass a rival, to hurt an ex-lover, or to increase their standing in the strange and twisted world of high-stakes politics. The gentry hired them because they possessed fortunes and could afford to pay for their games. To them, that is what life was—one big chess match with real knights, kings, and pawns. There was no good or evil, no right or wrong. It was all just politics. A game within a game with its own set of rules and no values. Their squabbles however, did provide a fertile field for them to harvest profits. Not only were the nobles rich and petty, they were also dim-witted. How else could Royce and Hadrian receive payment from the Earl of Chadwick to intercept letters Alenda Lanaklin sent to Degan Gaunt only to turn around and double their profit by stealing them back? They simply asked Albert to contact Alenda with the news Ballentyne had her letters and an offer to help her get them back. Their business was profitable, but ugly. Just another game he played in a world where heroes were legends and honor was a myth.

He tried to rationalize that what he and Royce did was not that horrible. After all, Alenda could certainly afford it. People like Mason and Emerald needed the money more than a wealthy marquis' daughter. Besides, perhaps it taught her a valuable lesson that might save her father's reputation and lands. Yet, it was still just a way of lying to himself. Trying to convince his conscience that what he was doing was right, or at least not wrong. He desired to do a job with merit, one with which he could actually save a man's life, one with intentions that resembled what he remembered as virtuous.

"Sure," he said.

# 4

When Hadrian finished speaking, the silence in the Dark Room was thick with anticipation. Only three men were present and when Hadrian stopped both he and Albert turned their attention to Royce. As expected, the thief did not look pleased and began slowly shaking his head even before he spoke. "I can't believe you took this job," he scolded.

"Look, I know it is short notice, but his story checks out, right?" Hadrian asked. "You followed him back to the castle. He is a guest of King Amrath. He didn't make any side trips. I can verify he appears to be from Calis, and none of Gwen's girls heard anything to contradict his claims. The job looks clean."

"*Two hundred gold tenents* to slip a sword out an open window —you don't find that suspicious?" Royce asked with a tone of amazed disbelief.

"Personally, I would call it a dream come true," Albert mentioned.

"Maybe they do things differently in Calis. It's pretty far away," Hadrian argued.

"It's not *that* far," Royce shot back. "And how is it this DeWitt is walking around with that much coin? Does he always travel to international trade meetings carrying bags bursting with gold? Why did he bring it?"

"Maybe he didn't. Maybe he sold a valuable ring tonight, or perhaps he obtained a loan using the good name of the Duke DeLorkan. It's even possible that he got it from the duke himself.

I am certain the two of them didn't ride up here on a couple of ponies. The duke likely travels in a huge caravan of wagons. To them, several hundred gold coins might not be unusual."

Hadrian's voice became more serious. "You weren't there. You didn't see this guy. He's facing a virtual execution tomorrow. How much is gold worth if you're dead?"

"We just got done with a job. I was hoping to take a few days off, and now you've signed us up for a new one." Royce sighed. "You say DeWitt was scared?"

"He was sweating."

"So, that's what this is really about. You want to take the job because it's for a good cause. You think risking our necks is worth it so long as we can pat ourselves on the back afterwards."

"Pickering will kill him—you know it. And he's not the first."

"He won't be the last either."

Hadrian sighed and, folding his arms across his chest, sat back in his chair. "You're right; there will be others. So, imagine we pinch the sword and get rid of the damn thing. The count never sees it again. Think of all the happy men who could finally look at Belinda without fear."

Royce chuckled. "So, now it's a public service?"

"And there is the two hundred gold tenents," Hadrian added. "That's more money than we've made all year. Cold weather is coming, and with that coin, we could sit out the winter."

"Well, at least now you are talking some sense. That would be nice," Royce admitted.

"And it's only a couple hours of work, just a quick climb and grab. You're the one always telling me how bad the security is at Essendon Castle. We'll be done and in bed before dawn."

Royce bit his lower lip and grimaced, refusing to look at Hadrian.

Hadrian saw his opening and pressed his advantage. "You remember how cold it was on top of that tower. Just think how cold it will be in a few months. You can spend the winter safe and warm, eating richly and drinking your favorite wine. Then of course," Hadrian leaned closer, "there's the snow. You know how you hate the snow."

"All right, all right. Grab the gear. I'll meet you in the alley."

Hadrian smiled. "I knew there was a heart in there somewhere."

Outside, the night was even colder than it had been. A slick frost formed on the roads. Winter snows would indeed be falling soon. Despite what Hadrian thought, Royce did not actually hate snow. He liked the way it blanketed the Lower Quarter, dressing it up in an elegant white gown. Nevertheless, its beauty came with a cost; tracks remained in snow and made his job much harder. Hadrian was right, after tonight they would have enough cash set aside to spend the whole winter in quiet hibernation. With that much money, they could even consider opening a legitimate business. He thought about it every time they scored big, and he and Hadrian discussed it on more than one occasion. A year ago, they talked seriously about opening a winery, but it did not suit them. That was always the problem. Neither could think of any lawful business that was right for them.

He stopped in front of Medford House. Appearing to grow out of The Rose and Thorn, The House was nearly as large as the tavern. Gwen had linked the two buildings by additions so customers could move back and forth freely without exposing themselves to the elements, or public scrutiny. Gwen DeLancy was a genius. He had never known anyone like her. She was clever and intelligent beyond reason, and she was more open and sincere than anyone he had ever met. She was a paradox to him, an impossible mystery he could not solve—she was an honest person.

"I thought you might stop by," Gwen said, stepping out onto the porch of The House and wrapping a cape about her shoulders. "I was watching for you through the doorway."

"You have good eyes. Most people never see me when I walk a dark street."

"You must have wanted to be seen then. You were coming to visit me, weren't you?"

"I just wanted to be sure you received your portion of the payment last night."

Gwen smiled. As she did, Royce could not help but notice how beautifully her hair shimmered in the moonlight.

"Royce, you know you don't have to pay me. I'd give you anything you asked for."

"No," Royce insisted. "We use your place as a base. It's dangerous, and for that, you get a part of the profit. We've been over this."

She stepped closer and took his hand. Her touch was soothingly warm amidst the chilling air. "I also wouldn't own The Rose and Thorn if it wasn't for you. There's a very good chance I wouldn't even be alive."

"I have no idea what you speak of, your ladyship," Royce said as he performed a formal bow. "I can prove I wasn't even in town that night."

She stared at him with the same smile. He loved to see her happy, but now her brilliant green eyes searched for something, and Royce turned away, letting go of her hand.

"Listen, Hadrian and I are taking that job. We have to do it tonight so I need to— "

"You're a strange man, Royce Melborn. I wonder if I'll ever really know you."

Royce paused and then softly said, "You already know me better than any woman should, more than is safe for either of us."

Gwen stepped toward him again, her heeled shoes crunching on the frosty ground, her eyes intense with pleading. "Be careful, won't you?"

"I always am."

With his cloak billowing in the wind, he walked away. She watched him until he entered a shadow and was gone.

# PART 3
## CONSPIRACIES

The crowned falcon standard flew from the highest tower of Essendon Castle, marking the presence of the king. Essendon was the royal seat of Avryn and the kingdom of Melengar, and although not especially large or powerful, it was nevertheless an old and respected realm. The castle, an imposing structure of elaborate gray walls and towers, stood at the center of Medford, the hub of the city's four distinct quarters of Gentry Square, Artisan Row, the Common Quarter, and the Lower Quarter. Like most cities in Avryn, Medford lay behind the protection of a strong outer wall; nevertheless, the castle also had its own fortifications partitioning it from the general city. This inner wall, crowned with crenellated parapets where skilled archers kept watch from behind stone merlons, did not completely encircle the castle. Instead, it connected to a large, imposing keep that served as its rear barrier. The height of the keep and the wide moat surrounding its base kept the king's home well protected.

During the day, merchants wheeled carts to the castle wall and positioned themselves on either side of the gate, forming a tent city of bustling vendors, entertainers, and lenders who sought to do business with the castle inhabitants. This wave of local commerce receded at sunset because citizens of the city could not pass within fifty feet of the walls from dusk until dawn. This restriction was strictly enforced by royal archers who rarely hesitated to fire at those who ventured too close at night. Pairs of guards, dressed in chain mail with steel helms bearing the falcon standard of Melengar, patrolled the perimeter of the castle. They walked casually, with thumbs in their sword belts, often discussing events of the day or their off duty plans.

Royce and Hadrian watched the pace of the guard's routine for an hour before moving toward the rear of the keep. Just as DeWitt had explained, negligent gardeners had ignored a spider-work of thick-stemmed vines tracing their way up the stone. Unfortunately, the vines did not reach as high as the windows. On this frosty late autumn night, the swim across the moat was bone chillingly cold. The ivy, however, proved to be quite reliable, and the climb was as easy as ascending a ladder.

"I now know why DeWitt didn't want to do this himself," Hadrian whispered to Royce as they hung from the ivy. "After being frozen in that water, I think if I fell right now I would shatter on impact."

"Just imagine how many chamber pots are dumped into it each day," Royce mentioned as he drove a small, ringed spike into the seam between two stone blocks.

Hadrian looked up at the many windows he presumed led to bedrooms and cringed at the implications. "I could have lived without that bit of insight." He pulled a strap harness from his satchel and fastened it to the eyelet of the spike's ring.

"Just trying to take your mind off the cold," Royce said, tapping in another spike.

Although tedious and tense, the process was surprisingly fast, and they reached the lowest window before the guards completed their circuit. Royce reached out and tested the shutter. As promised, it was open. He pulled it gently back, just a hair, and peered inside. A moment later, he climbed in and waved Hadrian up.

A small bed draped in a rich burgundy canopy took up the center of one wall. A dresser with a washbasin stood beside it. The only other piece of furniture was a simple wooden chair. A modest tapestry of hounds hunting deer covered much of the opposite wall. Everything was neat but sterile. There were no boots near the door, no jacket thrown across the chair, and the bed covers showed no wrinkles. The room was unused.

Hadrian remained silent near the window as Royce moved across the room to the door. He watched as the thief's feet tested the surface of the floor before committing his weight. Royce mentioned once how he had been in an attic on a job when he hit a weak board and fell through the bedroom ceiling. This floor was stone, but even stones had loose mortar or contained ingenious hidden traps or alarms. Royce made it to the door where he crouched and paused to listen. He motioned a sign for walking with his hand and then began counting on his fingers for Hadrian to see. There was a pause, and then he repeated the signal again. Hadrian crossed the room to join his friend and the two sat waiting for several minutes in silence.

Eventually Royce lifted the door latch with gloved hands but did not open it. Outside they could hear the heavy footfalls of hard boots on stone, first one set, and then a second. As the steps faded, Royce opened the door slightly and peered out. The hall was empty.

Before them lay a narrow hallway lit by widely spaced torches, whose flames cast flickering shadows, which created an illusion of movement on the walls. They entered the hall, quietly closed the door behind them, and quickly moved approximately fifty feet to another door. Ornate and elaborately carved, it had gilded hinges and a metal lock. Royce tried the door and then shook his head. He knelt and pulled a small kit of tools from his belt pouch while Hadrian moved to the far side of the hall. From where he stood, he could see the length of the corridor in both directions as well as a portion of the stairs that entered from the right. He stood ready for any trouble, which came sooner than he expected.

A sound echoed in the corridor to his right, and Hadrian could hear the faint noise of hard heels on stone coming in their direction. Still on his knees, Royce worked the lock as the steps grew closer. Hadrian moved his hand to the hilt of his sword when at last the thief quickly opened the door. Trusting to luck that the room was empty, the two slipped inside. Royce softly closed the door behind them, and the footsteps passed without pause.

They were in the royal chapel. Banks of candles burned on either side of the large room. Supporting a glorious vaulted ceiling, elaborate marble columns rose near the chamber's center. Four rows of wooden pews lined either side of the main aisle. Cinquefoil-shaped adornments and blind-tracery moldings common to the Nyphron Church decorated the walls. Alabaster statues of Maribor and Novron stood behind the altar. Novron, depicted as a strong handsome man in the prime of his youth, was kneeling, sword in hand. The god Maribor, sculpted as a powerful, larger-than-life figure with a long beard and flowing robes, loomed over Novron, placing a crown upon the young man's head. The altar itself consisted of an ornately carved wooden cabinet with three broad doors and a rose-colored marble top. Upon it, two more candles burned and a large gilded tome lay open.

DeWitt had told Hadrian he left the sword behind the altar, and they headed toward it. As they approached the first set of pews, both men froze in mid step. Lying there, face down in a pool of freshly spilled blood, was the body of a man. The rounded handle of the nondescript dagger protruded from his back. While Royce made a quick survey for Pickering's sword, Hadrian checked the man for signs of life. The man was dead, and the sword was nowhere to be found. Royce tapped Hadrian on the shoulder and pointed at the gold crown that had rolled to the far side of a pillar. The full weight of the situation registered with both of them—it was time to leave.

They headed for the door. Royce paused only momentarily to listen to ensure the hall was clear. They slipped out of the chapel, closed the door, and moved down the hall toward the bedroom.

"*Murderers!*"

The shout was so close and so terrifying that they both spun with weapons drawn. Hadrian had his bastard sword in one hand, his short sword in the other. Royce held a brilliant white-bladed dagger.

Standing before the open chapel door was a bearded dwarf.

"*Murderers!*" The dwarf cried again, but it was not necessary. The sounds of footfalls could already be heard, and an instant later, soldiers, with weapons drawn, poured into the hallway from both sides.

"*Murderers!*" the dwarf continued pointing at them. "They've killed the king!"

Royce lifted the latch to the bedroom door and pushed, but the door failed to give way. He pulled, and then pushed again, but the door would not budge.

"Drop your weapons, or we'll butcher you where you stand!" a soldier ordered. He was a tall man with a bushy moustache that bristled as he gritted his teeth fiercely.

"How many do you think there are?" whispered Hadrian. The walls echoed with the sounds of more soldiers about to arrive.

"Too many," Royce replied.

"Be a lot less in a minute," Hadrian assured him.

"We won't make it. I can't get the door opened; we have no exit. I think someone spiked it from the inside. We can't fight the entire castle guard."

"Put them down now!" The soldier in charge shouted and took a step closer while raising the level of his sword.

"Damn." Hadrian let his blades drop. Royce followed suit.

"Take them," the soldier barked.

# 2

Alric Essendon awoke, startled by the commotion. He was not in his room. The bed he was lying in was a fraction of the size and lacked the familiar velvet canopy. The walls were bare stone, and only a small dresser and wash table decorated the space. He sat up, rubbing his eyes and soon realized where he was. He had accidentally fallen asleep, apparently several hours ago.

He looked over at Tillie, her bare back and shoulder exposed above the quilt. Alric wondered how she could sleep with all the shouting going on. He rolled out of bed and felt around for his nightshirt. Determining his clothing from hers was easy to do even in the dark. Hers was linen; his was silk.

Awakened by his movement, Tillie groggily asked, "What's wrong?"

"Nothing, go back to sleep," Alric replied.

She could sleep through a hurricane, but his leaving always woke her. That he had fallen asleep was not her fault, but he blamed her just the same. Alric hated waking up here. He hated Tillie even more, and was conscious of the paradox. Throughout the day, her need for him attracted Alric, but in the morning, it repulsed him. Of all the castle servants, however, she was by far the prettiest. Alric did not care for the noble ladies his father invited to court. They were haughty, formal, and considered their virginity more valuable than the crown. He found them dull and irritating. His father thought differently. Alric was only nineteen, but already his father was pressuring him to pick a bride.

"You'll be king someday," Amrath told him. "Your first duty to the kingdom is to sire an heir." His father spoke of marriage as if it was a profession, and that was how Alric saw it as well. For him, this, or any form of work, was best avoided—or at least postponed as long as possible.

"I wish you could spend the whole night with me, my lord," Tillie babbled at him as he pulled his nightshirt over his head.

"Then you should be grateful I dozed as long as I did." With his toes he felt along the floor for his slippers and, finding them, he slid his feet into the warm fleece lining.

"I am, my lord."

"Good night, Tillie," Alric said as he reached the door and stepped outside.

"Good— " Alric closed the door before she finished.

Tillie usually slept with the other maids, in a dorm near the kitchens. Alric brought her to the little vacant bedroom on the third floor of the castle for privacy. He did not like taking girls to his room—his father's bedroom was right next door. The vacant room was on the north side of the castle, and because it received less sunlight, it was always cooler than the royal chambers. He pulled his nightshirt tight and shuffled down the corridor toward the stairs.

"I've checked all the upper floors, Captain, he's not there," Alric heard someone say from just up the steps. By his curt tone, he guessed the speaker to be a sentry. He spoke to them rarely, but when he did, they were always abrupt as if words were a commodity in short supply.

"Continue the search, down to the prisons if necessary. I want every room examined, each pantry, cabinet, and wardrobe. Do you understand?"

Alric knew that voice well, it was Wylin, the master-at-arms.

"Yes, sir, right away!"

Alric heard the sentry trotting down the steps, and he saw the soldier stop abruptly the moment he met Alric's gaze. "I found him, sir!" he shouted with a hint of relief.

"What's going on, Captain?" Alric called out even as Wylin and three other castle guards rushed down the steps.

"Your Royal Highness!" the captain knelt briefly, bowing his head, and then rose abruptly. "Benton!" he snapped at the solider. "I want five more men here protecting the prince *right now*. Move!"

"Yes, sir!" the soldier snapped a salute and ran back up the stairs.

"Protecting me?" Alric said. "What's going on?"

"Your father's been murdered."

"My father? What?"

"His Majesty, the king...we found him in the royal chapel stabbed in the back. Two intruders are in custody. The dwarf Magnus confirmed it. He saw them murder your father, but he was powerless to stop them."

Alric heard Wylin's voice, but he could not understand the words. They did not make sense. *My father is dead?* He had just spoken with him before he went to Tillie's room not more than a few hours ago. *How could he be dead?*

"I must insist that you remain here, Your Highness, under heavy guard until I finish sweeping the castle. They may not be alone. I am presently conducting a— "

"Insist what you like, Wylin, but get out of my way. I want to see my father!" Alric demanded, pushing past him.

"King Amrath's body has been taken to his bedroom, Your Highness."

*His body!*

Alric did not want to hear any more. He ran up the steps, his slippers flying off his feet.

"Stay with the prince!" Wylin shouted after him.

Alric reached the royal wing. There was a crowd in the corridor that moved aside at his approach. As he reached the chapel, its door lay open with several of the chief ministers gathered inside.

"My prince!" he heard his Uncle Percy call to him from inside, but he did not stop. He was determined to reach his father.

*He couldn't be dead!*

He rounded the corner, passed his own room, and rushed into the royal suite. Here the double doors were open as well. Several ladies in nightgowns and robes stood just outside weeping loudly. Inside, a pair of older women busied themselves wringing out pink-stained linens in a washbasin.

To the side of the bed stood his sister Arista, dressed in a burgundy and gold gown. Her arms wrapped around the bedpost, which she gripped so tightly that her fingers were white. She stared at the figure on the mattress with eyes that were dry but wide with horror.

On the pale white sheets of the royal bed lay King Amrath Essendon. He still wore the same clothes Alric had seen him in before he retired for the night. His face was pale, his eyes were closed, and near the corner of his lips, there was a tiny tear of dried blood.

"My prince—I mean, Your Royal Majesty," his uncle corrected himself as he followed him into the bedchamber. His Uncle Percy always looked older than his father did—his hair was very gray, his face wrinkled and drooping; however, he possessed the trim elegant build of a swordsman. He was still in the process of tying up his robe as he entered. "Thank Maribor you are safe. We thought you might have met a similar fate."

Alric was at a loss for words. He just stood staring at the still body of his father.

"Your Majesty, do not worry. I will take care of everything. I know how hard this must be. You're still a young man and— "

"What are you talking about?" Alric looked at him. "Take care of what? What are you taking care of?"

"A number of things, Your Majesty. There is the securing of the castle, the investigation as to how this happened, the apprehension of those responsible, arrangements for the funeral, and of course, the eventual coronation."

"Coronation?"

"You are king now, sire. We will need to arrange your crowning ceremony, but that, of course, will wait until we have everything else settled."

"But I thought…Wylin told me the murderers have been captured."

"He captured two of them. I'm just making certain there aren't anymore."

"What will happen to them?" He looked back at the still form of his father. "The killers, what will happen to them?"

"That is up to you, Your Royal Majesty. Their fate is yours to decide, unless you would prefer I handle the matter for you, since it can be quite unpleasant."

Alric turned to his uncle. "I want them to die, Uncle Percy. I want them to suffer horribly and then die."

"Of course, Your Majesty, of course. I assure you they will."

The dungeons of Essendon Castle lay buried two stories beneath the earth. Ground water seeped through cracks in the walls and wet the face of the stone. Fungus grew in the mortar between stone blocks, and mold coated the wood of doors, stools, and buckets. The foul, musty smell mixed with the stench of decay, and the corridors echoed with the mournful cries of doomed men. Despite the rumors told in Medford's taverns, the castle dungeons had a limited capacity. Needless to say, the prison staff found room for the king-killers. They moved prisoners to provide Royce and Hadrian with their own private cell.

News of the king's death did not take long to spread, and for the first time in years, the prisoners had something exciting to talk about.

"Who'da thought I'd outlast old Amrath," a graveled voice muttered. He laughed, but the laughter quickly broke into a series of coughs and sputters.

"Any chance the prince might review our sentences on account of all this?" A weaker, younger voice asked. "I mean it's possible, isn't it?"

This question was met with a lengthy silence, more coughing, and a sneeze.

"The guard said they stabbed the bastard in the back right in his own chapel. What does that say about his piety?" A new bitter voice questioned. "Seems to me he was asking for a bit too much from the man upstairs."

"The ones that done it 'ere in our old cell. They moved me and Danny out to make room. I saw 'em when they shifted us, two of 'em, one big, the other little."

"Anyone know 'em? Maybe they was trying to break us out and got sidetracked, eh?"

"Gotta have some pretty big brass ones to kill a king in his own castle. They won't get a trial, not even a fake one. I'm surprised they've lived this long."

"Gonna want a public torture before the execution. Things been quiet a long time. Haven't had a good torture in years."

"So why ya think they did it?"

"Why don't you ask 'em?"

"Hey, over there? You conscious in that cell of yours? Or did they beat you stupid?"

"Maybe they're dead."

They were not dead, but neither were they talking. Royce and Hadrian stood chained to the far wall of their cell, their ankles locked in stocks, and their mouths gagged with leather muzzles. They had only been there for the better part of an hour, but already the strain on Hadrian's muscles was painful. The soldiers had removed their gear, cloaks, boots, and tunics, leaving them with nothing but their britches to fight the damp chill of the dungeon.

They hung listening to the rambling conversations of the other inmates. The conversation halted at the sound of heavy approaching footfalls. The door to the cellblock opened and banged against the interior wall.

"Right this way, Your Royal Highness—I mean, Your Royal Majesty," the voice of the dungeon warden said rapidly.

A metal key twisted in the lock, and the door to their cell creaked open. Four royal bodyguards led the prince and his uncle, Percy Braga inside. Hadrian recognized Braga, the Archduke and Lord Chancellor of Melengar, but he had never seen Alric before. The prince was young, perhaps no more than twenty. He was short, thin, and delicate in appearance with light brown hair that reached to his shoulders, and only the ghost of a beard. His stature and features must have come from his mother because the former king had been a bear of a man. He wore only a silk nightshirt with a massive sword strapped comically to his side by an oversized leather belt.

"These are the ones?"

"Yes, Your Majesty," Braga replied.

"Torch," Alric commanded, snapping his fingers impatiently as a soldier pulled one from the wall bracket and held it out for him. Alric scowled at the offer. "Hold it near their heads. I wish to see their faces." Alric peered at them. "No marks? They haven't been whipped?"

"No, Your Majesty," Braga said. "They surrendered without a fight and Captain Wylin thought it best to lock them up while he searched the rest of the castle. I approved his decision. We can't be certain these two acted alone in this."

"No, of course not. Who gave the order to gag them?"

"I don't know, Your Majesty."

"Do you wish their gags removed?" Percy inquired.

"No, Uncle Percy—oh, I can't call you that anymore, can I?"

"You're the king now, Your Majesty. You can call me whatever you wish."

"But it isn't dignified, not for a ruler, but *archduke* is so formal —I will call you, Percy, is that all right?"

"It is not my place to approve of your decisions any longer, sire."

"Percy it is then, and no, leave their gags on. I have no desire to hear their lies. What will they say except that they didn't do it? Captured killers always deny their crimes. What choice do they have? Unless they wish to take their last few moments of life to spit in the face of their king. I won't give them the satisfaction of that."

"They could tell us if they were working alone or for someone else. They could even tell us who that person or persons might be."

Alric continued to study them. His eyes focused on a twisted mark in the shape of an M on Royce's left shoulder. He squinted and then, out of frustration, snatched the torch from a guard and held it painfully close to Royce's face for a moment. "What is this here? Like a tattoo, but not quite."

"A brand, Your Majesty," Braga replied. "It is the Mark of Manzant. It would seem this creature was once an inmate of Manzant Prison."

Alric looked puzzled. "I didn't think inmates were released from Manzant, and I wasn't aware anyone has ever escaped."

Braga appeared puzzled as well.

Alric then moved to inspect Hadrian. When he observed the small silver medallion that hung around his neck, the prince lifted it, turned it over with mild curiosity, and then let it go with disdain.

"It doesn't matter," Alric said. "I really don't think they look like the type to volunteer information. In the morning have them hauled out to the square and tortured. If they say anything of merit, have them beheaded."

"If not?"

"If not, quarter them slowly. Draw their bowels into the sun and have the royal surgeon keep them alive as long as possible. Oh, and before you do, make certain heralds have time to make several announcements. I want a crowd for this. People need to know the penalty for treason."

"As you wish, sire."

Alric started for the door, and then stopped. He turned and struck Royce across the face with the back of his hand. "He was my father, you worthless piece of filth!" The prince walked out, leaving the two hanging helplessly and awaiting the dawn.

Hadrian could only guess how long they had been hanging against the wall; perhaps two or three hours had passed. The faceless voices of the other inmates grew less frequent until they stopped entirely, silenced with boredom or sleep. The muzzle covering his mouth became soaked with spit and he found it difficult to breathe. His wrists were sore where the shackles rubbed and his back and his legs ached. To make matters worse, the cold tightened his muscles, making the strain even more painful. Not wanting to look at Royce, he alternated between closing his eyes and staring at the far wall. He did his best to avoid thinking about what would happen when daylight came. Instead, his mind was full of thoughts of self-incrimination—this was his fault. His insistence on breaking rules landed them where they were. Their death was on his hands.

The door opened, and once more, a royal guard, this time accompanied by a woman, entered the cell. She was tall, slender, and dressed in a gown of burgundy and gold silk, which shimmered like fire in the torch light. She was pretty, with auburn hair and fair skin.

"Remove their gags," she ordered briskly. The jailers rushed to unbuckle the straps and pull off the muzzles. "Now leave us, all of you."

The jailers promptly exited.

"You too, Hilfred."

"Your Highness, I'm your bodyguard. I need to stay to— "

"They are chained to the wall, Hilfred," she snapped and then took a breath to calm herself. "I am fine, now please leave and guard the door. I want no interruptions by anyone. Do you understand?"

"As you wish, Your Highness." The guard bowed and stepped out, closing the door behind him.

She moved forward, carefully studying the two of them. On her belt was a jeweled kris dagger. Hadrian recognized the long wavy blade as the type used by eastern occultists for magical enchantments. Presently he was more concerned with its other use —as a deadly weapon. She toyed with the dragon-shaped hilt as if she might draw it forth and stab them at any moment.

"Do you know who I am?" she asked Hadrian.

"Princess Arista Essendon," Hadrian replied.

"Very good." She smiled at him. "Now who are you and don't bother lying. You will be dead in less than four hours, so what is the point?"

"Hadrian Blackwater."

"And you?"

"Royce Melborn."

"Who sent you here?"

"A man by the name of DeWitt," Hadrian replied. "He is a member of the Duke DeLorkan's group from Dagastan, but we weren't sent to kill your father."

"What were you sent to do?" Her painted nails clicked along the silver handle of the dagger, her eyes intent on them.

"To steal Count Pickering's sword. DeWitt said the count challenged him to a duel here last night at a dinner party."

"And what were you doing in the chapel?"

"That's where DeWitt said he hid the sword."

"I see…" She paused a moment as her mask of stone wavered. Her lips began to tremble, and her eyes well up with tears. She turned away from them, trying to compose herself. Her head was bowed and Hadrian could see her small body lurching.

"Listen," Hadrian said, "for what it's worth, we didn't kill your father."

"I know," she said her back still turned.

Royce and Hadrian exchanged glances.

"You were sent here tonight to take the blame for the murder. Both of you are innocent."

"Are you—" Hadrian began, but stopped. For the first time since their capture, he felt hopeful, but thought better of it. He turned to Royce. "Is she being sarcastic? You can usually tell better than I."

"Not this time," Royce said, his face tense.

"I just can't believe he's really gone," Arista muttered. "I kissed him goodnight—it was only a few hours ago." She took a deep breath and straightened before turning to face them. "My brother has set plans for the two of you. You'll be tortured to death this morning. They're building a platform where you will be drawn and quartered."

"We have already heard the details from your brother," Royce said dismally.

"He is the king now. I can't stop him. He is determined to see you punished."

"You could talk to him," Hadrian offered hopefully. "You could explain that we're innocent. You could tell him about DeWitt."

Arista wiped her eyes with the insides of her wrists. "There is no DeWitt. There was no dinner party here last night, no duke from Calis, and Count Pickering hasn't visited this castle in months. Even if any of that were true, Alric wouldn't believe me. Not a person in this castle will believe me. I am an emotional girl; that's what they'll say. 'She is distraught. She is upset.' I can do no more to stop your execution tomorrow than I could do to save my own father's life tonight."

"You knew he was going to die?" Royce asked.

She nodded, fighting the tears again. "I knew. I was told he would be killed, but I didn't believe it." She paused for a moment to study their faces. "Tell me, what would you do to get out of this castle alive before morning?"

The two glanced at each other in stunned silence.

"I'm thinking anything," Hadrian said. "How about you, Royce?"

His partner nodded. "I'd have to say I'm good with that."

"I can't stop the execution," Arista explained, "but I can see to it that you get out of this dungeon. I can return your clothes and weapons, and I can tell you a way to reach the sewers that run under this castle. I think they will take you out of the city. You should know that I have never personally explored them."

"I...I wouldn't think so," Hadrian said, not really certain he was hearing everything correctly.

"It is imperative that when you escape, you leave the city."

"I don't think that will be a problem," Hadrian explained. "We'd probably do that anyway."

"And one more thing, you must kidnap my brother."

There was a pause as they both stared at her.

"Wait, wait, hold on. You want us to *kidnap* the Prince of Melengar?"

"Technically, he's the King of Melengar now," Royce corrected.

"Oh, yeah. I forgot," Hadrian muttered.

Arista walked back to the cell door, peeked out the window, and then returned.

"Why do you want us to kidnap your brother?" Royce asked.

"Because whoever killed my father will kill Alric next, and before his coronation, I imagine."

"Why?"

"To destroy the Essendon line."

Royce stared at her. "Wouldn't that place you at risk as well?"

"Yes, but the threat to me will not be serious as long as Alric is thought to be alive. He is the crown prince. I am only the silly daughter. Besides, one of us has to stay here in order to run the kingdom and find my father's murderer."

"And your brother couldn't do that?" Hadrian asked.

"My brother is convinced *you* killed him."

"Oh, right—you have to forgive me. A minute ago I was about to be executed, and now I'm going to kidnap a king. Things are changing a bit fast for me."

"What are we supposed to do with your brother once we've gotten him out of the city?" Royce asked.

"I need you to take him to Gutaria Prison."

"I've never heard of the place," Royce said. He looked at Hadrian, who shook his head.

"I'm not surprised; few people have," Arista explained. "It is a secret ecclesiastical prison maintained exclusively by the Church of Nyphron. It lies on the north side of Windermere Lake. You know where that is?"

They both nodded.

"Travel around the edge of the lake; there is an old road that rises up between some hills; just follow it. I need you to take my brother to see a prisoner named Esrahaddon."

"And then what?"

"That's it," she said. "Hopefully, he will be able to explain everything to Alric well enough to convince him of what is going on."

"So," Royce said, "you want us to escape from this prison, kidnap the king, cross the countryside with him in tow while dodging soldiers who I assume might not accept our side of the story, and go to another secret prison so that he can visit an inmate?"

Arista did not appear amused. "Either that, or you can be tortured to death in four hours."

"Sounds like a really good plan to me," Hadrian declared. "Royce?"

"I like any plan where I don't die a horrible death."

"Good. I will have two monks come in to give you last rites. I'll have your chains removed and the stocks opened so you can kneel. You will take their frocks, lock them in your place, and silence them with the gags. Your things are right outside in the prison office. I will tell the warden that you're taking them for the poor. I'll have my personal bodyguard Hilfred escort you to the lower kitchens. They won't be active for another hour or so. You should have the place to yourselves. A grate near the basin lifts out for sweeping debris into the sewer. I will speak to my brother and convince him to meet me at the kitchens alone. I assume you are capable fighters?"

"He is." Royce bobbed his head toward Hadrian.

"My brother isn't so you should be able to subdue him easily. Be certain not to hurt him."

"This is likely a really stupid question for me to ask," Royce said, "but what makes you think we won't just kill your brother, leave his body in the sewer to rot, and then just disappear?"

"Nothing," she replied. "Like you, I simply don't have a choice."

# 5

The monks posed little problem and once dressed in their frocks, with hoods carefully drawn, they slipped out of their cell. Hilfred stood waiting just outside and quickly escorted them as far as the entrance to the kitchens where, without a word, he left them alone. Royce, who had always had better night vision, led the way through the dark labyrinth of massive pots and piled plates. Dressed as they were with loose sleeves and long, disabling robes, they navigated this sea of potential disaster where one wrong move could topple a ceramic stack and cause alarm.

So far, Arista's plan was a success. The kitchen was empty. They shed their clerical garb in favor of their own clothes and gear. They located the central basin under which was a massive iron grating. Although it was heavy, they were able to move it out of position without creating too much noise. They were pleasantly surprised to find some iron rungs leading into the void. In the depths below, they could hear the trickle of water. Hadrian looked around and found a pantry filled with vegetables. He felt around until he located a burlap sack filled with potatoes. He quietly dumped out the spuds, shook it as clean as he could, and then rooted around for twine.

They were still a long way from free, but the future was looking considerably better than it had only minutes before. Although Royce had not said a word, the fact that he was responsible bothered Hadrian. Waiting there together, the guilt and silence became overpowering.

"Aren't you going to say 'I told you so'?" Hadrian whispered.

"What would be the point in that?"

"Oh, so you're saying that you're going to hang on to this and throw it at me at some future, more personally beneficial moment?"

"I don't see the point in wasting it now, do you?"

They left the door to the kitchen slightly ajar, and before long, the distant glow of a torch appeared and Hadrian could hear approaching voices. At this signal, they took their positions. Royce took a seat at the table with his back to the entryway. He put the hood of his cloak up and pretended to hunch over a plate of food. Hadrian stood to one side of the door, his short sword raised above his head.

"For Maribor's sake, why here?"

"Because I'm offering the old man a plate of food and a place to wash."

Hadrian recognized the voices of Alric and Arista and surmised they were now just outside the kitchen door.

"I don't see why we had to leave the guards, Arista. There may still be danger. Other assassins could be loose and plotting to kill me, or even you. Have you thought of that?"

"That's why you need to talk to this man. He says he knows who hired the men who killed father, and he refuses to talk to a woman. I get the impression there may be a conspiracy at work here, and I'm not sure who to trust. He said he will only deal with you, and only if you are alone. Don't worry, he's an old man and you're a skilled swordsman. We have to find out what he has to say. Don't you want to know?"

"Of course, but what makes you think he knows?"

"I don't. I don't know anything for certain. But he says he knows. He's not asking for money, just a fresh start. That reminds me, here are some clothes to give him." There was a brief pause. "Look, he seems trustworthy to me. I think if he were lying, he would request gold or land. I'm reserving judgment until I know what he knows, and as I said, he won't tell me anything."

"It's just so—strange. Hilfred is not even with you. It's as if you're walking around without a shadow. It's unnerving is what it is. Just coming down here with you it's…well, you and I, we…you know. We're brother and sister, yet, we hardly see each other. In the last few years, I think I've only spoken to you a dozen times, and then only when we visit Drondil Fields on holiday. You always lock yourself up in that tower doing who knows what, but now — "

"I know, it's strange," Arista replied. "I agree. It's like the night of the fire all over again. I still have nightmares about that evening. I wonder if I'll have nightmares about tonight."

Alric's voice softened. "That's not really my point. It's just that we've never gotten along, not really. But now, well, you're the only family I have left. It seems strange to be saying it, but I suddenly find that matters to me."

"Are you saying you want to be friends?"

"Let's just say I want to stop being enemies."

"I didn't know we were."

"You've been jealous of me ever since mother told you elder daughters don't get to be queen as long as little brothers are around to be king."

"I have not!"

"I don't want to fight. Maybe I do want to be friends. I'm the king now, and I'll need your help. You're smarter than most of the ministers anyway, Father always said so. And you've had university training; that's more than I've had."

"Trust me, Alric I'm more than your friend. I'm your big sister, and I'll look out for you. Now go in there and see what this man has to say."

As Alric entered the door, Hadrian brought the hilt of his sword down on the back of his head. The prince collapsed to the floor with a dull thud. Arista rushed in.

"I said not to hurt him!" she scolded.

"He would be screaming for the guard right now otherwise," Hadrian explained. He tied a gag around the prince's mouth and placed the sack over his head. Royce was already up from his seat and securing Alric's ankles with twine.

"He's all right though?"

"He'll live," Hadrian told her as he secured the hands and arms of the unconscious prince.

"Which is a whole lot more than he had in store for us," Royce added, pulling tight the noose around the prince's ankles.

"Keep in mind he was certain you killed his father," the princess said. "How would you react?"

"I never knew my father," Royce replied indifferently.

"Your mother then."

"Royce is an orphan," Hadrian explained as they continued to wrap the prince in twine. "He never knew either of his parents."

"I suppose that explains a lot. Well then, imagine how you will treat the person who sent you to the chapel tonight, once you find him. I doubt you will be very charitable when coming face to face with him. In any case, you gave your word. Please do as I ask, and take good care of my brother. Don't forget I spared your lives tonight. I'm hoping that fact will keep you to your word."

She held out the bundle dropped by her brother. "Here is a set of clothes that should fit him. They used to belong to the steward's son, and I always thought he looked about the same size as Alric. Oh, and remove his ring but keep it safe. It bears the royal seal of Melengar and is proof of his identity. Without it, unless you encounter someone who knows his face, Alric is just another peasant. Return it to him when you reach the prison. He'll need it to get in."

"We'll hold up our end of the bargain," Hadrian told her as he and Royce moved the bundled body of the prince toward the open basin. Royce pulled the opulent dark blue ring from Alric's finger and stuffed it in his breast pocket. He then climbed to the bottom of the cistern. Using the rope tied around Alric's ankles, Hadrian lowered him head first to Royce. Once the prince was down, Hadrian grabbed the torch and dropped it to Royce. Then he entered the hole and dragged the grating back into position. At the bottom of the ladder was a five-feet-wide, four-feet-high arched tunnel in which a shallow river of filth flowed.

"Remember," the princess whispered through the metal grid. "Go to Gutaria Prison and speak to Esrahaddon. And please, keep my brother safe."

# 6

An incomprehensible series of mumbles emitted from the prince from under the potato sack. While they were not certain exactly what he was saying, Royce and Hadrian could tell the prince was doing his best to shout and was decidedly displeased with his situation.

The cold water backing up from the Galewyr River into the sewer woke him. They were waist deep in it now and while the smell was better, the temperature was not. Looking out through the end of the cistern, the first pale light of dawn revealed the difference between the forested horizon and the sky. Night was melting away fast, and they could hear the Mares Cathedral bell ringing for early service. The whole city would be waking soon.

Hadrian calculated they were below Gentry Square, not far from Artisan Row where the city met the river. Determining their location was an easy guess, because it was the only section of town with covered sewers. A metal grate enclosed the end of the sewer. Hadrian was relieved to find hinges and a lock sealing it instead of bolts. Royce made quick work of the lock, and the rusted hinges surrendered to a few solid kicks from Hadrian. With the way clear, Royce went out to scout while Hadrian sat at the mouth of the sewer with Alric.

The prince had worked his gag loose, and Hadrian could recognize his words now. "I'll have you flailed to death! Release me this instant."

"You'll be quiet," Hadrian replied, "or I'll let you go into the river and we'll see how well you tread water with your hands and feet tied."

"You wouldn't dare! I am the King of Melengar, you swine!"

Hadrian kicked Alric's legs out from under him, and the prince fell face down. After allowing him to struggle for a few moments, Hadrian pulled him up. "Now keep your mouth shut or I might leave you to drown next time." Alric coughed and sputtered but did not speak another word.

Royce returned, having slipped into the sewer soundlessly. "We are right on the river. I found a small boat by a fisherman's dock and took the liberty of commandeering it in His Majesty's name. It's just down the slope in a stand of reeds."

"No!" The prince protested and shook his shoulders violently. "You must release me. I am the king!"

Hadrian gripped him by the throat and into his ear whispered, "What did I tell you about talking? Not a sound or you swim."

"But— "

Hadrian dunked the prince again, pulled him up for a short breath, and dunked him once more. "Not another sound," Hadrian growled.

Alric sputtered, and Hadrian, dragging the prince with him, followed Royce down the slope.

The craft was little more than an oversized rowboat, bleached by the sun and filled with nets and small painted buoys. The heavy smell of fish from the boat helped to mask the stench of sewage. A tarp, stretched to form a little tent used to store gear or to serve as a shelter, covered the bow. They stuffed the prince underneath, pinning him there with the nets and buoys.

Hadrian pushed off the bank with a long pole he found in the boat. Royce used the wooden rudder to steer the small craft as the river did the work of propelling them downstream. Near the headwaters, the current of the Galewyr was strong, and forward momentum was no problem. They found themselves working to keep the boat in the center of the river as they moved swiftly westward. Just as the sky was turning from a charcoal gray to dull steel, they passed under the shadow of the city of Medford. From the river, they could see the great tower of Essendon Castle, its falcon standard flying at half-mast for the dead king. The flag was a good sign, but how long before they discovered the prince was missing and they removed it?

The river marked the southern edge of the city, skirting along Artisan Row. Large two-story warehouses of gray brick lined the bank, and great wooden wheels jutted out into the river, catching the current to power the millstones and lumberyards. Because the shallow waters of the Galewyr prevented the passage of deep-keeled ships, numerous docks serviced flat-bottomed barges that brought goods from the small seaport village of Roe. There were also piers built by the fishing industry, which led directly to fish markets, where pulleys raised large nets and dumped them onto the cutting floor. In the early morning light, the gulls had already begun to circle the docks where fisherman had started to clear the lines on their skiffs. No one paid particular attention to the two men in a small boat drifting down the river. Nevertheless, they stayed low in the boat until the last signs of the city disappeared behind the rising banks of the river.

The day's light grew strong, as did the pull of the current. Rocks appeared and the river trench deepened. Neither Royce nor Hadrian was an expert boatman, but they did their best dodging the rocks and shallows. Royce remained at the tiller, while Hadrian, on his knees, used the long wooden pole to push the bow clear of obstacles. A few times, they glanced off unseen boulders, and the hull lurched abruptly with a deep unpleasant thud. When it did, they could hear the prince whimper, but otherwise, he remained quiet, and their trip was a smooth one.

In time, the full face of the sun rose overhead, and the river widened considerably and settled into a gentle flow with sandy banks and rich green fields beyond. The Galewyr divided two kingdoms. To the south lay Glouston, the northern marchland of the kingdom of Warric. To the north was Galilin, the largest province in Melengar administered by Count Pickering. At one time, the river had been a hotly disputed division between two uneasy warlords, but those days were gone. Now, it was a peaceful fence between good neighbors and both banks remained lovely, untroubled pastoral scenes of the late season, filled with hay mounds and grazing cows.

The day became unusually warm. Being so late in the year, there were few insects about. The cicadas' drone had disappeared, and even the frogs were quiet. The only sound that remained was the soft gentle breeze through the dry grasses. Hadrian reclined across the boat with his head on the bundle of the steward son's old clothes and his feet on the gunwale. His cloak and boots were off and his shirt was open. Similarly, Royce lay with his legs up, idly guiding the boat. The sweet scent of wild salifan was strong in the air, the fragrance more pungent after surviving the year's first frost. Except for the lack of food, the day was turning out to be quite wonderful and would have been even if they had not just escaped a horrible death hours before.

Hadrian tilted his head back to catch the full light of the sun on his face. "Maybe we should be fishermen."

"Fishermen?" Royce asked dubiously.

"This is pretty nice, isn't it? I never realized how much I like the sound of water lapping against a boat before. I'm enjoying this: the buzzing of a dragonfly, the sight of the cattails, and the bank drifting lazily by."

"Fish don't just jump into the boat you know?" Royce pointed out. "You have to cast nets, haul them in, gut the fish, cut off their heads, and scale them. You don't just get to drift."

"Putting it that way makes it sound oddly more like work." Hadrian scooped a handful of water from the river and splashed it on his warm face. He ran his wet fingers through his hair and sighed contentedly.

"You think he's still alive?" Royce asked, nodding his head toward Alric.

"Sure," Hadrian replied without bothering to look. "He's probably sleeping. Why do you ask?"

"I was just pondering something. Do you think a person could smother in a wet potato bag?"

Hadrian lifted his head and looked over at the motionless prince. "I really hadn't thought about it until now." He got up and shook Alric, but the prince did not stir. "Why didn't you mention something earlier!" he said, drawing his dagger. He cut through the ropes and pulled the bag clear.

Alric lay still. Hadrian bent down to check if he was breathing. Just then, the prince kicked Hadrian hard, knocking him back toward Royce. Alric began feverishly untying his feet, but Hadrian was back on him before he cleared the first knot. He slammed Alric to the deck, pinning his hands over his head.

"Hand me the twine," Hadrian barked to Royce, who was watching the wrestling match with quiet amusement. Royce casually tossed him a small coil, and when Hadrian at last had the prince secured, he sat back down to rest.

"See," Royce said, "*that's* more like fishing; only fish don't kick, of course."

"Okay, so it was a bad idea." Hadrian rubbed his side where the prince had hit him.

"By brutalizing me, the two of you have sentenced yourselves to death! You know that, don't you?"

"That's a bit redundant don't you think, Your Majesty?" Royce inquired. "Seeing as how you already sentenced us to death once today."

The prince rolled onto his side tilting his head back, squinted against the brilliant sunlight.

"You!" he shouted amazed. "But how did you—Arista!" His eyes narrowed in anger. "Not jealous is she! My dear sister is behind all this! She hired you to kill my father, and now she plans to eliminate me so she can rule!"

"The king was *her* father as well. Besides, if we wanted to kill you, don't you think you'd already be dead?" Royce asked. "Why would we go to all the trouble of hauling you down this river? We could have slit your throat, weighed you down with rocks, and dumped you hours ago. I might add that such a fate would still be considerably better than what you had planned for us."

The prince considered this for a moment. "So it's ransom then. Do you intend to sell me to the highest bidder? Did she promise you a profit from my sale? You're both fools, if you believe that. Arista will never allow it. She'll see me dead. She has to in order to secure her seat on the throne. You won't get a copper!"

"Listen, you little royal pain in the ass, we didn't kill your father. In fact, for what it is worth, I thought old Amrath was a fair king, as far as they go. We also aren't ransoming or selling you."

"Well you certainly aren't trussing me up like a pig to get in my good graces. Now exactly what *are* you doing with me?" The prince struggled against his bonds but soon found them too tight to bother.

"If you really want to know," Hadrian said, "as strange as it may seem, we are trying to save your life."

"You're what?" Alric asked stunned.

"Your sister seems to think someone residing in the castle— the same lot that killed your father—is plotting to kill everyone in the royal family. Because you would be the next likely target, she freed us to smuggle you out for your own safety."

Alric pulled his legs up under him and worked his way to a sitting position with his back resting up against the pile of white and red striped buoys. He stared at the two of them for a moment. "If Arista didn't hire you to kill my father, then exactly what were you doing in the castle tonight?"

Hadrian provided a quick summary of his meeting with DeWitt to which the prince listened without interruption.

"And then Arista came to you in the dungeon with this story asking you to abduct me to keep me safe?"

"Trust me," Hadrian said, "if there was another way to get out of there, we would have left you."

"So you actually believe her? You're dumber than I thought," Alric said, shaking his head. "Don't you see what she's doing? She's out to have the kingdom for herself."

"If that were so, why would she have us kidnap you?" Royce asked. "Why not just have you killed like your father?"

Alric thought a moment, his eyes drifting to the floor of the boat and then he nodded. "She most likely tried, only I wasn't there." He looked back at them. "I wasn't in my room last night like I usually am. I slipped out for a rendezvous with a young lady and fell asleep in her room until I heard the noise. It is very likely an assassin did come to my room, only I was not there. After that, I had a guard with me at all times until Arista convinced me I had to come alone to the kitchen. I should have known she was betraying me."

He swung his bound legs into the mound of nets. "I just never thought she could be so cold as to kill our father, but that's how she is, you see. She is extremely clever. She told you this story about a traitor, and it was believable because it was true. She only lied about not knowing who it was. Once her assassin missed me, she used you. It was more likely that you'd agree to a kidnapping rather than murder, so she set you up."

Royce did not answer but glanced at Hadrian.

"There was this boat," the prince went on looking around him, "perfect for your needs waiting at the river's edge."

Alric dipped his head at the tarp next to him. "How nice to have a boat with a cover like this to hide me under. With a nice boat, and a river, you wouldn't be tempted to stray off the water. You can't go upstream from the city. The headwaters are too rough. You have to go toward the sea. She knows exactly where we are, and where we'll be. Did she say where to take me? Is it somewhere down this river?"

"Lake Windermere."

"Ah, the Winds Abbey? It's not far from Roe, and this river travels toward it. How convenient! Of course, we'll never make it," the prince told them. "She'll have killers waiting along the bank. They will murder us. She'll say you two killed me just as you killed my father. And, of course, her guards killed you when you tried to flee. She'll have a wonderful burial for me and my father. The next day she will call Bishop Saldur to perform her coronation."

Royce and Hadrian sat in silence.

"Do you need more proof?" the prince went on. "You say this fellow that hired you was called DeWitt? You said he was from Calis? Arista returned from a visit there only two months ago. Perhaps she made some new friends. Perhaps she promised them land in Melengar in return for help with a troublesome father and brother who stood between her and the crown."

"We need to get off this river," Royce told Hadrian.

"You think he's right?" Hadrian asked.

"Doesn't matter at this point, even if he's wrong, the owner of this boat will report it stolen. When news leaks out that the prince is missing, they will connect the two."

Hadrian stood up and looked downstream. "If I were them, I would send a group of riders down the river bank in case we stopped and another set of riders running fast down the Westfield road to catch us at Wicend Ford. It would only take them three or four hours."

"Which means they could already be there," Royce concluded.

"We need to get off this river," Hadrian said.

# 7

The boat came into view of Wicend Ford, a flat, rocky area where the river widened abruptly and became shallow enough to cross. Farmer Wicend had built a small stock shelter of split rails close to the water, allowing his animals to graze and drink unattended; it was a pretty spot. Thick hedges of heldaberry bushes lined the bank, and a handful of yellowing willows bent so low toward the river that their branches touched the water and created ripples and whimsical whirlpools along the surface.

The moment the boat entered the shallows hidden archers launched a rain of arrows from the bank. One struck the gunwale with a thud. A second and third found their target in the royal falcon insignia emblazoned on the back of the prince's robe. The figure in the robe fell from view into the bottom of the boat. More arrows found their marks in the chest of the tiller man, who dropped into the water, and the pole man, who merely slumped to one side.

From behind the screen of bushes and willows, six men emerged dressed in browns, dirty greens, and autumn golds. They entered the river, waded out, and caught the still drifting boat.

"It's official, we're dead," Royce declared comically. "Interestingly enough, the first arrows hit Alric."

The three of them were lying concealed in the tall field grass atop the eastern hill overlooking the river upstream of the ford. Less than a hundred yards to their right lay the Westfield road. From there, the road ran along the riverbank all the way to Roe, where the river joined the sea.

"Now do you believe me?" the prince asked.

"It only proves that someone is indeed trying to kill you and that they are not us. They're not soldiers either, or at least they aren't in uniform, so they could be anyone," Royce told them.

"How can he see so much—the arrows, their clothing—I can only see movement and color from this distance?" Alric asked.

Hadrian shrugged.

The prince was now dressed in the clothes of the steward's son: a loose-fitting gray tunic, worn and faded wool knee-length britches, brown stockings, and a tattered, stained wool cloak which was too long. On his feet, he wore a pair of shoes that were little more than soft leather bags tied at his ankles. Although no longer bound, Hadrian kept hold of a rope tethered around the prince's waist. Hadrian also carried the prince's sword for him.

"They're moving in on the boat," Royce announced.

All Hadrian could really see were shadowy movements under the trees until one of the men stepped out into the sunlight to grab the bow of the boat.

"It won't be long before they discover they've only killed three bushels of thickets wrapped in old clothes," Hadrian told Royce. "So I'd be quick."

Royce nodded and promptly trotted down the slope toward the stock shelter.

"What's he doing?" Alric asked in shock. "He'll get himself killed and us as well!"

"That's one opinion," Hadrian said. "Just sit tight."

Royce slipped into the shade of the trees, and Hadrian immediately lost sight of him. "Where'd he go?" the prince asked with a puzzled look on his face.

Once more Hadrian shrugged.

Below them, the men converged on the boat, and Hadrian heard a distant shout. He could not make out the words, but he saw someone holding up the Alric-bush complete with arrows. Two of the men remained with the boat while the others waded toward the bank. Just then, Hadrian caught sight of movement in the trees, a train of tethered horses trotting up the slope toward them. From the bank came shouts of alarm and cursing as the distant figures struggled to race across the field and up the hill.

When the horses drew nearer, he spotted Royce crouched down, hanging between the two foremost animals. Hadrian caught two of the horses, pulled the bridle off one, and quickly tied a lead line to the other horse's halter. He ordered Alric to mount. Angry shouts erupted as the archers spotted them. Two or three stopped to fit arrows but their uphill shots fell short. Before they could close the distance, the three mounted and galloped toward the road.

Royce led them a mile northwest to where the Westfield and Stonemill roads intersected. Here Hadrian, and by default Alric, rode west. Royce, leading the train of captured horses, stayed behind to cloud their tracks and then rode north. An hour later Royce, with only the horse he rode, caught up with them. They turned off the road into an open field and headed away from the river, but still moved generally westward.

The horses had built up a solid sweat and were puffing for air. When they reached the hedgerow lands, they slowed their pace. Eventually they reached the thickets, and there they stopped and dismounted. Alric found a spot clear of thorn bushes and sat down fussing with his tunic, which did not hang on him quite right. Royce and Hadrian took the opportunity to search the animals. There were no markings, symbols, papers, or emblems of any kind to identify the attackers. Moreover, except for a spare crossbow and a handful of bolts left on Hadrian's mount, they wore only saddles.

"You'd think they would have some bread at least. Who travels without water?" Hadrian complained.

"They clearly didn't expect to be out long."

"Why do you still have me tethered?" the prince asked irritated. "This is extremely humiliating."

"I don't want you getting lost," Hadrian replied with a grin.

"There's no reason to drag me around any further. I accept that you did not kill my father. My cunning sister merely fooled you.

It is quite understandable. She is very intelligent. She even fooled me. So, if you don't mind, I would like to return to my castle so I can deal with her before she consolidates her power and has the whole army turned out to hunt me down. As for you two, you can go wherever Maribor dictates. I really don't care."

"But your sister said—" Hadrian began.

"My sister just tried to have us all killed back there, or weren't you paying attention?"

"We have no proof it was her. If we let you return to Essendon, and she is right, you will be walking to your death."

"And what proof do we have it wasn't her? Do you still intend to escort me to wherever she told you to take me? Don't you think she'll have another trap waiting? I see my death far more probable on the road there than on any other road. Look, this is my life; I think it's fair for me to decide. Besides, what do you care if I live or die? I was about to have you two tortured to death. Remember?"

"You know," Royce paused a moment, "he's got a point there."

"We promised her," Hadrian reminded him, "and she saved our lives. Let's not forget that."

Alric threw his hands up and rolled his eyes. "By Mar! You *are* thieves, *aren't* you? It's not as if you have a sense of honor to contend with. Besides, she was also the one who betrayed you and put your lives in danger in the first place. Let's not forget *that*!"

Hadrian ignored the prince. "We don't know she is responsible, and we *did* promise."

"Another good deed?" Royce asked. "You'll remember where the last one ended us?"

Hadrian sighed. "There it is! Didn't have to save it too long, did you? Yes, I did screw up, but that isn't to say I am wrong this time. Windermere is only, what, ten miles from here? We could be there by nightfall. We could stop at the abbey. Monks have to help wayward travelers. It's in their doctrine or code or whatever. We could really use some food, don't you think?"

"They also might know something about the prison," Royce speculated.

"What prison?" Alric asked nervously getting to his feet.

"Gutaria Prison, it's where your sister said to take you."

"To lock me up?" the prince asked fearfully.

"No, no. She wants you to talk to someone there, some guy called...Esra...oh, what was it?"

"Haddon I think," Hadrian said.

"Whatever. Do you know anything about this prison?"

"No, I've never heard of it," Alric replied. "Although, it sounds like the kind of place unwanted royals go to disappear when a conniving sister steals her brother's throne."

His horse butted against his shoulder, and Royce rubbed its head while he contemplated the situation. "I'm too tired to think clearly. I don't think any of us can make an intelligent decision at this point, and given the stakes, we don't want to be hasty. We'll go as far as the abbey at least. We'll talk to them and see what they can tell us about the prison. Then we'll decide what to do from there. Does that sound fair?"

Alric sighed heavily. "If I must go, can I at least be given the dignity of controlling my own horse?" There was a pause before he added, "I give you my word as king. I will not try to escape until we reach this abbey."

Hadrian looked at Royce, who nodded. He then pulled the crossbow from behind his saddle. He braced it against the ground, pulled the string to the first notch, and loaded a bolt.

"It's not that we don't trust you," Royce said as Hadrian prepared the bow. "It's just that we've learned over the years that honor among nobles is usually inversely proportionate to their rank. As a result, we prefer to rely on more concrete methods for motivations—such as self-preservation. You already know we don't want you dead, but if you have ever been riding full tilt and had a horse buckle under you, you understand that death is always a possibility, and broken bones are almost a certainty."

"There's also the danger of missing the horse completely," Hadrian added. "I'm a good shot, but even the best archers have bad days. So to answer your question—yes, you can control your own horse."

# 8

They traveled at a moderate but steady pace for the remainder of the day. Royce guided them through fields, hedgerows, and forested trails. They stayed off the roads and away from the villages until at last there were no more of either. Even the farms disappeared as the land lost its tame face and they entered the wild highlands of Melengar. The ground rose, and forests grew thicker with fewer passable routes. Ravines led to bogs at their bottoms, and hills sloped up into cliffs. This rough country, the western third of Melengar, lacked farmable land and remained unsettled. The area was home to wolves, elk, deer, bears, outlaws, and anyone seeking solitude, such as the monks of the Winds Abbey. Civilized men shunned it, and superstitious villagers feared its dark forests and rising mountains. Myths abounded about water nymphs luring knights to watery graves, wolf men devouring the lost, and ancient evil spirits that appear as floating lights in the dense forest enticing children to their dark caves under the earth. Regardless of the legions of potential supernatural dangers, enough natural obstacles made the route one to avoid.

Hadrian never questioned his partner's choice of path or direction. He knew why Royce stayed clear of the Westfield Road, which provided a clear and easy path along the riverbank to the fishing village of Roe. Despite its isolation at the mouth of the Galewyr, Roe had grown from a sleepy little dock into a thriving seaport. While it held the promise of food, lodging, and imagined safety, it would also likely be watched. The other easy option was to travel north up the Stonemill Road—the route Royce pretended to take by leaving enough tracks to hopefully mislead anyone who followed into thinking they were headed for Drondil Fields. Each path held obvious benefits, which anyone looking for them would understand as well. As a result, they plodded and hacked their way through the wilds, following whatever animal trails they could find.

After a particularly arduous fight through a dense segment of forest, they came out unexpectedly on a ridge that afforded a magnificent view of the setting sun, which bathed the valley of Windermere and reflected off the lake. Lake Windermere was one of the deepest lakes in all of Apeladorn. Because it was too deep to support plant life, it was nearly crystal clear. The water shimmered in the folds and crevices of the three surrounding hills that shaped it in the form of a stretched, jagged triangle. The surrounding hills rose above the tree line, showing bald, barren peaks of scrub and stone. On the top of the southernmost hill, they could just make out a stone building. Aside from Roe, the Winds Abbey was the only sign of civilization for miles.

The party aimed toward the building and descended into the valley, but night caught up with them before they were halfway there. Fortunately, a distant light from the abbey provided them a waypoint. The weariness of being up for two stress-filled days combined with hard travel and no food was taking its toll on Hadrian, and he assumed the same of Royce, though he showed it less. The prince looked the worst. Alric rode just ahead of Hadrian. His head would droop lower and lower with each stride of his horse until he nearly fell from his saddle. He would catch himself, straighten, and then the process would begin again.

Despite the warm day, night brought with it a bitter chill, and in the soft light of the rising moon, the breath of men and horses began to fog the crisp night air. Above, the stars shone like diamond dust scattered across the heavens. In the distance, the call of owls and the shrill static of crickets filled the valley. Had the party not been so exhausted and hungry, they might have described the trip that night as beautiful. Instead, they merely gritted their teeth and focused on the path ahead.

They began climbing the south hill as Royce led them with uncanny skill along a switchback trail that only his keen eyes could see. The thin, worn clothes of the steward's son were a miserable defense against the cold, and soon the prince was shivering. To make matters worse, as they climbed higher, the temperature dropped and the wind grew. Soon trees began to shrink to stunted shrubs and the earth changed to lichen and moss covered stone. At last, they reached the steps of the Winds Abbey.

Clouds had moved in, and the moon was no longer visible. In the darkness, they could see very little except the steps and the light they had followed. They dismounted and approached the gate. A stone arch set within a peaked nave lay open on a porch of rock hewn from the hill itself. There was no longer the sound of crickets, nor hooting owls; only the unremitting wind broke the silence.

"Hello?" Hadrian called. After a time Hadrian called again. He was about to try a third time when he saw a light move within. Like a dim firefly weaving behind unseen trees, it vanished behind pillars and walls, reappearing closer each time. As it drew near, Hadrian saw that the strange will-o-wisp was a small man in a worn frock holding a lantern.

"Who is it?" he asked in a soft, timid voice.

"Wayfarers," Royce answered. "Cold, tired, and hoping for a place to rest."

"How many are you?" The man poked his head out and swung the lantern about. He paused to study each face. "Just the three?"

"Yes," Hadrian replied. "We've been traveling all day with no food. We were hoping to take advantage of the famous hospitality of the legendry Monks of Maribor. Do you have room?"

The monk hesitated only a moment and then said, "I...I suppose." He stepped back to allow them entrance. "Come in."

With only the bleak glow of the monk's lantern, which he kept low to light the floor, they could not see much beyond the stone walkway. By now, however, each was too tired for a tour even if the monk had been inclined to show off his home. The abbey had a heavy smell of smoke about it that prompted Hadrian to envision large, warm crackling hearths where beds might be.

"We didn't mean to wake you," Royce said softly.

"Oh, not me," the monk said. "I actually don't sleep much at all. I was busy with a book, right in the middle of a sentence when you called. Most unnerving I can tell you. It's a rare thing to hear someone shouting in the middle of the day up here, much less a dark night. You can sleep up this way— "

"We have horses," Hadrian interrupted.

"Really? How exciting," the monk replied, sounding impressed. "Actual riding horses, with saddles and everything? Oh, I would like to see them, but it's very late. Did you ride them here?"

"Yes," Hadrian said. "We thought having them ride us would be silly." The monk paused with a peculiar look on his face. "I was making a joke," Hadrian said.

"Ah!" the monk smiled. "Oh, yes—very funny. So, you can sleep—"

"What I meant to ask," Hadrian interrupted again, "is whether there is somewhere we can stable our horses for the night? A barn or perhaps a shed?"

"Oh, I see," The monk paused, tapping his lip thoughtfully. "Ah, well, we had a lovely stable, mostly for cows, sheep, and goats, but that's not going to work tonight. We also had some animal pens where we kept pigs, but that really won't work either."

"I suppose we could just tie them up outside somewhere if that's all right?" Hadrian asked. "I think I remember a little tree or two."

The monk nodded, appearing relieved to have the issue resolved.

After they stacked the saddles on the porch, the little man led them through an opening into what appeared to be a large ornately framed courtyard. Columns of freestanding stone rose beneath a cloudy sky, and various black silhouetted statues dotted the space.

The smoky smell was stronger here, but the only thing burning appeared to be the lantern in the monk's hand. They reached a small set of stone steps and the monk led the way down a set of two turns into what appeared to be a rough-hewn stone cellar.

"You can stay here," the monk told them.

The three stared at the tiny hovel, which Hadrian thought looked less inviting than the cells below Essendon Castle. Inside, it was very cramped, filled with piles of neatly stacked wood, tied bundles of twigs and heather, two wooden barrels, a chamber pot, a little table, and a single cot. No one said a word for a moment.

"It's not much, I know," the monk offered regretfully, "but at the moment, it's all I can offer you."

"We'll make do then, thank you," Hadrian assured him. He was so tired he didn't care so long as he could lie down and be out of the wind. "Can we perhaps get a few blankets? As you can see we really don't have any supplies with us."

"Blankets?" The monk looked concerned. "Well, there is one here." He pointed at the cot where a single thin blanket lay neatly folded. "I truly am sorry I can't offer you anymore. You can keep the lantern if you like. I know my way around without it." The monk left them without another word, perhaps fearful they would ask for something else.

"He didn't even ask us our names," the prince said.

"And wasn't that a pleasant surprise," Royce pointed out as he moved around the room with the lantern. Hadrian watched him take a thorough inventory of what little was there: a dozen or so bottles of wine hidden in the back, a small sack of potatoes under some straw, and a length of rope.

"This is intolerable," Alric said in disgust. "Surely an abbey of this size has better accommodations than this pit."

Hadrian found an old pair of burlap shoes that he cleared out before he lay down on the cellar floor. "I actually have to agree with the royal one there. I heard great things about the hospitality of this abbey. We do appear to be getting the dregs."

"Question is why?" Royce asked. "Who else is here? It would need to be several groups or a tremendously large party to turn us out to this hovel. Only nobility travel with such large retinues. They might be looking for us. They might be associated with those archers."

"I doubt it. If we were in Roe, I think we'd have more reason for concern," Hadrian said as he stretched and then yawned. "Besides, anyone who is here has turned in for the night and probably not expecting any late arrivals."

"Still, I'm going to get up early and look around. We might need to make a hasty departure."

"Not before breakfast," Hadrian said, sitting on the floor and kicking off his boots. "We need to eat and I know abbeys are renowned for their food. If nothing else you can steal some."

"Fine, but His Highness should not move about. He needs to keep a low profile."

Standing in the middle of the cellar with a sickened look on his face, Alric said, "I can't believe I am being subjected to this."

"Consider it a vacation," Hadrian suggested. "For at least one day you get to pretend you are nobody, a common peasant, the son of a blacksmith perhaps."

"No," Royce said preparing his own sleeping space, but keeping his boots on. "They might expect him to know things like how to use a hammer. And look at his hands. Anyone could tell he was lying."

"Most people have jobs that require the use of their hands, Royce," Hadrian pointed out. He spread his cloak over himself and turned on his side. "What could a common peasant do that monks wouldn't know the first thing about and wouldn't cause calluses?"

"He could be a thief or a whore."

They both looked at the prince, who cringed at his prospects. "I am taking the cot," Alric said.

# PART 4

## WINDERMERE

The morning arrived cold and wet. A solid gray sky cast a steady curtain of rain upon the abbey. The deluge streamed down the stone steps and pooled in the low pocket of the entryway. When the growing puddle reached Hadrian's feet, he knew it was time to get up. He turned over on his back and wiped his eyes. He had not slept well. He felt stiff and groggy, and the cold morning air chilled him to the bone. He sat up, dragged a large hand down the length of his face, and looked around. The tiny room appeared even more dismal in the drab morning light than the night before. He moved back away from the puddle and looked for his boots. Alric had the benefit of the cot, yet, he did not appear to have fared much better. Despite having a blanket wrapped tightly around him, he lay shivering. Royce was nowhere to be seen.

Alric opened one eye and squinted at Hadrian as he pulled his big boots on.

"Good morning, *Your Highness*," he said in a mocking tone. "Have a pleasant sleep?"

"That was the worst night I have ever endured," Alric snarled through clenched teeth. "I have never felt such misery as this damp, freezing hole. Every muscle aches; my head is throbbing, and I can't stop my teeth from chattering. I'm going home today. Kill me if you must, but nothing short of my death will stop me. A grave is certain to be better than this misery."

"So that would be a no?" Hadrian jested, rubbing his arms briskly. He got to his feet and looked out at the rain.

"Why don't you do something constructive and build a fire before we die of the cold," the prince grumbled, pulling the thin blanket over his head and peering out as if it were a hood. "I don't think we should build a fire in this cellar. Why don't we just run over to the refectory? That way we can warm up and get food at the same time. I am sure they have a nice roaring fire. These monks get up early, probably been laboring for hours making fresh bread, gathering eggs, and churning butter just for the likes of us. I know Royce wants you to stay hidden, but I don't think he expected winter would arrive so soon, or so wet. I think if you keep your hood raised, we should be fine."

The prince sat up with an eager look. "Even a room with a door would be better than this."

"That may be," they heard Royce say from somewhere outside, "but you won't find it here."

The thief appeared a moment later, his hood up and his cloak slick with rain. Once he ducked in out of the downpour, he snapped it like a dog shaking his fur. This sent a spray of water at Hadrian and Alric. They flinched and with a grimace the prince opened his mouth to speak, but he stopped short. Royce was not alone. Behind him followed the monk from the night before. He was soaked. His wool frock sagged with the weight of the water, and his hair laid plastered flat on his head. His skin was pale, his purple lips quivered, and his fingers were wrinkled as if he had been swimming too long.

"I found him sleeping outside," Royce said as he quickly grabbed an armful of the stacked wood. "Myron, take off that robe. We need to get you dry."

"Myron?" Hadrian said with an inquisitive look. "Myron Lanaklin?" Hadrian thought the monk nodded in reply, but he was shivering so hard it was difficult to tell.

"You know each other?" Alric asked.

"No, but we are familiar with his family," Royce said. "Give him the blanket."

Alric looked shocked and held tightly to his covering.

"Give it to him," Royce insisted. "It's *his* blanket. This fool gave us his home to stay in last night while he huddled in a wind-lashed corner of the cloister and froze."

"I don't understand," Alric said, reluctantly pulling the blanket off his shoulders. "Why would you sleep outside in the rain when—"

"The abbey burned down," Royce told them. "Anything that wasn't stone is gone. We weren't walking through a courtyard last night—that was the abbey. The ceiling is missing. The outer buildings are nothing but piles of ash. The whole place is a gutted ruin."

The monk slipped out off his robe, and Alric handed the blanket to him. Myron hurriedly pulled it around his shoulders, and sitting down drew his knees up to his chest, wrapping them in the folds as well.

"What about the other monks?" Hadrian asked. "Where are they?"

"I...I bu-buried them. In the garden mostly," Myron said through chattering teeth. "The gr-ground is softer there. I don't th-think they will mind. We all lo-loved the garden."

"When did this happen?"

"Night before last," Myron replied.

Shocked by the news, Hadrian did not want to press the monk further and a silence fell over the room. Royce continued building a fire using various pieces of wood and kindling from inside the hovel. He used some oil from the lantern and quickly built a fire near the entrance. Despite the storm's wind lashing the flames violently, the fire grew strong. As it did, the heat reflected off the stone walls, and soon the room began to warm.

No one said anything for a long time. Royce prodded the fire with a stick, churning the glowing coals so that they sparked and spit. They each sat watching the flames, listening to the fire pop and crackle while outside the wind howled and the rain lashed the hilltop. Without looking at the monk, Royce said in a somber voice, "You were all locked in the church when it was burned weren't you, Myron?"

The monk did not reply. His gaze remained focused on the fire.

"I saw the blackened chain and lock in the ash. It was still closed."

Myron, his arms hugging his knees, began to rock slowly.

"What happened?" Alric asked.

Still Myron said nothing. Several minutes passed. At last, the monk looked away from the fire. He did not look at them, but instead, he stared at some distant point outside in the rain. "They came and accused us of treason," he said with a soft voice. "There were maybe twenty of them, knights with helms covering their faces. They rounded us up and pushed us into the church. They closed the big doors behind us. Then the fire started.

"Smoke filled the church so quickly. I could hear my brothers coughing, struggling to breath. The abbot led us in prayer until he collapsed. It burned very quickly. I never knew it contained so much dry wood. It always seemed to be so strong. The coughing got quieter and less frequent. Eventually, I couldn't see anymore. My eyes filled with tears, and then I passed out. I woke up to rain. The men and their horses were gone and so was everything else. I was under a marble lectern in the lowest nave, and all my brothers were around me. I looked for other survivors, but there were none."

"Who did this?" Alric demanded.

"I don't know their names, or who sent them, but they were dressed in tunics with a scepter and crown," Myron said.

"Imperialists," Alric concluded. "But why would they attack an abbey?"

Myron did not reply. He merely stared out the window at the rain. A long time passed; finally Hadrian asked in a comforting voice. "Myron, you said they charged you with treason. What did they accuse you of doing?"

The monk said nothing. He just sat huddled in his blanket and stared. Alric finally broke the silence. "I don't understand. I gave no orders to have this abbey destroyed, and I can't believe my father did either. Why would one of my nobles carry out such an act, especially without my knowledge?"

Royce cast a harsh and anxious look at the prince.

"What?" Alric asked.

"I thought we discussed the importance of keeping a low profile."

"Oh, please." The prince waved a hand at the thief. "I don't think it will get me killed if the monk here knows I'm the king. Look at him. I've seen drowned rats more formidable."

"King?" Myron muttered.

Alric ignored the monk. "Besides, who is he going to tell? I'm heading back to Medford this morning anyway. Not only do I have a traitorous sister to deal with, but apparently, there also are things going on in my kingdom that I know nothing about. Such things can't be ignored."

"It might not have been one of your nobles," Royce said. "There are Imperialists in every kingdom in Apeladorn. I wonder. Myron, did it have anything to do with Degan Gaunt?"

Myron shifted nervously in his seat as an anxious look came over his face. "I need to string a clothesline to dry my robe," he said, getting up.

"Degan Gaunt?" Alric inquired. "That deranged revolutionary? Why do you bring him up?

"He's one of the leaders of the Nationalist Movement, and he's been seen around this area," Hadrian confirmed.

"The Nationalist Movement—ha! A grandiose name for that rabble," Alric sneered, "more like the peasant party. Those radicals who want the commoners to have a say in how they are ruled."

"So perhaps Degan Gaunt was using the abbey for more than a romantic rendezvous," Royce speculated. "Maybe he was meeting here with Nationalist sympathizers as well. That's why the Imperialists attacked. Perhaps it *was* your father, or at least had something to do with his death."

"I'm going to gather some water to make us some breakfast. I'm sure you are all hungry," Myron said as he finished hanging his robe and began collecting various pots to set out in the rain.

Alric took no notice of the monk as he focused on Royce. "My father would never have ordered such a heinous attack! He would be angrier at the Imperialists attack on the abbey than the Nationalist revolutionaries using it for meetings. My family has always been steadfast Royalists. We aren't waiting for any fictitious heir to return and reunite the Old Empire nor are we about to turn the reins of power over to a bunch of undeserving thugs."

"You prefer things exactly the way they are," Royce observed, "but being the king, that doesn't seem terribly surprising."

"You are no doubt a staunch Nationalist, in favor of common rule and the dissolution and redistribution of all noble lands," Alric told Royce. "That would solve all the problems of the world, wouldn't it? And that would certainly be in *your* favor."

"Actually," Royce said, "I don't have any political leanings. They get in the way of my job. Noble or commoner, people all lie, cheat, and pay me to do their dirty work. Regardless of who is on the throne, the sun still shines, the seasons still change, and people still conspire. If one needs to place labels on attitudes, I prefer to think of myself as an Individualist."

Alric sighed and shook his head in resignation. He stood up and held his hands out to the fire. "So how long before breakfast is ready, Myron? I'm starving."

"I'm afraid I don't have much to offer you." Myron said. He set up a small, elevated grate over the fire. "I have a few potatoes in a bag in the corner."

"That's all you have, isn't it?" Royce asked.

"I am very sorry," Myron replied, looking sincerely pained.

"No, I mean those potatoes are all the food *you* have. If we eat them, you'll be left with nothing."

"Oh, well," he shrugged off the comment. "I'll manage somehow. Don't worry about me," he said optimistically.

Hadrian retrieved the bag, looked in, and then handed it to the monk. "There are only eight potatoes in here. How long were you planning to stay?"

Myron did not answer for awhile until at last he said to no one in particular, "I'm not going anywhere. I have to stay. I have to fix it."

"Fix what, the abbey? That's an awfully big job for one man."

He shook his head. "The library, the books, that's what I was working on last night when you arrived."

"The library is gone, Myron," Royce reminded him. "The books were all burned. They're ash now."

"I know. I know," he said brushing his wet hair back from his eyes. "That's why I have to replace them."

"How are you going to do that?" Alric asked with a smirk. "Rewrite all the books from memory?"

Myron nodded. "I was working on page fifty-three of *The History of Apeladorn* by Antun Bulard when you came." Myron went over to a makeshift desk and brought out a small box. Inside were about twenty pages of parchment and several curled sheets of thin bark. "I ran out of parchment. Not much survived the fire, but the bark works all right."

Royce, Hadrian, and Alric shuffled through them. Myron wrote with small meticulous lettering, which extended to the edge of the page in every direction. No space was wasted. The text was complete, including page numbers not placed at the end of the parchments, but where the pages would have ended in the original document.

Staring at the magnificently rendered text, Hadrian asked, "How could you remember all of this?"

Myron shrugged. "I remember all the books I read."

"And did you read all the books in the library here?"

Myron nodded. "I had a lot of time to myself."

"How many books were in the library?"

"Three hundred eighty-two books, five hundred twenty-four scrolls, and one thousand two hundred thirteen individual parchments."

"And you remember every one?"

Myron nodded once more.

They all sat back staring at the monk in awe.

"I was the *librarian*," Myron said as if that would explain it all.

"Myron," Royce suddenly said, "in all those books did you ever read anything about a place called Gutaria Prison or a prisoner called Esra...haddon?"

Myron shook his head.

"I suppose it is unlikely anyone would write anything down concerning a secret prison," Royce said, looking disappointed.

"But, it was mentioned a few times in a scroll and once in a parchment. On the parchment, however, the name Esrahaddon was altered to *prisoner* and Gutaria was listed as *Imperial Prison*."

"Maribor's beard!" Hadrian exclaimed looking at the monk in awe. "You really did memorize the whole library, didn't you?"

"Why Imperial Prison?" Royce asked. "Arista said it was an ecclesiastical prison."

Myron shrugged. "I supposed because in imperial times the Church of Nyphron and the Empire were linked. *Nyphron* is the ancient term for *Emperor* derived from the name of the first Emperor, Novron. So, the Church of Nyphron is the *worshipers of the Emperor* and anything associated with the Empire could also be considered part of the Church."

"That's why members of the Nyphron Church are so intent on finding the heir," Royce added. "He would be their god, so to speak, and not merely a political leader."

"There were several very interesting books on the heir to the Empire," Myron said excitedly, "and speculation as to what happened to him— "

"What about the prison?" Royce asked.

"Well, that is a subject which isn't mentioned much at all. The only direct reference was in a very rare scroll called *The Accumulated Letters of Dioylion*. The original copy came here one night about twenty years ago. I was only fifteen at the time, but I was already the library assistant when a priest, wounded and near death, brought it. It was raining then, much as it is now. They took him to the healing rooms and told me to watch after his things. I took his satchel, which was soaked, and inside I found all sorts of scrolls. I was afraid the water might damage them so I opened them up to dry. While they lay open, I couldn't resist reading them. I usually can't resist reading anything.

"Although he didn't look much better two days later, the priest left and took his scrolls. No one could convince him to stay. He seemed frightened. The scrolls themselves were several correspondences made by Archbishop Venlin, the head of the Nyphron Church at the time of the breaking of the Empire. One of them was a post-imperial edict for the construction of the prison, which is why I thought the document was so important historically. It revealed the Church exercised governmental control immediately following the disappearance of the Emperor. I found it quite fascinating. It was also curious that the building of a prison had such high priority, considering the turmoil of that period. I now realize it was a very rare scroll, but of course, I didn't know that back then."

"Wait a minute," Alric interrupted, "so this prison was built what—nine hundred years ago and exists in my kingdom and I don't know anything about it?"

"Well, based on the date of the scroll, it would have been started —nine hundred and ninety-six years, two hundred and fifty-four days ago. The prison was a massive undertaking. One letter in particular spoke of recruiting skilled artisans from around the world to design and build it. The greatest minds and the most advanced engineering went into its creation. They carved the prison out of solid rock from the face of the mountains just north of the lake. They sealed it not only with metal, stone, and wood, but also with ancient and powerful enchantments. In the end, when it was finished, it was believed to be the most secure prison in the world."

"They must have had some really nasty criminals back then to go to so much trouble," Hadrian said.

"No," Myron replied matter-of-factly, "just one."

"One?" Alric asked. "An entire prison designed to hold just one man?"

"His name was Esrahaddon."

Hadrian, Royce and Alric shared looks of surprise.

"What in the world did he do?" Hadrian asked.

"According to everything I read, he was responsible for the destruction of the Empire. The prison was specifically designed to hold him."

They looked incredulously at the monk.

"And exactly how is he responsible for wiping out the most powerful Empire the world has ever known?" Alric asked.

"Esrahaddon was once a trusted advisor to the Emperor, but he betrayed him, killing the entire imperial family, except of course the one son who managed to miraculously escape; there are even stories that he destroyed the capital city of Percepliquis. The Empire fell into chaos and civil war after the Emperor's death. Esrahaddon was captured, tried, and imprisoned."

"Why not just execute him?" Alric asked, generating icy glares from the thieves.

"Is execution your answer to every problem?" Royce sneered.

"Sometimes it is the best solution," Alric replied.

Myron retrieved the pots from outside and combined the water into one. He added the potatoes and placed the pot over the fire to cook.

"Then Arista has sent us to bring her brother to see a prisoner who is over a thousand years old. Does anyone else see a problem with that?" Hadrian asked.

"See!" Alric exclaimed. "Arista is lying. She probably picked up the name Esrahaddon in her studies at Sheridan University and didn't realize when he lived. There is no way Esrahaddon could still be alive."

"He might be," Myron said casually, stirring the potatoes in the pot over the fire.

"How's that?" Alric queried.

"Because he's a wizard."

"When you say he was a wizard," Hadrian asked, "do you mean that he was a learned man of wisdom or that he could do card tricks and slight of hand or maybe he was able to brew a potion to help you sleep? Royce and I know a man like that, and he is a bit of all three, but he can't hold off death."

"According to the accounts I have read," Myron explained, "wizards were different back then. They called magic *The Art*. Most of the knowledge of the Empire was lost when it fell. For instance, the ancient skills of Teshlor combat, which made warriors invincible, or the construction techniques that could create vast domes, or the ability to forge swords that could cut stone. Like these, the art of true magic was lost to the world with the passing of the true wizards. Reports say in the days of Novron, the Cenzars—that's what they called wizards—were incredibly powerful. There are stories of them causing earthquakes, raising storms, even blacking out the sun. The greatest of these ancient wizards formed into a group called the Great Cenzar Council. Members were part of the inner circle of government."

"Really," Alric said thoughtfully.

"Did you ever read anything about exactly where the prison was located?" Royce asked.

"No, but there was a bit about it in Mantuar's *Thesis on Architectural Symbolism in the Novronian Empire*. That's the parchment I mentioned where the name Esrahaddon was changed to prisoner and Gutaria was listed as Imperial Prison. Stuffed on a back shelf for years, I found it one day while clearing an old portion of the library. It was a mess, but it mentioned the date of construction, and a bit about the people commissioned to build it. If I hadn't first read *The Letters of Dioylion*, I never would have made the connection between the two because, as I said, it never mentioned the name of the prison or the prisoner."

"I don't understand how this prison could exist in Melengar without my knowing about it," Alric said shaking his head. "And how does Arista know about it? And why does she want me to go there?"

"I thought you determined she was sending you there to kill or imprison you," Hadrian reminded him.

"That certainly makes more sense to me than a thousand year old wizard," Royce said.

"Maybe," Alric muttered, "but…." The prince, his eyes searching the ground before him for answers, tapped a finger on his lips. "Consider this, if she really wanted me dead, why choose such an obscure place? She could have sent you to this monastery and had a whole army waiting, and no one would hear a scream. It's unnecessarily complicated to drag me to a hidden place no one has heard of. Why would she mention this Esrahaddon or Gutaria at all?"

"Now you think she's telling the truth?" Royce asked. "Do you think there really is a thousand-year-old man waiting to talk to you?"

"I wouldn't go that far, but…well, consider the possibilities if he does exist. Imagine what I could learn from a man like that, an advisor to the last Emperor."

Hadrian chuckled at the comment. "You're actually starting to sound like a king now."

"It might merely be the warmth of the fire or the smell of boiling potatoes, but I am starting to think it might be a good idea to see where this leads. And look, the storm is breaking. The rain will be stopping soon I think. What if Arista isn't trying to kill me? What if there really is something there I need to discover, something that has to do with the murder of our father?"

"Your father was killed?" Myron asked. "I'm so sorry."

Alric took no notice of the monk. "Regardless, I don't like this ancient prison existing in my kingdom without my knowledge. I wonder if my father knew about it, or his father. Perhaps none of the Essendons were aware of it. A thousand years would predate the founding of Melengar by several centuries. The prison was built when this land still lay contested during the Great Civil War. If it is possible for a man to live for a thousand years, if this Esrahaddon was an advisor to the last Emperor, I think I should like to speak to him. Any noble in Apeladorn would give his left eye for a chance to speak to a true imperial advisor. Like the monk said, so much knowledge was lost when the Empire fell, so much forgotten over time. What might he know? What advantages would a man like that be to a young king?"

"Even if he's just a ghost?" Royce asked. "It's unlikely there is a thousand-year-old man in a prison north of this lake."

"If the ghost can speak, what's the difference?"

"The difference is I liked this idea a lot better when you *didn't* want to go," Royce said. "I thought Esrahaddon was some old baron your father exiled who had put a contract out on you, or maybe the mother of an illegitimate half-brother who was imprisoned to keep her quiet. But this? This is ridiculous!"

"Let's not forget you promised my sister," Alric smiled. "Now let's eat. I'm sure those potatoes are done by now. I could eat them all."

Once more Alric drew a reproachful look from Royce.

"Don't worry about the potatoes," Myron told him. "There are more in the garden I am sure. These ones I found while digging in the—" he stopped himself.

"I'm not worried, Monk, because you are coming with us," Alric told him.

"Wha…What?"

"You obviously are a very knowledgeable fellow. I'm sure you will come in handy, in any number of situations that may lay before us. So you will serve at the pleasure of your king."

Myron stared back. He blinked two times in rapid succession, and his face went suddenly pale. "I'm sorry, but I…I can't do that," he replied meekly.

"Maybe it would be best if you came with us," Hadrian told him. "You can't stay here. Winter is coming and you'll die."

"But you don't understand," Myron protested with an increasing anxiety in his voice and shaking his head adamantly. "I…I can't leave."

"I know. I know," Alric raised his hand to quell the protest. "You have all these books to write. That's a fine and noble task. I am all for it. More people need to read. My father was a big supporter of the University at Sheridan. He even sent Arista there. Can you imagine that? A girl at university? In any case, I agree with his views on education. Look around you, man! You have no parchment and likely little ink. If you do write these tomes, where will you store them? In here? There is no protection from the elements; they will be destroyed and blown to the wind. After we visit this prison, I will take you back to Medford and set you up to work on your project. I'll see to it you have a proper scriptorium, perhaps with a few assistants to aid you in whatever it is you need."

"That is very kind, but I can't. I'm sorry. You don't really understand— "

"I understand perfectly. You're obviously Marquis Lanaklin's third son, the one he sent away to avoid the unpleasant dividing of his lands. You're rather unique—a learned monk, with an eidetic mind, and a noble as well. If your father doesn't want you, I certainly could use you."

"No," Myron protested, "it's not that."

"What is it then?" Hadrian asked. "You're sitting here, cold and wet in a stone and dirt hole, wrapped in only a blanket looking forward to a grand feast consisting of a couple of boiled potatoes, and your king is offering to set you up like a landed baron and you're protesting?"

"I don't mean to be ungrateful, but I…well, I…I've never left the abbey before."

"What do you mean?" Hadrian asked.

"I've never left. I came here when I was four years old. I've never left—ever."

"Surely, you've traveled to Roe, the fishing village?" Royce asked. Myron shook his head. "Never to Medford? What about the surrounding area, you've at least gone to the lake, to fish or just for a walk?"

Myron shook his head again. "I've never been off the grounds. Not even to the bottom of the hill. I am not quite sure I can leave. Just the thought makes me nauseous." Myron checked the dryness of his robe. Hadrian could see his hand was shaking even though he had stopped shivering some time ago.

"So that's why you were so fascinated by the horses," Hadrian said mostly to himself. "But have you seen horses before?"

"I have seen them from the windows of the abbey when on rare occasions we would receive visitors who had them. I've never actually touched one. I've always wondered what it would be like to sit on one. In all the books, they talk about horses, jousts, battles, and races. Horses are very popular. One king—King Bethamy—he actually had his horse buried with him. There are many things I have read about that I've never seen. Women for one. They are also very popular in books and poems."

Hadrian's eyes widened. "You've never seen a woman before?"

Myron shook his head. "Well some books did have drawings which depicted ladies—"

Hadrian hooked a thumb at Alric. "And I imagined the prince here lived a sheltered life."

"But you've at least seen your sister," Royce said. "She's been here."

Myron did not say anything. He looked away and set about removing the pot from the fire and placing the potatoes on plates.

"You mean she came here to meet with Gaunt and never even tried to see you?" Hadrian asked.

Myron shrugged. "My father came to see me once about a year ago. The abbot had to tell me who he was."

"So you weren't a part of the meetings here at all?" Royce observed. "You weren't hosting them? Making arrangements for them?"

"No!" Myron screamed at them, and he kicked one of the empty pots across the room. "I—don't—know—anything—about —Gaunt—and—my—sister!" He backed up against the cellar wall as tears welled up in his eyes, and he panted for breath. No one said a word as they watched him standing there, clutching his blanket, and staring at the ground.

"I'm…I'm sorry. I shouldn't have yelled at you. Forgive me," Myron said, wiping his eyes. "No, I've never met my sister, and I saw my father only that once. He swore me to silence. I don't know why. Gaunt—Alenda—Nationalists—Imperialists —I don't know about any of it. They never met here. Maybe nearby, I'm not sure. I never even heard Gaunt's name until I learned about it from the abbot the night of the fire." There was a distance in the monk's voice, a hollow painful sound.

"Myron," Royce began, "you didn't survive because you were under a stone lectern, did you?"

The tears welled up once again and the monk's lips quivered. He shook his head. "They made us watch," Myron said, his voice choked and hitched in his throat. "They wanted to know about Alenda and Gaunt. They beat the abbot in front of us with sticks. They beat him bloody. He finally told them my sister gave secret messages to Gaunt hidden in love letters. The abbot told them about my father's visit. That's when they questioned me." Myron swallowed and took a ragged breath. "But they never hurt me. They never touched me. They asked if my father was siding with the Nationalists, and who else was involved. I didn't say a word. I didn't know anything. I swear I didn't. But I could have said something. I could have lied. I could have said, 'Yes, my father is a Nationalist, and my sister is a traitor!' But I didn't. I stood completely silent and never opened my mouth. Do you know why?"

Myron looked at them with tears running down his cheeks. "I didn't tell them because my father made me swear to be *silent*." Myron returned to the barrel and sat down. "I watched *in silence* as they sealed the church. I watched *in silence* as they set it on fire. And *in silence*, I listened to my brothers' screams. It was my fault. I let my brothers die because of an oath I made to a man who was a stranger to me, who had given me away when I was four years old." Myron began to cry uncontrollably. He slid down the wall into a crumpled ball on the dirt, his arms covering his face.

"They would have killed them anyway, Myron," Royce told him. "No matter what you said, they still would have died. Once they found out the monks were helping Gaunt, their fate was sealed."

Hadrian finished serving the potatoes, but Myron refused to take a single bite. Hadrian stored two of the potatoes away in hope he might get Myron to eat them later.

By the time the measly meal ended, the monk's robe was dry, and he dressed. Hadrian approached him and placed his hands on Myron's shoulders. "As much as I hate to say it, the prince is right. You have to come with us. If we leave you here, you'll likely die."

"But I..." he looked frightened. "This is my home. I'm comfortable here. My brothers are here."

"They're all dead," Alric said bluntly.

Hadrian scowled at the prince and then turned to Myron. "Listen, it's time to move on with your life. There's a lot more out there besides books. I would think you'd want to see some of it. Besides, your *king*," he said the last word sarcastically, "needs you."

Myron sighed heavily, swallowed hard, and nodded in agreement.

2

The rain lightened, and by midday, it stopped completely. After they packed Myron's parchments and whatever supplies they could gather from the abbey's remains, they were ready to leave. Royce, Hadrian, and Alric waited at the entrance of the abbey, but Myron did not join them. Eventually Hadrian went looking for him and found the monk in the ruined garden. Ringed by soot-stained stone columns, it would have formed the central courtyard between all the buildings. There were signs of flowerbeds and shrubs lining the pathway of interlocking paving stones now covered in ash. At the center of the cloister, a large stone sundial sat upon a pedestal. Hadrian imagined that before the fire, this sheltered cloister had been quite beautiful.

"I'm afraid," Myron told Hadrian as he approached. The monk was sitting on a blackened stone bench, his elbows on his knees, his chin on his palms staring at the burnt lawn. "This must seem strange to you. But everything here is so familiar. I could tell you how many blocks of stone make up this walkway or the scriptorium. I can tell you how many windowpanes were in the abbey, the exact day of the year, and time of day, the sun peaks directly over the church. How Brother Ginlin used to eat with two forks because he vowed never to touch a knife. How Brother Heslon was always the first one up and always fell asleep during vespers."

Myron pointed across from them at a blackened stump of a tree. "Brother Renian and I buried a squirrel there when we were ten years old. A tree sprouted the following week. It grew white blossoms in spring, and not even the abbot could tell what species it was. Everyone in the abbey called it the Squirrel Tree. We all thought it was a miracle, that perhaps the squirrel was a servant of Maribor and he was thanking us for taking such good care of his friend."

Myron paused a moment and used the long sleeves of his robe to wipe his face as his eyes stared at the stump. He pulled his gaze away and looked once more at Hadrian. "I could tell you how in winter the snow could get up to the second-story windows, and it was like we were all squirrels living in this cozy burrow, all safe and warm. I could tell you how each one of us were the very best at what we did. Ginlin made wine so light it evaporated on your tongue, leaving only the taste of wonder. Fenitilian made the warmest, softest shoes. You could walk out in the snow and never know you left the abbey. To say Heslon could cook is an insult. He would make steaming plates of scrambled eggs mixed with cheeses, peppers, onions, and bacon, all in a light spicy cream sauce. He'd follow this with rounds of sweet bread, each topped with a honey-cinnamon drizzle, smoked pork rounds, salifan sausage, flaky powdered pastries, freshly churned sweet butter, and a ceramic pot of dark mint tea. And that was just for breakfast."

Myron smiled, his eyes closed with a dreamy look on his face.

"What did Renian do?" Hadrian asked. "The fellow you buried the squirrel with? What was his specialty?"

Myron opened his eyes but was slow to answer. He looked back at the stump of the tree across from them and he said softly, "Renian died when he was twelve. He caught a fever. We buried him right there, next to the Squirrel Tree. It was his favorite place in the world." He paused, taking a breath that was not quite even. A frown pulled at his mouth, tightening his lips. "There hasn't been a day that has gone by since then that I haven't said good morning to him. I usually sit here and tell him how his tree is doing. How many new buds there were, or when the first leaf turned or fell. For the last few days I've had to lie because I couldn't bring myself to tell him it was gone."

Tears fell from Myron's eyes, and his lips quivered as he looked at the stump. "All morning I've been trying to tell him goodbye. I've been trying…" he faltered, and paused to wipe his eyes. "I've been trying to explain why I have to leave him now, but you see Renian is only twelve, and I don't think he really understands." Myron put his face in his hands and wept.

Hadrian squeezed Myron's shoulder. "We'll wait for you at the gate. Take all the time you need."

When Hadrian emerged from the entrance, Alric barked at him. "What in the world is taking so bloody long? If he's going to be this much trouble, we might as well leave him."

"We aren't leaving him, and we will wait as long as it takes," Hadrian told them. Alric and Royce exchanged glances, but neither said a word.

Myron joined them only a few minutes later with a small bag containing all of his belongings. Although he was obviously upset, his mood lightened at the sight of the horses. "Oh my!" he exclaimed. Hadrian took Myron by the hand like a young child and led him over to his speckled white mare. The horse, its massive body moving back and forth as the animal shifted its weight from one leg to another, looked down at Myron with large dark eyes.

"Do they bite?"

"Not usually," Hadrian replied. "Here, you can pat him on the neck."

"It's so…*big*," Myron said with a look of terror on his face. He moved his hand to his mouth as if he might be sick.

"Please, just get on the horse, Myron," Alric's tone showed his irritation.

"Don't mind him," Hadrian said. "You can ride behind me. I'll get on first and pull you up after, okay?"

Myron nodded, but the look on his face indicated he was anything but okay. Hadrian mounted and then extended his arm. With closed eyes, Myron reached out his arm and was pulled up by Hadrian. The monk held on tightly and buried his face in the large man's back.

"Remember to breathe, Myron," Hadrian told him as he turned the horse and began to walk back down the switchback trail.

The morning started cold but it eventually warmed some. Still, it was not as pleasant as it was the day before. They entered the shelter of the valley and headed toward the lake. Everything was still wet from the rain, and the tall fields of autumn-browned grass soaked their feet and legs as they brushed past. The wind came from the north now and blew into their faces. Overhead, a chevron of geese honked against the gray sky. Winter was on its way. Myron soon overcame his fear and picked his head up to look about.

"Dear Maribor, I had no idea grass grew this high. And the trees are so tall! You know I had seen pictures of trees this size but always thought the artists were just bad at proportion."

The monk began to twist left and right to see all around him. Hadrian chuckled. "Myron, you squirm like a puppy."

Lake Windermere appeared like gray metal pooling at the base of the barren hills. Although it was one of the largest lakes in Avryn, the fingers of the round cliffs hid much of it from view. Its vast open face reflected the desolate sky and appeared cold and empty. Except for a few birds, little else moved on the stony clefts. The whole place was unsettling.

They reached the western bank. Thousands of fist-sized rocks, rubbed smooth and flat by the lake, made a loose cobblestone plain where they could walk and listen to the quiet lapping of the water. From time to time, rain would briefly fall. They would watch it come across the surface of the lake, the crisp horizon blurring as the raindrops broke the stillness, and then it would stop while the clouds above swirled undecidedly.

Royce, as usual, led the small party. He approached the north side of the lake and found what appeared to be the faint remains of a very old and unused road leading toward the mountains beyond.

Myron's wriggling was finally subsiding. He sat behind Hadrian but did not move for quite some time. "Myron, are you okay back there?" Hadrian asked.

"Hmm? Oh, yes, I'm sorry. I was watching the way the horses walk. I've been observing them for the last few miles. They are fascinating animals. Their back feet appear to step in exactly the same place their front feet left an instant before. Although, I suppose they aren't feet at all, are they? Hooves! That's right! These are hooves! *Enylina* in Old Speech."

"Old Speech?"

"The ancient imperial language. Few people outside the clergy know it these days. It is something of a dead language. Even in the days of the empire it was only used in church services, but that has gone out of style and no one writes in it anymore."

With that Myron became silent once more.

They turned away from the lakeside and started into a broad ravine that turned rocky as they climbed. The more they progressed the more apparent it was to Royce that they were traveling on what was once a road. The path was too smooth to be wholly natural, and yet over time, rocks had fallen from the heights and cracks formed where weeds forced themselves out of the crevices. Centuries had taken their toll, but there remained a faint trace of something ancient and forgotten.

Royce and Alric were riding more or less together. Hadrian and Myron lagged behind due to their horse carrying two. Before long, the ground stopped rising and leveled. Royce reined in his mount.

"Why are we stopping?" Alric asked.

"Have you forgotten that this might be a trap?"

"No," the prince said, "I am quite aware of that fact."

"Good, then in that case good luck, Your Majesty," Royce told him.

"You're not coming?"

"Your sister only asked us to bring you here. If you want to get yourself killed, that is your affair. Our obligation is complete."

"Then I suppose this is a perfect time to tell you I am officially bestowing the title of *Royal Protectors* upon you and Hadrian. Now that I am certain you aren't trying to kill me. You two will be responsible for defending the life of your king."

"Really? How thoughtful of you, Your Highness," Royce grinned. "I also suppose this is a good time to tell you, I don't serve kings—unless they pay me."

"No?" Alric smiled wryly. "All right then, consider it this way. If I live to return to Essendon Castle, I will be happy to rescind your execution order and will forget your unlawful entry of my castle. If however, I should die here, or if I'm taken captive and locked away forever in this prison, you will never be able to return to Medford. My uncle will identify you, if he hasn't already, and you will be labeled murderers of the highest order. I'm sure there are already men searching for you. Uncle Percy seems like a courtly old gentleman, but believe me, I have seen his other side and he can be downright scary. He's the best swordsman in Melengar. Did you know that? So if sovereign loyalty isn't good enough for you, you might consider the simple practical benefits of keeping me alive."

"The ability to convince others that your life is worth more than theirs must be a prerequisite for being king."

"Not a prerequisite, but it certainly helps," Alric replied with a grin.

"It will still cost you," Royce said and the prince's grin faded. "Let's say one hundred gold tenents."

"One hundred?" Alric protested.

"It's what DeWitt promised, so it seems only fair. And if we are to be your security, you'll do as I say. I can't protect you if you don't, and since we aren't just playing with your silly little life, but my future as well, I will have to insist."

Alric huffed and glowered, but he eventually nodded. "Like all good rulers, it is understood there are times when we know it is best to listen to skilled advisors. Just remember who I am, and who I will be when I return to Medford."

As the fighter and the monk caught up, Royce said, "Hadrian, we've just been promoted to Royal Protectors."

"Does it pay more?"

"Actually it does. It also weighs less. Give the prince back his sword."

Hadrian handed the huge sword of Amrath to Alric, who slipped the broad, ornate baldric over one shoulder and strapped on the weapon. Wearing it looked a bit less foolish now that he was dressed and mounted, but Royce thought it was still too large for him.

"Wylin took this off my father and handed it to me…was it only two nights past? It was Tolin Essendon's sword, handed down from king to prince for seven hundred years. We are one of the oldest unbroken families in Avryn."

Royce dismounted and handed the reins of his horse to Hadrian. "I'm going to scout up ahead and make sure there are no surprises waiting." He left with surprising swiftness in a hunched run. He entered the shadows of the ravine and vanished.

**4**

"How does he do that?" Alric asked.

"Creepy, isn't it?" Hadrian remarked.

"How did he do what?" Myron asked, studying a cattail he plucked just before they left the lakeside. "These things are marvelous by the way."

They waited for several minutes and when they heard a bird song, Hadrian ordered them forward. The broken road weaved to and fro a bit until they could once again see the lake below. They were now much higher, and the lake looked like a large bright puddle. The road narrowed until at last it stopped. To either side hills rose at a gradual slope. Directly in front the path ended at a straight sheer cliff extending upward several hundred feet.

"Are we in the wrong place?" Hadrian asked.

"It's supposed to be a *hidden* prison," Alric reminded them.

"I just assumed," Hadrian said, "being up here in the middle of nowhere was what was meant by hidden. I mean, if you didn't know the prison was here, would you come to such a place?"

"If this was made by the best minds of what was left of the Empire," Alric said, "it is likely to be hard to find and harder to enter."

"Legends hold it was mostly constructed by dwarves," Myron explained.

"Lovely," Royce said miserably. "It's going to be another Drumindor."

"We had issues getting into a dwarf-constructed fortress in Tur Del Fur a few years back," Hadrian explained. "It wasn't pretty. We might as well get comfortable; this could take a while."

Royce searched the cliff. The stone directly before the path was exposed as if recently sheered off, and while moss and small plants grew among the many cracks elsewhere, none was found anywhere near the cliff face.

"There's a door here I know it," the thief said, running his hands lightly across the stone. "Damn dwarves. I can't find a hinge, crack, or seam."

"Myron," Alric asked, "did you read anything about how to open the door to the prison? I've heard tales about dwarves having a fondness for riddles and sometimes they make keys out of sounds, words that when spoken unlock doors."

Myron shook his head as he climbed down off the horse.

"Words that unlock doors?" Royce looked at the prince skeptically. "Are these fairytales you're listening to?"

"An invisible door sounds like a fairytale to me," Alric replied. "So it seems appropriate."

"It's not invisible. You can see the cliff, can't you? It's merely well hidden. Dwarves can cut stone with such precision you can't see a gap."

"You do have to admit, Royce, what dwarves can do with stone is amazing," Hadrian added.

Royce glared over his shoulder at him. "Don't talk to me."

Hadrian smiled. "Royce doesn't much care for the wee folk."

"Open in the name of Novron!" Alric suddenly shouted with a commanding tone, his voice echoing between the stony slopes.

Royce spun around and fixed the prince with a withering stare. "Don't do that again!"

"Well, *you* weren't making any progress. I just thought perhaps since this was, or is, a Church prison, maybe a religious command would unlock it. Myron, is there some standard Church saying to open a door? You should know about this. Is there such a thing?"

"I am not a priest of Nyphron. The Winds Abbey was a monastery of Maribor."

"Oh, that's right," Alric said, looking disappointed.

"I mean I know *about* the Church of Nyphron," Myron clarified, "but I'm not a member of that religion so I wouldn't be privy to any secret codes or chants or such."

"What I don't understand," Hadrian said, dismounting and tying his horse to a nearby tree, "is why Arista sent us here knowing we couldn't get in?"

The day was growing dark and the wind had picked up, heralding another possible storm. Hadrian was careful to lash the horses tightly for fear the wind might spook them. Alric walked about, rubbing his legs and muttering about being saddle sore. Myron continued to watch the horses with fascination, summoning the nerve every so often to stroke their necks.

"Would you like to help me unsaddle them?" Hadrian asked. "I don't think we'll be leaving soon."

"Of course," the monk said eagerly. "Now, how do I do that?"

Together, Hadrian and Myron relieved the animals of their saddles and packs, and stowed their gear under a small rock ledge. Hadrian suggested Myron gather some grass for the animals while he approached Royce, who sat on the path staring at the cliff. Occasionally, the thief would get up, examine a portion of the wall, and sit back down grumbling.

"Well? How's it going?"

"I hate dwarves," Royce replied.

"Most people do."

"Yes, but I have a reason. The bastards are the only ones that can make boxes I can't open."

"You'll open it. It won't be pretty, and it won't be soon, but you'll open it."

Royce sat on his haunches, his cloak draped out around him. His eyes remained focused, but he was frustrated. "I can't even see it. If I could see it then maybe, but how can I break a lock when I can't even find the door?"

"Maybe more information would help," Hadrian suggested. He looked around and found Myron walking back to the horses with a few handfuls of weeds he had plucked. "Myron, tell me, what is the difference between Nyphrons and you monks?"

"Well, how much do you know about religion in general?" Royce let out a small chuckle. Hadrian ignored him. "Just start at the beginning, Myron. And pretend I don't know much at all."

"Oh," the monk nodded. "Well," he began as if reciting a well-remembered liturgy, "Erebus created Elan, which, of course, is the known world, everything we see, the sky and ground. He made it so his children would have a place to rule. He had three sons and one daughter. His eldest son he named Ferrol. Ferrol is a master of magic and created the elves. His second son was Drome. He is the master craftsman, and he created the dwarves. His youngest son is Maribor and he created Man. His daughter is Muriel, and she created the animals, the birds, and the fish in the sea.

"Now, Ferrol being the oldest, his children, the elves, dominated the entire surface of Elan. Drome's children also grew great and controlled the world underground. Maribor's children, mankind, had no place. We struggled to survive in the most wretched, desolate places that the elves and dwarves didn't want.

"Then it came to pass that Erebus, in a drunken rage, forced himself on Muriel. From this union was born Uberlin, the Dark One. He, too, created children in Elan, and they are the Ghazel, the Dacca, and all the other creatures of shadow. Outraged at the crime, Ferrol, Drome, and Maribor attacked their father and slew him. Uberlin tried to defend his father, and they turned on him. They nearly killed Uberlin as well, but Muriel, sickened at her father's death, begged for his life. Instead, they cast Uberlin down and locked him within the depths of Elan.

"His children, however, grew in number and began to take what little the children of Maribor had managed to acquire. Losing their tiny footholds, mankind begged Maribor for help, and he heard their pleas. He tricked his brother Drome into forging the great sword Rhelacan, although in some very old text it is referred to as a great horn. He convinced his other brother Ferrol to enchant the weapon. Then Maribor came to Elan in disguise and slept with a mortal woman. The union brought forth Novron the Great. Armed with the Rhelacan, Novron led mankind in a war against the elves, the dwarves, and the forces of shadow. In a few short years, mankind subdued them all.

"Angry about the subjugation of their children by a demigod, Ferrol and Drome unleashed Uberlin with the promise of permanent freedom if he slew Novron. Twisted and misshapen after eons of darkened captivity, their half brother met Novron in battle. They fought for three days that shook Elan. In the end, Uberlin, severely wounded, crawled back into the bowels of the world, but Novron was worse. The mortal son of Maribor was pierced through the heart and died, his spirit returning to his father's side.

"Novron's son became the new Emperor, and soon the Great Church of Nyphron was established to pay homage to Novron as god and the son of Maribor. The Nyphron Church became the official religion of the Empire, but farther away from the imperial capital of Percepliquis, people remembered the old ways and continued to worship Maribor as they always had. The people called these wandering priests of the old religion Monks of Maribor. Eventually, with the fall of the Empire, the monks became more prominent and established monasteries. There is much more to the story, of course, but that is a basic overview," Myron said.

"So," Hadrian began, "you monks worship Maribor while the Nyphron worship Novron?"

"Close," the monk said, "the Nyphron also worship Maribor, they just put emphasis on Novron. The main differences are really in the manner of worship. The Church focuses on public worship. They are very involved in guiding society, as they believe the birth of Novron demonstrates Maribor wanted his worshipers to take a direct hand in controlling the fate of mankind. As such, they are very involved in politics and warfare. We monks believe in a more personal devotion to Maribor. We seek out his will in the quiet places, through the ancient rituals and in this silence; he speaks to us in our hearts. We don't so much seek to do what Maribor wants, but rather to merely learn to know Maribor better."

"Well, thank you, Myron," Hadrian said. "That was very educational, but I'm afraid I didn't find anything in that which would help us with our current situation."

"I'm sorry I wasn't a help," Myron said in a disappointed tone.

During the monk's tale, Hadrian had found a comfortable seat next to Alric, with his back against the cliff wall. After checking on the horses once more, Myron joined them. Royce remained studying the cliff. No one disturbed his concentration.

Storm clouds covered the sky and darkened the ravine. What light remained was an odd hue adding a sense of the surreal to the landscape. Soon the wind began gusting through the pass, blowing dirt into the air. In the distance, they could hear the low rumble of thunder.

"Any luck with the door, Royce?" Hadrian asked. His legs were outstretched, and he tapped the tips of his boots together. "Because it looks like we're in for another cold, wet night, only tonight we won't have any shelter."

Royce muttered something none of them caught.

Down below them, framed by the walls of the ravine, they could still see the shimmering surface of the lake. It was still a pale gray, but now it shined like a mirror facing the sky. Every now and then, it would flash brilliantly when lightning flickered in the distance.

Royce grumbled again.

"What's that?" Hadrian asked.

"I was just thinking about what you said earlier. Why *would* she send us here if she knew we couldn't get in? She must have thought we could, maybe to her it was obvious."

"Maybe it's magic," Alric said, pulling his cloak tighter.

"Enough with the enchanted words," Royce told him. "Locks are mechanical. Believe me, I know a bit about this subject.

Dwarves are very clever and very skilled, but they don't make doors that unlock by a sound."

"I just brought it up because Arista could do some, so maybe getting in is easy for her."

"Do some what?" Hadrian asked.

"Magic."

"Your sister is a witch?" Myron asked disturbed.

Alric laughed. "You could certainly say that, yes, but it has little to do with her magical capabilities. She studied at Sheridan University for a few years learning magical theory. It never amounted to much, but she was able to do a thing or two. She *magically* locks the door to her room, and I am certain she made the Countess Amril terribly sick one day when she betrayed a trust and told a squire Arista fancied him. Poor Amril was covered in boils for a week."

Royce looked over at Alric. "What do you mean magically locks her door?"

"There's never been a lock on it, but no one can open it but her."

"Did you ever see your sister unlock her door?"

Alric shook his head. "I wish I had."

"Myron," Royce said, turning to the monk, "did you ever read about unusual locks, or keys? Maybe something associated with dwarves?"

"There's the tale of *Iberius and the Giant*, where Iberius uses a key forged by dwarves to open the giant's treasure box, but it wasn't magical. It was just big. There's also the Collar of Liem, from the *Myth of the Forgotten*, that refused to unlock until the wearer was dead—I guess that doesn't help you. There's also gemlocks."

"What are gemlocks?"

"They're not magical either, but they were invented by dwarves. Gems interact with other stones by creating a low resonance, or subtle vibrations. Gemlocks were created to be used when an individual key was impractical, for example when a great number of people needed to access the contents of a locked container, or when someone needed to be able to open a lock but would not be able to have access to a single key. All they needed to have was a gem of matching type. The wealthy sent messages in gemlocked boxes, using expensive stones for keys which made it hard for a poor courier to obtain. For particularly clever locks, the gemlock might require a specific cut, which modified the resonance. Truly gifted crafters could make a lock that actually changed with the seasons, allowing different gems to unlock it at different times of the year. This is what gave rise to the idea of birthstones, for certain stones have more strength at certain times."

"That's it," Royce interrupted.

"What's it?" Alric asked. Royce reached into his breast pocket and pulled out a dark blue ring. Alric jumped to his feet. "That's my father's ring! Give it to me!"

"Fine," Royce said tossing it toward the prince. "Your sister told us to return it to you when we got to the prison."

"She did?" Alric looked surprised. He slipped the ring on his finger, and like his sword, it did not quite fit and spun around from the weight of the gem. "I thought she took it. It has the royal seal. She could have used it to muster the nobles, to make laws, or to announce herself as steward. With it, she could have taken control of everything."

"Maybe she *was* telling the truth," Hadrian suggested.

"Let's not make snap judgments," Royce cautioned. "First, let's see if this works. Your sister said you would need the ring to get into the prison. I thought she meant to identify you as the king, but I think she meant it a bit more literally. If I'm correct, touching the stone with the ring will cause giant doors to open."

They all gathered at the cliff face close to Alric in anticipation of the dramatic event.

"Go ahead, Alric—do it."

He turned the ring so the gem was on top, made a fist, and attempted to touch it to the cliff. As he did, his hand disappeared into the rock. Alric recoiled, wheeling backward with a cry.

"What happened?" Royce asked. "Did it hurt?"

"No, it just felt sort of cold, but I can't touch it."

"Try it again," Hadrian said.

Alric did not look at all happy with the suggestion but nodded just the same. This time he pressed farther, and the whole party watched as his hand disappeared into the wall up to his wrist before he withdrew it.

"Fascinating," Royce muttered, feeling the solid stone of the cliff. "I didn't expect that."

"Does that mean he has to go in alone?" Hadrian asked.

"I'm not sure I want to enter solid stone alone," Alric said with fear in his voice.

"Well, you may have no choice," Royce responded, "assuming you still want to talk to the wizard. But let's not give up yet. Give me the ring a moment."

Despite his earlier desire for the ring, Alric now showed no concern at handing it over. Royce slipped it on, and when he pressed his hand to the cliff face, it passed into the mountainside just as easily as Alric's had. Royce pulled his hand back, then he took the ring off, and holding it in his left hand, he reached out with his right. Once more, his hand passed through the stone.

"So you don't have to be the prince, and you don't have to be wearing it. You only need to be touching it. Myron, didn't you say something about the gem creating a vibration?"

Myron nodded. "They create a specific resonance with certain stones types."

"Try holding hands," Hadrian suggested.

Alric and Royce did so, and this time, both could penetrate the stone.

"That's it." Royce declared. "One last test. Everyone join hands. Let's make sure it works with four." They all joined hands and each was able to pierce the surface of the cliff. "Everyone, make sure you remove your hands before breaking the chain."

"Okay, we need to make some decisions before we go any further. I've seen some unusual things before, but nothing like this. I don't have a clue what will happen to us if we go in there. Well, Hadrian, what do you think?"

Hadrian rubbed his chin. "It's a risk to be sure. Considering some of the choices I've made recently, I'll leave this one up to you. If you think we should go then that is good enough by me."

"I have to admit," Royce responded, "my curiosity is piqued, so if you still want to go through with this, Alric, we'll go with you."

"If I had to go in alone, I would decline," Alric said. "But, I also am curious."

"Myron?" Royce asked.

"What about the horses? Will they be all right?"

"I'm sure they will be fine."

"But what if we don't come back? They'll starve, won't they?"

Royce sighed. "It's us or the horses. You'll have to choose."

Myron hesitated. Lightning and thunder tore through the sky, and it began to rain. "Can't we just untie them, so in case we don't—"

"I don't intend to make plans based on our expected deaths. We'll need the horses when we come out. They're staying; are you?"

The wind sprayed rain into the monk's face as he stole one last look at the horses. "I'll go," he said finally. "I just hope they'll be all right."

"Okay," Royce told them, "this is how we'll do it. I'll go first wearing the ring. Alric comes in behind me, then Myron, and Hadrian will take up the rear. When we get inside, we break the chain in reverse order: Hadrian first, then Myron, and Alric last. Enter in the same place I do, and don't pass me. I don't want anyone setting off any traps. Any questions?"

All but Myron shook their heads. "Wait a second," he said as he trotted off toward where they stored their gear. He gathered the lantern and tinder kit he had brought from the abbey and paused a moment to pet the horses' wet noses one more time. "I'm ready now," he said when he returned to the party.

"All right, here goes, everyone hang on and follow me," Royce said as they rejoined their chain and moved forward. One by one, they passed through the rock cliff. Hadrian was last. When the barrier reached his shoulder, he took a deep breath as if he was swimming, and with that, Hadrian dipped his head inside the stone.

# PART 5

## ESRAHADDON

They entered into total darkness. The air was dry, still, and stale. The only sound came from the rainwater dripping from their clothes. Hadrian took a few blind steps forward to make sure he was completely through the barrier before releasing Myron's hand. "See anything, Royce?" he asked in a whisper so quiet it could scarcely be heard.

"No, not a thing. Everyone stay still until Myron gets the lantern lit."

Hadrian could hear Myron fiddling in the dark. He tilted his head, searching in vain for anything to focus on. There was nothing. He could have had his eyes closed. Myron scraped the tiny metal lever on his tinder pad, and a burst of sparks emitted from the monk's lap. In the flare, Hadrian saw faces glaring from the darkness. They appeared briefly and vanished with the dying brilliance.

No one moved or spoke as Myron scrapped the pad again. This time the tinder caught fire, and the monk lit the wick of the lantern. The light revealed a narrow hallway, only five feet wide, and a ceiling which was so high it was lost in darkness. Lining both walls were carvings of faces, as if people standing on the other side of a gray curtain were pressing forward to peer at them. Seemingly caught in a moment of anguish frozen forever in stone, their terrible ghastly visages stared back at them with gaping mouths and wild eyes.

"Pass up the light," Royce ordered softly.

As the lantern moved from Myron to Royce, its light shone on more faces. To Hadrian, it seemed as if they screamed at the intruders, but the corridor remained still and silent. Some of the figures had eyes wide with fear, while others were shut tight, perhaps to avoid seeing something too frightening to look at.

"Someone certainly had a morbid taste in decorating," Royce said, taking the lantern.

"I'm just thankful they're only carvings. Imagine if we could hear them," Alric said.

"What makes you think they're carvings?" Hadrian asked, reaching out to gingerly touch the nose of a woman with glaring eyes. He half expected warm skin and was grateful when his fingers met cold stone. "Maybe they let go of their gemstones too soon."

Royce held the lantern up high. "The passage keeps going."

"More faces?" Alric asked.

"More faces," the thief confirmed.

"At least we're out of the rain," Hadrian said, trying to sound cheerful. "We could still be back..." When he turned around, he was shocked. The corridor extended behind them seemingly without end. "Where's the wall we just came through?" He took a step and reached out. "It's not an illusion. The hallway keeps going." Turning back, Hadrian saw Royce pressing on the sides of the corridor, unlike the wall outside, his hand did not penetrate the surface.

"Well, this is going to make matters difficult," the thief muttered.

"There must be another way out, right?" Alric asked, his voice a bit shaky.

The thief looked back, then forward, and sighed. "We might as well travel in the direction we entered. Here, Alric, take your ring back, although I'm not sure what good it will do you in here."

Royce led them down the corridor. He checked and tested anything that appeared suspicious. The passage went on for what seemed like eternity. Despite the hallway appearing perfectly straight and level, Hadrian began to wonder if the dwarves had built in an imperceptible curve that made the hallway loop back onto itself to form a circle. He also worried about the amount of oil left in Myron's lantern. It would not be long before they were cast back into utter darkness.

The lack of variation in their surroundings made it impossible to judge exactly how long they had been walking. After awhile something luminescent appeared in the distance. A tiny light bobbed and weaved. As the light drew closer, the echo of sharp, deliberate footsteps accompanied it. At last, Hadrian could discern the figure carrying a lamp. He was tall, trim, and wore a long-hooded hauberk. Over this was a scarlet and gold tabard that shimmered in the lamplight. The tabard was marked with a regal coat of arms depicting a celestial crown and a jeweled scepter above a shield divided into quarters and supported on either side by combatant lions. At his side was an ornate sword, and on his head, a pointed silver helm exquisitely etched with gold ivy trim. Below the helm was a pair of dark eyes, and an even darker look.

"Why are you here?" His tone was reproachful and threatening.

There was a pause before Royce replied. "We are here to see the prisoner."

"*That* is not allowed," he responded firmly.

"Then Esrahaddon is still alive?" asked Alric.

"*Do not speak that name!*" thundered the sentry. He cast a tense look over his shoulder into the darkness. "Not here, not *ever* here. You should not have come."

"That may be, but we are here and we need to see Esra—the prisoner," Royce replied.

"That will not be possible."

"Make it possible," Alric ordered. His voice was loud and commanding. He stepped out from behind the others. "I am King

Alric of Melengar, lord of this land wherein you stand. You will not tell me what *is* and what *is not* possible within the boundaries of my own kingdom."

The sentry took a step back and eyed Alric critically. "You lack a crown, *king*."

Alric drew his sword. Despite its size, he handled it smoothly and extended the point at the sentry. "What I lack in a crown, I more than make up for in a sword."

"A sword will not avail you. None who dwell here fear death any longer." Hadrian could not tell whether it was the weight of the sentry's words or the weight of the sword, but Alric lowered his blade. "Do you have proof of your rank?"

Alric extended a clenched hand. "This is the seal of Melengar, symbol of the House of Essendon and emblem of this realm."

The sentry stared at the ring and nodded. "If you are the reigning sovereign of the realm, you do have the right to enter. But know this, there is magic at work here. You will do well to follow me closely." He turned and led them back the way he had come.

"Do you recognize the emblem on the guard?" Hadrian whispered to Myron as they followed him.

"Yes, that is the coat of arms of the Novronian Empire, worn by the Percepliquis Imperial City Guard. It is very old."

Their guide led them out of the corridor filled with faces, and Hadrian was grateful to be free of it. The hallway opened into a massive cavern with a vaulted ceiling carved from and supported by pillars of natural stone. Torches lining the walls revealed a magnificent expanse. It appeared large enough to hold all of Medford. They traversed it by crossing narrow bridges that spanned chasms and traveling through open arches that rose like great trees whose branches supported the mountain above.

There was no visible sign of wood, fabric, or leather. Everything—chairs, benches, desks, tables, shelves, and doors—was made of stone. Huge fountains hewn from rock gurgled with water from unseen springs. The walls and floors lacked the adornment of tapestries and carpets. Instead, carved into virtually every inch of the stone were intricate markings—strange symbols of elaborate twisted designs. Some of them were chiseled with a rough hand, while others were smoothly sculpted. At times, from the corner of his eye, Hadrian thought he saw the carved markings change as he passed them. Looking closely, he discovered it was not an illusion. The shifts were subtle, like cobwebs moving in the wake of their passing.

They moved deeper, and their escort did not pause or waver. He walked at a brisk pace, which at times caused Myron, who had the shortest legs, to trot in order to keep up. Their footfalls bounced off the hard walls throughout the stone chamber. The only other sounds Hadrian heard were voices, distant whispers of hidden conversations, but they were too faint for him to make out the words. Whether the sounds were from inhabitants around an unseen corner, or the result of some trick of the stone, it was impossible to tell.

Farther in, sentinels began to appear, standing guard along their path. Most were dressed identical to their guide, but others found deeper in the prison wore black armor with a simple white emblem of a broken crown. Sinister-looking helms hid their faces as they stood at perfect attention. None of them moved or said a word.

Once more Hadrian asked Myron about the emblem these men wore.

"The crest is used by the ancient order of the Seret Knights," the monk explained quietly. "They were first formed eight hundred years ago by Lord Darius Seret, who was charged by Patriarch Venlin with the task of finding the lost Heir of Novron. The broken crown is symbolic of the shattered Empire which they seek to restore."

Finally they reached what Hadrian assumed was their final destination. They entered an oval chamber with an incredibly tall door dominating the far wall. Carved of stone, it stood wreathed in a glittering array of fine spider web-like designs, which appeared organic in nature. Like the veins of a leaf or the delicate, curling tendrils of sprawling roots, the doorframe spread out until its artistry was lost in the shadows. On either side of the door stood dramatic obelisks covered with runes cut deep in beveled stone. Between these and the door, blue flames burned in braziers mounted on high pedestals.

A man sat on a raised chair behind a six-feet-tall stone desk that was exquisitely sculpted with intricate patterns of swirling lines. On two sides of the worktable, barrel-thick candles twice the height of a man burned. So many melted wax tears streaked down their sides that Hadrian thought they might once have been as tall as the great door.

"Visitors," their guide announced to the clerk who, until then, had been busy writing in a massive book with a black feathered quill. The man looked up from his work. His gray beard hung all the way to the floor. Deeply lined with wrinkles, his face looked like the bark of an ancient tree.

"What are your names?" the clerk asked.

"I am Alric Brendon Essendon, son of Amrath Essendon, King of Melengar, Lord of the Realm, and I demand an audience with the prisoner."

"The others?" the clerk motioned toward the rest.

"They are my servants, the Royal Protectors and my chaplain."

The clerk rose from his seat and leaned forward to examine each party member in more detail. He looked into each of their eyes for a moment before he resumed his seat. He dipped his feather quill and turned to a new page. After a few moments of writing, he asked, "Why do you wish to see the prisoner?" With his quill poised, he waited for a reply.

"My business is not your concern," Alric answered in a kingly voice.

"That may be, however, this prisoner is *my* concern, and if you have dealings with him, it *is my business.* I will know your purpose, or I will not grant you entry, king or not."

Alric stared at the clerk for sometime before relenting. "I wish to ask him questions concerning the death of my father."

The clerk considered this a moment, then scratched his quill on the page of the great book. When he finished, he looked up. "Very well. You may enter the cell, but you must obey our rules. They are for your own safety. The man to whom you wish to speak is no ordinary man. He is a thing, an ancient evil, a demon that we have successfully trapped here. Above all else, we are dedicated to keeping him confined. As you might imagine, he very much desires to escape. He is cunning and perpetually tests us. Constantly he is looking for a weakness, a break in a line, or a crack in the stone.

"First, proceed directly down the path to his confinement; do not tarry. Second, stay in the gallery; do not attempt to descend to his cage. Third, and this is the most important, do nothing he asks. No matter how insignificant it may sound. Do not be fooled by him. He is intelligent and cunning. Ask him your questions; then leave. Do not deviate from these rules. Do you understand?" Alric nodded. "Then may Novron have mercy on you."

Just then, the great doors split along the central seam and slowly started to open. The loud grinding of stone on stone echoed until at last the doors stood wide. Beyond them lay a long stone bridge that spanned an abyss. The bridge was three-feet wide, as smooth as glass, and appeared no thicker than a sheet of parchment. At the far end of the span rose a column of black rock. An island-like tower, its only visible connection to the world appeared to be the delicate bridge.

"You may leave your lantern. You will have no need for it," the clerk stated. Royce nodded but kept the lantern nevertheless.

As they stepped through the doorway, Hadrian heard a sound like singing, a faint mournful song as if a thousand voices joined in a somber dirge. The sad, oppressive music brought to mind the worst memories of his life and filled him with a misery so great it sapped his resolve. His feet felt weighted, his soul chilled. Moving forward became an effort.

Once the party crossed the threshold, the great doors began to close, shutting with a thundering boom. The chamber was well lit, although the light source was not apparent. It was impossible to judge the height or the depth of the chasm. Both stretched into seeming emptiness.

"Are other prisons like *this*?" Myron asked, his voice quivering as they began to inch their way across the bridge.

"I would venture to guess this is unique," Alric replied.

"Trust me, I know prisons," Royce told them. "This *is* unique."

The party fell into silence during the crossing. Hadrian was in the rear concentrating on the placement of his feet. Part way across he paused and glanced up briefly to check on the others. Myron was holding his arms out at his sides like a tightrope walker. Alric, half-crouching, reached out with his hands as if he might resort to crawling at any minute. Royce, however, strode casually forward with his head tilted up, and he frequently turned from side to side to study their surroundings.

Despite its appearance, the bridge was solid. They successfully crossed it to a small arched opening into the black tower. Once off the bridge, Royce turned to face Alric. "You were fairly free about revealing your identity back there, Your Majesty," he reproached the monarch. "I don't recall discussing a plan where you walk in and blurt out, 'Hey, I'm the new king, come kill me.'"

"You don't actually think there are assassins in here, do you? I know I thought this was a trap, but look at this place! Arista never could have arranged this. Or do you honestly think others will be able to slip in the same cliff door we entered through?"

"What I think is that there is no reason to take unnecessary chances."

"Unnecessary chances? Are you serious? You don't consider crossing a slick, narrow bridge over a gorge, which is who knows how high, not a risk? Assassins are the least of our worries."

"Are you always this much trouble to your security?"

Alric's only response was a look of disdain.

The archway led to a narrow tunneled corridor, which eventually opened into a large round room. Arranged like an amphitheater, the gallery contained descending stairs and stone benches set in rings, each lower than the one before it, which focused all attention to the recessed center of the room. At the bottom of the steps was a balcony, and twenty feet below it lay a circular stage. Once they descended the stairs, Hadrian could see the stage was bare except for a single chair and the man who sat upon it.

An intense beam of white light illuminated the seated figure from high above. He did not appear terribly old, with only the start of gray entering into his otherwise dark, shoulder-length hair. Dark, brooding eyes gazed out from beneath a prominent forehead. No facial hair marred his high cheekbones, which surprised Hadrian because the few wizards and magicians he knew about all wore long beards as a mark of their profession. He wore a magnificent robe the color of which Hadrian could not quite determine. The garment shimmered somewhere between dark blue and smoky gray, but where it was folded or creased, it looked to be emerald green or at times even turquoise. The man sat with the robe gathered around him, his hands, lost in its folds, placed on his lap. He sat still as a statue, giving no indication he was aware of their presence.

"What now?" Alric whispered.

"You talk to him," Royce replied.

The prince looked around thoughtfully. "That man down there can't really be a thousand years old, can he?"

"I don't know. In here, anything seems possible," Hadrian said.

Myron looked around the room and up toward the unseen ceiling, a pained expression on his face. "That singing…it reminds me of the abbey, of the fire, as if I can hear them again…screaming." Hadrian gently put a hand on Myron's shoulder.

"Ignore it," Royce told the monk and then turned to glare at Alric. "You have to talk to him. We can't leave until you do. Now go ahead and ask him what you came here to find out."

"What do I say? I mean, if he is, you know, really a wizard of the Old Empire, if he actually served the last Emperor, how do I approach him?"

"Try asking what he's been up to," Hadrian suggested, which was met by a smirk from Alric. "No, seriously look down there. It's just him and a chair. He has no books, no cards, nothing. I nearly went crazy with boredom cooped up in The Rose and Thorn last winter during a heavy snowfall. How do you suppose he's spent *a thousand years* just sitting in that chair?"

"And how do you not go insane, listening to that sound all that time," Myron added.

"Okay, I've got something." Alric turned to address the wizard. "Excuse me, sir." The man in the chair slowly raised his head and blinked in response to the bright light from above. He looked weary, his eyes tired. "Sorry to disturb you. I am Alric Ess—"

"I know well who thou art," Esrahaddon interrupted. His tone was relaxed and calm, his voice gentle and soothing. "I have expected thou ere long." He raised an arm to shelter his eyes and peered at them. "Where doth thy sinlister be?"

"My what?"

"Thy *sinlister*, Arista art her name."

"Oh, my *sister*."

"*Sis-ter*," the wizard repeated carefully and sighed, shaking his head.

"She is not here."

"Why did she not come?"

Alric looked first to Royce and then to Hadrian.

"She asked us to come in her place," Royce responded.

Looking at the thief, the wizard asked, "And thou art?"

"Me? I'm nobody," Royce replied.

Esrahaddon narrowed his eyes at the thief and raised one eyebrow. "Perhaps, perhaps not."

"My sister instructed me to come here and speak with you," Alric said, drawing the wizard's attention back to him. "Do you know why?"

"Because I told her to."

"Neat trick since you're locked in here," Hadrian observed.

"*Neat?*" Esrahaddon questioned. "Dost thou mean to say, 'twas a clean thing? Or a well-done effort?" The four men responded with looks of confusion. "No matter, Arista hath been in the habit of visiting me for the last year. At least I think it hath been a year. 'Tis quite difficult to tell the time in this gaol. She fancies herself a student of The Art, only there art no schools for wizards left. She learned all she could and then sought me. She wished to be mine apprentice and I her grinder. I was bored, as thee can imagine. So I obliged her. She entertained me with news of the outside world and teacheth me to speak the new language style. I taught her some *neat tricks*." His attention turned to Hadrian as he accentuated the last words.

"Tricks?" Alric asked concerned. "What kind of tricks?"

"Do not worry, dear boy, 'tis nothing of consequence. I believe thy father 'twas ill not long ago. I teacheth her to make a henth bylin." They all looked at him puzzled. Esrahaddon's gaze left them. He appeared to search for something. "Arista called it a…a…" His face strained with concentration. "Alas, I cannot remember."

"A healing potion?" Myron asked.

The wizard eyed the monk carefully. "Yes, that is what she called the henth bylin—a healing potion."

"You taught her to make a potion to give to my father?"

"Frightening, is it not? Such a devil as I, administering potions to a king. 'Tis nothing to concern thyself. I did not poison thy father. She had the same concern. I instructed her to bring a taste of the draught, and I drank it myself to prove there was no danger. She also sampled it for her own peace of mind. Neither of us died, nor grew horns, and thy father felt better, yes?"

"That doesn't explain why Arista sent me here."

"Was thy father recently killed?"

"Yes," Alric said.

"That wouldst be why. I told her if thy father was killed, or died in a mysterious accident, to send thou here. She did not believe me. Why should she? But I suppose thy father's death changed her mind. 'Tis a shame." Esrahaddon looked deliberately at Hadrian, Royce, and then Myron. "Ye three must be the scrapegars? The ones accused of the murder? I told Arista not to trust anyone except the accused killers as they wouldst most likely be completely innocent."

"Do you know, then, who killed my father?"

"I do not have a name, if that is what thou ask. I am not a fortune-teller, nor am I clairvoyant. I merely know how things work. Thy father was killed by a man to be sure, but that man is in league with an organization. I suspect it is the same one which holds me captive."

"The Nyphron Church," Myron muttered softly, yet still the wizard heard and his eyes narrowed once more at the monk.

"Why would the Church of Nyphron wish to kill my father?"

"Sadly, 'twas nothing more than a foolish case of mistaken identity. 'Twas merely a potion exercise for Arista and a remedy for thy sick father, but the Church, well, they listen to me day and night. Overhearing mine instructions to thy sinlist—*sis-ter*, they must have assumed thy father wert the Heir of Novron."

"Wait a minute," Alric interrupted, "the Church doesn't want to murder the heir. Their whole existence revolves around restoring him to the throne and creating a new Imperial Era."

"'Tis what they want thee to thinketh. In truth, they wish him dead. They desire the bloodline erased. 'Tis the true reason why they seeketh the Heir even after all this time. And why they have imprisoned me for all these years."

"Why?"

"Because I know it was the Church who betrayed the Emperor, who murdered him and every member of his family save one. If the heir is found, it wilt prove my innocence and their treachery."

"The way we heard the story *you* were the one who killed the imperial family. You are responsible for the destruction of the entire Empire," Hadrian said.

"And where didst ye learn that, the Church? Dost thou really think one man could do so much? Dost thou hast any idea just how ludicrous that sounds?"

"What makes you think they killed the Emperor?" Alric inquired.

"I do not think. I *know*. I was there, and 'twas I who saved the Emperor's only son from death at their hands. I helped him escape in those last desperate hours of the Empire."

"So you are telling us that you lived at the time of the Emperor. Do you expect us to believe that you are over nine hundred years old?" Royce asked.

"I do not expect anything. I am merely answering Thy Majesty's question."

"That's *just* an answer like this is *just* a prison," Royce countered.

"I still don't understand what all this has to do with my father. Why would the Church kill him?"

"'Tis because I showed an interest in him. When the Empire fell, I was not killed like so many others. They kept me alive through powerful enchantments for centuries because I alone know what happened to the Emperor's son and can find an heir if one still exists. They keep me alive in hope that I wilt lead them to him. As I said they art always listening. When I helped thy sister learn magic and I cured thy father of sickness, they must have thought I deemed it important for him to live. They must have suspected that Arista, thy father, and thou were descendents of the heir. While I thought there might be a danger, I did not think they would be so bloodthirsty in their eagerness to end the Novron line. I warned the princess if something happened to her father, something strange, unexpected, and deadly, that she and thou might be the next targets."

"And that is why you wanted me brought here? To explain all this to me, to make me understand?"

"No. That is why thy sister asked thou to come. I brought thou here for another reason entirely."

"And what is that?"

The wizard looked up at them, his expression revealing a hint of amusement. "To help me escape."

No one said anything. Myron took the moment to sit down on the stone bench behind him and whispered to Hadrian, "You were right. Life outside the abbey *is* much more exciting than books."

"You want us to help you to escape?" Royce asked incredulously. He held out his hands and looked around the black stone fortress. "From *here*?"

"'Tis necessary I am afraid."

"'Tis also impossible. I have gotten out of a number of difficult situations in my time, but nothing like this."

"And thou art aware of only a small fraction of the measures used to contain me. All thou sees art the walls, guards, and the abyss. There art also magical forces at work. Magical locks art on *all* the doors here, just as 'twas on the door through which ye entered the gaol. They disappear upon closing. 'Tis the same enchantment on the bridge ye came across. Go look and ye wilt find it so. 'Tis no longer there. 'Tis not invisible—'tis gone."

Royce raised an eyebrow skeptically. "Alric, I need your ring." The prince handed it to the thief, who climbed the steps and disappeared into the tunnel. He returned a few minutes later and gave the ring back to Alric. A slight shake of his head confirmed what Hadrian already suspected.

Hadrian turned his attention back to the wizard, and Esrahaddon continued. "Still, 'tis not the most serious of the barriers in use here. Perhaps ye saw the runes which line these walls? They create a powerful magical force protecting the stone from magic or physical damage. These enchantments create a magical barrier. Inside this field, no new magic can be cast, and the passing of time is suspended. It is why I have lived for so long. None of ye has aged a second since ye entered this cell. Due to the field created by the runes, what ye perceive as a singing noise, ye will not get hungry or thirsty, or at least not more than ye were when ye entered. Ye will not become sleepy. Ye wilt remain just as ye art. 'Tis really quite remarkable all the trouble they went through to contain me."

"I don't believe you," Alric challenged.

"Put a hand to thy chests. Ye wilt find the lack of a beating heart."

Myron inched his hand across his breast and let out a tiny squeak.

"And with all these obstacles, you expect us to help you escape?" Hadrian said.

"I am counting on it," the wizard replied with an impish grin.

"Although I am dying to ask how," Royce said. "I am even more compelled to ask why? If they went through this much effort to seal you here, it seems to me they might have had a good reason. You've told us what we came to hear. We're done. So why would we be foolish enough to try and help you escape?"

"Because ye hast little choice in the matter."

"We have a great many choices," Alric countered bravely. "I am king and rule here; it is you who is powerless."

"Oh, I will not be the one stopping ye. As ye understand rightly, I *am* helpless, a prisoner with no ability to do much of anything. They were very careful to ensure my subjugation. 'Tis the guards who will stop ye. When thee call for them, they wilt not come. They can hear ye. They hath heard every word we hath spoken. Just as they killed your father, they wilt also kill you, Your Majesty."

"But if they are listening, they also know I am not the heir," Alric said, the courage in his voice melting away.

"They cannot be sure if thou art or not. It wilt not matter to them. They wilt not take a chance. Besides, now that I told thee of their secret, they wilt never let thee leave—any of ye.

Thee wilt be imprisoned here, just as I am, or they wilt kill thee outright."

Alric's concern showed on his face as he looked first to Hadrian and then to Royce. "He may be right," the thief said quietly.

Concern turned to panic, and the prince began to shout commands for their release. There was no response, no sound of the great door opening nor of approaching protectors to escort them to the exit. Everyone except the wizard looked worried. Alric wrung his hands, and Myron stood and held onto the rail of the balcony, as if letting go would allow the world to spin away from him.

"It was a trap after all," Alric said. He turned to Royce. "My apologies for doubting your sound paranoia."

"Even I didn't expect this. Perhaps there's another way out." Royce took a seat on one of the observation benches and assumed the same contemplative look he had worn when he was trying to determine how to get inside the prison.

Everyone remained silent for some time. Finally, Hadrian approached Royce and whispered, "Okay, buddy, this is where you tell me you have this wonderfully unexpected plan to get us out of here."

"Well, I do have one. But it seems almost as frightening as the alternative."

"What's that?"

"We do what the wizard says."

They looked down at the man casually seated in the chair. His robe looked a slightly different shade of blue now. Hadrian waved the others over and explained Royce's plan.

"Could this be a trick?" Alric asked quietly. "The clerk did warn us not to do anything he said."

"You mean the nice clerk who took away our bridge and refuses to let us out?" Royce replied. "I am not seeing an alternative, but if any of you have another idea, I am willing to hear it."

"I'd just like to feel my heart again," Myron said holding his palm to his chest and looking sick. "This is very disturbing. I almost feel like I'm actually dead."

"Your Majesty?"

Alric looked up at the thief with a scowl. "I just want to say, for the record, as far as Royal Protectors go, you're not very good."

"It's my first day," Royce replied dryly.

"And already I am trapped in a timeless prison. I shudder to think what might have happened if you had a whole week."

"Listen, I don't see we have a choice here," Royce told the group. "We either do what the wizard says and hope he can get us out, or we accept an eternity of sitting here listening to this dreadful singing."

The mournful wail of the music was so wretched that Hadrian knew listening to it would eventually drive him mad. He tried to ignore it, but like Myron, it brought forth unpleasant memories of places and people. Hadrian saw the disappointment on his father's face when he left to join the military. He saw the tiger covered in blood, gasping for breath as it slowly died, and he heard the sound of hundreds chanting the name "*Galenti!*" He had reached his conclusion. Anything was better than staying there.

Royce stood and returned to the balcony where the wizard waited calmly below. "I assume if we help you escape, you will see to it we get out as well?"

"Of course."

"And there is no way to determine if you are telling the truth right now?"

The wizard smiled. "None whatsoever, I am afraid."

Royce sighed heavily. "What do we have to do?"

"Very little. I only need the king to recite a simple bit of poetry."

"*Poetry?*" Alric pushed past Hadrian to join Royce at the balcony, "What poetry?"

The wizard stood up and kicked his chair to one side to reveal two stanzas of text crudely scratched into the floor.

"'Tis amazing what beauty ye can create given time," the wizard said with obvious pride. "Speak it and it wilt be so."

Hadrian silently read the lines brightly illuminated by the beam of the overhead light.

---

As lord of this realm and keeper of keys,
a decree was made and a councilman seized.
Unjustly I say, and the time it is nigh
to open the gate and let his soul fly.
By virtue of gift granted to me,
by rightful birth, the sovereign I be.
Hereby I proclaim this royal decree,
Esrahaddon the wizard, this moment is free.

---

"How is that possible?" Alric asked. "You said spells don't work here."

"They do not, and thou art no spell-caster. Thou art merely granting me freedom as the law allows the rightful ruler of this land. The law predates Melengar, a law that made foolish assumptions about the longevity of power and those who would hold it. At this moment, thou do. Thou art the rightful and undisputed ruler of this land, and as such, the locks art thine to open. Not the physical ones mind thee, but the magical ones, because they art formed not of steel, but of words, and words in time can change their meaning.

"When this gaol stood on imperial ground, 'twas controlled by the Church of Nyphron who built this place. The Patriarch was the undisputed ruler, but civil war came; the Empire fell. Warlords sprang up as the central power weakened. These warlords became kings, and new lines appeared on the maps. Melengar was born and this land became the realm of House Essendon. What was once only the privilege of the leader of the Church of Nyphron has fallen to thou. After nine centuries of educational neglect, my jailers hath forgotten how to read their own runes!"

In the distance, Hadrian heard the grinding of stone on stone. Outside the cell, the great door was opening. "Speak those words, my lord, and thou wilt end nine hundred years of wrongful imprisonment."

"How does this help?" Alric asked. "You said I can't open the physical locks, and this place is filled with guards. How does this get us out?"

The wizard smiled a great grin. "Thy words wilt release the magical field, allowing me the freedom to use The Art once more."

"You'll cast a spell. You'll disappear!"

Footsteps thundered on the bridge, which had apparently reappeared. Hadrian ran up the gallery stairs to look down the tunnel. "We have guards coming! And they don't look happy."

"If you're going to do this, you'd better make it fast," Royce told Alric.

"They've swords drawn," Hadrian shouted. "Never a good sign."

Alric glared down at the wizard. "I want your word you won't leave us here."

"Thou have it, my lord," the wizard inclined his head respectfully.

"This better work," Alric muttered and began reading aloud the words on the floor below.

Royce raced to join his partner who was already positioning himself at the mouth of the tunnel. Hadrian planned to use its confined space to limit the advantage of the guard's numbers. The larger fighter planted his feet while Royce took up position slightly behind him. In unison, they drew their weapons, preparing for the impending onslaught. At least twenty men stormed the gallery. Hadrian could see their eyes and recognized what burned there. He had fought numerous battles and he knew the many faces of combat. He had seen fear, recklessness, hatred, even madness.

What came at him now was rage—blind, intense rage. Hadrian studied the lead man, estimating his footfalls to determine which leg his weight would land on when he came within striking range. He did the same with the man behind him. Calculating his attack, he raised his swords, but the prison guards stopped. Hadrian waited with his swords still poised, yet the guards did not advance.

"Let us be leaving," he heard Esrahaddon say from behind. Hadrian whirled around and discovered the wizard was no longer on the stage below. Instead, he moved casually past him, navigating around the stationary guards. "Come along," Esrahaddon called.

Without a word, the group hurried after the wizard. He led them through the tunnel and across the newly extended bridge. The prison was oddly silent, and it was then that Hadrian realized the music had stopped. The only remaining sound was their footfalls against the hard stone floor.

"Relax and just keep walking," Esrahaddon told them reassuringly.

They did as instructed, and no one said a word. To pass the clerk, who stood peering through the great door, they needed to come within inches of his anxiety-riddled face. As Hadrian attempted to slip by without bumping him, he saw the man's eye move. Hadrian stiffened. "Can they see or hear us?"

"No, not really. They might sense something. The hairs on the back of their neck might stand, and they might feel a disturbance in the air as thou moves by, but no, they do not know we are here."

The wizard led them without hesitation, making turns, crossing bridges, and climbing stairs with total confidence.

"Maybe we're dead?" Myron whispered, glaring at each frozen guard he passed. "Maybe we're *all* dead now. Maybe we're ghosts."

Hadrian thought Myron might be on to something. Everything was so oddly still, so empty. The fluid movement of the wizard and his billowing robe, which now emitted a soft silvery light far brighter than any lantern or torch, only heightened the surreal atmosphere.

"I don't understand. How is this possible?" Alric asked, stepping around a pair of black-suited guards who watched the third bridge. He waved his hand before the face of one of them, who did not respond.

"Actually, 'tis only this way because we are in this gaol. No one person hath the power to stop time, but this gaol was designed for just such a purpose. 'Tis a giant *Ithinal*. What we once called a magic box. Within these walls the matrices of enchantments art complex. Many of my old colleagues created this place, and according to what Arista hath told me, I may be the only one who can still understand the ancient language. Because this gaol was designed to affect magic and time, I merely ever so slightly adjusted a fiber or two within the weave to throw the five of us out of phase."

"So, the guards can't see us, but that doesn't explain why they are just standing there." Hadrian said. "We disappeared, and you're free. Why are they not searching? Shouldn't they be locking doors to trap us?"

"Because nothing hath happened, as far as they art concerned. We art still where we were. For everyone else in this gaol, 'tis the moment young Alric spoke the last word in my poem. 'Tis why they dost not appear to be moving to us."

"You turned it inside out!" Myron exclaimed.

"Exactly," Esrahaddon said, looking with an appraising eye over his shoulder at the monk. "'Tis thrice thou hath impressed me. What did thou say thy name was?"

"He didn't," Royce answered for him.

"Thou dost not trust people, dost thou my black-hooded friend? 'Tis quite wise. More people should be as careful, particularly when dealing with wizards." Esrahaddon winked at the thief.

"What does he mean by 'turning it inside out'?" Alric asked. "So, time has stopped for them while we are free?"

"In the crudest terms that is correct. Time still moves for them, but very slowly. While unaware of it, they wilt remain very close to the instant the field changed for all time, or at least until some-one alters the pattern engraved on the stone."

"I am starting to see now why they were afraid of you," Alric said.

"They kept me locked up for nine hundred years for saving the son of a man we all swore our lives to serve and protect. I think that I am being exceedingly kind. There art, after all, many worse moments in which to be trapped for all eternity."

They reached the great stair that led to the main entrance corridor and began the long exhausting climb up the stone steps. "How did you stay sane?" Hadrian asked. "Or did the time slip by in an instant like it is for them?"

"The time did slip by, but not as fast as thou might thinketh. A year for me passed in about the length of a day."

"Almost three years," Myron calculated.

"Not nearly as bad as I thought," Hadrian remarked, "but still, three years of just *sitting* there —"

"I was not just sitting there. I fought a battle each day. 'Twas a force of great effort to fend off their attacks to learn my secrets. And I had to decipher the runes etched all around me. I was never bored. Moreover, I have learned patience as a practitioner of The Art. Although there were times.... Well, who is to say what it means to be sane?"

When they approached the hall of faces, Esrahaddon looked down its length and paused. Hadrian noticed the wizard stiffen." What is it?" he asked.

"Those art the workers who built this gaol. I came here during the last few days they wert building this place. There was a small city of tents and shacks around the lake then. Hundreds of artisans and their families traveled here at the imperial call to do their part out of patriotism for their fallen Emperor. Such was the character of His Imperial Majesty. They all mourned his passing, and few in the vast and varied Empire would not have gladly given their lives for him. They labeled me the betrayer, and I could see the hatred in their eyes as they passed me on their way to work. They were proud to be the builders of my tomb."

The wizard's gaze moved from face to face. "I recognize some of them: the stone cutters, the sculptures, the cooks, and their wives and children. The Church could not let them go for fear they would talk. They sealed them in. All these people, all these artists ensnared by a lie and murdered just to keep me here. How many people died, I wonder? How much was lost just to hide one absurd secret, which even a millennium hath not erased?"

"There's no door down there," Alric warned the wizard.

Esrahaddon looked up at Alric as if awoken from a dream. "Of course there is a door," he said and promptly led them down the corridor at a brisk walk. "Thou wert merely out of phase with it before."

Here, in the darkest segment of the prison, Esrahaddon's robe grew brighter still, and he looked like a giant firefly. In time, they came to a solid stone wall, and without hesitation or pause, Esrahaddon walked through it. The rest quickly followed.

The bright sunlight of a lovely, clear autumn morning nearly blinded them the moment they passed through the barrier. Blue sky and the cool fresh air was a welcome change. Hadrian took a deep breath and reveled in the scent of grass and fallen leaves, a smell he had not even noticed prior to entering the prison. "That's strange. It should be nighttime and raining, I would think. We couldn't have been in there more than a few hours. Could we?"

"Funny things can happen when ye play with time." Esrahaddon threw his head back and faced the sun. He stood and took long deep breaths of air, sighing contentedly with each exhale. "The question ye should be asking thyselves is what day 'tis? Today could be the same day you entered, or the one after. In theory, 'tis possible to be tens or hundreds of years in the future." The wizard appeared amused at the shock on their faces. "Don't worry too much. Most likely ye only skipped a few days or hours."

"That's rather unnerving," Alric said, "losing time like that."

"I have lost nine hundred years. Everyone I knew is dead, the Empire is gone, and who knows what else hath happened. If what thy sister tells me is correct, much hath changed in the world while I have been gone."

"By the way," Royce mentioned, "no one uses the words *'tis* or *hath* anymore and certainly not *thou* or *thy*. You sound like a history book."

The wizard nodded. "I noticed none of ye spoke properly. In my day, various classes had different forms of speech. Properly educated people used more sophistication than the lower classes as a mark of their rank. I assumed all of ye were merely of a lower station or, in the case of the king, poorly educated."

Alric glared. "It is you who sound strange, not us."

"I see. Then I wilt have to learn to speak as all of—*you*— do. Even though—it is—very difficult and sounds crude and guttural."

Hadrian, Royce, and Myron began the task of saddling the horses, which remained standing where they had left them. Myron smiled, obviously happy to be with the animals once again. He petted them while eagerly asking how to tie a cinch strap.

"We don't have an extra horse, and Hadrian is riding double already," Alric explained. He glanced at Royce, who showed no indication of volunteering. "Esrahaddon will have to ride with me I suppose."

"That won't be necessary. I will be going my own way."

"Oh no you're not. You're coming back to my castle with me. I have a great deal to speak with you about. You were the advisor to the Emperor and are obviously very gifted and knowledge-able. I have great need for such an advisor. You will be my Royal Counselor."

"No. 'Twill…" He sighed and then continued. "*It will* come as a shock to—*you*—but I did not escape for the purpose of helping you with *your* little problems. I have more important matters to which I must attend, and I have been too long from them."

The prince appeared taken aback. "What matters could you possibly have after nine hundred years? After all, it's not as if you have to get home to tend to your livestock. If it is a matter of compensation, you will be well paid and live in as much luxury as I can afford. And if you are thinking of shopping around, only Ethelred of Warric is likely to offer as much and trust me, you don't want to work for the likes of him. He's a dogmatic Imperialist and a loyal church supporter."

"I am not looking for compensation."

"No? Look at you. You have nothing, no food, no place to sleep. I think you should consider your situation a bit more before refusing me. Besides, gratitude alone should compel you to help me."

"Gratitude? Has the meaning of that word changed as well? In my day, it meant to show appreciation for a favor."

"And it still does. I saved you. I released you from that place."

Esrahaddon raised an eyebrow. "Didst thou help me escape as a favor to me? I think not. Thou freed me to save thyself. I owe thee nothing, and if I did, I repaid thee when I brought thou out."

"But the whole reason I came here was to gain your assistance. I am inheriting a throne handed down by blood! Thieves abducted and dragged me across the kingdom in my first two days as king. I still don't know who killed my father or how to find them. I am in great need of help. You must know hundreds of things the greatest minds of today have never known—"

"Thousands at least, but I am still not going with you. You have a kingdom to secure. My path lies elsewhere."

Alric's face grew red with frustration. "I insist you return with me and become my advisor. I can't just let you wander off. Who knows what kind of trouble you could cause. You're dangerous."

"Yes indeed dear prince, so allow me to givest thee a bit of free council: doth not use the word *insist* in conjunction with me. Thine hath but only a small spill to contend with, do not tempt a deluge."

Alric stiffened.

"How long before the Church starts hunting you?" Hadrian asked casually.

"What dost thou…." The wizard sighed. "What do *you* mean?"

"You locked things up nicely in the prison so no one will know you escaped. Of course, if we were to return and start bragging about how we broke you out, that might start inquiries."

The wizard leveled his gaze at Hadrian. "Art thee attempting to blackmail me?"

"Why would I do that? As you already know, I have nothing to do with this, being just a scapegoat and all. Not to mention it would be pretty stupid of me to threaten a powerful wizard. The thing is though, the king here, he is not as bright as I am. He very well might get drunk and tell stories at the first tavern he arrives at, as nobles often do." Esrahaddon glanced at Alric, whose red face now turned pale. "Fact is, we came all this way to find out who killed Alric's father, and we really don't know much more than we did before we set out."

Esrahaddon chuckled softly. "Very well, I will give you some assistance. Tell me how did your father die exactly?"

"He was stabbed with a knife," Alric explained.

"What kind of knife?"

"A common rondel military dagger." Alric held his hands about a foot apart. "About this long. It had a flat blade and a round pommel. It was really nothing special."

Esrahaddon nodded. "Where was he stabbed?"

"In his private chapel."

"I meant where physically?"

"Oh, in the back, upper left side, I think."

"Were there any windows or other doors in the chapel?"

"None."

"Who found the body?"

"These two." Alric pointed at Royce and Hadrian.

The wizard smiled and shook his head. "No, beside them, who announced the death of the king? Who raised the alarm?"

"That would be Captain Wylin, my master-at-arms. He was on the scene very quickly and apprehended them."

Hadrian thought about the night King Amrath had been killed. "No, that's not right. There was a dwarf there. He must have come around the corner of the hallway just as we left the room. He probably saw the king's body lying on the floor of the chapel and shouted. Right after he yelled, the soldiers came, and surprisingly fast, I might add."

"Did you actually see this dwarf approach from the corridor?" the wizard asked.

"No," Hadrian replied, and Royce confirmed with a shake of his head.

"And when you entered the chapel, was the king's body visible from the doorway?"

Hadrian and Royce shook their heads.

"That solves it then," the wizard said, as if everything was perfectly clear. The party stared back at him in confusion. Esrahaddon sighed. "The dwarf killed Amrath."

"That's not possible," Alric challenged. "My father was a big man, and the dagger thrust was downward. A dwarf couldn't possibly have stabbed him in the upper back."

"You said your father was in his chapel. As any good pious king, he was no doubt kneeling with head bowed. The dwarf killed him as he prayed. I suspect the dwarf was someone your father knew. Someone he would not be alarmed to see in the chapel."

"But the door was locked when we entered," Hadrian said. "And there was no one in the room besides the king."

"No one you could *see* at least. The dwarf must have been hiding inside the room when you entered. Did the chapel have an altar with a cabinet?"

"Yes, it did."

"They did a millennium ago as well. Religion changes very slowly. The cabinet was no doubt too small for a man to crouch in, but I'm sure it could easily accommodate a dwarf. After he killed the king, he locked the door and waited for you two to find the body." Esrahaddon paused. "That cannot be right you—*two*

*—to?*" He rolled his eyes and shook his head. "If you have done this to language, I fear to know the fate of all else.

"With the door locked, a night guard or a cleaning steward would not find the body prematurely. Only a skilled thief would be able to enter, which I assume at least one of *you* is." He looked directly at Royce as he said the last part. "After you left, the dwarf crept out, opened the door, and sounded the alarm, trapping you before you could get away."

"So, the dwarf is the agent of the Church?"

"No." The wizard sighed with a look of frustration. "Unless things have changed drastically since I was last about, there is not a dwarf alive who would carry a common dagger. The traits of dwarves change even slower than religion. He was given the dagger by the one who hired him. Find that person and you will find the true killer."

Stunned, everyone looked at the wizard." That's incredible," Alric said.

"Actually, it is not difficult to determine. After so many years you learn a great many things." The wizard inclined his head toward the cliff. "Getting out of there *was hard*. Speaking as you do *is hard*. Determining the murderer of King Amrath was…was…soft."

"Soft?" Hadrian asked. "You mean easy."

"How is easy the opposite of hard? This does not make sense."

Hadrian shrugged. "And yet, it is."

Esrahaddon looked frustrated. "See what I mean? Now, you have what you came here for, or at least as much assistance as I can lend in this matter. Therefore, I will be on my way. As I said, I have to attend to my own affairs. I assume my help was sufficient to prevent any loose tongues?"

"You have my hand on it," Alric said reaching out.

The wizard looked down at Alric's open palm and smiled. "Your word is enough." He turned away and without so much as a parting gesture began walking down the slope.

"You're going to walk? You know it's a long way to anywhere from here," Hadrian yelled after him.

"I am looking forward to the trip," the wizard replied without glancing back. Following the ancient road, he rounded the corner and slipped out of sight.

The remaining party members mounted their horses. Myron seemed more comfortable with the animals now and climbed confidently into his seat behind Hadrian. He even neglected to hold on until they began down the ravine back in the direction from which they had come. Hadrian expected they would pass Esrahaddon on the way down, but they reached the bottom of the ravine without seeing him.

"Not your run-of-the-mill fellow, is he?" Hadrian asked. He was continuing to look around for any signs of the wizard.

"The way he was able to get out of that place, makes me wonder exactly what we did here today by letting him out," Royce said.

"No wonder the Emperor was so successful." Alric frowned and knotted the ends of his reins. "Although I can tell it didn't come without aggravation. You know, I don't extend my hand often, but when I do I expect it to be accepted. I found his reaction quite insulting."

"I'm not sure he was being rude by not shaking your hand. I think it is just because he couldn't," Myron told them. "Shake your hand that is."

"Why not?"

"In *The Letters of Dioylion*, they told a bit about Esrahaddon's incarceration. The Church had both of his hands cut off in order to limit his ability to cast spells."

"Oh," Alric said.

"Why do I get the impression this Dioylion fellow didn't die a natural death?" Hadrian asked.

"He's probably one of those faces in the hallway." Royce spurred his horse down the slope.

# PART 6

## REVELATIONS BY MOONLIGHT

"I heard you were looking for me, Uncle?" Princess Arista swept into his office. She was followed by her bodyguard Hilfred, who dutifully waited by the door. Still dressing in clothing mourning her father's death, she wore an elegant black gown with a silver bodice. Standing straight and tall with her head held high, she maintained her regal air.

The Archduke Percy Braga rose as she entered. "Yes, I have some questions for you." He resumed his seat behind the desk. Her uncle was dressed in black as well. His doublet, cape, and cap were dark velvet, causing his gold chain of office to stand out more than usual. His eyes looked weary from lack of sleep, and a thickening growth of stubble shadowed his face.

"Do you now?" she said glaring at him. "Since when does the Lord Chancellor summon the acting queen to answer *his* questions?"

Percy raised his eyes to meet hers. "There is no proof your brother is dead, Arista. You are not queen yet."

"No proof?" She walked over to Braga's chart table where maps of the kingdom lay scattered everywhere. They were littered with flags marking where patrols, garrisons, and companies were deployed. She picked up the soiled robe she saw there, it bore the Essendon falcon crest. Poking her fingers through the holes cut in the back she threw it on his desk. "What do you call this?"

"A robe," the archduke responded curtly.

"This is my brother's, and these holes look as though a dagger or arrow would fit through them nicely. Those two men who murdered my father killed Alric as well. They dumped his body in the river. My brother is dead, Braga! The only reason I have not already ordered my coronation is that I'm observing the appropriate mourning period. That time will soon be over, so you should mind how you speak to me, Uncle, lest I forget we are family."

"Until I have his body, Arista, I must consider your brother alive. As such, he is still the rightful ruler, and I will continue to do everything in my power to find him regardless of your interference. I owe that much to your father who entrusted me with this position."

"In case you haven't noticed, my father is dead. You should pay more attention to the living, or you won't be the Lord Chancellor of Melengar for long."

Braga started to say something and then stopped to take a calming breath. "Will you answer my questions or not?"

"Go ahead and ask. I will decide after I hear them." She casually walked back to the chart table and sat on it. She crossed her long legs at the ankles and absently studied her fingernails.

"Master Wylin reports that he has completed his interviews with the dungeon staff." Braga got up and moved from behind his desk to face Arista. In his hand, he held a parchment, which he glanced at for reference. "He indicates you visited the prisoners after your brother and I left them. He says you brought two monks with you who were later found gagged and hanging in place of the prisoners. Is that true?"

"Yes," she replied without embellishment. The archduke continued to stare at her, the silence growing between them. "I am a superstitious woman by nature, and I wanted to be certain they had last rites so their ghosts didn't remain after their execution."

"There is a report you ordered the prisoners unchained?" Braga took another step closer to her.

"The monks told me the prisoners needed to kneel. I saw no danger in it. They were in a cell with an army of guards just outside."

"They also reported you entered with the monks and had the door closed behind you." The archduke took another step. He was now uncomfortably close, studying her manners and expression.

"Did they also mention I left before the monks did? Or that I wasn't there when the brutes grabbed them?" Arista pushed off the desk, causing her uncle to step back. She casually slipped past him and walked to the window which looked down at the castle court-yard. A man was chopping and stacking wood for the coming winter. "I will admit it wasn't the smartest thing I've ever done, but I never thought they would escape. They were just *two men*!" She continued to stare out the window absently. Her gaze drifted from the woodcutter to the trees that had lost all their leaves. "Now is that all you wanted to know? Do I have the Chancellor's permission to return to my duties as queen of this realm?"

"Of course, my dear." Braga's tone turned warmer. The princess left the window and moved toward the exit. "Oh, but there is one last thing."

Arista paused at the doorway and glanced over her shoulder. "What is it?"

"Wylin also reports the dagger used to kill your father is missing from the store room. Do you have any idea where it might be?"

She turned to face him. "Are you now accusing me of *stealing*?"

"I am simply asking, Arista," the archduke huffed in irritation. "You don't need to be so obstinate with me. I am merely trying to do my job."

"*Your job?* I think you are doing much more than *your job*. No, I don't know anything about the dagger, and stop pestering me with accusations thinly veiled as inquiries. Do it again and we shall soon see who rules here!"

Arista stormed out of Braga's office, leaving Hilfred to jog a step to keep up with her. She promptly crossed the keep to the residences. Asking Hilfred to stand guard, she rushed up the steps of her personal tower. She entered her room, slammed the door shut, and locked it with a tap from the gemstone in her necklace.

Breathing heavily, she paused a moment, with her back pressed against the door. She tried to steady herself. She felt as if the room were swaying like a young tree in a breeze. She had been feeling that way often lately. The world seemed to be constantly swirling around her. Yet, this was her sanctuary, her refuge from the world. Here was the one place she felt safe, where she kept her secrets, where she could practice her magic, and where she dreamed her dreams.

For a princess, her room was very modest. She had seen the bedrooms of the daughters of earls and even one baroness who had finer abodes. By comparison, hers was quite small and austere. It was, however, by her own choice. She could have her pick of the larger, more ornately decorated bedrooms in the royal wing, but she chose the tower for its isolation and the three windows, which afforded a view of all the lands around the castle. Thick burgundy drapes extended from ceiling to floor, hiding the bare stone. She had hoped they might keep the chill out as well, but unfortunately, they did not. Winter nights were often brutally cold despite her efforts to keep the little fireplace roaring. Still the soft presence of the drapes made it seem warmer just the same. Four giant pillows rested upon a tiny canopy bed. There was no room for a larger one. Next to the bed was a small table with a pitcher inside a washbasin. Beside it stood a wardrobe, which had been passed down to her from her mother along with her hope chest. The solidly made trunk with a formidable lock sat at the foot of her bed. The only other pieces of furniture in the room were her dressing table, a mirror, and a small chair.

She crossed the room and sat at her dressing table. The mirror, which stood beside it, was of lavish design. The looking glass was clearer than most and was framed on either side by two elegant swans swimming away from one another. This too, had once belonged to her mother. She fondly remembered nights sitting before it, watching through its reflection as her mother brushed her hair. On the table, she kept her collection of hairbrushes. She had many, one from each of the kingdoms her father had visited on matters of state. There was a pearl-handled brush from Wesbaden, and an ebony one with fine fish-bone teeth from the exotic port city of Tur Del Fur. Looking at them now brought back memories of days when her father would return home with a hand hidden behind his back and a twinkle in his eye. Now, the swan mirror and the brushes were all that remained of her parents.

With a sudden sweep of her hand, she threw the brushes across the room. *Why had it come to this?* She cried softly; it did not matter. She had work yet to do. There were things she had started which must now be finished. Braga was getting more suspicious each day—time was running out.

She unlocked and opened her hope chest. From inside, she removed the bundle of purple cloth she had hidden there. How ironic, she thought, for her to have used that cloth. Her father had wrapped the last hairbrush he had given her in it. She laid the bundle on her bed and carefully unfolded it to reveal the rondel dagger. The blade was still stained with her father's blood.

"Only one more job left for you to do," she told the knife.

# 2

The Silver Pitcher Inn was a simple cottage located on the outskirts of the province of Galilin. Fieldstone and mortar composed the lower half, while whitewashed oak beams supported a roof of thick field thatch, gone gray with time. Windows divided into diamond panes of poor quality glass underscored by helda-berry bushes lined the sides. Several horses stood tied to the posts out front, with still more visible in the small stable to the side.

"Seems like a busy place for so far out," Royce observed.

Traveling east, they had ridden all day. Just as before, the trip through the wilds proved exhausting. As the evening light faded, they reached the rural farmland of Galilin. They passed through tilled fields and meadows, at last stumbling upon a country lane. Because none of them knew for certain where they were, they decided to follow the road to a landmark. To their pleasant surprise, The Silver Pitcher Inn was the first building they found.

"Well, Majesty," Hadrian said, "you should be able to find your way back to the castle from here, if that is still your destination."

"It is about time I got back," Alric told him, "but not before I eat. Does this place have decent food?"

"Does it matter?" Hadrian chuckled. "I'd be happy for a bit of three-day-ripe field mouse at this point. Come on, we can have a last meal together, which, since you have no money on you, I will be paying for. I hope you'll let me deduct it from my taxes."

"No need. We'll tack it on to the job as an additional expense," Royce interjected. He looked at Alric and added, "You haven't forgotten you still owe us one hundred tenents, have you?"

"You'll get paid. I'll have Uncle Percy set the money aside. You can pick it up at the castle."

"I hope you don't mind if we wait a few days, just to make sure."

"Of course not," the prince nodded.

"And if we send a representative to pick up the money for us?" Alric stared at him. "One who has no idea how to find us in case he is captured?"

"Oh please, aren't you being just a tad bit too cautious now?"

"No such thing," Royce replied.

"Look!" Myron shouted suddenly pointing at the stable.

All three of them jumped fearfully at the sudden outburst.

"There's a *brown* horse!" the monk said in amazement. "I didn't know they came in *brown*!"

"By Mar, monk!" Alric shook his head in disbelief, an expression Royce and Hadrian mirrored.

"Well, I didn't," Myron replied sheepishly. His excitement however, was still evident when he added, "What other colors do they come in? Is there a green horse? A blue one? I would so love to see a blue one."

Royce went inside and returned a few minutes later. "Everything looks all right. A bit crowded, but I don't see anything too out of the ordinary. Alric, be sure to keep your hood up and either spin your ring so the insignia is on the inside of your hand, or better yet, remove it altogether until you get home."

Just inside the inn was a small stone foyer where several cloaks and coats hung on a forest of wall pegs. A handful of walking sticks of various shapes and sizes rested on a rack to one side. Above, a shelf held an assortment of tattered hats and gloves.

Myron stood just inside the door, gaping at his surroundings. "I read about inns," he said. "In *Pilgrim's Tales*, a group of wayward travelers spend a night at an inn where they decided to tell stories of their journeys. They made a wager for the best one. It's one of my favorites, although the abbot didn't much care for my reading it. It was a bit bawdy. There were several accounts about *women* in those pages and not in a wholesome fashion either." He scanned the crowd excitedly. "Are there women here?"

"No," Hadrian replied sadly.

"Oh. I was hoping to see one. Do they keep them locked up as treasures?"

Hadrian and the others just laughed.

Myron looked at them mystified then shrugged. "Even so, this is wonderful. There's so much to see! What's that smell? It's not food, is it?"

"Pipe smoke," Hadrian explained. "It probably was not a popular activity at the abbey."

A half-dozen tables filled the small room. A slightly askew stone fireplace with silver tankards dangling from mantle hooks dominated one wall. Next to it stood the bar, which was built from rough and unfinished tree logs complete with bark. Some fifteen patrons lined the room, a handful of which watched the group enter with passing interest. Most were rough stock, woodsmen, laborers, and traveling tinkers. The pipe smoke came from a few gruff men seated near the log bar, and a cloud of it hovered at eye level throughout the room, producing an earthy smell that mingled with the burning wood of the fireplace and the sweet scent of baking bread. Royce led them to an open round table near the window where they could see the horses outside.

"I'll order us something," Hadrian volunteered.

"This is a beautiful place," Myron declared, his eyes darting about the room. "There is *so* much going on, so many conversations. Speaking at meals wasn't allowed at the abbey, so it was always deathly silent. Of course, we got around that rule by using sign language. It used to drive the abbot crazy because we were supposed to be focusing on Maribor, but there are times when you simply have to ask someone to pass the salt."

No sooner had Hadrian reached the bar than he felt someone press up behind him menacingly.

"You should be more careful, my friend," a man in a green hood said softly.

Hadrian turned slowly and chuckled softly when he saw who it was. "I don't have to, Albert. I have a shadow who watches *my* back." Hadrian gestured at Royce, who had slipped up behind the Viscount Winslow.

Albert, who wore a dirty, tattered cloak with the hood pulled up, turned to face a scowling Royce. "I was just making a joke."

"What are you doing here?" Royce whispered.

"Hiding..." Albert started, but he fell quiet when the bartender came over with a pitcher of foaming beer and four mugs.

"Have you eaten?" Hadrian asked.

"No." Albert looked longingly at the pitcher.

"Could I get another mug and another plate of supper?" Hadrian asked the hefty man behind the bar.

"Sure, thing," the bartender responded as he added another mug. "I'll bring the food over when it is ready."

They returned to the table with the viscount trailing them. Albert looked curiously at Myron and Alric for a moment.

"This is Albert Winslow, an acquaintance of ours," Hadrian explained as Albert pulled a chair over to their table. "These are—"

"Clients," Royce cut in quickly, "so no business talk, Albert."

"We've been out of town...traveling, the last few days," Hadrian said. "Anything been going on in Medford?"

"A lot," he said quietly as Hadrian poured the ale. "King Amrath is dead."

"Really," Hadrian feigned surprise.

"The Rose and Thorn has been shut down. Soldiers tore through the Lower Quarter. A bunch of folks were rounded up and sent to prison. There's a small army surrounding Essendon Castle and the entrances to the city. I got out just in time."

"An army around the castle? What for?" Alric asked.

Royce motioned for him to calm down. "What about Gwen?"

"She's okay—I think," Albert replied, looking curiously at Alric. "At least she was when I left. They questioned her and roughed up a few of her girls, but nothing more than that. She's been worried about you. I think she expected you to return from... traveling...days ago."

"Who are *they*?" Royce asked, his voice several degrees colder.

"Well, a lot of them were royal guards, but they had a whole bunch of friends as well. Remember those strangers in town we talked about a few days ago? They were involved. They were marching with some of the royal guards, so they must be working for the crown prince I would think." Again, Albert glanced at Alric. "They were combing the entire city and asking questions about a pair of thieves operating out of the Lower Quarter. That's when I made myself scarce. I left town and headed west. It was the same all over. Patrols are everywhere. They have been ripping apart inns and taverns, hauling people into the streets. I've stayed one step ahead of them so far. Last thing I heard a curfew was ordered after nightfall in Medford."

"So, you just kept heading west?" Hadrian asked.

"Until I got here. This is the first place I came to that hadn't been ransacked."

"Which would explain the large turnout," Hadrian mentioned. "Mice leave a sinking ship."

"Yeah, a lot of people decided Medford wasn't so friendly anymore," Albert explained. "I figured I would stick around here for a few days and then start back and test the waters as I go."

"Has there been any word concerning the prince or princess?" Alric asked.

"Nothing in particular," the viscount responded. He took a drink, his eyes lingering on the prince.

The rear door to the inn opened and a slim figure entered. He was filthy, dressed in torn rags and a hat that looked more like a sack. He clutched a small purse tightly to his chest and paused for only a moment, his eyes darting around the room nervously. He walked quickly to the rear of the bar, where the innkeeper filled a sack of food in exchange for the purse.

"What do we have here?" asked a burly fellow from one of the tables as he got to his feet. "Take off the hat, *elf*. Show us them *ears*."

The ragged pauper clung to his bag tightly and looked toward the door. When he did, another man from the bar moved to block his path.

"I said take it off!" the burly man ordered.

"Leave him alone, Drake," the innkeeper told him. "He just came in for a bit of food. He ain't gonna eat it here."

"I can't believe you sell to *them*, Hall. Haven't you heard they're killing people up in Dunmore? Filthy things." Drake reached out to pull the hat off but the figure aptly dodged his reach. "See how they are? Fast little things when they want to be, but lazy bastards if you try to put 'em to work. They ain't nothing but trouble. You let 'em in here, and one day they'll end up stabbing you in the back and stealing you blind."

"He ain't stealing anything," Hall said. "He comes in here once a week to buy food and stuff for his family. This one has a mate and a kid. Poor things are barely alive. They're living in the forest. It's been a month since the town guard in Medford drove them out."

"Yeah?" Drake said. "If he lives in the forest, where's he getting the money to pay for the food? You stealing it, ain't you, boy? You robbing decent people? Breaking into farms? That's why the sheriffs drive 'em out of the cities, 'cause they're all thieves and drunks. The Medford guard don't want 'em on their streets, and I don't want 'em on ours!"

A man standing behind the vagabond snatched his hat off, revealing thick matted black hair and pointed ears.

"Filthy little elf," Drake said. "Where'd you get the money?"

"I said leave him be, Drake," Hall persisted.

"I think he stole it," Drake said and pulled a dagger from his belt.

The unarmed elf stood fearfully still, his eyes darting back and forth between the men who menaced him and the door to the inn.

"Drake?" Hall said in a lower, more serious tone. "You leave him be, or I swear you'll never be served here again."

Drake looked up to see Hall, who was considerably larger than he, holding a butcher knife.

"You wanna go find him in the woods later, that's your business. But I won't have no fighting in my place." Drake put the dagger away. "Go on, get out," Hall told the elf, who carefully moved past the men and slipped back out the door.

"Was that really an *elf*?" Myron asked, astonished.

"They're half-breeds," Hadrian replied. "Most people don't believe pure-blood elves exist anymore."

"I actually pity them," Albert said. "They were slaves back in the days of the Empire. Did you know that?"

"Well actually, I…" Myron started, but he stopped short when he saw the slight shake of Royce's head and the look on his face.

"Why pity them?" Alric asked. "They were no worse off than the serfs and villeins we have today. And now they are free, which is more than the villeins can say."

"Villeins are bound to the land, true, but they aren't slaves," Albert corrected. "They can't be bought and sold; their families aren't torn apart, and they aren't bred like livestock and kept in pens or butchered for entertainment. I heard they used to do that to the elves, and sure, they're free now, but they aren't allowed to be part of society. They can't find work, and you just saw what they have to go through just to get food."

Royce's expression had grown colder than usual, and Hadrian knew it was time to change the subject. "You wouldn't know it to look at him," he said, "but Albert here is a nobleman. He's a viscount."

"Viscount Winslow?" Alric said. "Of what holding?"

"Sad to say, none," Albert replied, taking a large drink of ale. "Granddad, Harlan Winslow, lost the family plot when he fell out of favor with the King of Warric. Although, truth be told, I don't think it was ever anything to boast about. From what I heard, it was a rocky patch of dirt on the Bernum River. King Ethelred of Warric gobbled it up a few years ago.

"Ah, the stories my father told me of grandfather's trials and tribulations trying to live with the shame of being a landless noble. My dad inherited a little money from him, but he squandered it trying to keep up the pretense he was still a wealthy nobleman. I myself have no problem swallowing my pride if it will fill my stomach." Albert squinted at Alric. "You look familiar, have we met before?"

"If we did, I'm certain it was in passing," Alric replied.

The meal arrived and chewing replaced conversation. The food was nothing special: a portion of slightly overcooked ham, boiled potatoes, cabbage, onions, and a loaf of old bread. Yet, after nearly two days of eating only a few potatoes, Hadrian considered it a veritable feast. As the light outside faded, the inn boy began lighting the candles on each table, and they took the opportunity to order another pitcher.

While sitting there relaxing, Hadrian noticed Royce repeatedly looking out the window. After the third glance, he leaned over to see what was so compelling. With the darkness outside, the window was like a mirror. All Hadrian could see was his own face.

"When was The Rose and Thorn raided?" Royce asked.

Albert shrugged. "Two or three days ago, I guess."

"I meant what time of day?"

"Oh, evening. At sunset I believe, or just after. I suppose they wanted to catch the dinner crowd," Albert paused and sat up suddenly as his expression of contentment faded into one of concern. "Oh...ah...I hate to eat and run, but if it's all right with you boys, I'm going to make myself scarce again." He got up and exited quickly through the rear door. Royce glanced outside again and appeared agitated.

"What is it?" Alric asked.

"We have company. Everyone stay calm until we see which way the wind is blowing."

The door to The Silver Pitcher burst open, and eight men dressed in byrnie with tabards bearing the Melengar falcon poured into the room. They flipped over a few tables near the door, scattering drinks and food everywhere. Soldiers brandishing swords glowered at the patrons. No one in the inn moved.

"In the name of the king, this inn and all its occupants are to be searched. Those resisting or attempting to flee will be executed!"

The soldiers broke into groups. One began pulling men from their tables and shoved them against the wall, forming a line. Others charged up the steps to the loft, while a third set descended into the tavern's cellar.

"I do an honest business here!" Hall protested as they pushed him up against the wall with the rest.

"Keep your mouth shut or I'll have this place torched," a man entering said. He did not wear armor, nor the emblem of Melengar. Instead, he was dressed in fine practical clothing of layered shades of gray.

"It was a pleasure having your company, gentlemen," Alric told those at the table, "but it seems my escort is here."

"Be careful," Hadrian told him as the prince stood up.

Alric moved toward the center of the room, pulled back his hood, and stood straight with his chin held high. "What is it you are looking for, good men of Melengar?" he asked in a loud clear voice that caught the attention of everyone in the room.

The man in gray spun around and when he saw Alric's face, he showed a surprised smile. "Well! We are looking for *you*, Your Highness," he said with a gracious bow. "We were told you were kidnapped, possibly dead."

"As you can see, I am neither. Now release these good people."

There was a brief hesitancy on the part of the soldiers, but the man in gray nodded, and they changed their stance to stand at attention. The man in gray moved promptly to Alric. His eyes looked the prince up and down with a quizzical expression. "Your choice of dress is a bit unorthodox, is it not, Your Majesty?"

"My choice of dress is none of *your* concern, sir…"

"It's baron, Your Highness, Baron Trumbul. Your Majesty is needed back at Essendon Castle. Archduke Percy Braga ordered us to find and escort you there. He has been worried about your welfare, considering all the recent events."

"As it happens, I was heading that way. You can, therefore, please the archduke and me by providing escort."

"Wonderful, my lord. Do you travel alone?" Trumbul looked at the others still seated at the table.

"No," Alric replied, "this monk is with me, and he will be returning to Medford as well. Myron, say goodbye to those nice people and join us." Myron stood up and with a smile waved at Royce and Hadrian.

"Is that all? Just the one?" The baron glanced at the remaining two of the party.

"Yes, just the one."

"Are you certain? It was rumored you might have been captured by two men."

"My dear baron," Alric replied sternly, "I think I would remember such a thing as that. And the next time you take it upon yourself to question your king, it may be your last. It is lucky for you that I find myself in a good mood, having just eaten and being too tired to take serious offense. Now give the innkeeper a gold tenent to pay for my meal and your disruption."

No one moved for a moment, and then the baron said, "Of course, Your Majesty. Forgive my impudence." He nodded to a soldier who pulled a coin from his purse and flipped it toward Hall. "Now, Your Highness, shall we be going?"

"Yes," Alric replied. "I hope you have a carriage for me. I have had my fill of riding, and I am hoping to sleep the rest of the way back."

"I am sorry, Your Majesty, we do not. We can commandeer one just as soon as we reach a village, and hopefully some better clothes for you as well."

"That will have to do, I suppose."

Alric, Myron, Trumbul, and the troops left the inn. There was a brief discussion only partially heard through the open door as they arranged mounts. Soon, the sound of hooves retreated into the night.

"That was Prince Alric Essendon?" Hall asked, coming over to their table and trying to see out their window. Neither Royce nor Hadrian replied.

After Hall returned to the bar, Hadrian asked, "Do you think we should follow them?"

"Oh, don't start that. We did our good deed for this month, two in fact, if you count DeWitt. I'm content to just sit here and relax."

Hadrian nodded and drained his mug of ale. They sat there in silence while he stared out the window, drumming his fingers restlessly on the table.

"What?"

"Did you happen to notice the weapons that patrol was wearing?"

"Why?" Royce asked, irritated.

"Well, they were wearing Tiliner rapiers instead of the standard falchion swords carried by the Medford Royal Guard. The rapiers had steel rather than iron tangs, but unmarked pommels. Either The Royal Armory has upgraded their standards or those men are hired mercenaries most likely from eastern Warric. Not exactly the kind of men you'd hire to augment a search party for a lost Royalist king. And if I am not mistaken, Trumbul is the name of the fellow Gwen pointed out as being suspicious in The Rose and Thorn the night before the murder."

"See," Royce said, irritated, "this is the problem with these good deeds of yours; they never end."

The moon was rising as Arista placed the dagger on her window-sill. While it would still be sometime before the moonbeams would reach it, all the other preparations were ready. She had spent all day working on the spell. In the morning, she gathered herbs from the kitchen and garden. To find a mandrake root of just the right size had required nearly two hours. The hardest step, however, had been slipping down to the mortuary to clip a lock of hair from her father's head. By evening, she was grinding the mixture with her mortar and pestle while she muttered the incantations needed to bind the elements. She had sprinkled the resulting finely ground powder on the stained blade and had recited the last words of the spell. All that was required now was the moonlight.

She jumped when a knock on her door startled her. "Your Highness? Arista?" the archduke called to her.

"What is it, Uncle?"

"Can I have a word with you, my dear?"

"Yes, just a minute." Arista drew the curtain shut, hiding the blade on the sill. She placed her mortar and pestle in her trunk and locked it. Dusting off her hands, she checked her hair in the mirror. She went to the door, and with a tap of her necklace, she opened it.

The archduke entered still dressed in his black doublet, his thumbs hooked casually in his sword belt. His heavy chain of office shimmered in the firelight from Arista's hearth. He looked around her bedroom with a critical expression. "Your father never did approve of you living up here. He always wanted you down with the rest of the family. I actually think it hurt him a bit that you chose to separate yourself like this, but you have always been a solitary person, haven't you?"

"Does this visit have a point?" she asked with irritation as she took a seat on her bed.

"You seem very curt with me lately, my dear. Have I done something to offend you? You are my niece, and you did just lose your father and possibly your brother. Is it so impossible to believe I am concerned for your welfare? That I am worried about your *state of mind*? People have been known to do…unexpected things in moments of grief…or anger."

"My state of mind is fine."

"Is it?" he asked raising an eyebrow. "You have spent most of the last few days in seclusion up here, which cannot be healthy for a young woman who has just lost her father. I would think you would want to be with your family."

"I no longer have a family," she said firmly.

"*I* am your family, Arista. I am your *uncle*, but you don't want to see that, do you? You want to see me as your enemy. Perhaps that is how you deal with your grief. You spend all your time in this tower, and when you do step out of this stronghold of yours, it is only to attack me for my attempts to find your brother. I don't understand why. I have also asked myself why I've not seen you cry at the loss of your father. You two were quite close, weren't you?"

Braga moved to the dresser with the swan mirror and paused as he stepped on something. He picked up a silver-handled brush laying on the floor. "This brush is from your father. I was with him when he bought this one. He refused to have a servant select it. He personally went to the shops in Dagastan to find just the right one. I honestly think it was the highlight of the trip for him. You should take more care with things of such importance." He replaced it on the table with the other brushes.

He returned his attention to the princess. "Arista, I know you were afraid he was going to force you to marry some old, unpleasant king. I suspect the thought of being imprisoned within the invisible walls of marriage terrified you. But, despite what you might have thought, he *did* love you. Why do you not cry for him?"

"I can assure you, Uncle, I'm perfectly fine. I'm just trying to keep busy."

Braga continued to move around her small room, studying it in detail. "Well that's another thing," he said to her. "You're *very* busy, but you are not trying to find your father's killer? I would be, if I were you."

"Isn't that *your* job?"

"It is. I have been working continuously without sleep for days, I assure you. Much of my focus, however, as you should know, has been on finding your brother in the hopes of saving his life. I hope you can understand my priorities. You, on the other hand, seem to do little despite being the *acting queen*, as you call yourself."

"Did you come here to accuse me of being lazy?" Arista asked.

"Have you been lazy? I doubt it. I suspect you've been hard at work these last few days, perhaps weeks."

"Are you suggesting I killed my father? I ask only because *that* would be a very dangerous thing to suggest."

"I am not suggesting anything, Your Highness. I am merely trying to determine why you have shown so little sadness at the passing of your father and so little concern for the welfare of your brother. Tell me, dear niece, what were you doing in the oak grove this afternoon returning with a covered basket. I also heard you were puttering around the kitchen pantry."

"You've had me followed?"

"For your own good, I assure you," he said with a warm reassuring tone, patting her on the shoulder. "As I said, I am concerned. I have heard stories of some who took their own lives after a loss such as yours. That's why I watch you. However, in your case, it was unnecessary, wasn't it? Taking your own life is not at all what you have been up to."

"What makes you say that?" Arista replied.

"Picking roots and pilfering herbs from the kitchen, sounds more like you were working on a recipe of some kind. You know, I never approved of your father sending you to Sheridan University, much less allowing you to study under that foolish magician Arcadius. People might think you a witch. Common folk are easily frightened by what they don't understand, and the thought of their princess as a witch could be a spark that leads to a disaster. I told your father not to allow you to go to the university, but he let you leave anyway."

The archduke walked around the bed, absently smoothing her coverlets.

"Well, I am glad my father didn't listen to you."

"Are you? I suppose so. Of course, it really didn't matter. It wasn't such a terrible thing. After all, Arcadius is harmless, isn't he? What could he teach you? Card tricks? How to remove warts? At least that was all I thought he could teach you. But as of late, I have become—concerned. Perhaps he did teach you something of value. Perhaps he taught you a name…*Esrahaddon*?"

Arista looked up sharply and then tried to mask her surprise.

"Yes, I thought so. You wanted to know more. You wanted to know real magic, only Arcadius doesn't know much himself. He did, however, know someone who did. He told you about Esrahaddon, an ancient and evil wizard of the old order who knows how to unlock the secrets of the universe and control the primordial powers of the elements. I can only imagine your delight to discover such a wizard was imprisoned right here in your own kingdom. As princess, you have the authority to see the prisoner. You never asked your father for permission, did you? You never asked him because you thought he might say no. The way he almost did when you wanted to go to the university. You should have asked him, Arista. If you had, he would have explained that *no one* is allowed in *that* prison. He would have explained to you the way the Church explained it to him the day he was coroneted king. He would have told you how dangerous Esrahaddon is. What he can do to innocent people like you. That monster taught you real magic, didn't he, Arista? He taught you black magic, am I right?" The archduke narrowed his eyes, his voice losing even the pretense of warmth.

Arista did not reply. She sat in silence.

"What did he teach you, I wonder? Certainly not tricks or slight of hand. He probably didn't show you how to call lightning or how to split the earth, but I'm sure he taught you simple things. Simple, yet useful things, didn't he?"

"I have no idea what you're talking about," she said standing. Her voice betrayed a hint of fear. She wanted to put distance between the two of them. Crossing to the dressing table, she picked up a brush and began running it through her hair.

"No? Tell me, my dear, what happened to the dagger that killed your father and still bares his blood?"

"I told you I don't know anything about that." She watched him in the mirror.

"Yes, you did say that, didn't you? But somehow, I find that hard to believe. You are the only person who might have a purpose for that blade—a dark purpose. A very evil purpose."

Arista whirled on him, but before she could speak, Braga went on. "You betrayed your father. You betrayed your brother. Now you would betray me as well and with the same dagger! Did you really think me such a fool?"

Arista looked toward the window and could see, even through the heavy curtain, the moonlight had finally reached it. Braga followed her glance and a puzzled expression washed over his face. "Why does only one window have its curtains drawn?"

He turned, grabbed the drape, and threw it back revealing the dagger bathed in moonlight. He staggered at the sight of it, and Arista knew the spell had worked its magic.

# 4

They had not gone far, only a handful of miles. The traveling was slow and the lack of sleep combined with his full stomach made Alric so drowsy he feared he might fall from the saddle. Myron did not look much better, riding along behind a guard, his head drooping. They traveled down a lonely dirt lane past a few farms and over footbridges. To the left lay a harvested cornfield where empty brown stalks were left to wither. To the right stood a dark woodland of oak and hemlock, their leaves long since scattered to the wind; their naked branches reached out over the road.

It was another cold night, and Alric swore to himself he would never take another night ride as long as he lived. He was dreaming of curling up in his own bed with a roaring fire and perhaps a warmed glass of mulled wine when the baron ordered an unexpected halt.

Trumbul and five soldiers rode up beside Alric. Two of the men dismounted and took hold of the bridles of the prince and Myron's horses. Four additional men rode ahead, beyond Alric's sight, while three others turned and rode back the way they had come.

"Why have we stopped?" Alric asked, yawning. "Why have the men split up?"

"It's a treacherous road, Your Majesty," Trumbul explained. "We need to take precautions. Vanguards and rear guards are necessary when escorting one such as you, during times such as these. Any number of dangers might exist out here on dark nights.

Highwaymen, goblins, wolves—there's no way to know what you might come across. There's even the legend of a headless ghost that haunts this road, did you know that?"

"No, I didn't," the prince said, not liking the casual tone the baron was suddenly taking with him.

"Oh yes, they say it is the ghost of a king who died at this very spot. Of course, he wasn't really a king. He was a crown prince who might have been a king. You see, as the tale goes the prince was returning home one night in the company of his brave soldiers when one of them took it upon himself to chop the poor bastard's head off and put it in a sack." Trumbul paused as he pulled a burlap bag off his horse and held it up to the prince. "Just like this one here."

"What are you playing at, Trumbul?" Alric inquired nervously.

"I am not playing at all, your Royal High-and-Mightiness. I just realized I don't need to return you to the castle to be paid, I only need to return *part* of you. Your head will do fine. It saves the horse the effort of carrying you the entire way, and I have always had a fondness for horses. So whatever I can do to help them, I try to do."

Alric spurred his mount, but the man holding the reins held it firmly, and the horse only pivoted sharply. Trumbul took advantage of the animal's sudden lurch and pulled the prince to the ground. Alric attempted to draw his sword, but Trumbul kicked him in the stomach. With the wind knocked out of him, Alric doubled over in the dirt, laboring to breathe.

Trumbul then turned his attention to Myron who sat in his saddle with a look of shock as the baron approached him.

"You look familiar," Trumbul said as he pulled Myron roughly off the horse. He held the monk's head toward the moonlight. "Oh yes, I remember. You were the not-so-helpful monk at the abbey we burned. You probably don't remember me, do you? I was wearing a helm with a visor that night. We all were. Our employer insisted that we hide our faces." He stared at the monk whose eyes were beginning to well with tears. "I don't know if I should kill you or not. I was originally told to spare your life so you could deliver a message to your father, but you don't seem to be heading that way. Besides, keeping you alive was related to that job, and unfortunately for you, we have already been paid for its completion. So it seems what I do is completely at my discretion."

Without warning, Myron kicked the baron in the knee with such force that it broke the baron's grip on the monk, who leapt over a fallen log and bolted into the darkness of the trees snapping twigs and branches as he ran into the night. Screaming in pain, the baron collapsed to the ground. "Get him!" he yelled, and two soldiers chased after Myron.

A commotion erupted in the trees. Alric heard Myron cry for help followed by the sound of a sword drawn from a scabbard. Another scream ended as quickly as it began, cut abruptly short. The silence returned. Still holding his leg, Trumbul cursed the monk. "That will teach the little wretch!"

"You all right, Trumbul?" asked the guard holding Alric's horse.

"I'm fine, just give me a second. Damn, that little monk kicked hard."

"He won't be kicking anyone anymore," another soldier added.

The baron slowly climbed to his feet and tested his leg. He walked over to where Alric lay and drew his sword. "Grab him by the arms and hold him tight. Make sure he doesn't cause me any trouble, boys."

The guard Myron was riding behind dismounted and took Alric's left arm while another secured his right. "Just make sure you don't hit us by accident," he said.

Trumbul grinned in the moonlight. "I never do anything by accident. If I hit you, you've done something to deserve it."

"If you kill me, my uncle will hunt you down no matter where you try to hide!"

Trumbul chuckled at the young prince. "Your uncle is the one who will pay us for your head. He wants you dead."

"What? *You lie!*"

"Believe what you will," the baron laughed. "Turn him over so I get a clear stroke at the back of his neck. I want a pretty trophy. I hate it when I end up having to hack and hack."

Alric struggled, but the two soldiers were stronger than he was. They twisted the prince's arms behind his back, forced him to his knees, and shoved his head to the ground.

There was the sound of snapping twigs from the thick brush by the side of the road. "About time you two climbed out of there," Trumbul said as the two guards returned from killing the monk. "You got back just in time for the night's finale."

The two soldiers holding Alric twisted his arms harder to keep him from moving. The prince struggled with all his strength, screaming into the dirt. "No! Stop! You can't! *Stop!*" His efforts were useless. The soldiers each had a firm grip and years of battle wielding swords and shields had turned their arms to steel. The prince was no match for them.

Alric waited for the blow. Instead of hearing Trumbul's blade whistling through the night air, he heard an odd gurgle, then a thud. The guards loosened their hold on him. One let go entirely, and Alric heard his rapid footfalls as he sprinted away. The other hauled the prince up, holding him tightly from behind. The baron lay dead on the ground. Two men stood on either side of the body. In the darkness, Alric saw only silhouettes, but they did not match the men who had chased Myron into the trees. The nearest to the baron held a knife, which seemed to glow with an eerie radiance in the moonlight. Next to him stood a taller, broader man who held a sword in each hand.

"Everyone, over here!" shouted the soldier who still shielded himself with Alric.

The two guards holding the horses dropped the reins and drew their swords. Their faces, however, betrayed their fear.

"Your friends aren't coming," Alric heard Royce's voice. "They're already dead."

The two guards wielding swords looked at each other then raced down the road in the direction of The Silver Pitcher Inn. The last remaining soldier holding Alric, looked around wildly. As Royce and Hadrian took a stride toward him, he cursed abruptly, let go of the prince, and bolted into the trees. Before Hadrian could close the gap between them, the man screamed. A moment later, Myron exited from the trees, dragging a bloodied sword behind him. He was pale, and a sickened look covered his face. When he reached the rest of the party, he dropped the sword, fell to his knees, and began to sob.

Alric could not stop shaking, as he wiped the tears and dirt from his face. Hadrian and Royce came over and helped him to his feet. He stood on wobbly legs and looked at those around him.

"They were going to kill me," he said. "They were going to *kill me!*" he screamed.

He abruptly pushed Royce and Hadrian away and, drawing his father's sword, drove it deep into the torso of the dead Trumbul. He staggered and stood there gasping, staring at the dead body before him, his father's sword swaying back and forth, the tip buried in the baron's back.

Soon men approached from both directions of the road. Many were from The Silver Pitcher Inn, and carried crude weapons. Some of them were wet with blood, but none appeared injured. Two of them led the horses that Royce, Hadrian, and Alric had been using since the Wicend Ford. There was also a thin figure in tattered rags wearing a shapeless hat. He bore only a heavy stick.

"Not a single one got past us," Hall declared as he approached the small group. "One tried to duck us, but the half-breed found him. I can see now why you asked him to come. Bastard can see better than an owl in the dark."

"As promised, you can keep the horses and everything on them," Hadrian said. "But make sure you bury these bodies tonight or you might find trouble in the morning."

"Is that really the prince?" one of the men asked, staring at Alric.

"Actually," Hadrian said, "I think you are looking at the new King of Melengar."

There was a quiet murmur of interest, and a few went through the bother of bowing, although Alric did not notice. He had retrieved his sword and was now searching Trumbul's body.

The men gathered in the road to look over the captured animals, weapons, and gear. Hall took charge of the division of loot and began to divvy it up as best he could.

"Give the half-elf one of the horses," Royce told him.

"What?" The innkeeper asked stunned. "You want us to give *him* a horse? Are you sure? I mean most of these men don't have a good horse."

Drake quickly cut in, "Listen, we all fought equally tonight. He can have a share like everyone, but that miserable filth ain't walking off with no horse."

"Don't kill him, Royce," Hadrian said hurriedly.

The prince looked up to see Drake backing up as Royce took a step toward him. The thief's face was eerily calm, but his eyes smoldered.

"What does the king say?" Drake asked quickly. "I mean—he is the king and all, right? Technically, 'em is *his* horses right? His soldiers was a ridin' 'em. We should ask him to decide...*okay*?"

There was a pause while Alric stood up and faced the crowd. The prince felt sick. His legs were weak, his arms hurt, and he was bleeding from scrapes on his forehead, chin, and cheek. He was covered in dirt. He came within seconds of death and the fear from it was still with him. He noticed Hadrian move away to where Myron was. The monk was still crying off to his right, and Alric knew he was a hair away from joining him, but he was the king. He clenched his teeth and looked at them. A score of dirty, blood-splattered faces looked back. He stood there unable to think clearly. His mind was still on Trumbul. He was still furious and humiliated. Alric glanced at Royce and Hadrian and then looked back to the crowd.

"Do whatever these two men tell you to do," he said slowly, clearly, and coldly. "They are my Royal Protectors. Any man who willfully disobeys will be executed." There was quiet in the wake of his voice. In the stillness, Alric pulled himself onto his horse. "Let's go."

Hadrian and Royce exchanged looks of surprise and then helped Myron up. The monk was silent now and walked in a daze. He no longer looked around; instead, he focused on his blood-covered hands. Hadrian pulled Myron up behind him.

As they started down the road, Royce stopped his horse near Hall and Drake and quietly told them both, "See to it the half-elf gets a horse and keeps it, or when I return, I will hold everyone in this hamlet accountable—and for once—it will be legal."

The four rode along in silence for some time. Finally, Alric hissed. "It was my own uncle." Despite his efforts, his eyes began to water.

"I've been thinking about that," Hadrian mentioned. "The archduke stands next in line for the throne after you and Arista. But being family, I figured he'd be just as big a target as you, only he's not a blood uncle is he? His last name is Braga not Essendon."

"He married my mother's sister."

"Is she alive?"

"No, she died years ago, something to do with a fire." Alric slammed his fist on the saddle's pummel. "He taught me the blade! He showed me how to ride! He is *my uncle*! And he's trying to kill me!"

Nothing was said for awhile, and then Hadrian finally asked, "Where are we going?"

Alric shook his head as if coming out of a dream. "What? Oh, to Drondil Fields, Count Pickering's castle. He is…was…one of my father's most trusted nobles, a staunch Royalist, and the most powerful leader in the kingdom. If he is still loyal, I will raise my army there and march on Medford within the week. And Maribor help the man, or *uncle*, who tries to stop me!"

**5**

"Is this what you wanted to see?" the archduke asked Arista, picking up the dagger. He held it out so she could read the name "Percy Braga" clearly spelled out on the blade in her father's blood. "It looks like you have indeed learned a thing or two from Esrahaddon. This however, proves nothing. I certainly didn't stab your father with it. I wasn't even near the chapel when he was killed."

"But you did it. You ordered it. You might not have driven the dagger into his body, but you were the one who killed my father!" Arista wiped the tears from her eyes. "He trusted you. We all trusted you. You were part of our family!"

"There are some things more important than family, my dear—secrets, terrible secrets which must remain hidden at all costs. As hard as it may be for you to believe, I do care for you, your brother and your—"

"Don't you dare say it!" she shouted at him. "You murdered my father!"

"It was necessary. If you only knew. If you could understand what is truly at stake."

"Esrahaddon told me everything."

"Esrahaddon told you what he wanted you to know. Do you think that old wizard is your friend? He used you, just as he's trying to use us, just as he has always used people. He's the reason your father had to die, and he's the reason Alric will die as well."

"And me?"

"Three unusual deaths look a little too suspicious. One murder is fine, and Alric's disappearance is actually a great help. I suspect he will meet death in some quiet remote area far from here. But if you were to be found murdered, well, that may prove to be difficult to explain. You, however, my dear, have made my job much easier than you might imagine. It will be easy for me to convince others you hired those two thieves to kill your father and your brother. You see, I already planted the seeds that something was amiss. The night your father was killed, I had Wylin and a squad of men at the ready. Having failed the double-murder, you sought to correct matters by freeing the killers. We have several witnesses who can attest to the arrangements you made that evening. You would have been smarter to send a handmaid and then poison her. Alric will be found dead, and you will be found guilty of the murders. I planned on holding your trial after Alric's body was found, but now…" He looked at the dagger and his name glistening on the shining metal blade, "now I will have to accelerate my timetable.

"I will announce your trial at once and call all the nobles to court. They will hear of your treachery, your betrayals, and your foul acts. They will learn how education and witchcraft turned you into a power craving killer."

"You won't dare! If you put me before the nobles I will tell them the truth!"

"That will be difficult because, for the safety of the nobles, I will have to keep you gagged to prevent you from casting spells upon us. I would have your tongue cut out now except that might look suspicious as I haven't yet called for the trial."

Braga looked around the bedroom once more and nodded. "I was wrong. I do approve of this choice of room after all. I had other plans for this tower once, but now, I think sealing you in here until the trial will keep you nicely isolated. And with the amount of time you've spent by yourself, practicing your crafts, no one will notice a difference."

He walked out, taking the dagger with him. As he left, she saw a bearded dwarf with a hammer in hand standing outside the door. When it closed, she heard pounding and knew she had been locked in.

# PART 7
## DRONDIL FIELDS

The four rode on through most of the night. They finally stopped when Myron toppled from the horse after falling asleep behind Hadrian. Leaving the horses saddled, they slept only briefly in a thicket. Soon they were back on the road, traveling through an orchard of trees. Each plucked an apple or two and ate the sweet fruit as they rode. There was little to see until the sun rose. Then a few workers began to appear. An older man drove an ox cart filled with milk and cheese. Farther down the lane, a young girl carried a basket of eggs. Myron watched her intently as they passed by and she looked up at him, smiling self-consciously.

"Don't stare, Myron," Hadrian told him. "They will think you're up to something."

"They are even prettier than horses," the monk remarked, glancing back repeatedly over his shoulder as the girl fell behind them.

Hadrian laughed. "Yes, they are, but I wouldn't tell them *that*."

Ahead a hill rose and on top of it, stood a castle. The structure was nothing like Essendon Castle; it looked more like a fortress than a house of nobility.

"That's Drondil Fields," Alric told them. The prince had barely said anything since his ordeal the night before. He did not complain about the long ride or the cold night air. Instead, he rode in silence with his eyes fixed on the path that lay ahead. As they came into view of the castle, he began speaking with a tone of pride and warmth in his voice. "It's the oldest and strongest fortress in Melengar. They built it with thick walls of granite shaped like a five-pointed star making it impossible to find a blind wall to scale.

"It was once the home of Brodic Essendon, who in the turmoil of the civil wars following the fall of the Empire, subdued these lands to become warlord. His son, Tolin the Great, finished the work his father started. He defeated the forces of Lothomad the Bald and proclaimed himself the first king of Melengar. That was the last battle of a long war, which carved the kingdom out of the political chaos of the post-imperial era.

"They fought the battle just down there, in those fields to the left of the hill. They belonged to a farmer named Drondil and afterwards this whole area became known as Drondil Fields, or so the story goes.

"This was also the site where Tolin, his clansmen, and his warlords drew up the Drondil Charter, which divided Melengar into seven provinces. He rewarded his faithful warlords with the titles of counts and gave each of them a parcel of land. Once he was officially crowned king, Tolin felt it wasn't proper to live in such a gloomy fortress. He built Essendon Castle in Medford and, before moving there, Tolin entrusted Galilin, the largest and richest of the provinces, to his most loyal general Seadric Pickilerinon. Seadric's son assumed control of the province a short time later, after his father died of a terrible fever. He was the one who shortened his name to Pickering.

"The Essendons and Pickerings have always been close. We often spend Wintertide and Summersrule here with them. There is no direct blood relation, but it is as if we are kin. I grew up with Count Pickering's sons and they are like my brothers. Of course, the other nobles aren't happy about that, particularly those who actually *are* blood-relatives. Nothing has ever come of their jealousies, though since no one would dare challenge a Pickering. They have a legendary family tradition with swords."

"We are well acquainted with that little bit of trivia," Hadrian muttered, but it did not stop the prince from continuing.

"Rumor has it that Seadric learned the ancient art of Tek'chin from the last living member of the Knights of the Order of the Fauld, the post-imperial brotherhood who tried to preserve at least part of the ancient skills of the legendary Teshlor Knights. The Teshlor, the greatest warriors ever to have lived, once guarded the Emperor himself. Like everything, they were lost with the Empire. What Seadric learned from the Order of the Fauld was just a tiny bit of the Teshlor skill, just one discipline, but that knowledge was faithfully passed from father to son for generations, and the secret give the Pickerings an uncanny advantage in combat.

"This hill never used to look like it does now," Alric explained, gesturing to the trees growing on the slope all the way up to the walls. "It used to be cut clear to afford no cover to would-be attackers. The Pickerings planted this orchard only a couple of generations ago. Same with those rosebushes and rhododendrons. Drondil Fields hasn't seen warfare in five hundred years. I suppose the counts didn't see the harm in some fruit, shade, and flowers. The great fortress of Seadric Pickilerinon," Alric sighed, "now little more than a country estate."

"Here now, hold on there!" an overweight gate warden ordered as they approached the castle. He was holding a pastry in one hand and a pint of milk in the other. His weapon lay at his side. "Where do you think you're all going, riding up here as if this were your fall retreat?"

Alric pulled back his hood, and the warden dropped both his pastry and milk. "I...I'm sorry, Your Highness," he stumbled, snapping to attention. "I had no idea you were coming today. No one said anything to me." He wiped his hands and brushed the crumbs from his uniform. "Is the rest of the royal family coming as well?" Alric ignored him, continuing through the gate and across the plank bridge into the castle. The others followed him without a word as the astonished warden stared after them.

Like the outside of the castle, the interior courtyard did little to remind one of a fortress. The courtyard was an attractive garden of neatly trimmed bushes and the occasional small, carefully pruned tree. Colorful banners of greens and gold hung to either side of the keep's portico, rippling in the morning breeze. The grass looked carefully tended, although it was mostly yellow now with winter dormancy. Carts and wagons, most filled with empty bushel baskets possibly used to harvest the fruit, lay beneath a green awning. A couple of apples still lay in the bottom of one of them. A stable of horses stood near a barn where cows called for their morning milking. A shaggy black-and-white dog gnawed a bone at the base of the fieldstone well, and a family of white ducks followed each other in a perfect line as they wandered freely, quacking merrily as they went. Castle workers scurried about their morning chores, fetching water, splitting wood, tending animals, and quite often nearly stepping on the wandering ducks.

Near a blacksmith shed, where a beefy man hammered a glowing rail of metal, two young men sparred with swords in the open yard. Each of them wore helms and carried small heater shields. A third sat with his back to the keep steps. He was using a slate and a bit of chalk to score the fighters' match. "Shield higher, Fanen!" the taller figure shouted.

"What about my legs?"

"I won't be going after your legs. I don't want to lower my sword and give you the advantage, but you need to keep the shield high to deflect a down stroke. That's where you're vulnerable. If I hit you hard enough and you aren't ready, I can drive you to your knees. Then what good will your legs be?"

"I'd listen to him, Fanen," Alric yelled toward the boy. "Mauvin's an ass, but he knows his parries."

"Alric!" The taller boy threw off his helm and ran to embrace the prince as he dismounted. At the sound of Alric's name, several of the servants in the courtyard looked up in surprise.

Mauvin was close to Alric in age but was taller and a good deal broader in the shoulders. He sported a head of wild dark hair and a set of dazzling white teeth, which shone as he grinned at his friend.

"What are you doing here, and by Mar, what are you dressed up as? You look frightful. Did you ride all night? And your face —did you fall?"

"I have some bad news. I need to speak to your father immediately."

"I'm not sure he's awake yet, and he is awfully cranky if you wake him early."

"This can't wait."

Mauvin stared at the prince and his grin faded. "This is no casual visit then?"

"No, I only wish it was."

Mauvin turned toward his youngest brother and said, "Denek, go wake Father."

The boy with the slate shook his head. "I'm not going to be the one."

Mauvin started toward his brother. "Do it now!" he shouted, scaring the young boy into running for the keep.

"What is it? What's happened?" Fanen asked, dropping his own helm and shield on the grass and walking over to embrace Alric as well.

"Has any word reached you from Medford in the last several days?"

"Not that I know of," Mauvin replied, his face showing more concern now.

"No riders? No dispatches for the count?" Alric asked again.

"No, Alric, what is it?"

"My father is dead. He was murdered in the castle by a traitor."

"What!" Mauvin explained, taking a step back. It was a reaction rather than a question.

"That's not possible!" Fanen exclaimed. "King Amrath dead? When did this happen?"

"To be honest, I'm not sure how long it has been. The days following his murder have been confusing, and I've lost track of the time. If word has yet to reach here, I suspect it hasn't been more than a few days."

All the workers stopped what they were doing and stood around listening intently. The constant ringing of the blacksmith's hammer ceased and the only sound in the courtyard was the distant mooing of a cow and the quacking of the ducks.

"What's this all about?" Count Pickering asked as he stepped out of the castle holding up an arm to shield his squinting eyes from the morning's bright sun. "The boy came in panting for air and said there was an emergency out here."

The count, a slim, middle-aged man with a long, hooked nose and a well-trimmed prematurely gray beard, was dressed in a gold and purple robe pulled over his nightshirt. His wife Belinda came up behind him, pulling on her robe and peering out into the courtyard nervously. Hadrian took advantage of Pickering's sun-blindness to chance a long look. She was just as lovely as rumor held. The countess was several years younger than her husband, with a slender, stunning figure and long golden hair, which spilled across her shoulders in a way she would never normally show in public. Hadrian now understood why the count guarded her jealously.

"Oh my," Myron said to Hadrian as he twisted to get a better view. "I don't even think of horses when I look at her."

Hadrian dismounted and helped Myron off the horse. "I share your feelings, my friend, but trust me, that's one woman you *really* don't want to stare at."

"Alric?" the count said. "What in the world are you doing here at this hour?"

"Father, King Amrath has been murdered," Mauvin answered in a shaky voice.

Shock filled Pickering's face. He slowly lowered his arm and stared directly at the prince. "Is this true?"

Alric nodded solemnly. "Several days ago. A traitor stabbed him in the back while he was at prayer."

"Traitor? Who?"

"My uncle, the Archduke and Lord Chancellor—Percy Braga."

Royce, Hadrian, and Myron followed their noses to the kitchen after Alric had left for a private meeting with Count Pickering. There they met Ella, a white-haired cook who was all too happy to provide them with a hearty breakfast in order to have first chance at any gossip. The food at Drondil Fields was far superior to the meal they ate at The Silver Pitcher Inn. Ella brought wave upon wave of eggs, soft powdered pastries, fresh sweet butter, steaks, bacon, biscuits, peppered potatoes, and gravy along with a jug of apple cider, and an apple pie baked with maple syrup for dessert.

They ate their fill in the relative quiet of the kitchen. Hadrian repeated little more than what Alric had already revealed in the courtyard however, he did mention that Myron had lived his life in seclusion at the monastery. Ella seemed fascinated by this and questioned the monk mercilessly on the subject. "So, you never saw a woman before today, love?" Ella asked Myron who was finishing the last of his pie. He was eating heartily and there was a ring of apples and crust around his mouth.

"You're the first one I've ever spoken to," Myron replied as if he were boasting a great achievement.

"Really," Ella said smiling with a feigned blush. "I am so honored. I haven't been a man's first in years." She laughed but Myron only looked at her puzzled.

"You have a lovely home," Myron told her. "It looks very…sturdy."

She laughed again. "It's not mine, ducky, I just work here. It belongs to the nobles, like all the nice places do. Us normal folk, we lives in sheds and shacks and fights over what they throw away. We're sorta like dogs that way, aren't we? 'Course, I ain't complaining. The Pickerings aren't a bad lot. Not as snooty as some of the other nobles who think the sun rises and falls because it pleases them. The count won't even have a chambermaid. He won't let no one help him dress neither. I've even seen him fetch water for himself more than once. He's downright daft that one. His boys take after him too. You can see it in the way they saddle their own horses. That Fanen, why just the other day I seen him swinging a smith's hammer. He was having Vern show him how to mend a blade. Now I asks you, how many nobles you see trying to learn the blacksmith trade? Can I get anyone another cup of cider?"

They all shook their heads and took turns yawning.

"Lenare, now she takes after her mother. They're a pair, they are. Both are pretty as a rose and smell just as sweet, but they do has their thorns. The temper those two have is frightful. The daughter is worse than the mother. She used to train with her brothers and was beating the stuffing out of Fanen until she discovered she was a lady and that ladies don't do such things."

Myron's eyes closed, his head drooped, and suddenly the chair toppled as the monk fell over. He woke with a start and struggled to his knees. "Oh, I am terribly sorry, I didn't mean to—"

Ella was so busy laughing she couldn't answer and simply waved her hand at him. "You've had a long night, dear," she finally managed to say. "Let me set you up in the back before that chair bucks you off again."

Myron hung his head and said quietly, "I have the same problem with horses."

Alric told his story to the Pickerings over breakfast. As soon as he finished, the count shooed his sons out and called for his staff to begin arranging for a full-scale mobilization of Galilin. While Pickering dispatched orders, Alric left the great hall and began wandering through the halls of the castle. This was the first time he had been alone since his father's death. So much had happened, he really had not had time to think. He felt as though he was caught up in the current of a river, whisked along by the events unfolding around him. Now it was time to take control of his destiny.

Alric saw few people in the corridors. Aside from the occasional suit of armor or painting on the wall, there was little to distract his thoughts. Drondil Fields, though smaller than Essendon, felt larger due to its horizontal layout, which sprawled across the better part of the hilltop. Where Castle Essendon had several towers and lofty chambers rising many stories high, Drondil Fields was only four stories at its tallest point. As a fortress, fireproofing was essential so the roof was made of stone rather than wood, requiring thick walls to support their weight. Because the windows were small and deep, they let in little light, which made the interior cavelike.

He remembered running through these corridors as a child chasing Mauvin and Fanen. They had held mock battles, which the Pickerings always won. He had always trumped them by bringing up that he would be king someday. At the age of twelve, it had been wonderful to be able to taunt a friend who had bested him with, "Sure, but I'll be king. You will have to bow to me and do as I say." The thought that in order to become king his father would have to die had never really occurred to him. Nor had he known what being the king really meant.

*I am king now.*

Being king was always something he had imagined to be far, far in the future. His father had been a strong man, not much older than Pickering. Alric had looked forward to many years as prince of the realm. Only a few months ago, at the Summersrule Festival, he and Mauvin had made plans to go on a year-long trip to the four corners of Apeladorn. They had wanted to visit Delgos, Calis, Trent, and even planned to seek the location of the fabled ruined city of Percepliquis. To discover and explore the ancient capital of the Old Novronian Empire was a childhood dream of theirs. They wanted to find fortune and adventure in the lost city. Mauvin hoped to discover the rest of the lost arts of the Teshlor Knights, and Alric was going to find the ancient crown of Novron. While they had mentioned the trip to their fathers, neither one brought up Percepliquis. They knew they would not be allowed to travel there. Walking the fabled halls of Percepliquis was probably the boyhood dream of every youth in Apeladorn. For Alric though, his adolescence was over.

*I am king now.*

Dreams of endless days of reckless adventures, exploring the frontier while drinking bad ale, sleeping beneath the open sky, and loving nameless women blew away like smoke in the wind. In its place came visions of stone rooms filled with old men with angry faces. He had only occasionally watched his father hold court, listening while the clergy and the nobles demanded less taxes and more land. One earl had even demanded the execution of a duke and the custody of his lands for the loss of one of his prized cows. His father sat, in what Alric felt must have been dull misery, as the court secretary read the many petitions and grievances on which the king was required to rule. As a child, he had thought being king meant doing whatever he wished. But over the years, he saw what it really meant—compromise and appeasement. A king could not rule without the support of his nobles and the nobles were never happy. They always wanted something and expected the king to deliver.

*I am king now.*

To Alric, being king felt like a prison sentence. The rest of his life would be spent in service to his people, his nobles, and his family, just as his father had done. He wondered if Amrath had felt the same way when his own father had died. It was something he never considered before. Considering Amrath as a man and the dreams he might have sacrificed was a foreign concept to the young prince. He wondered if his father had been happy. Thinking of him now, the image that came to mind was his bushy beard and bright smiling eyes. His father had smiled a great deal. Alric wondered if it was due to his enjoyment of being king or because being with his son gave him a much-needed break from the affairs of state. Alric felt a sudden longing to see his father once more. He wished he had taken time to sit and talk with him, man to man, to ask for his father's council and guidance in preparation for this day. He felt completely alone and uncertain about whether he could live up to the tasks that lay before him. More than anything, he just wished he could disappear.

**4**

The shrill ring of clashing metal awakened Hadrian. After Ella's breakfast, he wandered into the courtyard. The weather was turning distinctly colder but he found a place to nap on a soft patch of lawn that caught the full face of the sun. He thought he had only closed his eyes for a moment, but when he opened them again, it was well past noon. Across the yard the Pickering boys were back at sparring.

"Come at me again, Fanen," Mauvin ordered, his voice muffled by his helm.

"Why? You're just going to whack me again!"

"You have to learn."

"I don't see why," Fanen protested. "It's not like I'm planning a life in the soldiery or the tournaments. I'm the second son. I'll end up at some monastery stacking books."

"Second sons don't go to abbeys, third sons do." Mauvin lifted his visor to grin at Denek. "Second sons are the spares. You have to be trained and ready in case I die from some rare disease. If I don't, you'll get to roam the lands as a bachelor knight fending for yourself. That means a life as a mercenary or on the tournament circuit. Or if you are lucky, you'll land a post as a sheriff or a marshal or master-at-arms for some earl or duke. These days, it is almost as good as a landed title really. Still, you won't get those jobs, or last long as a merc or swordsman, unless you know how to fight. Now come at me again, and this time pivot, step, and lunge."

Hadrian walked over to where the boys were fighting and sat on the grass near Denek to watch. Denek, who was only twelve years old, glanced at him curiously. "Who are you?"

"My name is Hadrian," he replied as he extended his hand. The boy shook it, squeezing harder than was necessary. "You're Denek right? The Pickering's third son? Perhaps you should speak with my friend Myron, seeing as how I hear you are monastery bound."

"Am not!" he shouted. "Going to the monastery, I mean. I can fight as well as Fanen."

"I wouldn't be surprised," Hadrian said. "Fanen is flat-footed, and his balance is off. He's not going to improve much either, because Mauvin is teaching him, and Mauvin is favoring his right and rocks back on his left too much."

Denek grinned at Hadrian and then turned to his brothers. "Hadrian says you both fight like girls!"

"What's that?" Mauvin said, whacking aside Fanen's loose attack once more.

"Oh, ah, nothing," Hadrian tried to recant and glared at Denek, who just kept grinning. "Thanks a lot," he told the boy.

"So, you think you can beat me in a duel?" Mauvin asked.

"No, it's not that, I was just…explaining I didn't think Denek here would have to go to the monastery."

"Because we fight like girls," Fanen added.

"No, no, nothing like that."

"Give him your sword," Mauvin told Fanen.

Fanen threw his sword at Hadrian. It dove point down in the sod not more than a foot before his feet. The hilt swayed back and forth like a rocking horse.

"You're one of the thieves Alric told us about, aren't you?" Mauvin swiped his sword deftly through the air in a skillful manner that he had not used in his mock battles with his brother. "Despite this great adventure you all have been on, I don't recall Alric mentioning your great prowess with a blade."

"Well, he probably just forgot," Hadrian joked.

"Are you aware of the legend of the Pickerings?"

"Your family is known to be skillful with swords."

"So, you *have* heard? My father is the second best swordsman in Avryn."

"He's the best," Denek snapped. "He would have beaten the archduke if he had his sword, but he had to use a substitute, which was too heavy and awkward."

"Denek, how many times do I have to tell you, when speaking of one's reputation, it does not boost your position to make excuses when you lose a contest. The archduke won the match. You need to face that fact," Mauvin admonished. Turning his attention back to Hadrian he said, "Speaking of contests, why don't you pick up that blade, and I will demonstrate the Tek'chin for you."

Hadrian picked up the sword and stepped into the dirt ring where the boys had been fighting. He made a feint followed by a stab, which Mauvin easily deflected.

"Try again," Mauvin encouraged.

Hadrian tried a slightly more sophisticated move. This time he swung right and then pivoted left and cut upward toward Mauvin's thigh. Mauvin moved with keen precision. He anticipated the feint and knocked the blade away once more.

"You fight like a street thug," Mauvin assessed.

"Because that's what he is," Royce assured them as he approached from the direction of the keep, "a big, dumb street thug. I once saw an old woman batter him senseless with a butter churn." He shifted his attention to Hadrian. "*Now* what have you gotten yourself into? Looks like this kid will hand you a beating."

Mauvin stiffened and glared at Royce. "I would remind you I am a count's son, and as such, you will address me as *lord*, or at least *master*, but not *kid*."

"Better watch out, Royce, or he'll be after you next," Hadrian said, moving around the circle, looking for an opening. He tried another attack but that, too, was blocked.

Mauvin moved in now with a rapid step. He caught Hadrian's sword hilt-to-hilt, placed a leg behind the fighter, and threw him to the ground.

"You're too good for me," Hadrian conceded as Mauvin held out a hand to help him to his feet.

"Try him again," Royce shouted.

Hadrian gave him an irritated look and then noticed a young woman entering the courtyard. It was Lenare. She wore a long gown of soft gold, which nearly matched her hair. She was as lovely as her mother, and walked over to join the group.

"Who is this?" she asked, motioning at Hadrian.

"Hadrian Blackwater," he said with a bow.

"Well, Mister Blackwater, it appears my brother has beaten you."

"It would appear so," Hadrian acknowledged, still dusting himself off.

"It is nothing to be ashamed of. My brother is a very accomplished swordsman—too accomplished, in fact. He has a nasty tendency to chase away any would-be suitors."

"They are not worthy of you, Lenare," Mauvin said.

"Try him again," Royce repeated. There was a perceptible note of mischief in his voice.

"Shall we?" Mauvin asked politely with a bow.

"Oh, please do," Lenare bade him, clapping her hands in delight. "Don't be afraid. He won't kill you. Father doesn't like them to actually hurt anyone."

With an evil smirk directed toward Royce, Hadrian turned to face Mauvin. This time he made no attempt to defend himself. He stood perfectly still holding his blade low. His gaze was cool and he stared directly into Mauvin's eyes.

"Put up a guard you fool," Mauvin told him. "At least *try* to defend yourself."

Hadrian raised his sword slowly, more in response to Mauvin's request than as a move to defend. Mauvin stepped in with a quick flick of his blade designed to set Hadrian off his footing. He then pivoted around behind the larger man and sought to trip him up once more. Hadrian, however, also pivoted and, swinging a leg, caught Mauvin behind the knees, dropping him to the dirt.

Mauvin looked curiously at Hadrian as he helped him to his feet. "Our street thug has some surprises, I see," Mauvin muttered with a smile.

This time, Mauvin struck at Hadrian in a fast set of sweeping attacks, most of which never caught anything but air as Hadrian avoided the strokes. Mauvin moved in a flurry, his blade traveling faster than the eye could follow. The steel rang now as Hadrian caught the strokes with his blade, parrying them aside.

"Mauvin, be careful!" Lenare shouted.

The battle rapidly escalated from friendly sparring to serious combat. The strokes moved faster, harder, and closer. The shrill ring of the blades began to echo off the courtyard walls. The grunts and curses of the fighters became grimmer. The match went on for some time, the two fighting toe to toe. Suddenly Mauvin executed a brilliant maneuver. Feinting left, he swung right, following through the stroke and spinning fully around exposing his back to Hadrian. Seeing his opponent vulnerable, Hadrian made the obvious riposte, but Mauvin miraculously caught his blade instinctively without seeing it. Pivoting again, Mauvin brought his own sword to Hadrian's undefended side. Before he could finish the blow however, Hadrian closed the distance between them and Mauvin's swing ran behind the larger man's back. Hadrian trapped the boy's sword arm under his own and raised his sword to the boy's throat. There was a gasp from Mauvin's siblings. Royce simply chuckled with sinister relish. Releasing his grip, Hadrian set Mauvin free.

"How did you do that?" Mauvin asked. "If performed correctly, which it was, the Vi'shin Flurry has no defense!"

Hadrian shrugged. "It does now." He threw the sword back toward Fanen. It landed point first between the boy's feet. Unlike the previous time, it dove in edge first so the hilt did not swing.

With his eyes on Hadrian and an expression of awe on his face, Denek turned to Royce and said, "That must have been an awfully wicked old lady and a big butter churn."

**5**

"**A**lric?"

The prince had wandered into one of the castle storerooms and was sitting in the thick nave of a barrel-vaulted window looking out at the western hills. The sound of his friend's voice roused him from deep thoughts, and it was not until then that he realized he was crying.

"I don't want to disturb," Mauvin said, "but father's been looking for you. The local nobles have started to arrive, and I think he wants you to talk to them."

"It's okay," Alric said, wiping his cheeks and glancing once more longingly out the window at the setting sun. "I've been here longer than I thought. I guess I lost track of the time."

"It's easy to do in here." He walked around the room and took a bottle of wine out of a crate. "Remember the night we snuck down here and drank three of these?"

Alric nodded. "I was really sick."

"So was I, and yet, we still managed to make the stag hunt the next day."

"We couldn't let anyone know we were drinking."

"I thought I was going to die, and when we got back, it turned out Arista, Lenare, and Fanen had already turned us in the night before."

"I remember."

Mauvin studied his friend carefully. "You'll make a good king, Alric. And I'm sure your father would be proud."

Alric did not say anything for a moment. He picked up a bottle from the crate and felt its weight in his hand. "I'd better get back. I have responsibilities now. I can't hide down here drinking wine like the old days."

"I suppose we could if you really wanted to," Mauvin grinned devilishly.

Alric smiled and threw his arms around him. "You're a good friend. I'm sorry we'll never get to Percepliquis now."

"It's all right; besides, you never know. We might get there someday."

As they left the storeroom, Alric dusted dirt off his hands that he picked up from Mauvin's back during their embrace. "Is Fanen getting so good now that he was able to put you in the dirt?"

"No, it was the thief you brought with you, the big one. Where did you find him? His skill at sword fighting is unlike anything I've ever seen. It's actually rather remarkable."

"Really? Coming from a Pickering, that is high praise indeed."

"I'm afraid the Pickering legend won't last long at this rate: father loses to Percy Braga, and now I get thrown in the dirt by a common ruffian. How long will it be before we are being challenged for our land and title by the other nobles without fear?"

"If your father had his sword that day..." Alric paused. "Why didn't your father have his sword?"

"Misplaced it," Mauvin said. "He was certain it was in his room, but the next morning, it was gone. A steward found it later the same day laying somewhere strange."

"Well, sword or no, I can tell you, Mauvin, I think your father is still the best swordsman in the kingdom."

# 6

Royce, Hadrian, and Myron continued to enjoy the hospitality of the Pickerings with a hearty lunch as well as supper served to them in the warm comfort of Ella's kitchen. They spent most of the day napping, recovering lost sleep from the previous days. By nightfall, they were beginning to feel like themselves again.

Hadrian had a newfound shadow as Denek followed him wherever he went. After supper, he asked the three to come watch the marshalling of the troops from one of his favorite spots. The boy led them to the parapet above the main gate. From there, they could see both the grounds outside the castle and inside the courtyard without being underfoot.

Around early evening people began to arrive. Small groups of knights, barons, squires, soldiers, and village officials trickled in and formed camps outside the castle. Tall poles bearing the banners of various noble houses stood in the courtyard, signaling their presence in accordance with their sworn duty. By moonrise, eight standards and about three hundred men gathered in camps around bonfires. Their tents littered the hillside and extended throughout the orchards.

Vern, along with five other blacksmiths from various villages, worked late sharing his forge and anvil. They were hammering out last minute requests. The rest of the courtyard was equally active with every lamp lit, and each shop busy. Leather workers adjusted saddle stirrups and helms. Fletchers fashioned bundles of arrows, which they stacked like cord wood against the stable wall. Woodcutters created large rectangular archer shields. Even the butchers and bakers worked hard preparing sack meals from smoked meats, breads, onions, and turnips.

"The green one with the hammer on it is Lord Jerl's banner," Denek told them. The weather had turned sharply cold again, and his breath created a frosty fog. "I spent a summer at their estate two years ago. It is right on the edge of the Lankster Forest, and they love to hunt. They must have two dozen of the realm's best hounds. It's where I learned to shoot a bow. I bet you know how to shoot a bow real well, don't you, Hadrian?"

"I've been known to hit the forest from the field on occasion."

"I bet you could outshoot any of Jerl's sons. He's got six, and they all think they are the best marksmen in the province. My father never taught us archery. He said it didn't make sense because we would never be fighting in ranks. He taught us to concentrate on the sword. Although I don't know what good it will do me if I'm sent to a monastery. I'll be stuck doing nothing but reading all day."

"Actually there is a great deal more than that to do in an abbey," Myron explained, pulling the blanket around his shoulders tighter. "In spring, most of your time will be spent gardening, and in autumn, there is the harvest, preserving, and brewing. Even in winter, there is the mending and cleaning. Of course the bulk of your time is spent in prayer, either communal in the chapel or silently in the cloister. Then there is—"

"I think I'd rather be a foot soldier," Denek sighed with a grimace. "Or maybe I could join you two and become a thief! It must be a wonderfully exciting life running all over the world, accomplishing dangerous missions for king and country."

"You'd think that, wouldn't you?" Hadrian muttered softly.

Below them, a single rider rode up quickly to the front gate.

"Isn't that the banner of Essendon?" Royce asked, pointing to the falcon flag the rider carried.

"Yeah," Denek said surprised, "it's the king's standard. He's a messenger from Medford."

They looked at each other puzzled as the messenger entered the castle and did not re-emerge. They went on talking with Myron, who was trying in vain to convince Denek life in the monastery was not bad at all, when Fanen came running up the catwalk.

"There you are!" He shouted at them. "Father has half the castle turned out looking for you."

"Us?" Hadrian asked.

"Yes," Fanen nodded. "He wants to see the two thieves in his chambers right away."

"You didn't steal the silver or anything did you, Royce?" Hadrian asked.

"I would bet it has more to do with your flirting with Lenare this afternoon and threatening Mauvin just to show off," Royce retorted.

"That was your fault," Hadrian said, jabbing his finger at him.

"It's nothing like that," Fanen interrupted them. "The Princess Arista is going to be executed for treason tomorrow morning!"

Once long ago, the great hall of Drondil Fields was the site of the first court of Melengar. It was here that King Tolin drafted and signed the Drondil Charter, officially bringing the kingdom into existence. Now, old and faded, the parchment was mounted on one wall in a place of honor. Around it, massive burgundy drapes hung tied back by gold chords with silken tassels. Today, the hall served as the council chambers of Count Pickering; Royce and Hadrian hesitantly entered the hall.

At a long table in the center of the room sat a dozen men dressed in the finery of nobles. Hadrian recognized most of the men and could make some good guesses at the identities of those he did not know. There were earls, barons, sheriffs, and marshals; the leadership of eastern Melengar sat assembled before them. At the head of the table was Alric and, at his right, Count Pickering. Standing behind his father was Mauvin, and as Hadrian and Royce entered, Fanen took up position next to his brother. Alric was dressed in fine clothes, no doubt borrowed from one of the Pickerings. Less than a day passed since Hadrian last saw the prince, but Alric looked much older than he remembered.

"Have you told them why they were summoned?" Count Pickering asked his son.

"I told them the princess was to be executed," Fanen replied. "Nothing more."

"I've been summoned by Archduke Percy Braga," Count Pickering explained holding up the dispatch, "to report to Essendon

Castle as witness for the immediate trial of Princess Arista on the grounds of witchcraft, high treason, and murder. He has accused her not only of killing Amrath but also Alric." He dropped the dispatch on the table and slammed his hand down on it in disgust. "The blackguard means to have the kingdom for his own!"

"It is worse than I feared," Alric summarized for the thieves, "My uncle planned to kill me and my father and then blame both murders on Arista. He will execute her and take the kingdom for himself. No one will be the wiser. He'll fool everyone into thinking he is the great defender of the realm. I'm sure his plan will work. Even I was suspecting her only a few days ago."

"It's true. It has long been rumored that Arista has dabbled in the arcane arts," Pickering confirmed. "Braga will have no trouble finding her guilty. People are afraid of what they don't understand. The thought of a woman with magical powers is terrifying to old men in comfortable positions. Even without the fear of witchery, most nobles are uncomfortable with the thought of a woman monarch. The verdict will be assured. Her sentence will be handed down quickly."

"But if the prince were to arrive," Baron Enild said, "and show himself alive then—"

"That's exactly what Braga wants," Sir Ecton declared. "He can't find Alric. He's searched for days and couldn't locate him. He wants to draw him out before he has a chance to gather an army against him. He's counting on the prince's youth and lack of experience. He wants to manipulate the prince to react with emotion instead of reason. If he can't find Alric, he will lure the prince to him."

"Less than half our forces have mustered so far," Pickering grumbled despairingly. He walked to the great map of Melengar, which hung opposite the ancient charter, and slapped the western half of the map. "Our most powerful knights are the farthest from here, and because they have the most men to rally, it will take them longer to report. I don't expect them for another eight hours, maybe as long as sixteen.

"Even if we resign ourselves to employing only Galilin's forces, the earliest we could be ready to attack wouldn't be until tomorrow evening. By then Arista will be dead. I could march with what troops I have, leaving orders for the others to follow, but doing so would risk the whole army by dividing our forces. We cannot jeopardize the realm for the sake of one woman, even though she is the princess."

"Judging from the mercenaries we encountered at the inn," Alric told them, "I suspect the archduke anticipates an assault and has strengthened his forces with purchased arms loyal only to him."

"He will likely have scouts and ambushes prepared," Ecton said. "At first sight of our march, he will tell the other nobles assembled for the trial that we are working for Arista and that they need to defend Essendon against us. There is simply no way for us to march until we have more forces."

"Waiting," Alric said sadly, "will surely see Arista burned at the stake. Now, more than ever, I feel guilty for not trusting her. She saved my life. Now hers is in jeopardy, and there is little I can do about it." He looked at Hadrian and Royce. "I can't simply sit idly by and let her die! But to act prematurely would be folly."

The prince stood and walked over to the thieves. "I have inquired about you two since we arrived. You've been holding out on me. I thought you were common thieves. So, imagine my surprise when I discovered you two are famous." He glanced around at the other nobles in the room. "Rumor has it you two are unusually gifted agents known for taking difficult, sometimes nearly impossible assignments of sabotage, theft, espionage, and, even on rare occasions, assassinations. Don't bother denying it. Many in this room have already confided in me that they have used your services in the past."

Hadrian looked at Royce and then around at the faces of the men before them. He nodded uncomfortably. Not only were some of the men past clients, some had been targets as well.

"They tell me you are independents and are not aligned with any established guilds. It is no small feat to operate with such autonomy. I have learned more in a few hours from them than I did after days riding with you. What I do know, however—what I discovered for myself—is that you saved my life twice, once to honor a promise to my sister and once for no reason I can discern. Last night, you challenged the might of the Lord Chancellor of Melengar and came to my aid against a superior force of trained killers. No one asked you to, no one would have faulted you for letting me die. You could expect no reward for saving me and yet, you did it. Why?"

Hadrian looked at Royce who stood silent. "Well," he began as he glanced at the floor. "I guess…we'd just grown kind of fond of you I suppose."

Alric smiled and addressed the room. "The life of the Prince of Melengar—the would-be king—was saved, not by his army, not by his loyal bodyguards, nor by a grand fortress—but by two treacherous, impudent thieves who didn't have the good sense to ride away."

The prince stepped forward and placed a hand on each of their shoulders. "I am already deeply in your debt, and have no right to ask, but I must beg you now to display the same poor judgment once again and save my sister. Please, steal her from Braga's clutches and you can name whatever price you wish."

"Another last-minute, good-deed job," Royce grumbled as he stuffed supplies into his saddlebag.

"True," Hadrian said, slinging his sword belt over his shoulder, "but this is at least a *paying* job."

"You should have told him the real reason we saved him from Trumbul—because we wouldn't see the hundred tenents otherwise."

"That was *your* reason. Besides, how often do we get to do royal contracts? If word gets around, we'll be able to command top salaries."

"If word gets around, we'll be hanged."

"Okay, good point. But remember, she did save our skins. If Arista hadn't helped us out of the dungeon, we'd be ornaments for the Medford Autumn Festival right now."

Royce paused and sighed. "I didn't say we weren't doing it, did I? Did I say that? No, I didn't. I told the little prince we'd do it. Just don't expect me to be happy about it."

"I just want to make you feel better about your decision," Hadrian said. Royce glared at him. "Okay, okay, I'll see about the horses now." He grabbed his gear and headed for the courtyard where a light snow was starting to fall.

Pickering had provided the thieves with two of his swiftest stallions and any supplies they thought they might need. Ella had a late night snack and a sizable travel meal prepared for them. They took heavy woolen cloaks to brace against the cold and dark scarves that they wrapped around the lower half of their faces to keep the chill of the wind off their cheeks.

"I hope we will meet again soon," Myron told them as they prepared their mounts. "You two are the most fascinating people I have ever met, although I suppose that isn't saying a lot is it?"

"It's the thought that counts," Hadrian told him and gave the monk a bear hug, which caught the little man by surprise. As they climbed into their saddles, Myron bowed his head and muttered a soft prayer.

"There," Hadrian told Royce, "we've got Maribor on our side. Now you can relax."

"Actually," Myron said sheepishly, "I was praying for the horses. But I *will* pray for you as well," he added hastily.

Alric and the Pickerings came out to the courtyard to see them off. Even Lenare joined them, wrapped in a white fur cape. The fluffy muffler was wrapped so high on her shoulders that it hid the lower portion of her face. Only her eyes could be seen.

"If you can't get her out," Pickering said, "try to stall the execution until our forces can arrive. Once they do, however, you'd better have her secured. I am certain Braga will kill her out of desperation. Oh, and one more thing, don't try to fight Braga. He's the best swordsman in Melengar. Leave him for me." The count slapped the elegant rapier he wore at his side. "This time I'll have my own sword, and the archduke will feel its sting."

"I will be leading the attack on Essendon," Alric informed them. "It is my duty as ruler. So if you do reach my sister and if I should fall before the end of this, let her know I'm sorry for not trusting her. Let her know…" he faltered for a moment, "let her know I loved her and I think she will make a fine queen."

"You'll tell her yourself, Your Majesty," Hadrian assured him.

Alric nodded and then added, "And I'm sorry about what I said to you before. You two are the best Royal Protectors I could ever hope for. Now go. Save my sister or I'll have you both thrown back in my dungeon!"

They bowed respectfully in their saddles, then turned their horses and urged them into a gallop. They rode out the gate into the cold black of night.

# PART 8
## TRIALS

The morning of Arista Essendon's trial arrived along with the first snow. Despite not having slept, Percy Braga did not feel the least bit tired. Having set the wheels in motion the previous morning by sending the trial announcements, he had a hundred details demanding his personal attention. He was just rechecking his witness list when there was a knock at the door to his office and a servant entered.

"I'm sorry to disturb you, sir," the man said with a bow. "Bishop Saldur is here. He said you wanted to see him."

"Of course, of course, send him in," the archduke replied.

The elderly cleric entered, wearing his dress robes of black and red. Braga crossed the room and kissed his ring as he bowed. "Thank you for seeing me so early, your grace. Are you hungry?" May I arrange for some breakfast to be brought for you?"

"No, thank you, I've already eaten. At my age, one tends to wake early whether one wants to or not. What exactly did you want to see me about?"

"I just wanted to make sure you didn't have any questions about your testimony today. We could go over it now if you do. I've scheduled some time."

"Ah, I see," the bishop replied, nodding slowly. "I don't think that will be necessary. I have a clear understanding of what is required."

"Wonderful, then I think everything is in order."

"Excellent," the bishop said and glanced toward the decanter. "Is that brandy I see?"

"Yes, would you like some?"

"Normally I wouldn't indulge so early, but this is a special occasion."

"Absolutely, your grace."

The bishop took a seat near the fire as Braga poured two glasses of brandy and handed one to the bishop. "To the new Melengar regime," the archduke proposed. The crystal rang clear like a bell as their glasses touched. Then each took a deep drink.

"There's just something about a bit of brandy on a snowy day," Saldur remarked with a tone of satisfaction in his voice. The cleric had white hair and gentle looking eyes. Sitting in the glow of the fire, casually cupping the glass in his wrinkled hand, he appeared the quintessential kindhearted grandfather. Braga knew better. He could not have risen to his present position without being ruthless. As bishop, Saldur was one of the chief officers of the Nyphron Church and the ranking clergy in the kingdom of Melengar. He worked and resided in the great Mares Cathedral, an edifice just as imposing, and certainly more beloved, than Castle Essendon. As far as influence was concerned, Braga estimated that of the nineteen bishops who comprised the leadership of the faithful, Saldur must be in the top three.

"How long before the trial?" Saldur asked.

"We'll begin in about an hour or so."

"I must say you've handled this very well, Percy." Saldur smiled at him. "The Church is quite pleased. Our investment in you was substantial, but it would appear we made a wise choice. When dealing with timetables as long as we are, it's difficult to be sure we've put the right people in place. Each of these annexations needs to be handled delicately. We don't want anyone suspecting us of stacking the deck the way we are. When the time comes, it has to appear as if all the monarchies voluntarily accept the formation of the New Empire. I must admit, I had some doubts about you."

Braga raised an eyebrow. "I'm surprised to hear you say that."

"Well, you didn't look as though you had the makings of a king when we arranged your marriage to Amrath's sister. You were a scrawny, pretentious, little—"

"That was nearly twenty years ago," Braga protested.

"True enough. However, at the time, all I noticed about you was your skill with a sword and your staunch Imperialist view. I was afraid, being so young you might—well, who knew if you'd stay loyal, but you proved me wrong. You've grown into an able administrator, and your ability to adapt in the face of unexpected events, like this sudden timetable shift Arista caused, proves your capability to manage problems effectively."

"Well, I'll admit it hasn't gone exactly as I planned. Alric's escape was unexpected. I clearly underestimated the princess, but at least she was good enough to provide me a convenient means to implicate her."

"So, exactly what are you planning to do about Arista's little brother? Do you know where he is?"

"Yes, he is at Drondil Fields. I have several reports of the mustering of Galilin. Troops are converging at Pickering's castle."

"And you're not concerned about that?"

"Let's just say I wished I could have caught the little brat before he reached Pickering. But I'll be turning my attentions to him as soon as I conclude with his sister. I hope to take care of him before he can bolster too much support. He's been quite elusive. He slipped through my fingers at the Wicend Ford. Not only did he escape, but he also took horses from my men. I thought he would be easy to find, and I had scores of troops watching every road, valley and village, but for several days he just vanished."

"And that's when he got through to Pickering?"

"Oh, no," Braga said. "I actually managed to catch him. A patrol picked him up at The Silver Pitcher Inn."

"Then I don't understand. Why isn't he here?"

"Because my patrol never came back. An advance rider brought the news Alric was captured, but the rest of them disappeared. I investigated and heard some amazing rumors. According to my reports, two men traveling with the prince organized the locals and staged an ambush on the men bringing Alric in."

"Do you know who these two men were who came to Alric's aid?"

"I have no names, but the prince called them his Royal Protectors. I'm certain, however, they're the same two thieves I setup to take the blame for Amrath's death. Somehow, the prince has managed to retain their services. He must have offered them riches, perhaps even land and title. The boy is more clever than I thought. But no matter, I have made adequate arrangements for him and his friends. I've been bolstering the ranks of the Melengar army for the last several weeks with mercenaries loyal to my money. Amrath never knew. One of the perks of being the Lord Chancellor is not having to get the royal seal on all orders."

There was another knock at the door, and the servant once again entered. "The Earl of Chadwick is here to see you, my lord."

"Archibald Ballentyne? What is he doing here? Get rid of him."

"No, wait," the bishop intervened. "I asked the earl to come. Please send him in." The servant bowed and left, closing the door behind him.

"I wished you had discussed this with me," Braga said. "Forgive me, your grace, but I have too much going on today to entertain a visit from a neighboring noble."

"Yes, yes. I know you are quite busy, but the Church has its own matters to attend to. As you well know, you're not the only kingdom we administer to. The Earl of Chadwick possesses a certain interest to us. He is young, ambitious, and easily impressed by success. It will do him good to see firsthand just what kinds of things are possible with the right *friends*. Besides, having an ally on your southern border has benefits for you as well."

"Are you suggesting I try and sway him away from King Ethelred?"

"Ethelred is a good Imperialist, I admit, but there can be only one Emperor. There's no reason it couldn't be you, assuming you continue to prove yourself worthy. Ballentyne has many assets that could help in that endeavor. "

"I'm not even king yet and you're talking Emperor?"

"The Church hasn't lasted for three thousand years by not thinking ahead. Ah, here he is. Come in, come in, Archibald." Archibald Ballentyne entered, brushing the snow from his cloak and stomping his feet. "Toss your cloak aside and come to the fire. Warm up, lad. The carriage ride must have been a cold one."

Archibald crossed the room and kissed the ring of the still seated bishop, "Good morning, your grace," he said, then turned and bowed graciously to the archduke. "My lord."

He swept off his cloak and shook it out carefully. Perplexed, he looked around. "Your servant left before taking my cloak."

"Just throw it anywhere," Braga instructed.

The earl looked at him aghast. "This is imported damask with gold thread embroideries." Just then, the servant reentered with a large comfortable chair. "Ah, there you are. Here take this, and, for Maribor's sake, don't hang it from a peg." He passed his cloak to the servant, who bowed and left.

"Brandy?" Braga asked.

"Oh, good lord, yes," Archibald replied. Braga handed him a glass, the bottom of which was filled with a smoky amber liquid.

"I appreciate your coming, Archibald," the bishop said. "I'm afraid we won't have much time to talk just now, there is quite a bit of turmoil in Melengar today. But as I was telling Braga, I thought it might be beneficial for the three of us to have a quick chat."

"I'm always at your service, of course, your grace. I appreciate any opportunity to meet with you and the new King of Melengar,"

Archibald said nonchalantly. Saldur and Braga exchanged looks. "Oh, come now, it can hardly be a secret. You are the archduke and Lord Chancellor. With King Amrath and the prince dead, if you execute Arista, you'll wear the crown. It's really rather nicely done. I commend you. Murder in broad daylight, right before the nobles—they'll cheer you on as you steal their crown."

Braga stiffened. "Are you accusing me of—"

"Of course not," the earl stopped him. "I accuse no one. What care do I have for the affairs of Melengar? My liege is Ethelred of Warric. What happens in your kingdom is none of my affair. I was merely offering my *sincere* congratulations," he raised his glass and nodded at the bishop, "to both of you."

"Do you have a name for this game, Ballentyne?" Braga asked tentatively as both he and Saldur watched the young earl closely.

Archibald smiled again. "My dear gentlemen, I am playing no game. I'm being truthful when I say I am simply in awe. All the more because of my own recent failure. You see, I tried a gamble myself, to increase my station, only it was less than successful."

Braga became quite amused with this primly dressed earl. He understood what the bishop saw in him and he was curious now. "I'm very sorry to hear you suffered difficulties. Exactly what were you attempting?"

"Well, I acquired some letters and tried to blackmail the Marquis of Glouston into marrying his daughter to me so I could obtain his Rilan Valley. I had the messages locked in my safe in my private tower and was prepared to present them to Victor in person. Everything was perfect, but...poof." Archibald made an exploding gesture with his fingers. "The letters vanished. Like a magic trick."

"What happened to them?" Saldur asked.

"They were stolen. Thieves sawed a hole in the roof of my tower and, in just a matter of minutes, slipped in and snatched them from underneath my very nose."

"Impressive," Saldur judged.

"Depressing is what it was. They made me look like a fool."

"Did you catch the thieves?" Braga asked.

Archibald shook his head. "Sadly no, but I finally figured out who they are. It took me days to reason it out. I did not tell anyone I possessed those letters. So, the only ones who could have taken them are the same thieves which I hired in the first place. Cunning devils. They call themselves Riyria. I'm not sure why they stole them, perhaps they planned to charge me twice. I won't give them the satisfaction of course. I'll hire someone else to intercept the next set from the Winds Abbey."

"So, the letters you had were correspondences between the Marquis of Glouston and the Nationalists?" Saldur asked.

Archibald looked at the bishop surprised. "That's an amazing guess, your grace. You are very close. No, they were love letters between his daughter and her Nationalist lover Gaunt. I planned to have Alenda marry me instead to spare Victor the embarrassment of his daughter being involved with a commoner."

Saldur chuckled.

"Have I said something funny?"

"You had more in your hands than you knew," Saldur informed him. "Those weren't love letters. Those were coded messages from Victor Lanaklin carried by Alenda to Gaunt. The Marquis of Glouston is a traitor to his kingdom and the Imperial cause. With that treasure you could have had all of Glouston and Victor's head as a wedding gift."

Archibald stood silent and then swallowed the rest of his brandy in one mouthful.

"But you won't be able to obtain additional letters. There will be no more meetings at the Winds Abbey. Regrettably, I was forced to ask the archduke here to teach the monks a lesson for hosting such meetings. The abbey was burned along with the monks."

"*You* killed your fellow shepherds of Maribor's flock?" Archibald asked Saldur.

"When Maribor sent Novron to us it was as a warrior to destroy our enemies. Our god is not squeamish at the sight of spilled blood, and it is often necessary to prune weak branches to keep the tree strong. Killing the monks was a necessity, but I did spare one, the son of Lanaklin so he could return home and let his father know the deaths were on his hands. We can't have Monarchists and Nationalists allying themselves can we?" Saldur smiled at him. The elderly cleric took another sip of his drink, the moment passed and once more Braga observed the persona of the saintly grandfather returned.

"So, you were after Glouston, Archibald?" Braga said, refilling the earl's glass. "Perhaps I misjudged you. Tell me, my dear earl, were you more upset you lost the land or Alenda?"

Archibald waved his hand in the air as if he was shooing a fly. "She was merely an added benefit. It's the land I wanted."

"I see." Braga glanced at Saldur, who smiled and nodded. "You may still get it." Braga resumed speaking to the earl. "With me on the throne of Melengar, I will want a strong Imperialist ally guarding my southern border with Warric."

"King Ethelred would call that treason."

"And what would you call it?"

Archibald smiled and drummed his fingernails on the beautiful cut-crystal of the royal brandy glass, making it ring with a pleasant song. "Opportunity."

Braga sat back down and stretched out his feet to the fire. "If I help you obtain the marchland from Lanaklin, and you throw your allegiance to me, Melengar will replace Warric as the strongest kingdom in Avryn. Similarly, *Greater* Chadwick will be its most powerful province."

"That's assuming Ethelred doesn't declare war," Archibald warned. "Kings often frown upon losing a quarter of their realm, and Ethelred is not the type to take such an action without retaliation. He enjoys fighting. What's more, he's good at it. He has the best army in Avryn now."

"True," Braga said, "but he has no able general to command it. He doesn't have anyone near the talent of your Sir Breckton. That man is gifted when it comes to leading men. If you broke with Warric, could you count on his loyalty to you?"

"Breckton's loyalty to me is unwavering. His father, Lord Belstrad, is a chivalrous knight of archaic dimensions. He beat those values into his sons. Neither Breckton nor his brother—what's his name, the younger Belstrad boy who went to sea—*Wesley*, would dishonor themselves by opposing a man they have sworn their allegiance to. I do admit, however, their honor can be an inconvenience. I remember once a servant dropped my new fustian hat in the mud, and when I commanded Breckton to cut off the clumsy oaf's hand in punishment, he refused. Breckton went on for twenty minutes explaining the code of chivalry to me. Oh yes, my lord, he is indeed loyal to House Ballentyne, but I would rather have a less loyal man who simply obeys without question. It is entirely possible that should I break with Warric, Breckton might refuse to fight at all, but I'm certain he would not oppose me. Personally, I would be more concerned with Ethelred himself. He is a fine commander in his own right."

"True," Braga acknowledged, "but so am I. I would welcome him engaging me personally. I already have a standing veteran army and a number of mercenaries at the ready. I will be able to muster superior numbers should that prove necessary. The result will be that he would lose all of Warric, and that could provide me the keys to the rest of Avryn and, perhaps, all of Apeladorn."

This time Archibald chuckled. "My, but I do appreciate your ability to *think big*. I can see there would be many advantages to my joining with you. Do you really have your sights on the title of Emperor?"

"Why not? If I am poised to conquer, the Patriarch will be eager to throw his allegiance to me just as the Church did with Glenmorgan. If I promise certain rights to the Church, he may even declare me the Heir. Then no one will stand against me. In any case, this is for another day. We are getting ahead of ourselves." Braga turned his attention toward the bishop. "I want to thank you, your grace, for arranging this meeting. It was very educational. But now it is nearly midmorning, and I think it is time to get Arista's trial underway. I would, however, like to invite you to stay, Archibald. As it turns out, I think I may be able to offer you a gift to show you my commitment to you as a newfound friend of Melengar."

"I'm flattered, my lord. I'd welcome the opportunity to spend time with you, and I'm sure whatever gift you may have will be a generous one."

"You mentioned the thieves who spoiled your move against Victor Lanaklin called themselves Riyria?"

"Yes, I did. Why do you ask?"

"Well, it appears we share a common interest in these two rogues. They have also been a rather painful thorn in my own side. As you already discovered, they pay no respect to people who hire them and are willing to turn against their employers. I, too, hired them for a task and now find them working against me. I have reason to believe they may be coming here today, and I have set plans in motion to capture them. If they do indeed make an appearance, I will try them along with Arista. It is quite possible all three will be burning at the stake by early evening."

"You are, indeed, most generous, my lord," Archibald replied, with a nod of his head and a smile on his lips.

"I thought you might enjoy that. You mentioned when you arrived that Alric is dead and that is indeed the notion I've been circulating. Unfortunately, it is not so…that is not yet. Arista actually arranged for those thieves to smuggle Alric out of this castle on the night of Amrath's death. I believe he has hired them and they will attempt to save her. Evidence indicates they used the sewers to exit the castle so I've taken extra precautions there. The grate in the kitchen has been sealed, and Wylin, the castle's master-at-arms, waits with his best men hidden to close the river grate behind them. I even failed to post guards near there to make it more enticing. With luck, the fool of a prince might actually play the boyish hero and come with them. If he does—checkmate!"

Archibald nodded with obvious pleasure. "You really are very impressive."

Braga raised his glass in tribute, "To me."

"To you," Archibald drank to Braga's health.

There was a loud pounding on the door. "Come!" Braga called irritated.

"Lord Chancellor!" One of Braga's hired soldiers burst into the room. His cheeks and nose were red, his armor dripping wet. On his head and shoulders a small bit of snow remained.

"Yes? What is it?"

"The wall guard reports foot prints in the snow leading to the river near the sewers, my lord."

"Excellent," Braga replied draining his glass. "Take eight men and support Wylin from the river. I don't want them escaping. Remember, if the prince is with them, kill him on sight. Don't let Wylin stop you. Either way, I want the thieves alive. Lock them in the dungeons and gag them as before. I will use them as further incriminating evidence against Arista and burn the whole lot together." The soldier bowed and left hurriedly.

"Now, gentlemen, as I was saying, let's join the magistrate and the other nobles. I'm anxious to get this trial underway." They all stood and, walking three abreast, they exited the large double doors as one.

## 2

The morning sun magnified by the snow entered the river grate as a stark white light. The wintry radiance splintered along the glistening subway ceiling, revealing ancient stone caked in mildew and moss. The light reflected off the frozen sweat of the sewer walls, bouncing back and forth until at last it scattered into the all-consuming darkness. In the gloom, the soldiers waited, crouching and cold. Their feet were ankle-deep in filthy cold water, which streamed between their legs running from the castle drains to the river. For the better part of four hours, they lingered in silence, but now they could hear the sound of footsteps approaching. The sloshing of the dirty water echoed off the sewer walls, and the distant movement of shadows played upon the stone.

With a motion of his hand, Wylin ordered his troop to hold their position and maintain their silence. He wanted to be certain the rearguard was in place, and his prey was in sight before he made his move. There were many avenues in the sewers where two men could run and hide in the dark. He did not want to be chasing the rats through a maze of tunnels. Not only was it unpleasant down there, but Wylin knew the archduke wanted the thieves for the morning festivities and would not be pleased with a long delay.

Soon they came into view. Two men, one tall and broad, the other shorter and slimmer, each dressed in warm winter cloaks with hoods pulled high rounded the corner slowly, pausing from time to time to look about.

"Remind me to compliment His Majesty on the quality of his sewers," one of them mentioned in a mocking tone.

"At least the slime is warmer than the river," the other replied.

"Yeah, too bad this is happening on the coldest day of the year. Why couldn't it be the middle of summer?"

"That would be warmer for sure, but could you imagine the smell?"

"Speaking of smell, do you think we're getting close to the kitchen yet?"

"You're the one leading; I can't see a thing in here."

Wylin waved his arm. "*Move in, now! Take them!*"

The castle guard rushed from their positions in an adjoining tunnel and charged the two men. From behind, more soldiers raced forward, blocking any retreat. The troops encircled the two, swords drawn and shields at the ready.

"Careful," Wylin said, "the archduke says they are full of surprises."

"I'll show you surprises," one of the soldiers from the rear said and stepping forward struck the tall one with the pommel of his sword dropping him to the ground. Another used his shield and the second man fell unconscious.

Wylin sighed and glared at his ranks then shrugged. "I was planning on letting them walk, but this works too. Chain 'em, gag 'em, and drag 'em to the dungeons. And for Maribor's sake, get their heads up before they drown. Braga wants them alive." The soldiers nodded and went to work.

"This hearing of the High Court of Melengar has been assembled in good order to review allegations made against the Princess Arista Essendon by the Lord Chancellor, the Archduke of Melengar, Percy Braga." The strong voice of the chief magistrate boomed across the chamber. "Princess Arista stands duly accused of treason against the crown, the murder of her father and brother, and the practicing of witchcraft."

The largest room in the castle, the Court of Melengar had a cathedral ceiling, stained-glass windows, and walls rimmed in emblems and shields of the noble houses of the kingdom. Bench seats and balconies were overflowing with spectators. The nobles and the city's affluent merchants pressed in to see the royal trial of the princess. Outside, many common people had been gathering since dawn and waited in the snow as runners reported the proceedings. A wall of armor-clad soldiers held them at bay.

The court itself was a boxed set of bleachers composed of tiered armchairs where the ranking nobles of the kingdom sat. Several of the seats were vacant, but enough had arrived to serve Braga's purpose. Still frosty with the morning chill, most of the court wore fur wraps as they waited for the fire in the great hearth to warm the room. At the front of the court stood the empty throne, its vacancy looming like an ominous specter before the court. Its presence was a stark reminder of the gravity and scope of the trial. The verdict could decide who would sit there next and control the reins of the kingdom.

"This judicial court, comprised of men of good standing and sound wisdom, will now hear the allegations and the evidence. May Maribor grant them wisdom."

The chief magistrate took his seat and a heavyset man with a short beard wreathing his small mouth stood up. He was dressed in expensive looking robes that flowed behind him as he paced before the jury, eyeing each man carefully.

"Lords of the Court," the lawyer said addressing the bleachers with a dramatic sweep of his arm. "Your noble personages have by now learned that our good king Amrath was murdered seven days past in this very castle. You may also be aware Prince Alric is missing, presumed abducted and murdered. But how could such things as these happen within a king's own castle walls? A king *might* be murdered, a prince *might* be abducted, but both in the same night one after the other? How is this possible?"

The crowd quieted as they struggled to hear.

"How is it possible that two killers slipped inside the castle unnoticed, stabbed the king to death, and, despite being caught and locked in the dungeon, were able to escape? This in itself is incredible, because the cell in which they were locked was heavily guarded by skilled soldiers. Not only were they imprisoned, they were also chained by their wrists and ankles to the wall. But what is beyond amazing, what is beyond belief, is that after managing their miraculous escape, the two did not flee! No, indeed! Informed while in captivity that they would be drawn and quartered at dawn —a most painful and gruesome death to be certain—for their most heinous crime, these two killers remained in a castle filled with hundreds of soldiers ready to thrust them back into their cell. Rather than flee for their lives, instead they sought out the prince, the most heavily guarded and high-profile personage in the castle, and kidnapped him! I ask you again, how is this possible? Were the castle guards asleep? Were they so totally incompetent as to let the killers of the king walk out? Or could it be that the assassins had help?

"Could a guard have done this? A foreign spy? Even a trusted baron or earl? No! None of them would have the authority to enter the dungeon to *see* the killers of the king much less free them. Nay, gracious lords, no person in the castle that night had the authority to enter those jails so easily, save one—Princess Arista! Being the daughter of the victim, who could deny her the right to spit in the faces of the men who murdered her father so brutally? Only she wasn't there to defile the killers, she came to help them finish the job she started!"

The crowd murmured.

"This is an outrage!" an elderly man protested from the bleachers. "To accuse the poor girl of her father's death, you should be ashamed! Where is she? Why is she not present to dispute these claims?"

"Lord Valin," the lawyer addressed him, "we are honored to have you with us today. This court will call the princess forth shortly. She is not here for the presenting of facts as it is a tedious and unpleasant matter, and this court does not want the princess to endure it. Likewise, those called to testify can speak freely, without the presence of their future queen, should she be found innocent. And there are still other, more unpleasant reasons of which I will elaborate upon in due time."

This did not appear to change Lord Valin's mood, but he made no further protest and sat back down.

"The court of Melengar calls Reuben Hilfred to testify."

The lawyer paused as the big soldier still dressed in ring mail and the tabard of the falcon stood before the court. His stance was proud and straight, but his expression was anything but pleased.

"Hilfred," the lawyer addressed him," what is your position here at Essendon Castle?"

"I am personal bodyguard to Princess Arista," he told the court in a loud clear voice.

"Tell us Reuben, what is your rank?"

"I am sergeant-at-arms."

"That's a fairly high rank, isn't it?"

"It is a respected position."

"How did you attain this rank?"

"I was singled out for some reason."

"For some reason? For some reason?" the lawyer repeated, laughing gaily. "Is it not true you were recommended for promotion by Captain Wylin for your years of consistent and unwavering loyalty to the crown? Moreover, is it not true that the *king himself* appointed you to be his daughter's personal bodyguard after you risked your life and saved Arista from the fire that killed the queen mother? Were you not also presented with a commendation for bravery by the king? Are not all these things true?"

"Yes, sir."

"I sense in you a reluctance to be here, Reuben. Am I correct?"

"Yes, sir."

"It is because you are loyal to your princess, and you do not wish to be a part of anything which might harm her. That is an admirable quality. Still, you are also an honorable man, and as such, you must speak truthfully in your testimony before this court. So tell us, Reuben, what happened the night the king was murdered?"

Hilfred shifted his weight uncomfortably from one foot to the other and then took a breath and spoke. "It was late, and the princess was asleep in her bed. I was on post at the tower stairs when the king was found. Captain Wylin ordered me to check on Princess Arista. Before I reached her door, she came out, startled by the noise."

"How was she dressed?" the lawyer asked.

"In a gown, I am not sure which."

"But she was dressed? Was she not? Not in a robe or night clothes?"

"Yes, she was dressed."

"You've spent years guarding Arista. Have you ever known her to sleep in her gowns?"

"No."

"Never?"

"Never."

"But I assume you've no doubt stood outside her door when she went to dress for meals or to change after traveling. Does she have servants to help her dress?"

"Yes."

"How many?"

"Three."

"And how long is the fastest you recall her dressing?"

"I am not certain."

"Make a guess, the court will not hold you to the exact time."

"Perhaps twenty minutes."

"Twenty minutes with three servants. That is actually quite fast considering all the ties and toggles that require lacing for most ladies' clothing. Now how long would you say it was between the discovery of the king's body and the time the princess came out of her room?"

Hilfred hesitated.

"How long?" the lawyer persisted.

"Perhaps ten minutes."

"Ten minutes, you say? And when she came out of her room, how many servants were with her?"

"None, that I saw."

"Amazing! The princess woke up unexpectedly in the dark and managed to dress herself fully in a lavish gown in ten minutes without the help of a single servant!"

The lawyer paced the floor, his head down in thought, a finger tapping his lips. He paused with his back to Hilfred. Then, as if a sudden thought occurred to him, he spun abruptly.

"Tell us, how did she take the news of the king's death?"

"She was shocked."

"Did she weep?"

"I am sure she did."

"But did you *see* her?"

"No."

"Then what happened?"

"She went to Prince Alric's chambers to find him and was surprised he wasn't there. She then—"

"Please stop there just a minute. She went to *Alric's* chambers? She learns her father is murdered and her first inclination is to go to her brother's room? Did you not find it odd she didn't immediately rush to her father's side? After all, no one suggested any harm had come to Alric, had they?"

"No."

"What happened next?"

"She went to view her father's body, and Alric arrived."

"After the prince sentenced the prisoners to death, what did the princess do?"

"I don't understand what you mean," Hilfred replied.

"Is it true she went to visit them?" the lawyer questioned.

"Yes, she did."

"And were you with her?"

"I was asked to wait outside the cell."

"Why?"

"I don't know."

"Has she often asked you to wait outside when speaking with people?"

"Sometimes."

"Often?"

"Not often."

"Then what happened?"

"She called for monks to give last rights to the murderers."

"She called for monks?" the lawyer repeated with a clear note of skepticism in his voice. "Her father is murdered and she is concerned about the *murderers'* souls? Why did she call for two monks? Was one not sufficient to do the job for both? For that matter, why not call the castle priest?"

"I don't know."

"And did she also order the murderers unchained?"

"Yes, to be able to kneel."

"And when the monks entered the cell did you go with them?"

"No, again she asked me to remain outside."

"So, the monks could enter, but not her trusted bodyguard? Not even when the known killers of her father were unchained and free? Then what?"

"She came out of the cell. She wanted me to stay behind and escort the monks to the kitchen after they were done giving last rites."

"Why?"

"She didn't say."

"Did you ask?"

"No, sir. As a man-at-arms, it is not my place to question the orders from a member of the royal family."

"I see, but were you pleased with these orders?"

"No."

"Why?"

"I was fearful more assassins might be in the castle, and I didn't wish the princess to be out of my sight."

"In point of fact, wasn't Captain Wylin in the process of searching the castle for additional threats, and didn't he make everyone aware he felt the castle was unsafe?"

"He did."

"Did the princess explain to you where she was going so you could find her after performing your duty to the monks?"

"No."

"I see. And how do you know the two you escorted to the kitchens were the monks? Did you see their faces?"

"Their hoods were up."

"Did they have their hoods up when they entered the cell?"

Hilfred thought a moment and then shook his head. "I don't think so."

"So, on a night when her father is killed, she orders her personal bodyguard to leave her unprotected and to escort two monks down to the empty kitchens—two monks who decided suddenly to pull their hoods up inside the castle, hiding their faces? And what about the murderers' possessions? Where were they?"

"They were in the custody of the cell warden."

"And what did she say to the warden concerning them?"

"She told him she was going to have the monks take them for the poor."

"And did they take them?"

"Yes."

The lawyer softened his address. "Reuben, you don't strike me as a fool. Fools don't rise to the rank and position you have achieved. When you heard the killers escaped, and the monks were found chained in their place, did it cross your mind that maybe the princess had arranged it?"

"I assumed the killers attacked the monks after the princess left the cell."

"You didn't answer my question," the lawyer said. "I asked if it crossed your mind?"

Reuben said nothing.

"Did it?"

"Perhaps, but only briefly."

"Let us turn our attention to more recent events. Were you present during the conversation between Arista and her uncle in his study?"

"Yes, but I was asked to wait outside."

"To wait just outside the door correct?"

"Yes."

"Therefore could you hear what transpired inside?"

"Yes."

"Is it true the princess entered the archduke's office, where he was diligently working at locating the prince, and informed him that Prince Alric was clearly dead and that no search was needed? That he would make a better use of his time..." he paused here and turned to face the nobles, "...*to begin preparations for her coronation as our queen!*"

There was a decidedly unpleasant murmur from the crowd, and a few of the court whispered and nodded to one another.

"I don't remember her using those words."

"Did she, or did she not, indicate the archduke should stop looking for Alric?"

"Yes."

"And did she threaten the archduke, insinuating she would soon hold her coronation, and once she was queen, he might find he was no longer the Lord Chancellor?"

"I believe she did say something to that effect, but she was angry—"

"That will be all, sergeant-at-arms; that's all I asked. You can step down." Hilfred began to leave the witness box when the lawyer spoke again. "Oh, I'm sorry…just one last thing. Have you ever seen or heard the princess cry over the loss of her father or brother?"

"She is a very private woman."

"Yes or no?"

Hilfred hesitated, "No, I haven't."

"I am prepared to call the cell warden to corroborate the testimony of Hilfred if the court feels his account of the events is not truthful," the lawyer told the magistrates.

They conferred in whispers, and then the chief magistrate replied, "That won't be necessary; the word of the sergeant-at-arms Hilfred is recognized as honorable and we will not question it here. You may proceed."

"I'm sure you are as perplexed as I was," the lawyer said, addressing the bleachers in a sympathetic voice. "Many of you know her. How could this sweet girl attack her own father and brother? Was it just to gain a throne? It's not like her, is it? I ask you to bear with me. The reason should become quite clear in a moment. The court calls Bishop Saldur to testify."

Eyes from the gallery swept the room looking for the cleric as the old man slowly stood up from his seat and approached the witness box.

"Your grace, you have been in this castle on many occasions. You know the royal family extremely well. Can you shed some light on her highness' motivations?"

"Gentlemen," Bishop Saldur spoke to the court and judges in his familiar warm and humble tone, "I have watched over the royal family for years and this recent tragedy is heartbreaking and dreadful. The accusation the archduke brings against the princess is painful to my ears for I feel almost like a grandfather to the poor girl. However, I cannot hide the truth, which is—she *is* dangerous."

This brought a round of whispers between the spectators.

"I can assure each of you she is no longer the sweet innocent child whom I used to hold in my arms. I have seen her, spoken to her, watched her in her grief—or rather the lack of grief—for her father and brother. I can tell you truly her lust for knowledge and power has caused her to fall into the arms of evil." The bishop paused, dropping his head into his hands and shaking it. He looked up with a remorse-filled face and said, "It is the result of what happens when a woman is educated and in Arista's case, introduced to the wicked powers of black magic."

There was a collective gasp issued from the crowd.

"Against my advice, King Amrath allowed her to attend the university where she studied sorcery. She opened herself up to the forces of darkness, and it created in her a craving for power. Education planted an evil seed in her, and it flowered into the horrible deaths of her father and her brother. She is no longer a princess of the realm, but a *witch*. This is evident by the fact she hasn't wept for her father. You see, as a learned bishop of the Church, I know—witches cannot cry."

The crowd gasped again. From somewhere in the gallery, Braga heard a man say, "I knew it!"

The lawyer called Countess Amril to the court, and she testified that two years earlier Arista had hexed her when she told the handsome squire Davens that the princess fancied him. Amril went on to describe how she suffered horribly for days of sickness and boils as a result.

Next, the lawyer called the monks, who like Countess Amril, were eager to relate how they had been ill-used by the princess. They told how she had insisted the thieves be unchained despite their assurance it was not necessary and explained they were attacked the moment she left the room.

The crowd's reaction grew louder, and even Lord Valin looked troubled.

Percy Braga observed the audience with satisfaction from his seat at the rear of the magistrates. The faces of the gentry were filling with anger. He had successfully coaxed the spark into a flame and the flame would soon be a blaze.

In the crowd, he spotted Wylin moving in the wings toward him.

"We have them, my lord," Wylin reported in a whisper. "They are gagged and locked in the dungeon. A little banged up by two of my overzealous men, but alive."

"Excellent, and has there been any movement on the roads? Has there been any indication nobles loyal to the traitor Arista may attack?"

"I don't know, sir. I came directly from the sewers."

"Very well, get to the gate and sound the horn if you see anything. I'm concerned there may be an assault from Pickering of Drondil Fields. Oh, and if you see that wretched little dwarf, tell him it is time to bring the princess down."

"Of course, your lordship." Wylin pulled a small parchment rolled into a tube from his tabard. "I was passed this on my way in. It just arrived via messenger addressed to you." Braga took the missive from Wylin and the master-at-arms left with a bow.

Braga grinned at the ease of it all. He wondered if the princess in her distant tower prison could sense her coming death. Her own beloved citizens would soon be begging—nay demanding—her execution. He had yet to present the storeroom administrator who would attest to the stolen dagger that was later found in Arista's possession. And then of course, there were now the thieves. He would hold them until the last and drag them out to the floor gagged and chained. The mere sight of them was likely to start a riot. He would have Wylin explain how he apprehended them trying to save the princess. The magistrates would have no choice but to rule against Arista and grant him the throne.

He would still have to deal with the possibility of Alric attacking, but that could not be helped now. He was certain he would defeat Alric. Several of the more disgruntled eastern lords already agreed to join him the moment he was crowned king. Once the trial was complete and Arista dead, he planned to hold the coronation. By tomorrow, he would marshal the kingdom. Alric would cease to be a prince and become a fugitive.

"The court calls storage clerk Kline Druess," the lawyer was saying, "who was in charge of keeping the knife used to kill the king."

*More damning evidence*, Braga thought as he unrolled the scroll that Wylin had presented him. It had no seal, no emblem of nobility, only a simple string tie. He read the message, which was as simple as its package:

You missed us in the sewers.

We now have the princess.

Your time is growing short.

The archduke crumpled the note in his fist and glared around at the numerous faces in the crowd wondering if whoever wrote it was watching him. His heart began beating faster, and he stood up slowly trying not to draw attention to himself.

The lawyer caught sight of his movement and gave him a curious look. Braga dismissed his concern with a slight wave of his hand. He left the court, forcing himself to walk slowly and calmly. The moment he passed out through the chamber doors, and out of sight of the crowd, he trotted through the castle halls, his cape whipping behind him. In his fist, he held on to the note, crushing it.

*It wasn't possible*, he thought, *it couldn't be!* Hearing footfalls approaching rapidly from behind, he stopped and spun, drawing his sword.

"Is there a problem, Braga?" Archibald Ballentyne inquired. He held his hands up defensively before the point of the archduke's blade. Braga silently threw the crumpled note at him and resumed his march toward the dungeon.

"It's those thieves, those damned thieves," the Earl of Chadwick called out as he ran after Braga. "They're demons! Magicians! Evil mages! They are like smoke, appearing and disappearing at will."

Archibald caught up with Braga and they descended the stairs to the detention block where the door guard dodged aside just in time to avoid the archduke. After trying the door and finding it locked, Braga hammered on it. The warden promptly left his desk and brought his keys for the red-faced archduke.

"My lord, I—"

"Open the cell to the prisoners Wylin's men just brought in. Do it now!"

"Yes, my lord." Fumbling with his great ring of keys, the warden moved quickly to the cell hall. Two castle guards stood watch to either side of a door and promptly stepped aside at his approach.

"Have you two been here since the prisoners were brought in?" Braga asked the guards.

"Aye, my lord," the guard on the left replied, "Captain Wylin ordered us to stand guard and to allow absolutely no admittance to anyone except him or you."

"Very good," he said. Then, to the warden, he added, "Open it."

The warden unlocked the door and entered the cell. Inside, Braga saw two men chained to the wall, stripped to their waist with gags in their mouths. They were not the same men he saw the night of the king's murder.

"Remove the gags," Braga ordered the warden. "Who are you? What are you doing here?"

"M-m-my name's Bendent, your lordship, I'm just a street sweeper from Dock Street—honest—we weren't doing nothing wrong!"

"What were you two doing in the sewers under this castle?"

"Hunting rats, sir," the other one said.

"*Rats?*"

"Yes, sir, honest, we was. We was told there was a big event here in the castle this morning and the castle kitchen was complaining about rats climbing up from the sewers. 'Cause of the cold, you see, sir. We was told we'd get paid a silver tenet for every rat we done killed and brought out—only…"

"Only what?"

"Only we never seen no rats, your lordship."

"Before we found any, we were knocked out by soldiers and brought here."

"See? What did I tell you?" Archibald told Braga. "They took her already. They stole her right from under your nose just like they took my letters!"

"They couldn't have. There's no way to get up to Arista's tower. It is too high, and it can't be climbed."

"I'm telling you, Braga, these men are skilled. They scaled my Gray Tower well enough, and it is one of the tallest there is."

"Trust me, Archibald. Arista's tower can't be climbed."

"But they did it," Ballentyne insisted. "I didn't think it was possible when they did it to me either, not until I opened the safe and my prize was gone. Now your prize is gone, and what will you do with that crowd out there when you have no princess to burn!"

"It's just not possible," Braga repeated, pushing Ballentyne out of his way. "You two," he said to the guards still standing outside the cell as he walked out, "come with me and bring one of those gags. It's time the princess came down for her court appearance!"

Braga led them through the castle and up six flights of stairs to the residence level. The hallway here was empty. All of the servants were gathered with the others, listening to the proceedings of the trial.

They passed the royal chapel and continued up the hallway to the next door. "Magnus!" Braga shouted, throwing the door open. Inside a dwarf with a braided brown beard and a broad flat nose lay on a bed. He was dressed in a blue leather vest, large black boots, and a bright orange puffed sleeved shirt that made his arms appear huge.

"Is it time?" the dwarf asked. Hopping off the bed, he yawned and rubbed his eyes.

"Is there any chance someone could have gotten up in her tower and stolen Arista out of there?" Braga asked urgently.

"None whatsoever," the dwarf said with a tone of total confidence. Braga looked back and forth between Ballentyne and the dwarf, scowling.

"I have to know for certain. Besides, she needs to come down for the burning anyway and I must get back to the trial. Archibald, go get Wylin, my master-at-arms; he's stationed at the castle gate. Tell him to come to the royal residence wing and provide assistance guarding the princess. I need tight security on this girl. Do you understand me, tight!" Braga now turned his attention to the dwarf. "You'll have to fetch her. Take these guards with you, one of them has a gag. Make sure they use it before bringing her down." To the guards the archduke added, "The princess has been corrupted by dark magic; she's a witch and can play tricks with your mind, so don't let her talk to you. Get her and bring her to the court." The guards nodded and the dwarf led them down the hallway in the direction of the tower.

"I'll do as you say, Percy, but I'm sure she is already gone," Archibald insisted. "These bastards are incredible. They're like ghosts, and they have no fear at all. They work right under your nose, steal you blind, and then have the audacity to send you a note *telling* you what they have done!"

Braga paused in thought. "Yes, why *did* they do that?" he asked himself. "If they took her, why let me know? And if they didn't, they must have suspected I would immediately check to…" He glanced over his shoulder in the direction the dwarf had gone. "Get Wylin up here, *now!*" he shouted at the earl and shoved him on his way.

Braga ran up the hallway, following the dwarf and the two guards. They were just entering the north corridor, which led directly to the tower when he caught up to them.

"Stop where you are!"

The dwarf turned around, with a puzzled expression on his face. The guards responded differently. The larger of the two pivoted, drawing his sword, and moved to block the archduke's passage.

**4**

"Time to move, Royce," Hadrian said, casting off his helm. The standard issue sword of the Melengar guard felt heavy and awkward in his grip.

Royce removed his helm as well, as he moved past the dwarf, running quickly down the hall.

"Stop him, you fool!" Braga ordered the dwarf, but he was too slow to react. The thief was already far down the hall and the small dwarf ran after him. Braga drew his own sword and turned his attention to Hadrian.

"Do you know who I am? I know we met in the dungeon recently when you were hanging in chains, but are you aware of my reputation? I am Archduke Percy Braga, Lord Chancellor of Melengar, and more importantly, the winner of the title of Grand Circuit Tournament Swords Master, for the last five years in a row. Do you have any titles? Any ribbons won? Any awards bestowed? Are there trophies shelved for your handling of a sword? I have bested the best in Avryn, even the famous Pickering and his magic rapier."

"The way I heard it, he didn't have his sword the day you two dueled."

Braga laughed. "That sword story is just that—a story. He uses it as an excuse to account for his losses or when he is afraid of an opponent. His sword is just a common rapier with a fancy hilt."

Braga moved in and swiped at Hadrian in a savagely fast attack that drove him backward. He struck again and Hadrian had to leap backwards to avoid being slashed across the chest.

"You're fast. That's good, it will make this more interesting. You see, Mister Thief, I'm sure you have the situation here all wrong. You may be under the impression that you are holding me at bay while your friend races to the rescue of the damsel in distress. How noble for a commoner like yourself. You must entertain dreams of being a knight to be so idealistic." Braga lunged, dipped, and slashed. Hadrian fell back again, and once more, Braga smiled and laughed at him. "The truth is, you are not holding me at all. I am holding you."

The archduke feinted left and then short-stroked toward Hadrian's body. He dodged the attack, but it put him off balance and off guard. Although Braga's stroke missed, it allowed him the opportunity to punch the hilt of his sword hard into Hadrian's face, throwing him back against the corridor wall. His lip began to bleed. Immediately, Braga lashed out again, but Hadrian had moved, and the archduke's sword sparked across the stone wall.

"That looked like it hurt."

"I've had worse," Hadrian said. He was panting slightly, his voice less confident.

"I must admit, you two have been quite impressive. Your reputation is certainly well earned. It was very clever of you two, slipping in the sewers behind those rat catchers, using them as a decoy. It was also intelligent of you to send that note causing me to direct you right to the princess, but your genius ended there. You see, I can kill you whenever I want, but I want you alive. I need at least one person to execute. The mob will insist on that. In a few moments, Wylin and a dozen guards will come up here, and you will be taken to the stake. Meanwhile, your friend, whom you are sure is rescuing Arista, will be the instrument of her death and his as well. You could run and warn him, but oh—that's right—you are keeping me at bay, aren't you?"

Braga grinned evilly and attacked again.

**5**

Royce reached a door at the end of the hall and was not surprised to find it locked. He pulled his tools from his belt. The lock was traditional, and he had no trouble picking it. The door swung open, but immediately Royce knew something was wrong. He felt, more than heard, a click as the door pulled back. His instincts told him something was not right. He looked up the spiral stairs that disappeared around the circle of the tower. Nothing looked amiss, but years of experience told him otherwise.

He tentatively put a foot on the first step and nothing happened. He moved to the second, and the third, inching his way up. Listening for any telltale sounds, he searched for wires, levers, or loose tiles. Everything appeared safe. Behind him down the hallway, he could hear the faint sounds of swordplay as Hadrian entertained the archduke. He needed to hurry.

He moved up five more steps. There were small windows, no more than three feet tall and only a foot wide, just enough to allow light to pass through, but nothing else. The brilliant wintry sun revealed the staircase in a colorless brilliance. Weight, rather than mortar, held the smooth stone walls together. The steps were likewise made of solid blocks of stone also fitted with amazing artisanship so that a sheet of parchment could not slip between the cracks.

Royce moved up to the sixth step, and as he shifted his weight to the higher stone block, the tower shook. In reaction, he instinctively started to step back and then it happened. The previous five steps collapsed. They broke and fell out of sight into an abyss below him. Royce shifted his weight forward again just in time to avoid falling to his death and took another off balance step upward. The moment he did, the previous step broke away and fell. The tower rumbled again.

"Your first mistake was picking the lock," Magnus told him.

Royce could hear the dwarf's voice from the doorway below. When he turned, he could see the dwarf standing just outside the door in the castle corridor. He stood there, spinning a door key tied to a string around his index finger, winding and unwinding it. He absently stroked the hair of his beard.

"If you open the door without using the key, it engages the trap," Magnus explained with a grin.

The dwarf began to pace slowly before the open door like a professor addressing a class. "You can't jump the hole you made to get back here. It's already too far. And, in case you are wondering, the bottom is a long way down. You started climbing this tower on the sixth floor of the castle, and the base of the tower extends to the bedrock below the foundation. I also added plenty of jagged rocks at the bottom, just for fun."

"You made this?" Royce asked.

"Of course, well—not the tower, it was here already. I spent the last half-year hollowing it out like a stone-eating termite." He grinned and flashed his eyes. "There's very little stone left in it. All those very solid looking blocks of rock you see are paper-thin. I left just the right amount of structure in place. The inside looks like a spider web made of stone rather than thread. Tiny strands of rock in a latticework of a classic crystalline matrix—strong enough to hold the tower up, but extremely fragile if the right thread is broken."

"And I take it each time I take a step up, the previous one will fall?"

The dwarf's grin widened. "Beautiful, isn't it? You can't go down, but if you go up, you get into an even worse state. The steps work as a horizontal support for the vertical planes. Without the steps to steady the structure, it will twist on itself and fall. Before you reach the top, the entire tower will collapse once enough supports fall away. Don't let my talk about hollow walls put you too much at ease. It is still stone, and the full weight of this tower remains immense. It will very easily crush you, and the lady at the top, should the fall and the sharp rocks at the bottom not manage to do the job. You've already weakened the structure to where it might fall on its own now. I can hear it with the blowing of the wind—the tiny little cracks and pops—all stone makes sounds as it grows, shrinks, twists, or erodes—it's a language I understand very well. It tells me stories of the past and of the future, and right now, this tower is singing."

"I hate dwarves," Royce muttered.

# PART 9

## RESCUERS

The water pitcher and basin hit the floor and shattered. The crash jolted Arista, who sat on her bed, disoriented and confused. The room was shaking. All summer the tower had felt strange, but nothing like this. She held her breath—waiting. Nothing happened. The tower stopped moving.

Tentatively, she slipped off the bed, crept gingerly toward the windows and looked out. She saw nothing to explain the tremor. Outside the world was blanketed white by a fresh layer of snow that was still falling. *Is that it?* She looked up at the tower's eaves. *Is it the snow, sliding off the roof?* It did not seem likely…it also did not matter. *How much time do I have left?*

She looked down. The crowd still circled the front gate of the castle. There must have been more than a hundred people there, all pressing for news of her trial. Around the perimeter of the castle, three times the usual number of guards patrolled in full armor. Her uncle was not taking any chances. Perhaps he thought the people of the city might rise up against him rather than see their princess burned? She knew better. No one cared if she lived or died. While she knew all the lords, earls and barons by name, and had sat down with them for dozen of meals, she knew they were not her friends. She did not have friends. Braga was right; she spent too much time in her tower. No one really knew her. She lived a solitary life, but this was the first time she ever really felt alone.

She had spent all night trying to determine exactly what words she would use when brought before the court. In the end, she concluded there was little she could do or say. She could accuse Braga of the murder of her father, but she had no proof. He was the one with all the evidence on his side. After all, she had released the two thieves, and she was responsible for Alric's disappearance. And what good did that do?

*What was I thinking?*

She handed her brother over to two unknown thugs. Alric personally explained his intent to torture them to death, and she left him to their mercy! What were the odds of his survival? What was a promise to thieves? She felt sick whenever she imagined them laughing at her expense as they drowned poor Alric in the river. Now they were likely halfway to Calis or Delgos, taking turns wearing the royal signet ring of Melengar. When the scouts had returned with Alric's robe, she was certain he was dead, and yet, why was there no body?

*Is it possible Alric still lives?*

No, she reasoned, it was far more likely Braga kept Alric's corpse hidden. Revealing it before her trial would allow her to make a bid for the throne. Once the trial was over, once she was found guilty and burned, he would miraculously reveal its discovery. It was very possible Braga had Alric's body locked away in one of the rooms below her, or somewhere in the vault.

It was all her fault. If she had not interfered, perhaps Alric might have taken charge and discovered Braga's treachery. Perhaps he could have saved both of them. Perhaps she was nothing more than a foolish girl after all. At least her death would put an end to the questions and the guilt consuming her. She closed her eyes and once more felt the unsteadiness of the world around her.

The Galilin host was now a full five hundred strong as it marched through the wintry landscape. Sixty knights dressed in full armor carried lances adorned with long forked banners. They snapped like serpents' tongues in the numbing wind. Myron had overheard Alric, when they were back at Drondil fields, arguing with the other nobles, about marching too soon. Apparently, they were still missing the strength of several lords, and leaving when they did was a risk. Pickering finally agreed to Alric's demands and convinced the others once Barons Himbolt and Rendon arrived, bringing another score of knights. To Myron, the force was impressive at any size.

At the head of the line rode Prince Alric, Myron, Count Pickering and his two eldest sons, as well as the land-titled nobles. Following them were the knights who rode together in rows four abreast. An entourage of squires, pages, and footmen traveled behind them. Farther back were the ranks of the common men-at-arms: strong, stocky brutes dressed in chain and steel with bullet-shaped helms, plate metal shin guards, and metal shank boots. Each was equipped with a kite shield, a short, broad-blade sword, and a long spear. Next in line were the archers in leather jerkins and woolen cloaks that hid their quivers. They marched holding their un-strung bows as though they were mere walking sticks. At the rear came the artisans, smiths, surgeons, and cooks, pulling wagons that hauled the army's supplies.

Myron felt foolish. After hours on the road, he was still having trouble keeping his horse from veering to the left into Fanen's gelding. He was starting to get the hang of the stirrups, but he still had much to learn. The front toe guard, which prevented his feet from resting on the soles, frustrated him. The Pickering boys took him under their wing and explained how only the ball of the foot was to rest on the stirrup brace. This provided better control and prevented a foot from catching in the event of a fall. They also told him how tight stirrups helped to hold his knees to the horse's sides. All of Pickering's horses were leg trained and could be controlled by the feet, thighs, and knees. They were taught this way so that knights could fight with one hand on a lance or sword and the other on a shield. Myron was working on this technique now, squeezing his thighs, trying to persuade the horse to steer right, but it was no use. The more he used his left knee, the more his right knee also squeezed to compensate. The result was confusion on the part of the animal, and it wandered over and brushed against Fanen's mount once again.

"You need to be more firm," Fanen told him. "Show her who's in charge."

"She already knows—*she* is," Myron replied pathetically. "I think I should just stick with the reins. It's not like I will be wielding a sword and shield in the coming battle."

"You never know," Fanen said. "Monks of old used to fight a lot, and Alric said you helped save his life by killing one of those mercenaries who attacked you. So you're one ahead of me there. I've never actually killed a man."

Myron frowned and dropped his gaze. "I wish he hadn't told anyone about that."

"Oh, it's nothing to be ashamed of. Slaying a villain in the service of your king is the stuff of legends and what heroes are made of."

"It didn't feel very heroic. It made me sick. I don't even know why I…no, that's a lie. I really have to stop doing that."

"Doing what?"

"Lying. The abbot told me once that lying was a betrayal to one's self. It's evidence of self-loathing. You see, when you are so ashamed of your actions, thoughts, or intentions, you lie to hide it rather than accept yourself for who you really are. The idea of how others see you becomes more important than the reality of you. It's like when a man would rather die than be thought of as a coward. His life is not as important to him as his reputation. In the end, who is the braver? The man who dies rather than be thought of as a coward or the man who lives willing to face who he really is?"

"I'm sorry, you lost me there," Fanen said with a quizzical look.

"It doesn't matter, besides, the prince asked me along strictly as a chronicler of events, not as a warrior. I think he wants me to record what happens today in a book."

"Well, if you do, please leave out the way Denek threw a fit at not being allowed to come. It will reflect badly on our family."

Everything they passed was new to Myron. He had seen snow, of course, but only in the courtyard and cloister at the abbey. He never saw how it settled on a forest or glittered on the edges of rivers and streams. They were traveling through populated country now, passing village after village; each one larger than the one before. Myron could only stare in fascination at the many different types of buildings, animals, and people he saw along the way. Each time they came into a town, the villagers came out to stare at them. They scurried out of their homes aroused by the ominous *thrump, thrump, thrump* of the soldiers marching. Some summoned the courage to ask where they were going, but the men said nothing under strict orders to maintain silence.

Children ran to the edge of the road where parents quickly pulled them back. Myron had never seen a child before, at least not since he had been one. It was not uncommon for a boy to be sent to the abbey at ten or twelve but rarely, if ever, before the age of eight. The smallest of the children fascinated Myron, and he watched them in amazement. They were like short drunk people, loud and usually dirty, but all were surprisingly cute and looked at him in much the same way that he looked at them. They would wave, and Myron could not help but wave back, although he assumed it was not very soldierly to do so.

The war host moved surprisingly fast. The foot soldiers, responding in unison to orders, alternated between periods of double-time marching with a more relaxed stride, which was only slightly slower. Each of them wore a grim face without a smile among them.

For hours, they marched. No one interfered with them. There were no advance formations lying in ambush, no challenges along the road. To Myron, the trip felt more like an exciting parade than the preparation for an ominous battle. Finally, he saw his first glimpse of Melengar in the distance. Fanen pointed out the great bell tower of Mares Cathedral and the tall spires of Essendon Castle, where no standard flew.

A vanguard rode up and reported a strong force entrenched around the city. The nobles ordered their regiments to form ranks. Flags relayed messages, archers strung their bows, and the army transformed themselves into blocks of men. In long lines of three across, they moved as one. The archers were summoned forward and moved ahead just behind the foot soldiers.

Ordered to the rear, Myron and Fanen rode with the cooks to watch and listen. From his new vantage point, Myron noticed part of the army had broken away from the main line and was moving to the right side of the city. When the ranks of men reached the rise, which left them visible to the castle walls, a great horn sounded in the distance.

One of their own answered the castle horn, and the Galilin archers released a barrage of arrows upon the defenders. The shafts flew and appeared to hang briefly in the air like a dark cloud. As they fell, Myron could hear the distant cries of men. He watched with anticipation as the mounted knights broke into three groups. One stayed on the road, while the other two took up flanking positions on either side. The main line increased their pace to a brisk walk.

When they heard the horn, Mason Grumon and Dixon Taft led their mob up Wayward Street, effectively emptying the Lower Quarter. It was the sign Royce and Hadrian told them to wait for; it was the signal to attack.

Ever since the two thieves woke them in the middle of the night, they spent their time organizing the resistance in the Lower Quarter of Medford. They spread news of Amrath's assassination by the archduke, of the innocence of the princess, and of the return of the prince. Those not moved by loyalty or justice were enticed by the chance to strike back at their betters. It was not difficult to convince the poor and the destitute to take up arms against the soldiery who policed them. In addition, there were those hoping for a possibility to do a little looting, or perhaps receive some reward from the crown if they prevailed.

They armed themselves with pitchforks, axes, and clubs. Makeshift armor was constructed by strapping whatever thin metal they could find under their clothing. In most cases, this meant commandeering a baking sheet from their wives. They had the numbers, but they looked a pathetic lot. Gwen had roused the Artisan Quarter, which provided not only strong workers but a few swords, bows, and bits of armor. With the city guards ordered to the perimeter and most of the Gentry Quarter at the trial, there was no one to stop them from openly organizing.

With Dixon at his side, Mason marched at the head of the commoner procession, his smithing hammer in one hand and a rough-hewn shield he had beaten together that morning in the other. Years of frustration and resentment steamed to the surface as the smith strode forward. Anger born from the life he had been denied overwhelmed him. When he could not pay the taxes on his late father's shop, it had been the city sheriff and his guards who came. When he refused to leave, they had beaten him unconscious and thrown him into the gutter of Wayward Street. Mason blamed the guards for most of his life's misfortunes. The beating had weakened his shoulders, and for years afterward, wielding his hammer was so painful he could only work a few hours each day. This, and his gambling habit, kept him in poverty. Of course, he never really considered the gambling to be the real problem; it was the guards who were responsible. It did not matter to him that the soldiers and the sheriff who beat him were no longer with the guard. Today was his chance to fight back, to repay in kind for the pain he had endured.

Neither he nor Dixon were warriors or athletic, but they were large men with broad chests and thick necks, and the crowd followed behind them as if the citizens of the Lower Quarter were plowing the city with a pair of yoked oxen. They turned onto Wayward Street and marched unchallenged into the Gentry Quarter. Compared to the Lower Quarter, it was like another world. The streets were paved with decorative tile work and lined with metal horse hitches. Along the avenue, enclosed street lamps and covered sewers accentuated the care taken for the comfort of the privileged few. Marking the center of the Gentry Quarter was a large spacious square. The great Essendon Fountain, with its statue of Tolin on a rearing horse above the pluming water, was its main landmark. Across from it, Mares Cathedral rose. In its towers high above, bells chimed loudly. They passed the fine three-story stone and brick houses with their iron fences and decorative gates. That the stables here looked better than the house Mason lived in was not lost on him. The trip through the square only added fuel to the fire that was sweeping across the city.

When they reached Main Street, they saw the enemy.

# 4

The sound of the horn brought Arista to the window once more. What she saw amazed her. In the distance, at the edge of her sight, she could see banners rising above the naked trees. Count Pickering was coming, and he was not alone. There were a score of flags comprising most of the western provinces. Pickering was marching on Medford with an army.

*Is it on my account?* She pondered the question and concluded the answer was no. Of all the nobles, she knew the Pickerings the best, but she doubted he marched for her. News of Alric's death must have reached him, and he was challenging Braga for the crown. Most likely, he had given no thought at all to her plight. Count Pickering merely saw his opportunity and he was reaching for it. The fact that the princess might still live was only a technicality. No one wanted a woman as their ruler. If he won, he would force her abdication of the throne in favor of himself, or perhaps Mauvin. She would be sent away. She might not be locked up, but she would never be truly free. At least if he won, Braga would never sit on the throne of Melengar—but, would Pickering win? She was no tactician and certainly not a general; still even she could see that the forces marching on the road lacked the numbers for a castle siege. Braga had his forces well entrenched. Looking at the courtyard below, she suddenly realized the attack was distracting everyone. If only she could manage to escape.

*Perhaps, this time it will be different.*

She rushed to her door and with a tap of her necklace, unlocked it. She grabbed the latch and pushed. As usual, the door refused to budge. "Damn that dwarf," she said aloud to herself. She pushed violently against the door, throwing her entire weight, such that it was, against it. The door did not give way.

There was another rumble, and her room shook once more. Dust fell from the rafters. *What is going on?* She staggered as the tower swayed like a ship at sea. She did not know what else to do. Terrified and bewildered, she returned to the illusionary safety of her bed. She sat there, hugging her knees, hardly breathing, her eyes darting at the slightest sound. The end was coming. One way or another, she was certain the end was coming soon.

The prince was new to combat and unsure what to expect. He had hoped that merely assembling a massive force would cause the city's defenders to surrender. The reality was altogether different. When they reached Medford, they found trenches built outside the walls filled with spearmen. His archers had launched three flights of arrows but still the defenders remained steadfast. Using shields, they fended off much of the barrage and sustained little noticeable damage.

*Who are they?* Alric wondered. *Are my own soldiers standing between me and my home? What lies has Braga spread among the guards? Or are they these all hired men? Did my gold pay for those lines of pointed steel?*

Alric sat on one of Pickering's horses draped with a caparison hastily adorned with rough sewn images of the Melengar falcon. The animal was as restless as its rider, shuffling its hooves and snorting great clouds of frosty fog. Alric held the reins with his right hand, his left holding his woolen cloak tight about his neck. His eyes rose above the heads of the spearmen to look on the city of his birth. The walls and towers of Medford appeared faint and dream-like through the falling snow. The vision slowly faded into white as an eerie silence muffled the world.

"Your Majesty," Count Pickering spoke, breaking the stillness.

"Another flight?" Alric proposed.

"Arrows will not conquer your city."

Alric nodded solemnly. "The knights then, send in the knights to break the line."

"Marshal!" the count shouted. "Order the knights to break the line!"

Gallant men in shining armor spurred their steeds and charged forward with banners dancing overhead. A whirlwind of snow launched into the sky by their passing obscured them from view. They vanished from sight, but still Alric listened to the thunder of their hooves.

The clash was dreadful. Alric felt it as much as heard it. Metal shrieked, men cried out, and until that moment Alric never knew it was possible for horses to scream. When the cloud of snow settled, the prince could at last see the bloody spectacle. Spears braced in the dirt pierced the breast of man and mount. Horses collapsed, throwing the knights to the ground where they lay, like turtles struggling to right themselves. Spearmen drew forth short swords and thrust downward, punching their sharp points into eye slits and the armor gaps at the armpit or groin.

"This is not going as well as I hoped," Alric complained.

"Battle rarely ever does, Your Majesty," Count Pickering assured him. "But this is a large part of what being king means. Your knights are dying. Are you going to leave them to their fate?"

"Should I send in the foot soldiers?"

"If I were you, I certainly would. You need to break a hole in that wall, and you'd better do so before your men decide you're incompetent and vanish into the forests around them."

"Marshal!" Alric shouted. "Marshal Garret, order the foot soldiers to engage immediately!"

"Yes, sire!"

A horn sounded and the men roared forward into battle. Alric watched as steel cut through flesh. The footmen fared better than the knights, but the defensive position of the city soldiers took a toll. Alric could hardly bear to watch. Never before had he seen such a sight—there was so much blood. The white snow was gone;

it was stained pink and, in some desperate places, had pooled to a dark red. Littering the grounds were body parts—arms lay severed, heads split open, and legs chopped off. The wall of men blended in a whirling mass of flesh, dirt, blood, and an endless cacophony of screams.

"I can't believe this is happening," Alric said, sounding and feeling sick. "This is my city. These are my people. My men!" He turned to Count Pickering. "I am killing my own men!" He was shaking now and tears filled his eyes, his face red. Hearing the shrieks and cries, he squeezed the pommel of his saddle until his hands hurt. He felt helpless.

*I am king now.*

He did not feel like a king. He felt like he did on the road near The Silver Pitcher when those men held him face down in the dirt. The tears were now streaming down his cheeks.

"Alric! Stop it!" Pickering snapped at him. "You mustn't let the men see you crying!"

Fury flared in Alric, and he spun on the count. "No? *No?* Look at them! They are dying for me. They are dying on *my* order! I say they do have a right to see their king! They *all* have a right to see their king!"

Alric wiped the tears from his cheeks and gathered his reins. "I'm tired of this. I'm tired of having my face put in the dirt! I won't stand it. I'm tired of being helpless. That's my city, built by my ancestors! If my people chose to fight, then, by Maribor, I want them to know it is me they fight!"

The prince put on his helm, drew his father's large sword and spurred his horse forward, not at the trench but at the castle gate itself.

"Alric, no!" Pickering shouted after him.

**M**ason rushed forward and drove his hammer through the helmet of the first guard he saw. Grinning with delight at his good fortune, he gathered the man's sword and looked up.

The mob had reached the main gate of the city. The great four-towered barbican of gray stone rose above them like a monstrous beast. It swarmed with soldiers shocked at the sight of the city rising against them. Surprise and the accompanying panic bought the mob time to clear the streets and reach the gate house. Mason heard Dixon shout, "For Prince Alric!" but the prince was the last thing on the smith's mind.

Mason picked out his next target—a tall guard absorbed in a swinging match with a street sweeper from Artisan Row. Mason stabbed the guard in the armpit and listened to him scream as he twisted the blade. The street sweeper grinned at the smith and Mason grinned back.

He had only killed two men but already Mason was slick with blood. His tunic felt heavy as it stuck to the skin of his chest and he could not tell if it was sweat or tears of blood dripping down his face. The grin he had shown to the sweeper remained on his face, glued to his lips by the thrill and elation. *This was freedom! This was living!* His heart thundered and his head swam as if he were drunk.

Mason swung his sword again, this time at a man already down on one knee. His swing was so strong the blade cut halfway through his victim's neck. He kicked the dead man aside and cried aloud in his victory. He spoke no words; words were valueless at such a moment. He shouted the fury that pounded in his heart. He was a man again, a man of strength, a man to be feared!

A horn sounded and Mason looked up once more. A captain of the castle guard was on the ramparts shouting orders, rallying his troops. They responded to the call and fell back into ranks struggling to defend the gate even as the mob closed in.

Mason stepped through the muddy, blood-soaked ground, which was now slick beneath his feet. He looked about and picked a new target. A castle guard with his back to the smith was in the process of retreating to the sound of his captain's voice. The smith aimed at the guard's neck, attempting to cleave off his head. His inexperience with a sword caused him to aim too high and the blade glanced off the man's helmet ringing it loudly. He raised the sword for another blow when the man unexpectedly turned around.

Mason felt a sharp, burning pain in his stomach. In an instant, all the strength and fury drained from him. He let go his sword. He saw, rather than felt, himself drop to his knees. He looked down at the source of the pain and watched the soldier withdraw a sword from his stomach. Mason could not believe what he was seeing. *How could all that steel have been inside me?*

The smith felt a warm wetness on his hands as he instinctively pressed them to his wound. Trying as best he could to contain his organs that were spilling out, the blood flowed through a gash at least a foot wide. He no longer felt his legs and lay helpless when, to his horror, he saw the soldier swing again, this time at his head.

Alric charged the castle barbican. Immediately, Count Pickering, Mauvin, and Marshal Garret led the reserve knights in behind him. Arrows rained down from the parapets above the great gates. One deflected off Alric's visor, and another struck deep into the horn of his saddle. One hit Sir Sinclair's horse in the flank, causing it to rear unexpectedly, but the knight remained mounted. Countless more struck the ground harmlessly. The enraged prince rode directly to the gate and standing up in his stirrups shouted, "I am Prince Alric Brendon Essendon! Open this gate in the name of your king!"

Alric was not certain anyone heard him as he stood there, his sword raised high over his head. Furthermore, having heard him, there was no reason to believe another arrow would not whistle down and end his life. Behind the prince, the remaining knights fanned out around him as the marshal attempted to build a wall around his monarch.

A second arrow did not fly, but neither did the gate open.

"Alric," Count Pickering shouted, "you must fall back!"

"I am Prince Alric Essendon! Open the gate *now*!" He demanded again, and this time he removed his helm and threw it aside backing his horse into full view of the ramparts.

Alric and the others waited. Count Pickering and Mauvin stared at the prince in terror and tried to persuade him to come away from the gate. Nothing happened for several tense moments as the prince and his bodyguards sat outside waiting, staring up at the parapets. From inside they heard the sounds of fighting.

A shout came from atop the walls of the city. "The prince! Open the gate! Let him in! It's the prince!" More shouts, a scream, and then suddenly the massive gate split open, and the great doors pulled back. Inside was a mass of confusion as uniformed guards fought a horde of citizens dressed up like tinkers wearing makeshift armor or stolen helms.

Alric did not pause. He spurred his mount and drove into the crowd. Mauvin, Count Pickering, Sir Ecton, and Marshal Garret struggled to form a personal defense for their king, but there was little need. At the sight of him, the defenders laid down their weapons. Word that the prince was alive spread, and those who saw him charging toward the castle, brandishing his father's sword roared with cheers.

# 8

Royce heard the horn wail as he stood trapped on the steps of the tower. "Sounds like a fight outside," Magnus mentioned. "I wonder who will win?" The dwarf scratched his beard. "For that matter, I wonder who is fighting?"

"You don't take much interest in your employer's business, do you?" Royce said studying the walls. When he tried to tap a spike into a seam, it broke like an eggshell. The dwarf was telling the truth about that.

"Only if it is necessary for the job. By the way, I wouldn't do that again. You were lucky you didn't hit a binding thread."

Royce cursed under his breath. "If you want to be helpful, why not just tell me how to get up and back?"

"Who said I was trying to be helpful?" The dwarf grinned at him wickedly. "I just spent half a year on this project. I don't want you to topple the whole thing in the first few minutes. I want to savor the moment."

"Are all dwarves this morbid?"

"Think of it as having built a sandcastle and wanting the pleasure of seeing it fall to a wave. I am on the edge of my toes waiting to see exactly how and when it will finally collapse. Will it be a misstep, a loss of balance, or something amazing and unexpected?"

Royce drew his dagger and held it by the blade for the dwarf to see. "Are you aware I could put this through your throat where you stand?"

It was a false threat, as he would not dare throw away such a vital tool at this moment. Still he expected a reaction of fear, or at least a mocking laugh. Instead, the dwarf did neither. He glared at the dagger his eyes wide.

"Where did you get that blade?"

Royce rolled his eyes in disbelief. "I'm a little busy here. If you don't mind." He resumed his study of the steps. He observed the way they curved up and around the central trunk of the tower, how the steps above formed the ceiling to the ones below. He looked up ahead and then behind him.

"The step I am on doesn't collapse if I am on it," Royce said to himself, but loud enough for the dwarf to hear. "It only falls if I step on the next one."

"Yes, quite ingenious, isn't it. As you might imagine, I'm quite proud of my work. I originally designed it to be an instrument of Arista's death. Braga hired me to set it up to look like an accident. A decrepit old tower in the royal residence collapses, and the poor princess is crushed in the process. Unfortunately, after Alric escaped, he changed his mind and decided to have her executed instead. I thought I would never get to see the fruits of all my hard work, but then you came along. How nice of you."

"All traps have weaknesses," Royce said. He looked ahead at the steps and smiled suddenly. Crouching he leapt forward not one, but two steps. The step in the middle slipped from its position and fell, but the original step he started from remained. "With no following step," Royce observed, "that step is now secure from breaking, isn't it?"

"Very clever," the dwarf replied, clearly disappointed.

Royce continued to leap two steps at a time until he moved around the circle out of sight of the dwarf. As he did, Magnus shouted, "It'll do you no good. The gap at the bottom is much too far for you to jump. You are still trapped!"

Trista was still crouched on her bed when she heard someone outside her door. It was probably that dreadful little dwarf or Braga himself coming to take her to the trial. She could hear a scraping and an occasional thud. She remembered too late that she had not resealed the door with her gemlock. As she moved toward the door, it swung open. To her surprise, it was neither Braga nor the dwarf. Instead, there in the doorway was one of the thieves from the dungeon.

"Princess," was all Royce said entering with a respectful though brief nod in her direction. He quickly moved passed her and seemed to be looking for something, his eyes roamed over the walls and ceiling of her bedroom.

"You? What are *you* doing here? Is Alric alive?"

"Alric's fine," Royce said as he moved about the room. He looked out the windows and examined the material of the drapes. "Well, that's not going to work."

"Why are you here? How…did you get here? Did you see Esrahaddon? What did he say to Alric?"

"I'm a bit busy just now, Your Highness."

"Busy? Doing what?"

"Saving you, but I'll admit, I'm not doing very well at the moment." Without asking permission, Royce opened her wardrobe and began sifting through her clothes. Then he rifled through her dresser drawers.

"What do you want with my *clothes*?"

"I'm trying to figure a way out of here. I suspect this tower is going to collapse in a few minutes, and if we don't get out soon, we'll die."

"I see," she said simply. "Why can't we just go down the stairs?" She got up and crept to the doorway. "Sweet Maribor!" she cried as she saw every other step missing.

"We can leap those but the last six or seven steps at the bottom are totally gone. It's too far to jump to the corridor. I was hoping maybe we could jump out the window to the moat, but that looks like instant death."

"Oh," was all she could utter. A scream was growing in her and she covered her mouth with her hand, holding it back. "You're right. You're not doing very well."

Royce looked under her bed and then stood up. "Wait a minute, you're a sorceress, aren't you? Esrahaddon taught you magic. Can you get us down? Levitate us, or turn us into birds or something?"

Arista smiled awkwardly. "I was never able to learn much from Esrahaddon and certainly not self-levitation."

"Can you levitate a board or stone we could jump to?"

Arista shook her head.

"And the bird thing?"

"Even if I could, which I can't, we'd stay birds because I couldn't turn us back after changing now could I?"

"So, magic is out," Royce said and began pulling the feather stuffed mattress off Arista's bed revealing the rope net beneath it. "Okay, then help me untie your bed."

"The rope isn't long enough to reach the bottom of the tower," Arista told him.

"It doesn't have to be," he replied, pulling the rope through the holes in the bed frame.

The tower shuddered, and dust cascaded from the rafters. Arista held her breath for a moment, her heart pounding in anticipation of a sudden plummet, but the tower steadied itself once more.

"Clearly we are running out of time." Royce coiled the length of rope over his shoulder and headed toward the door.

Arista paused only a moment to look back at the dressing table and the brushes her father gave her and then moved to what remained of the stairs.

"You're going to have to jump down. The steps that are still there should be very sturdy and it should be easier than jumping up. Just be sure you don't over jump, but if you do, I'll try to catch you." With that, he sprang down two steps so gracefully that she felt embarrassed for her own lack of confidence.

Arista stood on the landing and rocked back and forth, focusing on the first step. She leapt and landed on it a little too far forward. Waving her arms madly, she teetered on the edge struggling desperately against falling. Royce held out his hands ready to catch her, but she regained her balance. Shaking slightly she took a deep breath.

"Don't over jump!" he reminded her.

*No kidding*, she thought to herself. *As if I haven't learned that lesson already.*

The second jump was easier, and the third better still. Soon she developed a rhythm and moved down the steps at a brisk pace following Royce, who almost danced his way down. They were nearly to the bottom when Royce stopped.

"Keep going," he told her. "Stop when you reach the last step and wait there."

She nodded as he pulled the rope from around his shoulder and began tying it to the step he stood on. Arista continued to jump her way down, reminding herself not to be over confident. When she saw the open expanse at the bottom, her remaining confidence fled. The gaping hole falling away into darkness was enough to shake her back into terror.

"Well, well, princess!" the dwarf called to her. He stood in the open doorway of the corridor grinning, showing a mouth full of yellowed teeth. "I really didn't expect to see you again. Where's the thief? Did he fall to his death?"

"You disgusting little beast!" she cried at him.

The tower shifted once more. Its shuttering caused Arista to stagger a bit on the step and her heart to pound in fear. Clouds of dust and bits of rock rained down, clattering off the walls and steps. Arista cowered, covering her head with her arms until the shaking stopped and the debris settled.

"This old tower, she's almost ready to fall," the dwarf told her with a manic glee in his voice. "Such a pity to be so close to safety and yet still so very far. If only you were a frog you might leap it. As it is, you still don't have a way out."

A coil of rope fell from the heights above. Suspended by a stair, the rope dangled midway between the princess and the dwarf. Along the slender line, Royce descended like a spider. When he reached a point level with Arista, he stopped and began to swing.

"Now *that* is impressive!" the dwarf exclaimed and nodded showing his approval.

Royce swung onto the step next to Arista and tied the rope around his own waist. "All we have to do is swing across. Just hang on to me."

The princess gladly threw her arms around the thief's shoulders and squeezed tight, as much out of fear as for safety.

"You might have actually made it," the dwarf said, "and for that you have my respect, but you must understand I have a reputation to uphold. I can't have someone walking around boasting they escaped one of my traps." Then without warning, he abruptly closed the door, sealing them in.

# 10

Hadrian heard the wail of a horn as he faced Braga in the corridor of the royal residence. "I think it will be quite some time until Wylin and the castle guards arrive," he taunted the archduke. "I suspect the master-at-arms has more on his mind than responding to the demands of an earl from Warric to report to the royal residence when his castle is being stormed."

"Mores the pity for you as I no longer have the luxury of keeping you alive," Braga said as he lunged once more.

He swiped at Hadrian with lightning fast cuts. Hadrian danced away from Braga retreating farther and farther down the hall. The archduke showed perfect form, his weight centered on his back foot while only the toe of his front foot touched the ground, his back straight, his sword arm outstretched, and his other arm raised in an elegant bent L. Even the fingers of his free hand were elegantly posed as if they were holding up an invisible wine glass. His long black hair, peppered with lines of gray, cascaded down to his shoulders, and not a trace of perspiration was on his brow.

Hadrian in contrast acted clumsy and unsure. The Melengar sword was far inferior to any of his own blades. The tip wavered as he tried to hold it steady with both hands. He inched backward working to keep a distance between them.

The archduke lunged again. Hadrian parried and then dove past Braga, barely avoiding a return slice, which nicked a wall sconce. He took the opportunity to run down the hallway and slipped into the chapel. "Are we playing hide-and-seek now?" Braga goaded.

Braga entered and crossed swiftly to the altar where Hadrian stood. When the archduke swung at him, Hadrian stepped back, ducked a swiping stroke, and then leapt clear of a slash. Braga's attacks glanced off the statue of Novron and Maribor, taking part of the god's first three fingers off. Hadrian now stood before the wooden lectern, keeping his eyes on the archduke while he awaited the next attack.

"It's so poetic of you to choose to die in the same room as the king," Braga said. He swung right, and Hadrian glanced the stroke aside. Braga pivoted on his back foot and swung his sword overhead in a powerful, downward stroke. Expecting this attack, counting on it, Hadrian dove and slid across the polished marble floor on his stomach in the direction of the chapel door.

Hadrian got to his feet and turned in time to see Braga's stroke had sliced into the vertical grain of the lectern. His swing had been so forceful that the blade was now wedged in the wood and the archduke struggled to free it. Taking advantage of his distraction, Hadrian ran to the door, slipped out, and closed it behind him. Driving his sword into the jam, he wedged it shut.

"That should hold you for a while," Hadrian said to himself, pausing to catch his breath.

# 11

"That little worm!" Arista spat through clenched teeth at the closed door.

The tower shuddered again, and this time larger pieces fell. One block of stone plummeted down, taking out a step only a few feet from them. Both shattered on impact and fell into the abyss of the tower's foundation. With the loss of those blocks, the tower came free and began to twist and topple.

"Hang on!" Royce shouted as he pushed off the step. The two flew across the gap to the door. He grabbed hold of the large iron door ring, and they each found footholds on the ledge of the door jam.

"He locked it," Royce informed her. He looped one arm through the door ring and removed his lock-picking tools from his belt. With his free hand, he worked the lock. A deep, resonating thunder shook the castle, and suddenly the rope tied to Royce went slack. The thief dropped his tools and pulled out his dagger. He cut the rope around his waist just as the stone slab attached to it passed them heading down. The rest of the tower was collapsing now.

Royce drove his dagger deep into the wooden door for another handhold as the tower fell around them. Walls hollowed out by the dwarf, splintered into shards, which burst and flew in all directions. Rocks and stone pummeled them as Royce and Arista cowered under the scant protection of the narrow stone arch of the doorframe.

A fist-size stone struck Arista's back. She lost her tenuous foothold, and screamed as she fell. In an instant, Royce grabbed her. Grasping blindly, he caught the back of her dress and a substantial amount of hair. "I can't hold you!" he shouted.

He felt her sliding down his body, the back of her dress tearing. Royce gave up his own toehold, hanging by his arm hooked through the door ring, so that he could wrap his legs around her. The princess' fingers clawed his body frantically and finally finding his belt, she latched on.

Royce was temporarily blinded by a cloud of dust and powdered stone. When it settled, he found they were dangling in the brilliant sunlight on what was now an exterior wall of the castle's keep. The debris of the tower fell into the moat, making a pile of broken rocks seventy feet below. The crowd of trial watchers screamed and gasped pointing up at them. "It's the princess!" A voice shouted.

"Can you reach the ledge?" Royce asked.

"No! If I try, I'll fall. I can't— "

Royce felt her slipping again and tried to tighten his leg hold on her, but he knew it would not be enough.

"Oh no! My fingers—I'm slipping!"

Royce's arm, crooked in the ring, was wrenching his shoulder badly. His other hand, which gripped Arista's dress and hair, was slowing losing hold. She was sliding down once again; soon he would lose her altogether. Royce felt a tug on his arm. The door opened, and a strong hand reached out and grabbed Arista.

"I've got you," Hadrian told her as he hauled the princess up. Then he pulled the door open wide, dragging Royce into the hallway with it.

They lay on the floor exhausted and covered in bits of rock. Royce got to his feet and dusted off his clothes. "I thought I felt it unlock," he said, getting up and retrieving his dagger from the face of the door.

Hadrian stood in the threshold of the doorway looking out at the clearing blue sky. "Well, Royce, I love what you've done with the place."

"Where's the dwarf?" Royce asked looking around.

"I didn't see him."

"And Braga? You didn't kill him, did you?"

"No. I locked him in the chapel, but it won't hold. Which reminds me, could I borrow your sword? You're not going to use it anyway."

Royce handed him the falchion sword that had been part of his castle guard disguise. Hadrian took the weapon, slipped it from its sheath, and weighed it in his hand. "I tell you, these swords are terrible. They are heavy and have all the balance of a drunken three-legged dog trying to take a piss." He then looked at Arista and added, "Oh, excuse me…Your Highness. How are you doing, Princess?"

Arista got to her feet, "Much better now."

"For the record, we're even, right?" Royce asked her. "You saved us from prison and a horrible death, and now we've saved you."

"Fine," she agreed, wiping the dust from her torn dress. "But I would like to point out my rescue of you was far less death defying." She ran a hand through her disheveled hair. "That really hurt you know."

"Falling would have hurt more."

A loud bang echoed from down the hall.

"Gotta go," Hadrian told them, "his lordship is loose."

"Be careful," Arista shouted after him, "he's a renowned swordsman!"

"I'm really tired of hearing that," Hadrian grumbled as he started back up the hall. He had not gone far when Braga rounded the corner coming toward them.

"So, you got her out!" Braga bellowed. "I'll just have to kill her myself then."

"You'll have to get by me first I'm afraid," Hadrian told him.

"That won't be a problem."

The archduke charged Hadrian, swinging at him in a fury. He hammered stroke after stroke on the fighter in a rage. Hadrian fought to deflect the fierce blows, which fell so fast they whistled in the air. The look on Braga's reddening face was one of hatred as he continued to pummel Hadrian.

"Braga!" Alric shouted from the far end of the hall.

The archduke spun, panting for air.

Hadrian saw the prince standing at the far end of the corridor. He was dressed in plate armor and a white tabard marred by a spattering of blood. Alric's hand rested on the hilt of his sheathed sword, and at his side were the Pickerings and Sir Ecton, each with a grim and dangerous look upon his face.

"Put down your weapon," the prince ordered in a powerful voice. "It's over. This is my kingdom!"

"You filthy little creature!" he cursed at the prince. He turned his attention away from Hadrian and began walking toward the prince. Hadrian did not follow. Instead, he joined Royce and Arista to watch.

"Did you think I was after your precious little kingdom?" Braga bellowed. "Is that what you think? I was trying to save the *world*, you fools! Can't you see it? Look at him!" The archduke pointed at the prince. "Look at the little maggot prince!" he turned and pointed back at Arista. "And her, too! Just like their father; they aren't human!" Braga, his face still red from the fight, continued down the corridor toward Alric. "You would have filth rule you all, but not me. Not while there is breath in this body!"

Braga charged forward raising his sword as he moved. When he came within reach of Alric, he brought it down toward the prince. Before Alric could react, the attack was deflected. An elegant rapier caught Braga's blade mid-stroke. Count Pickering held Braga's sword in the air, and Sir Ecton pulled the prince out of harm's way.

"You have your sword, I see. So there will be no excuse for you this time, dear count."

"There will be no need for one. You are a traitor to the crown and in memory of my friend Amrath, I will end this."

Blades flashed. Pickering was as much a master of fencing as Braga, and the two moved elegantly, their swords appearing as extensions of their bodies. Reaching for their swords, Mauvin and Fanen started forward, but Ecton stopped them, "This is your father's fight."

Pickering and Braga fought to kill. Sword strokes swept faster than the eye could follow, their deadly blades whistling a song to each other, crashing in chorus. The incredibly lustrous blade of Pickering's rapier caught the faint light in the corridor and glowed as it streaked through the air like a wand of light. It flashed and sparked when steel met steel.

Braga lunged, nicked Pickering's side, and sweeping back, cut him shallowly across the chest. Pickering barely blocked a second stab with a sweeping parry, which allowed him an overhead stroke. Braga raised his sword to block, but Pickering ignored the defense. Instead he swung down with force and speed, streaking light from his sword.

Hadrian instinctually cringed. The high, overpowered stroke would leave Pickering vulnerable, open to a fatal riposte by Braga. Then the metal of the swords clashed. A brilliant spark flared as incredibly, Pickering's blade sheered Braga's sword in two. The count's stroke continued unabated into the archduke's throat. The Lord Chancellor collapsed to the floor, his head rolling a foot farther away.

Mauvin and Fanen rushed to their father's side, beaming with obvious pride and relief. Alric ran down the hall where his sister stood between the two thieves. "Arista!" he shouted as he threw his arms around her. "Thank Maribor you're all right!"

"You aren't angry with me?" she asked, pulling away from him with surprise in her voice.

Alric shook his head. "I owe you my life," he said hugging her again, "and as for you two—" he began, looking at Royce and Hadrian.

"Alric," Arista interrupted, "it was not their fault. They didn't kill father, and they didn't want to kidnap you. It was my doing. I was the one who forced them. They didn't do anything. I was—"

"Oh, you are quite wrong there, my dear sister. They did a *great* deal." Alric smiled and placed a hand on Hadrian's shoulder. "Thank you."

"You're not going to charge us for the tower I hope," Hadrian said. "But if you are, it was Royce's fault and should come out of his share."

Alric chuckled.

"My fault?" Royce growled. "Find that little bearded menace and take your payment out of *his* stubby little hide."

"I don't understand," Arista replied, looking confused. "You wanted them executed."

"You must be mistaken, dear sister. These two fine men are the Royal Protectors of Essendon, and it appears they have done a fine job today."

"Your lordship," Marshal Garret appeared in the hall and approached the count, glancing only briefly at the dead body of Braga. "The castle has been secured and the mercenaries are slain or have fled. It would appear the castle guard is still loyal to the House of Essendon. The nobles are anxious to hear about the state of affairs and are waiting in the court."

"Good," the count replied. "Tell them His Majesty will address them soon. Oh, and send someone to clean this mess up, will you?" The marshal bowed and left.

Alric and his sister walked hand-in-hand down the corridor toward the others. Hadrian and Royce followed behind them. "Even now it is hard for me to believe him capable of such treachery," Alric said, looking down at Braga's body. A large puddle of blood stretched across the floor of the hallway. Arista lifted the hem of her dress as she passed by to avoid staining it.

"What was all that ranting about us not being human?" Arista asked.

"He was clearly insane," Bishop Saldur said, approaching with Archibald Ballentyne in tow. Although he had never met the bishop in person, Hadrian knew who he was. Saldur greeted the prince and princess with a warm smile and fatherly expression. "It is so good to see you, Alric," he said, placing his hands on the boy's shoulders. "And my dear Arista, no one is more pleased than I about your innocence. I must beg your forgiveness, my dear, as I was misled by your uncle. He planted seeds of doubts in my mind. I should have followed my heart and realized you could not possibly have done the things he accused you of." He gently kissed her on one cheek and then the other.

The bishop looked down at the blood-soaked body at their feet. "I fear the guilt of killing the king was too much for the poor man, and in the end, he lost his mind completely. Perhaps he was certain you were dead, Alric, and seeing you in the hallway he took you for a ghost or a demon back from the grave to haunt him."

"Perhaps," Alric said skeptically, "well, at least it's over now."

"What about the dwarf?" Arista asked.

"Dwarf?" Alric replied. "How do you know about the dwarf?"

"He was the one who set the trap in the tower. He nearly killed Royce and me. Does anyone know where he has gotten to? He was just here."

"He's responsible for far more than that. Mauvin run and tell the marshal to organize a search immediately," Alric instructed.

"Right away," Mauvin nodded and ran off.

"I, too, am pleased you are all right, Your Highness," Archibald told the prince. "I was told you were dead."

"And were you here to pay your respects to my memory?"

"I was here by invitation."

"Who invited you?" Alric asked and looked at the slain corpse of Braga. "Him? What dealings does an Imperialist earl of Warric and a traitorous archduke have in Melengar?"

"It was a cordial visit, I assure you."

Alric glared at the earl. "Get out of my kingdom before I have you seized as a conspirator."

"You wouldn't dare," Archibald returned. "I am a vassal of King Ethelred. Seize me or even treat me roughly and you risk war—a struggle Melengar can ill afford, particularly now with an inexperienced boy at the helm."

Alric drew his sword, and Archibald took two steps back. "Escort the earl out before I forget Melengar has a treaty of peace with Warric."

"Times are changing, Your Highness," Archibald called to the prince as guards led him away. "The New Empire is coming, and there is no place for an archaic monarchy in the new order."

"Is there no way I can throw him in the dungeon, even for a few days?" Alric asked Pickering. "Can I try him as a spy perhaps?"

Before Pickering could reply, the Bishop Saldur spoke. "The earl is quite right, Your Highness, any hostile act made against Ballentyne would be considered by King Ethelred to be an act of war against Chadwick. Just consider how you would respond if Count Pickering here were hanged in Aquesta. You wouldn't stand for it anymore than he would. Besides, the earl is all bluster. He is young and merely trying to sound important. Forgive him his youth. Have you not made errors in judgment as well?"

"Perhaps," Alric muttered. "Still, I can't help but suspect that snake is up to no good. I just wish there was some way I could teach him a lesson."

"Your Highness?" Hadrian said, stopping him. "If you don't mind, Royce and I have friends in the city we'd like to check on."

"Oh, yes, of course, go right ahead," Alric responded. "But there is the matter of payment. You've done me a great service," he said, looking fondly at his sister. "I intend to honor my word. You can name your price."

"If it is all right, we'll get back to you on that," Royce said.

"I understand," the prince said, revealing a hint of concern, "But I do hope you will be reasonable in your request and not bankrupt the kingdom."

"You should address the court," Pickering told Alric.

Alric nodded and he, Arista, and Mauvin disappeared down the stairs. Pickering lingered behind with the two thieves.

"I think there's a chance that boy will actually make a decent king," he mentioned once the prince was too far away to hear. "I had my doubts in the past, but he seems to have changed. He is more serious, more confident."

"So, the sword is magic after all." Hadrian motioned toward the rapier.

"Hmm?" Pickering looked down at the sword he wore at his side and grinned. "Oh, well, let's just say it gives me an edge in a battle. That reminds me, why were you letting Braga beat you?"

"What do you mean?"

"I saw you fighting when we first came up. Your stance was defensive, your strokes all parries and blocks. You never once attacked."

"I was frightened," Hadrian lied. "Braga won so many awards and tournament competitions, and I haven't won any."

Pickering looked puzzled. "But not being noble born, you aren't allowed to enter a tournament."

Hadrian pursed his lips and nodded. "Now that you mention it, I suppose you're right. You'd best see to your wounds, your lordship. You're bleeding on your nice tunic."

Pickering glanced down and looked surprised to see the slice Braga gave him across the chest. "Oh, yes, well, it doesn't matter. The tunic is ruined from the cut anyway, and the bleeding seems to have stopped."

Mauvin returned and trotted over to them. He stood next to his father, his arm around his waist. "I have soldiers looking for the dwarf, but so far no luck." Despite the bad news, Mauvin was smiling broadly.

"What are you grinning at?" his father asked.

"I knew you could best him. I did doubt it for a time, but deep down, I knew."

The count nodded and a thoughtful expression came over his face. He looked at Hadrian. "After so many years of doubt, it was fortuitous I had the opportunity and good fortune to defeat Braga, particularly with my sons watching."

Hadrian nodded and smiled. "That's true."

There was a pause as Pickering studied his face and then he placed a hand on Hadrian's shoulder. "To be quite honest, I for one am very pleased you're not noble Mr. Hadrian Blackwater, quite pleased indeed."

"Are you coming, your lordship?" Sir Ecton called, and the count and his sons headed off.

"You didn't really hold back on Braga so Pickering could kill him, did you?" Royce asked after the two were left alone in the hallway.

"Of course not. I held him off because it's death for a commoner to kill a noble."

"That's what I thought." Royce sounded relieved. "For a minute, I thought you'd gone from jumping on the good-deed wagon to leading the whole wagon train."

"Sure the gentry appear all nice and friendly, but if I'd killed him, even though they wanted him dead anyway, you can be sure they wouldn't be patting me on the back saying good job. No, it's best to avoid killing nobles."

"At least not where there are witnesses," Royce said with a grin.

As they headed out of the castle, they heard Alric's voice echoing "...was a traitor to the crown and responsible for the murder of my father. He attempted to murder me and to execute my sister. Yet, due to the wisdom of the princess and the heroism of others, I am standing here before you."

This was followed by a roar of applause and cheers.

# PART 10
## CORONATION DAY

Sixty-eight people had died, and over two hundred bore wounds from what became known as the Battle of Medford. The timely attack by the citizenry at the gate precipitated the prince's entrance into the city, and arguably saved his life. Once news spread through the city of Alric's return, all resistance ended. This restored peace but not order. For several hours after the battle, roving gangs took the opportunity to loot shops and storehouses, mostly along the riverfront. A shoemaker died defending his cobbler shop, and a weaver was badly beaten. In addition to the general thieving, the sheriff, his two deputies, and a moneylender were murdered. Many believed there were those who took advantage of the chaos to settle old scores. The killers were never identified, and no one bothered to look for the looters. In the end, no one was even arrested; it was enough that the violence was over.

Most of the snow that had fallen the day of the battle had melted over the next few days, leaving only dirty patches hiding in the shadows. Still for the most part, the weather remained decidedly cold. Autumn was officially finished, and winter had arrived. In the freezing winds, a silent crowd stood outside the royal crypt for hours as they removed Amrath's body for the official state funeral. Many others were buried that same day. The funerals provided a cleansing of the entire city's grief, followed by a week-long period of mourning.

Among the dead was Wylin, the master-at-arms of Castle Essendon. He fell while directing the defenses at the castle gate. It was never determined if Wylin had been a traitor or had merely been deceived by the archduke's lies. Alric gave him the benefit of the doubt and granted him burial with full honors. Although Mason Grumon died, Dixon Taft, manager of The Rose and Thorn, survived the battle with only the loss of his left arm just above the elbow. He might have died, along with many others, except for the efforts of Gwen DeLancy and her girls. Prostitutes, it turned out, made excellent nurses. The maimed and wounded who lacked family to care for them filled Medford House for weeks. When word of this reached the castle, food, supplies, and linens were sent.

News spread throughout Melengar of Alric's heroic charge on the fortified gates. How he survived the hail of arrows, only to bravely fling off his helm and dare them a second time—it made for great barroom stories. Few thought much of the son of Amrath prior to the battle, but now he became a hero in the eyes of many. A somewhat lesser known tale gained popularity a few days later as it, too, circulated through the city's taverns. This outlandish yarn described how two criminals, falsely accused of the king's murder, had escaped a tortuous death by abducting the prince. The story grew with each telling, and soon these same thieves were said to have gone on a rollicking trip through the countryside with the prince, returning just in time to save the princess from the tower seconds before it collapsed. Some even claimed to have helped save the prince from a roadside execution while others insisted they personally saw the princess and one of the criminals dangling from the side of the castle after the collapse of the tower.

Despite extensive searches, the dwarf whose hand actually killed the king escaped. Alric posted a reward notice offering one hundred gold tenents on every crossroad sign and on the door of every tavern and church in the realm. Patrols rode the length of every road searching barns, storehouses, mills, and even under the spans of bridges, yet he was not found.

Following the week of mourning, work began on repairing the castle. Crews cleared away the debris, and architects estimated at least a year to rebuild the lost tower. Though the falcon flag flew above the castle, the city saw little of Prince Alric. He remained sequestered within the halls of power buried under hundreds of obligations. Count Pickering, acting as a counselor, remained in the castle along with his sons. He assisted the young prince in his efforts to assume his father's role.

One month to the day after the burial of King Amrath, the prince's coronation took place. By that time, the snows returned and the city was white once more. Everyone came to the ceremony, yet, only a fraction could fit inside the expansive Mares Cathedral where the coronation took place. The majority only caught a brief glimpse of their new monarch when he rode in an open carriage back to the castle or as he stood on the open balcony while trumpets blared.

It was a full day of celebration with minstrels and street performers hired to entertain the citizenry. The castle even provided free ale and rows upon rows of tables filled with all manner of food. In the evening, which came sooner with the shortening of the days, people crammed into the local taverns and inns that were full of out of town visitors. The locals retold the stories of the Battle of Medford and the now famous legend of *Prince Alric and the Thieves*. These stories were still popular and showed no sign of going out of fashion. The day was long and eventually even the lights in the public houses winked out.

One of the few buildings still burning a candle was in the Artisan Quarter. It was originally a haberdashery, but the previous owner, Lester Furl, had died in the battle the month before. Some said the plumed hat he wore that day caught the attention of an axe. Since then, the wooden sign of the ornate cavalier hat still hung above the door, but no hats were for sale in the window. Even late into the night, the light was always on; however, no one was ever seen entering or exiting the shop. A small man in a simple robe greeted those nosy enough to knock. Behind him, visitors saw a room filled with the dried, hairless skins of animals. Most soaked in tubs or were stretched out on frames. There were pumice stones, needles and thread, and folded sheets of vellum piled neatly along the walls. The room also contained three desks with upright tops over which large sheets of parchment lay with carefully written text. Bottles of ink rested on shelves and in open drawers. The man was always polite, and when asked what he sold in his shop, he would reply, "Nothing." He simply wrote books. Because few people could read, most inquiries ended there.

The fact was, there were very few books in the shop.

Myron Lanaklin sat alone in the store. He had written half a page of *Grigoles Treatise on Imperial Common Law* and then just stopped. The room was cold and silent. He stood up, walked to the shop window, and looked out at the dark, snowy street. In a city with more people than he saw in his lifetime, he felt utterly alone. A month had passed, but he had only finished half of his first book. He found himself spending most of his time just sitting. In the silence, he imagined he could hear the sound of his brothers speaking the evening vespers.

He avoided sleep because of the nightmares. They had started the third night he slept in the shop. They were terrible. Visions of flames and sounds of pleading coming from his own mouth as the voices of his family died in the inferno. Every night they died again, and every day he awoke on the cold floor of the tiny room in a world more silent and isolated than the abbey had ever been. He missed his home and the mornings he spent with Renian.

Alric made good on his promise. The new king of Melengar provided him the shop rent-free and all the materials needed for making his books. Never was there a mention of cost. Alric endeavored to support the literary sciences in his realm starting with Myron as his little pet project. Myron should have been happy, but he felt more lost each day. Although he had more food than ever before, and no abbot to restrict his diet, he ate little. His appetite dwindled along with his desire to write.

When he had first arrived at the shop, he felt obligated to replace the books, but as the days slipped by, he sat alone and confused. How could he *replace* the books? They were not missing. No shelf lay bare, no library stood wanting. What would he do if he ever completed the project? What would he do with the books? What would become of them? What would become of him? They had no home, and neither did he.

Myron sat down on the wooden floor in the corner, pulling his legs to his chest and rested his head against the wall. "Why did I have to be the one who lived?" he muttered to the empty room. "Why did I have to be left behind? Why is it I'm cursed with an indelible memory, so that I can recall every face, every scream, every cry?"

As usual, Myron wept. There was no one to see, so he let the tears run unchecked down his cheeks. He cried there on the floor in the flickering candlelight and soon fell asleep.

The knock on the door startled him. He stood up. It was still night. He could not have been asleep long; the candle still burned. Myron moved to the door and opening it a crack, peered out. On the stoop outside, two men in heavy winter cloaks stood waiting.

"Myron? Are you going to let us in or leave us to freeze?"

"Hadrian? Royce!" Myron exclaimed as he threw open the door. He embraced Hadrian immediately and then turned to Royce and paused, deciding a handshake would suit him better.

"So it's been a while," Hadrian said, shaking the snow off his boots. "How many books have you finished?"

Myron looked sheepish. "I've had a little trouble adjusting, but I will get them done. Isn't this place wonderful?" he said trying to sound sincere. "It was very generous of His Majesty to provide all this for me. I have enough vellum to last years and ink! Well, don't get me started. As Finiless wrote, 'More could not be gotten though the world be emptied to the breath of time.'"

"So you like it here?" Hadrian asked.

"Oh, I love it, yes; I really couldn't ask for anything more." A look exchanged between the two thieves, the meaning of which

Myron could not discern. "Can I get either of you something, tea perhaps? The king is very good to me. I even have honey to sweeten it."

"Tea would be nice," Royce said, and Myron moved to the counter to fetch a pot.

"So what are you two doing out so late?" Myron asked then laughed at himself. "Oh, never mind, I guess this isn't late for *you*. I suppose you work nights."

"Something like that," Hadrian said. "We just got back from a trip to Chadwick. We are heading back to The Rose and Thorn but wanted to stop by here on the way and deliver the news."

"News? What kind of news?"

"Well I thought it might be good news, but now I'm not so sure."

"Why's that?" the monk asked, pouring water into the pot.

"Well, it would mean leaving here."

"It would?" Myron turned suddenly, spilling the water.

"Well, yes, but I suppose if you're really attached to this place we could—"

"To go where?" Myron asked anxiously, setting down the pitcher forgetting the tea.

"Well," Hadrian began, "Alric offered us whatever we wanted as payment for saving Arista, but seeing as how Arista saved our life first, it didn't seem right asking for money, or land, or anything personal like that. We got to thinking just how much was lost when the Winds Abbey was destroyed. Not just the books mind you, but the safe haven for those lost in the wilderness. So we asked the king to rebuild the abbey just like it was."

"Are…are you serious?" Myron stammered. "And did he say yes?"

"To be honest, he sounded relieved," Royce said. "I think he felt as if there was a dagger dangling over his head for a month. I suppose he was afraid we'd ask for something ridiculous like his first born or the crown jewels."

"We might have, if we hadn't already stolen them," Hadrian chuckled, and Myron was not sure if he was joking or not.

"But if you really like this place," Hadrian, said whirling his finger in the air, "I suppose we—"

"No! No…I mean, I think you are right. The abbey should be rebuilt for the sake of the kingdom."

"Glad you feel that way because we need you to help the builders design it. I am assuming you could draw a few floor plans and maybe some sketches?"

"Certainly, down to the finest detail."

Hadrian chuckled. "I bet you can. I can see you're going to drive the royal architect to drink."

"Who will be the abbot? Has Alric contacted the Dibben Monastery already?"

"He sent out a messenger this morning as one of his first acts as king. You're going to have a few guest monks trickling in over the winter, and this spring all of you will have a great deal of work to do."

Myron was grinning widely.

"About that tea?" Royce inquired.

"Oh yes, sorry." He returned to pouring water into the pot. Stopping once more, he turned back to the thieves and his grin faded.

"I would so much love to return to my home and see it rise again. But…" Myron paused.

"What is it?"

"Won't the Imperialists simply come back? If they hear the abbey is there again…I don't think I could…"

"Relax, Myron," Hadrian said, "that's not going to happen."

"But how can you be sure?"

"Trust me, the Imperialists won't advocate another foray into Melengar," Royce assured the monk. The smile on the thief's face made Myron think of a cat, and he was happy not to be a mouse.

In the hours before dawn, the Lower Quarter was quiet. Damp-ened by the snow, the only sound came from the muffled hoof falls of mounts as they moved slowly up the alley to The Rose and Thorn.

"Do you need any of the money?" Royce asked Hadrian.

"I have enough. Deposit the rest with Gwen. What does that come to now?"

"Well, we're in pretty good shape. We have our share of the fifteen gold tenents for returning Alenda's letters, and the twenty from Ballentyne for stealing them in the first place, plus DeWitt's one hundred, and Alric's one hundred. You know, one day we're going to have to find DeWitt—and *thank him* for that job." Royce grinned.

"Do you think it was fair asking for the money along with the abbey?" Hadrian asked. "I have to admit the guy was starting to grow on me, and I hate to think we took advantage of him."

"The hundred was for going into Gutaria with him," Royce reminded him. "The abbey was for saving his sister. We didn't ask for *anything* Alric didn't agree to in advance. And he did say anything so we could easily have asked for land and noble rank."

"Why didn't we?"

"Oh? So you would like to be the Count Blackwater, would you?"

"It might have been nice," Hadrian said sitting up straighter in his saddle, "and you could be the infamous Marquis Melborn."

"Why infamous?"

"Would you prefer notorious? Nefarious perhaps?"

"What's wrong with *beloved*?"

Neither could hold a straight face at the thought.

"Come to think of it, we failed to bill the good king for saving him from Trumbul. Do you think—"

"It's too late, Royce," Hadrian told him.

Royce sighed, disappointed. "So, I think he wasn't too put out all things considered. Besides we *are* thieves, remember? Anyway, the bottom line is, we won't be starving this winter."

"Yes, we've been good little squirrels, haven't we?" Hadrian said.

"Maybe this spring we can start that fishing enterprise you wanted."

"I thought you wanted the winery?"

Royce shrugged.

"Well, you keep thinking. I'm going to go wake up Emerald and let her know I'm back. It's too cold to sleep alone tonight."

Royce passed the tavern and dismounted at Medford House. For some time, he stood, just staring at the top window while his feet grew colder and colder in the snow.

"You *are* going to come up, aren't you?" Gwen asked from the doorway. She was still dressed and as pretty as ever. "Isn't it awfully cold out there?"

Royce smiled at her. "You waited up."

"You said you'd be coming back tonight."

Royce pulled his saddlebag off his horse and carried it up the steps. "I have another deposit to make."

"Is that why you were standing in the snow for so long? You were trying to decide whether or not to trust me with your money?"

Her words stung him. "No!"

"Then why were you standing there so long?"

Royce hesitated. "Would you prefer me if I were a fisherman, or perhaps a wine maker?"

"No," she said, "I prefer you as you are."

Royce took her hand. "Gwen, you have to understand. It never ends well for someone like me. You'd be better off with a nice farmer or rich merchant. Someone you can raise children with, someone you can grow old with, someone who will stay at home and not leave you alone and wondering."

She kissed him.

"What was that for?"

"I'm a prostitute, Royce. There aren't many men who consider themselves unworthy of me. I prefer you just as you are and just as you will be. If I did have the power to change you, the only change I would make would be to convince you of that."

He put his arms around her, and she pulled him close. "I missed you," she whispered.

# 3

Archibald Ballentyne awoke with a start.

He had fallen asleep in the Gray Tower of Ballentyne Castle. The fire had burned out, and the room was growing cold. It was also dark, but the dim glow of the faint orange embers in the hearth gave a little light. There was an odd and unpleasant odor in the air, and he felt the weight of something large and round on his lap. He could not make it out in the darkness. It seemed like a melon wrapped in linen. He stood up and set the object in his chair. He moved aside the brass screen and, taking two logs from the stack nearby, placed them on top of the hot coals. He prodded the embers with a poker, blew on them, and coaxed the fire back to life. As he did, the room filled with light once more.

He set the poker back to its stand, replaced the screen, and dusted his hands off. As he turned around, he looked at the chair he had been sleeping in and immediately pin-wheeled backward in horror.

There on his seat was the head of the former Archduke of Melengar. The cloth, which was covering it, had partially fallen away revealing a large portion of what had once been Braga's face. The eyes were rolled back leaving white and milky orbs in their sockets. The yellowed skin, stretched and leathery, was shriveled. A host of some kind of worms moved in the gaping mouth, slithering in a heaving mass which made it almost appear as if Braga's tongue was trying to speak.

Archibald's stomach twisted in knots. Too frightened to scream, he looked around the room for intruders. As he did, he saw writing on the wall. Painted in what appeared to be blood, in letters a foot tall, were the words:

**NEVER INTERFERE WITH MELENGAR AGAIN**
**BY ORDER OF THE KING**
**...AND US**

.

Born in Detroit Michigan, Michael J. Sullivan has lived in Vermont, North Carolina and Virginia. He worked as a commercial artist and illustrator, founding his own advertising agency in 1996, which he closed in 2005 to pursue writing full-time. The Crown Conspiracy is his first published work. He currently resides in Fairfax, Virginia with his wife and three children.

You can read more about Michael and his works at:
*www.michaelsullivan-author.com.*

We hope you enjoyed this story. Be sure to check out
Michael J. Sullivan's forthcoming works as well as other
AMI authors. Your comments and thoughts concerning this book
or Aspirations Media are welcome.

**www.aspirationsmediainc.com**

If you're a writer or know of one who has a work that they'd love to
see in print—then send it our way. We're always looking for great
manuscripts that meet our guidelines. Aspirations Media is looking
forward to hearing from you and/or any
others you may refer to us.

Thank you for purchasing this
Aspirations Media publication.